About the

MOLLY GREEN has travelled the world, unpacking her suitcase in a score of different countries which often became her new place of work. On returning to England, she set up an estate agency business which she ran and expanded for twenty-five years. Eventually, she sold her business to give herself time and space to pursue her dream to write novels. She has since moved to a village near Lewes in East Sussex and is ably assisted with her writing by her one-eyed rescued cat, Bella.

You can keep up with Molly at mollygreenauthor.com

Also by Molly Green

Courage
for the
Cabinet
Girl

MOLLY GREEN

avon.

Published by AVON
A division of HarperCollins*Publishers* Ltd
1 London Bridge Street
London SE1 9GF

www.harpercollins.co.uk

HarperCollins*Publishers*
Macken House, 39/40 Mayor Street Upper,
Dublin 1, D01 C9W8, Ireland

A Paperback Original 2024

3

First published in Great Britain by HarperCollins*Publishers* 2024

Copyright © Denise Barnes 2024

Denise Barnes asserts the moral right to be identified as the author of this work.

A catalogue copy of this book is available from the British Library.

ISBN: 978-0-00-867954-5

This novel is entirely a work of fiction. References to real people, events or
localities are intended only to provide a sense of authenticity, and are used
fictitiously. All other characters and incidents portrayed in it are
the work of the author's imagination.

Typeset in Minion Pro by HarperCollins*Publishers* India

Printed and bound in the UK using 100%
Renewable Electricity at CPI Group (UK) Ltd

All rights reserved. No part of this text may be reproduced, transmitted,
down-loaded, decompiled, reverse engineered, or stored in or introduced into
any information storage and retrieval system, in any form or by any means,
whether electronic or mechanical, without the express written permission of the
publishers.

This book contains FSC™ certified paper and other controlled
sources to ensure responsible forest management.

For more information visit: www.harpercollins.co.uk/green

*For my father, Hatherleigh Percy Harold Barnes,
and my mother, Lilian Hilda Beatrice – or Molly,
as she was always known. They lived in London and were
married by special licence three days after war was declared,
enduring every moment of the terrifying Blitz.*

*In May 1940 when Winston Churchill had just
become Prime Minister, he walked down the spiral staircase
to the War Rooms and into the Cabinet Room.
Glancing round and in his gravelly voice, he told Brigadier
Leslie Hollis and the small group accompanying him:
'This is the room from which I will direct the war.'*

Chapter One

August 1939
Wimbledon, London

Katie Valentine jumped off the bus, ready for her walk home from Wimbledon Racetrack where she worked as a kennel maid. It was a warm Saturday night, and for once she'd managed to leave on time after the last race finished and she'd given the forty dogs a few biscuits and water and settled them in their baskets.

Her thoughts turned to the impending war that was on everyone's lips. Her father said only yesterday it was no longer 'if', but 'when'. She shuddered at the thought that life for millions of people could be turned upside down by one callous dictator far away in Germany – a country she'd never visited in spite of having a German mother. As a child, she'd often wondered why her parents had never taken her to see her German grandparents, why they never sent a birthday or a Christmas present, not even a card, but Mutti had always evaded her questions by blaming all sorts of illnesses, and by the time Katie was in her teens, she'd stopped mentioning them.

But what about her own life? Katie wondered. She certainly didn't want to stay at the racetrack after she'd witnessed the terrible injury her favourite dog, Tan Pet, had endured last month when a rogue spike on the metal fence that bordered the track had pierced his side as he'd raced round a corner. She'd never forgotten the callous owner who'd said he was no longer any good for racing so he'd have to be put down. No love for the animal, she'd realised bitterly. Tan Pet was simply there to make the owner money. She'd nursed the whimpering dog back to health, then taken him home to live, much to her mother's indignation that she hadn't been consulted.

Katie had put off giving in her notice until she'd found another job, but the trouble was that she'd gone straight from school to the racetrack without getting any formal qualifications, and there'd never been anything she'd rather do than work with animals. Katie chewed her lip. If there really *was* a war, she realised, it would have to take priority over any foolish dreams. Perhaps she should join the Forces like two of her old schoolfriends had announced they would do if the worst should happen.

Her mouth now parched and her pace beginning to drag with tiredness, she forced herself to quicken her steps until, after what seemed an eternity, she pushed the key into the front door keyhole.

'Ah, you are finally home,' Ursula Valentine said as Katie came into the kitchen, Tanny trotting behind her.

It was the same greeting her mother always gave, no matter what shift Katie had just finished.

'Where's Dad?' she asked, kissing her mother's cheek.

'In the sitting room reading his paper. Go and keep him company. Take the dog with you and I will bring you a cocoa.'

Oscar Valentine put down his paper. Tanny immediately rushed over, giving a short bark.

'Yes, good boy.' Her father patted the dog's golden head and looked at his daughter. 'Hello, love. Have you seen your mother?'

'Yes. She'll be in in a minute.'

'Did she say anything about—?' He broke off as his wife came into the room with a tray.

'We agreed I would speak to Katharina,' Ursula said, setting the mug of cocoa on the little table by the side of Katie, who frowned.

'She'll know sooner or later,' Oscar said mildly.

'What's all the mystery?'

'We've just had notification of Judith's will.' Her mother handed Katie a brown envelope with her name on.

Katie's heart jumped to see her beloved aunt's neat handwriting. She'd been devastated to learn of her recent death from lung cancer, far too early at only fifty. The doctor had put it down to her aunt's chain-smoking. Katie turned the envelope over. She narrowed her eyes. The envelope was addressed to her but although it was still sealed, the wrinkles on the flap showed that someone had tampered with it and not stuck it down again very accurately.

'Has this been opened?' Katie demanded, looking at both parents although she knew without doubt it was her mother's doing.

Ursula flushed. 'It came in a large envelope with the will. She's left us her old furniture and her collection of books. As if we need more books.' Her gaze hovered over the bookcases as though not wanting to meet her daughter's eye.

'Mutti, I'm asking why you felt able to open a letter clearly addressed to me.'

'I'm your mother. I need to know what Judith is writing about to my daughter.'

Katie shook her head, remembering the time she'd caught her mother reading her diary. How she'd said she needed to know what her daughter was up to. From that day, Katie had hidden her diary in a different place every night.

'Where are you going?' Ursula said as Katie rose from the chair.

'I'm taking my *private* letter upstairs where I can read it *privately* even though it's plain to see that it's no long *private*.'

At nineteen, she knew she was being childish, but really her mother was too bad. Katie picked up her cocoa and Tanny immediately followed her upstairs, his tail drooping as though he'd picked up his mistress's displeasure. In her room she ordered him to go to his basket, then sat on the bed and removed two sheets of paper from the envelope. Sadness threatened to overwhelm her again to think dear Aunt Judy was gone – she'd never see her again, have a giggle together and give her a hug – yet here she was, still speaking to her and obviously worrying about her. How often Katie had wished her aunt had been her real mother. Then she would berate herself for being disloyal. Mutti couldn't help the way she was. Turning back to the letter, Katie noticed it was dated 26th June, the day after the doctor told her aunt there was nothing more to be done.

My darling Katie,

When you read this I will, of course, no longer be here. But you have all your life ahead of you. And I don't want you to waste it at that racetrack. I know you love the dogs but your present job is a dead-end one. And you are amongst men who gamble!! I do not approve of such a situation and cannot bear to think of you wasting your life.

Katie bit her lip. Aunt Judy was sounding like her mother. Maybe the two women had more in common than they realised, though there always seemed to be a flicker of jealousy between them – or at least on the part of her mother.

To that end I bequeath you a sum of money which will pay for you to take a year's secretarial course at a good establishment. There will be enough money for you to live on so you can give in your notice immediately at that dreadful place.

4

I know you will rail against this but it will stand you in good stead to earn a proper salary and meet interesting people. You will find with those skills that all sorts of opportunities will be open to bright girls like you. There's no doubt we will be at war with Germany sooner or later and you'll have something concrete to offer, such as a secretary at the War Office in Whitehall. (I approached them myself once – successfully – in the Great War!)

After your secretarial training you will be able to pay the rent for a small flat for a year so you can leave home and make your own way in life. But this is just a temporary measure. You need a steady, well-paid job so you are never forced into marrying a man for the wrong reasons but always try to be financially independent. Any money left over, after you've put some away for a rainy day, you can splurge on some good-quality outfits and shoes ready for your new career. And you never need to be in want of a hat not seen on anyone else as I'm leaving you a dozen of my favourite ones for any occasion that will suit you down to the ground.

Katie couldn't help smiling. Her aunt had always dressed in the latest fashion with one of the hats she'd crafted herself perched on her head. They always looked right on Aunt Judy, no matter how outlandish. Now she'd inherited them.

This money is set aside for you only and is to be used only as I have outlined above.

Please remember I have your best interests at heart. You have always been like a daughter to me – the daughter I was never able to have.

Katie briefly put the letter aside. Poor Aunt Judy. She'd never married. When Katie had plucked up the courage one day to ask her why, her aunt's tone was unusually sharp.

'Why do you ask that?'

Katie bit her lip. Was she intruding on Aunt Judy's personal life?

'You're such an interesting person – you're well read, you've travelled, you're independent – any man worth his salt would be intrigued. Besides all that, you must have been very beautiful when you were young because you still are so I'm sure you didn't lack admirers.'

Her aunt remained tight-lipped.

After a few moments, Katie ventured, 'Did you never fall in love with anyone?'

Judy hesitated, her eyes clouding. Instinctively, Katie was sure there had been a special man in her aunt's life.

'You're right. I did have several admirers over the years. In fact, I had two serious proposals and even stupidly became engaged to both of them – though not at the same time.' She threw her niece one of her mischievous smiles. 'But I never found anyone I wanted to spend the rest of my life with.' Judy looked away, as though wondering if to say anything more. She cleared her throat and said quietly, 'Well, there was one, but it wasn't meant to be.'

Katie had wondered at the time who this man was and why their relationship had sounded doomed. She swallowed hard at the memory of her aunt's wistful expression, then read the closing sentences.

Don't be sad to learn that I am gone. I've packed more into my life than most people, and now I will have peace of mind knowing I have done my best for you.
All my love, my darling,
Judy XX
P.S. Nearly forgot! The sum of money which is now yours is £500.

Katie gasped. Five hundred pounds! That was a small fortune. Her aunt had earned a reasonable income after the war as a milliner for Bourne and Hollingsworth in Oxford Street, but as far as she knew, she wasn't rich by any means. And a secretarial course would only cost a fraction of that. If only her aunt hadn't insisted she learn shorthand and typing – because that's all it amounted to and she couldn't imagine anything more dull. It was too bad. She'd always thought her aunt knew her better than anyone. But she'd been wrong.

She read the letter again, more slowly this time, in case she'd missed something. But no, her aunt seemed determined to put her savings towards her niece's future – for which she was incredibly grateful – but in a job Katie would never have imagined herself doing.

You'd get some proper training, her inner voice whispered. *If you don't take up Aunt Judy's offer, what will you do? Stay at the racetrack that you now despise? Being paid a pittance so you'll never be independent?*

She sprang up from the bed and from his basket Tanny opened one eye, then trotted over. She put her face near his and he gave her cheek a lick.

But typing for some grey-haired old bank manager in an office? That's the last place she'd have thought of. Briefly, she closed her eyes

I cannot bear to think of you wasting your life.

Katie startled. It was as though Aunt Judy was speaking directly to her, begging her not to pass up this opportunity. She heaved a sigh. If her darling aunt thought she should do the course and gain her certificate, and was willing to fund it, then all right, she supposed she should at least give it some serious thought. Sleep on it, Dad always advised.

But if I did take the course, what then?

Where would that certificate in her hand lead her?

Later that night, Katie turned over yet again and switched on her bedside light. Ten past one and she still hadn't had a wink of sleep. She banged the pillow in frustration, then flung it over, hoping the cool side against her cheek would help slow down her brain. If she could only think of something else she could train for and give in her notice at the racetrack.

Trouble is, Katie mused, girls and women don't have so much choice as men. But there'd be a positive side if women and girls were also allowed to play their part – it would be an unexpected opportunity to contribute to the war effort. But would England really go to war with Germany – her own mother's country – for the second time? If so, it would break Mutti's heart, though Mr Chamberlain, the Prime Minister, had already warned Germany that if they invaded Poland, England would come to Poland's aid. And then the horror would begin.

A sudden tremor ran over her. It certainly felt like the country was on the brink of something momentous. If that turned out to be the case, and it meant getting herself a sensible qualification as Aunt Judy had practically ordered, then that's what she must do.

This time when she turned over, she fell instantly asleep.

The following morning, as soon as Katie opened her eyes, she felt ready to stick to her decision to apply for the secretarial course. She'd tell her mother at breakfast. At least Mutti would be relieved. Throwing on her dressing gown, she tied the cord, and, with Tanny bounding in front, ran down the stairs and into the kitchen where her mother stood in front of the stove stirring the porridge.

She turned round, her expression anxious. 'Good morning, Katharina. Did you have a good night?'

'Only after I'd thought about the secretarial course.'

Her mother fixed her eyes on Katie.

'And what have you decided, Katharina?'

'I'm giving in my notice this morning.'

Her mother gave a half smile, obviously of relief.

'Judith was sensible for once,' she said, as she ladled the porridge into two bowls and set them on the kitchen table. 'You'll get a steady job until one day you marry a nice young man.'

'I hope that day is far in the future,' Katie said, her mouth firm. 'And anyway, by the looks of things all the eligible men will have disappeared.'

'Do not speak such things, Katharina.' Her mother's voice was sharp as Katie poured out the tea. 'There will not be a war. Even Hitler does not want us to be enemies.' She paused. 'Why, he admires the British. He even copies some of their habits.' She raised her cup to her lips and looked at her daughter. 'Do you know that he often has a traditional English afternoon tea – just like us?'

Katie rolled her eyes. As if indulging in an afternoon tea made the dictator a normal, reasonable person.

'And he loves his dog.' Katie couldn't keep the sarcasm from her voice. When her mother was silent, she said, 'Mutti, you must face it. Hitler will have his way. He's determined to expand his territory. Look at what's happened with Austria. How he pretended it's what the Austrians wanted.'

'Some of them did want to join Germany as one country,' her mother argued.

'I bet it won't be long before they wish they never had.'

Her mother's bright blue eyes filled with tears.

'What is happening to my beautiful country? Have they not learnt anything from the last war?'

'I'm sure the German people themselves aren't in favour,' Katie said. 'But they don't have a voice. It's Hitler and the rest of the bloody Nazis that now have all the power.'

'I will not have you swear,' Ursula reprimanded. 'It is not

9

ladylike.' She gave Katie a stern look. 'That's what comes from working at that racetrack. .'

'There won't be much call for "ladies" if there's a war. Women and girls will have to muck in – like Dad said they did in the last one, so the men are free to fight.'

'I do not wish that for you,' Ursula said through pursed lips. 'It is for the men to fight. German women will remain in the home to look after their husbands and children.'

'What about the single German women?'

'They will not be allowed to involve themselves in fighting – even if they desired it.'

Katie stole a look at her mother, fourteen years younger than Dad. Her slight figure, most of the time enveloped in an apron, her delicate bone structure, the innocent china-blue eyes . . . A horrifying thought struck her. Her mother might be treated as the enemy. Sent back to Germany even. Katie swallowed hard. Mutti wouldn't survive in her native country without Dad.

'How did they take it when you told them you wouldn't be returning?' her father asked when Ursula had dished up supper that evening.

'They weren't pleased,' Katie said. 'I'm cheap labour but dedicated so I doubt they'll replace me that easily. I just told them war was inevitable and I had to do my bit.' She didn't elaborate and tell them Mr Jackson hadn't even thanked her or wished her luck – just told her she could leave after her shift on Saturday night.

'Neville Chamberlain will convince Herr Hitler that there must be a peaceful resolution,' Ursula remarked.

'I'm afraid, my dear, it's inevitable,' Oscar said ruefully. 'Chamberlain is an appeaser and Hitler doesn't respect that attitude and will take full advantage of him. No one is strong enough to oppose the wretched man – except possibly Winston

Churchill. *He* would never consider entering into any kind of negotiation with that dictator.' He shook his head. 'No, we must brace ourselves.' His glance took in both his wife and daughter. 'I certainly hope the government is bracing itself in turn. If it's not, we're in deep trouble.'

'It can't happen again. *Lieber Gott, es muss nicht.*' Ursula's voice cracked as she looked up at her husband, her eyes wide with terror. She fled the room in tears.

'Your mother is living in cloud-cuckoo-land if she thinks Chamberlain will save us at the last minute,' Katie's father continued.

'It's her way of trying to cope.'

'She has to face the truth some time,' he said, regarding his daughter thoughtfully. 'Talking of coping – I think you have a fair bit of adapting to do yourself, working in an office after being outside with the greyhounds all those months. Because I know your heart is in working with animals.'

'It looks like my heart might have to be put on one side for the time being,' Katie said with feeling.

September 1939

'This is London. You will now hear a statement by the Prime Minister.'

The sombre tones of Neville Chamberlain came over the wireless in the sitting room where Katie and her parents had gathered to listen.

'I am speaking to you from the Cabinet Room at 10 Downing Street. This morning the British Ambassador in Berlin handed the German Government a final note stating that unless we heard from them by eleven o'clock that they were prepared at once to withdraw their troops from Poland, a state of war would exist between us. I have to tell you now that no such undertaking has been received and that consequently this country is at war with Germany.'

'*Lieber Gott!*' Ursula Valentine shot out of her chair as though a bomb were about to drop on her head there and then.

'Hush, my dear, and listen to what more Chamberlain has to say.'

Ursula stared at him with frightened eyes.

Katie listened intently as the Prime Minister said he needed everyone's help to face Hitler's evil with calmness and courage, though Ursula looked dazed, as though she wasn't able to take in any more. Was her mother thinking she might be sent home – or worse, to prison? Dare she ask her father what the government might do with German people who lived in this country? Whatever the answer, they needed to be prepared.

She was just about to question him when a blood-curdling wail started up, then rose to a crescendo. She froze. Her mother screamed and dived under the table. That sound. Katie had heard it before on Pathé News. The air-raid warning. Good God, it couldn't – surely – have started already.

'It's all right, Ursula.' Oscar bent down to his wife, whose legs were sticking out from under the table. 'They won't have time to come over and bomb us the same moment we declare war on them. It'll be a practice to show the public what an air-raid siren sounds like. Come on out of there. We'll go outside and you'll see there are no German bombers in sight.'

'Just leave me,' came her whimper.

Her father sighed. 'Katie, come with me and we'll have a look.'

Neighbours gathered outside, their heads tilted upwards. There was nothing to see except a few innocent clouds.

'Dad, what will happen to Mutti?'

'What do you mean?'

'She's German.' Katie bit her lip. 'I think she's worried the government will send her back to Germany. Or even imprison her.' She turned to her father. 'They wouldn't do that, would they?'

'Well, they might start interning Germans who they're suspicious of, but they can't do anything to your mother. When we got married, she automatically became a British citizen.'

'Are you sure?'

'Quite.' He looked at her. 'I thought I'd reassured her on that.' He paused. 'I'd better go in and try to calm her down.'

Katie stared after his vanishing figure. It seemed surreal that they were now at war with Germany. Like a nightmare from which you try to wake up but can't. She shuddered. What would become of them all? At nineteen, her own life was only just beginning. Would it end before it had even started?

Chapter Two

June 1940

Katie heaved a sigh as she rolled a fresh sheet of paper, together with a piece of carbon paper backed by a sheet of flimsy copy paper, into her typewriter, ruing the moment she'd finally agreed to take a secretarial course at May Stanley's Secretarial School in Kensington a whole nine months ago. Thank goodness she'd be finished by the end of the month and be able to collect her certificate. After the initial shock, she hadn't disliked the course – in fact, to her surprise she'd even enjoyed learning Pitman's shorthand. It reminded her of grappling with German at the insistence of her mother, ultimately revelling in her top place in the small class. She hadn't been so keen on bookkeeping, yet with practice even that began to fall into place. But the thought of being shut in an office day after day, sitting at a typewriter producing the same kinds of letters over and over after taking dictation from some mumbling old fuddy-duddy, filled her with fear.

And now what everyone had dreaded, many burying their heads, had happened. It was still incredible that the country was in the throes of another world war – the Phoney War, the Americans called it, as so far there'd been no sign of the threatened invasion. The British went one better and named it the Bore War. Katie sighed as she propped up her shorthand notebook on the left-hand side of her desk and began transcribing the piece of dictation Miss Brown had given them an hour earlier, just before the tea-break. Some of the students must be struggling, she thought, as there was only the sound of a few typewriter keys being hammered. She kept her eye on her notebook and had soon finished typing the letter to a fictional company about their heating system. If only the subject matter was more interesting. But thank goodness she was pretty accurate with her typing. Just as well. One mistaken word only was allowed in a complete letter or report and that had to be erased very carefully so as not to smudge the carbon copy underneath, which in turn had to be amended. Miss Brown would hold up the sheet of typing to the light to spot if this correction was noticeable. A stencil was even worse – you were only allowed two incorrect letters, which you could dab with a bright pink liquid – almost like applying nail varnish – and type over. If there were more errors, the stencil would end up in the bin and that student would be ticked off for wasting it.

'I should have typed this straightaway instead of going to tea,' Maureen on the desk next to her grumbled under her breath. 'Now my shorthand's gone stale, I can't read some of it.'

'Jot down the bits you can,' Katie advised. 'Your brain will soon fill in the missing words.'

'My brain doesn't work like that.'

'Then you have to train it,' Katie said firmly.

At four o'clock in the afternoon, Miss Brown made her usual announcement.

'Thank you, girls. You've done well today. You may now pack up and go home.'

Katie had noticed quite soon after the course began that Miss Brown rarely criticised any of them, even though a couple of the girls still couldn't type without looking at the keys, and half their letters ended up in the waste-paper basket, full of mistakes. And poor Maureen always had difficulty transcribing her shorthand. Maybe Mrs Stanley didn't want to lose any students as she might be obliged to reimburse some of the fee.

The dozen girls pulled the covers over their machines and picked up their handbags, then darted for the door. Where were they all heading? She knew several girls had dates with their boyfriends this evening but not everyone, surely. Well, she didn't have a date. Katie blew out her cheeks, feeling a little envious. What would it be like to have a boyfriend taking her arm and maybe going to the cinema, sitting in the back row holding hands? But since she'd got the job at the racetrack six days a week, her old schoolfriends had stopped asking her to join them, as she was either working on a Saturday night or too tired to go to a dance. Certainly, the greyhound racetrack was not the place to meet the kind of young man her mother would approve of. But it would be nice if there was someone waiting for her.

Stop being ridiculous! You have too much happening already to worry about some non-existent man.

Mechanically, she drew the cover over her own typewriter, not in the mood to go home just yet. Maybe she'd go for a walk. Clear her mind. Maybe she could—

Her thoughts were interrupted by Miss Brown.

'Katie, Mrs Stanley would like to have a word with you in her office.'

The teacher's words took her by surprise. Apart from when Katie had had her interview with the owner, the woman had never spoken to her.

'Of course, Miss Brown.'

She mounted the dusty narrow staircase to an equally narrow landing and knocked on the first door she came to.

'Enter!'

Katie opened the door and stepped inside. The smell of smoke assailed her nostrils.

'Have a seat.' Mrs Stanley gestured to one of the chairs on the other side of the desk as she stubbed out the remains of her cigarette, causing the last of the smoke to curl towards Katie.

'You've done well in your course, Miss Valentine.' Mrs Stanley flipped through a file. 'Miss Brown says you are one of the fastest with your shorthand and typing and should be able to secure a good position in any company you choose. We would, of course, give you an excellent reference, if that's what you decide.'

Katie's heart dropped. It wasn't what she'd planned for the rest of her life. And if a bomb fell on her, what had there been to show for that life?

'Thank you,' she murmured.

'As I'm sure you know, Miss Brown became engaged at the weekend,' Mrs Stanley continued briskly. 'She and her fiancé plan to marry by the end of the year and move to Newcastle.' She paused to light a fresh cigarette.

What have Miss Brown's plans got to do with me?

'That means I'll need to recruit someone to step into her place and I'd like you to be that person.'

Katie startled. Had she heard right? Mrs Stanley wanted her as a teacher of shorthand and typing and bookkeeping? Oh, she couldn't think of anything worse. Stuck with a load of girls, probably no more enthusiastic than she'd been. But how to answer without sounding rude or ungrateful?

'Um, thank you for having such faith in me,' she finally stuttered.

Mrs Stanley leaned forward on her desk.

'Miss Brown strongly recommended you.' She inhaled deeply on her cigarette. 'I realise you're not yet twenty-one but you're mature for your age. And until Miss Brown leaves, you can be her understudy for the autumn term. She and I have every confidence you will do a splendid job.' She blew out a stream of smoke. 'I don't expect an immediate answer. You'll need to talk it over with your parents. That's natural. But perhaps by tomorrow I hope you'll be in a position to accept.'

Katie bit her lip. She didn't need to talk about a job offer with her parents. She was old enough to make up her own mind whether to accept a situation or not. Without doubt, her mother would say it was just the opportunity she should take. But would teaching girls shorthand and typing help with the war effort? No. Now she was about to take her final exams, she wanted to apply her skills to something that would place her nearer to the action that was bound to start sooner or later. Do her bit, as Mr Churchill, the new Prime Minister, had rallied the country to do in one of his marvellous speeches.

Besides, there'd been no mention of earnings. Katie's mind raced. Miss Brown had warned all the girls when they'd first begun the course and had to feign an interview with a future boss: never ask how much the employer was offering.

'No well-brought-up young lady would dream of discussing remuneration,' she'd said. 'You must hope that the employer will bring up the issue himself. Under no circumstances must you be the first. If they grant you a second interview and still don't, then you'd be within your rights to enquire once they'd offered you the position. Until then, it's vulgar to mention it.'

Well, vulgar or not, Katie thought, here goes.

'What would you be offering as a wage, Mrs Stanley?'

Katie almost giggled as Mrs Stanley's thin pencilled eyebrows practically disappeared into her hairline.

'That is to be discussed only if you accept the post.' Her voice had noticeably cooled.

'But how can I accept if I don't know what I'll be earning? It could make all the difference to my decision. In fact, I can't even make a decision if I don't know exactly what you have in mind.'

If her mother heard the way she was talking to one of her elders and betters, Katie knew she would be horrified. But surely she wasn't being unreasonable.

'I've never heard anything so extraordinary from a young woman.' Mrs Stanley rose to her feet, her dark skirt swirling round her ankles. 'Unless you have severe financial problems at home that you would need to discuss with me—' She raised a pencilled eyebrow.

Katie shook her head. 'Not that I know of, but I think it's only fair to be told. After all, I don't want to live with my parents for ever.' There was a silence. Before Katie realised what she was about to say, she blurted, 'I'm sure the men ask future employers what their salary is to be and no one turns a hair.'

She couldn't believe she was arguing with Mrs Stanley, whose face had darkened with anger.

'I think, Miss Valentine, I must reconsider my offer. I have a feeling you might turn out to be more trouble than you're worth!'

The late afternoon sun warmed Katie's bare arms as she wandered through Hyde Park, musing over Mrs Stanley's surprising offer, and how, moments later, she had just as surprisingly taken it back. Really, the woman was too cynical for words, interpreting her question as rude and assuming she must be a troublemaker.

Even if Mrs Stanley had offered to increase her wages from a guinea a week to twenty-five shillings, Katie knew it wouldn't have been enough to tempt her. She had to be interested and happy in her work – and being a teacher in May Stanley's Secretarial School was not the job that could make either possible.

Well, she wouldn't tell her parents any of this. Her mother in particular would never let her forget that she'd messed up such an opportunity by her apparently bad behaviour.

Relieved the decision had been taken out of her hands, Katie sat at one end of a park bench watching a young family play ball with their dog and breathing in the scent from the nearby rose bed. She'd take Tanny for a walk as soon as she was home. She tilted her head to look up at the sky. It was a clear blue – a perfect early summer afternoon. She couldn't imagine the sky filled with German planes dropping bombs on innocent people, as the country had been told would happen if Hitler had his way and they were invaded. But so far everything seemed calm and perfectly ordinary, and it was hard to believe it would ever be any other way than how it was at this very minute.

Chapter Three

Over the next three weeks, no matter how hard she tried to shrug off Miss Brown's noticeable change of manner, constantly finding fault with almost everything she did, Katie felt a burning resentment towards the teacher. As for Mrs Stanley, the woman couldn't even raise a smile and say, 'Good morning' whenever she passed by.

'I won't let them get me down,' Katie muttered to herself. 'Mrs Stanley's done me a favour. I know I would have hated teaching and would have felt awkward when there were bound to be some older girls who would have resented me and made my job difficult.'

The atmosphere was worse at the end of June when the certificates were given out after the final examination. Katie was pleased to come second in the class – until she learnt that Daphne had come top, even with consistently lower marks than Katie's throughout the nine months. But she managed to swallow her indignation and took her certificate, saying 'Thank you' and looking Miss Brown and Mrs Stanley straight in the eye. Let them think what they liked.

Katie kept her dignity while she marched out of the building, her head high and her spine pulled straight to make the most of every inch of her petite frame. But when she turned the corner, she couldn't stop the tears.

'You all right, love?' A plump, middle-aged woman walking towards her stopped in her tracks.

Furiously, Katie brushed her face with her hand.

'Something in my eye,' she mumbled.

'If you're sure.' The woman gave her a kind smile as she passed by.

Katie was lost in her jumbled thoughts when she heard her name.

'Katie, wait!'

She turned round. It was Daphne, of all people. Had she come to gloat? She almost walked on but out of curiosity she stopped. Daphne ran up, breathing fast.

'I'm glad I caught up with you,' she said. 'Look, why don't we go somewhere and have a cup of tea.'

'I don't see the point,' Katie said coolly. 'I want to forget all about Mrs Stanley and her damned school.'

She shouldn't swear, but, face to face with the girl who'd unfairly beaten her in the final exams, she felt humiliation hot on her cheeks.

'So do I,' Daphne said surprisingly. 'I couldn't wait to get my certificate and leave that place.'

'Really?' Katie's eyes widened. 'I actually quite enjoyed it.'

'Oh, I didn't mind the training itself,' Daphne said. 'It was that pathetic Miss Brown. And I never took to Mrs Stanley.' She took Katie's arm to steer her out of the way of two young boys. 'So thank God it's over.' She stopped abruptly. 'There's a Lyons' teashop round the corner – and it's my treat.'

Suddenly, tea seemed a good idea to Katie.

Daphne pushed the door open to a clattering noise. From where Katie was standing, there wasn't an empty table in sight. Nippies in their black dresses, white aprons and distinctive white caps, rushed to and fro, holding trays high.

'Table over there,' one of the waitresses said, her head jerking to a corner where an elderly couple were rising to their feet. 'Wait here a mo while I clear it.'

Two minutes later the girls were settled at the table and the same waitress handed them a menu.

'Tea for two, please,' Daphne said, then looked towards Katie. 'Would you like a toasted teacake? I'm having one.'

Katie nodded. 'Thank you, that would be nice.'

'With real butter, please,' Daphne added to the waitress, who scribbled the order on her notepad and hurried away.

'Now, Katie, I want to know exactly what brought about the change with Miss Brown, suddenly finding fault with everything you did when we'd almost completed the course.'

Katie bit her lower lip. Daphne's eyes were looking directly at her. She was a vivacious girl, Katie thought, maybe a couple of years older than herself, and they'd never been unfriendly. Maybe she'd feel better if she got it off her chest.

'It all started when Miss Brown became engaged and recommended to Mrs Stanley that I be trained in her place,' Katie began. She filled Daphne in with a few more details. 'So Mrs Stanley took back her offer after I'd asked her for the second time what my wages would be. She said I'd be a troublemaker.'

Daphne threw back her dark head and roared with laughter. 'She really said that?'

'Yes. And it was the last straw—' Katie stopped. No, she had more pride than to mention it to Daphne.

'When I came top and didn't deserve it,' Daphne finished.

'How did you know I was going to say that?'

'Because I would have felt the same as you. Furious. They're totally unprofessional, but it's not going to make any difference to your future. The certificate merely says we've passed and are now qualified secretaries.' Daphne's hazel eyes sparkled. 'I can't think of anything more exciting – can you?'

Daphne's tone was so blatantly sarcastic, Katie couldn't help chuckling.

'I'd like to be friends,' Daphne said, 'so how about it?'

23

Katie's temporary grudge against Daphne immediately fell away. The girl had sought her out and explained. She hadn't tried to lord it over her in any way. And right now, it would be good to have a friend with whom she had something in common, even if it was only the secretarial course.

'I'd like that, too.'

Over tea and buttery toasted teacakes the conversation inevitably turned to the subject of how the war was going.

'So far the Germans haven't done that much – well, not to us, at any rate,' Katie added.

'Hmm. Don't speak too soon.' Daphne buttered the second half of her teacake. 'Have you seen the papers today?'

'No,' Katie said. 'I usually read it after Dad's read it and that's not until the evening.' She looked at Daphne. 'Why? Has something happened?'

'You could say that.' Daphne's face was grim. 'The Nazis invaded the Channel Islands yesterday. More than likely it'll be us next.'

Katie stared at Daphne in horror, swallowing at the enormity of what Daphne had just said.

'Dear Lord.' The teacake dropped from her fingers.

'I imagine it will end in total world war.' Daphne pulled out a packet of cigarettes and shook one out to Katie. She took it, hoping it might calm her thudding heart, and Daphne lit the two cigarettes with a silver lighter. 'No one can change Hitler's determination to add to his Fatherland. Look at how he swiped Czechoslovakia. It came out of nowhere and they had no defence. It was frightening. Then poor Poland, Norway and Denmark, half of France—' She broke off with a heavy sigh.

'I can't keep up with all Hitler's doings.'

'My father, who's an army officer, talks a lot about it,' Daphne said. 'He thinks we all need to be aware of what's going on, and I agree. It'll affect us all sooner or later.'

'Do you really think we're next on Hitler's plan?' Katie said.

'I'm sure. He won't want to leave us out. We're a challenge but he thinks we'll give in like a baby.' She gave Katie a rueful smile. 'He definitely doesn't know the British.'

'My mother won't believe Hitler would dare to invade us – not when it's only twenty years since the last one.' Should she say anything about her mother's nationality? Would it matter? After all, her father had never told her she must hide the fact. She coughed a little from the cigarette, the smoke irritating her throat. She wasn't used to smoking but had wanted to be polite. 'It's worse for her.'

'In what way?' Daphne leaned forward over the table.

'Because she's German.'

Daphne's smile faded. 'Oh, too bad. She could be in for a rough time.'

'That's what I'm worried about.'

'So what do you think you'll do now?'

'I did want to see something of the world before I settled down.'

'Get married, you mean?'

'Maybe sometime in the future, but not yet.' It was too soon for Katie to mention her dream of setting up an animal centre.

'Do you have a boyfriend?'

Katie felt her cheeks grow warm. Roderick would no longer count. She'd met him at a dance and they'd gone out a few times. He'd even kissed her. But then he'd told her he was going into the Army. She hadn't seen him for several months and to her surprise hadn't missed him. Soon his letters stopped altogether. He must have felt the same about her.

'Not any longer,' was all she said. 'How about you?'

Daphne pulled her mouth into a grim line. 'I fell for the wrong chap. He thought he could push me around – literally. He did it once too often and I ditched him. But I have the feeling he still hasn't got the message. So now I'm going to apply to the ATA.'

'What's that?'

'The Air Transport Auxiliary – where the pilots deliver aeroplanes to the soldiers.'

Katie's jaw dropped. 'Can you actually fly a plane?'

Daphne hesitated. 'I haven't got my licence yet, but I was having lessons until the school closed when the war started. My dream is to be a pilot. Difficult in a man's world.' She gave a rueful smile. 'But now we're at war, suddenly the clouds have broken loose and apparently the ATA has started to recruit female pilots to ferry planes around, as well as finish training them if they're not yet qualified.' She stubbed her cigarette into the ashtray with more vehemence than it warranted. 'I want to be where the action is.' She looked at Katie. 'I imagine having a German mother you speak German very well.'

'Pretty much. My mother was determined I learn even when I was little.'

'I'm sure it will stand you in good stead.' Daphne finished her tea and looked at her watch. 'Well, I must be going but let's not lose contact.' She rose to her feet. 'Are you on the telephone?'

'Yes.'

'Then give me your number and I'll keep in touch. Perhaps we can go to the pictures one evening.'

'I'd like that.'

How strange that something horrid had turned into something so nice, Katie mused, as she put out her hand for the bus to stop. It looked as though Daphne came from a good family, judging by that expensive silver cigarette lighter, and the way she always dressed to perfection. And fancy her being a pilot. Katie smiled to herself. Daphne had certainly made her think again about what women could do if they were determined.

In a much better frame of mind, Katie alighted at the bus-stop and walked the short distance to her home. All was quiet when she opened the door and called out, but there was a delicious smell of apples and cinnamon. Her mother had been making *Apfelstrudel*. Even though she'd just finished a toasted teacake, Katie's mouth watered. She wandered to the kitchen but it was deserted. The *Apfelstrudel* was on a baking tray and still warm to Katie's light touch. Her mother must have gone to Mrs Shelton's while it was cooling.

Forcing herself not to cut even a sliver to taste it – Ursula liked to be in control of her baking – Katie went to her bedroom and kicked off her shoes. Oh, that was better. She put on a pair of flat sandals and opened the middle drawer of her dressing table to find a comb to grip back her hair. On the top was Aunt Judy's letter, still in its envelope. She hadn't looked at it since she'd opened it a year ago. Idly, she picked it up and read the contents again.

All right, Aunt Judy, I did as you instructed. I have my certificate. Now what do I do?

Her eyes ran down the page and a flurry of words jumped out at her as though for the first time:

'There's no doubt we will be at war with Germany sooner or later,' she read out slowly, 'and you'll have something concrete to offer such as a secretary at the War Office in Whitehall.'

She'd even gone on to say she'd successfully approached them in the Great War. For the first time, Katie wondered in what capacity.

Well, dear Aunt Judy, we are *at war now. The Nazis have just invaded the Channel Islands. It's hard to believe but it could be us next.*

Maybe the War Office was where she should apply. Katie's heart fluttered. She hadn't thought of that and now it was staring her in the face. But she was getting ahead of herself. Yet something told her if she *did* apply, she might well be offered a job. Until then she wouldn't mention it to her parents – it might be tempting fate. Wishing she could hug her aunt for thinking ahead about her niece's future, and with renewed energy, Katie ran down the stairs to greet her mother, who had just come through the front door.

Katie was suddenly struck by how Ursula had begun to look as if she were well into middle age. Her fair hair was already salt and pepper, even though she was only forty-two. But she must have been a beauty in her day, Katie thought, with her fine bone structure and bright blue eyes. It must have been her delicate blonde appearance that had captured her father's heart. For once overwhelmed by the frail figure, she said, 'Hello, Mutti,' and kissed her cheek. 'Go and sit down and I'll make *you* a cup of tea for a change.'

Chapter Four

July 1940

Katie heard the letterbox rattle as she was getting dressed. She'd written to Whitehall a few days ago, crossing her fingers that they would at least give her an interview. With Tanny rushing in front, she hurried down the stairs and picked up the morning post. Two bills and a brown typed envelope. Her heart raced as she turned it over. But it was addressed to her father.

She blew out her cheeks. It had been a week now and she wondered if she should give up and look for something else. Her father's newspaper advertised vacancies for females but what was on offer didn't appeal. Nannies and nurses and cleaners and kitchen staff in hotels and restaurants, waitresses in Lyons' teashops, filing clerks . . . nothing where she could use her new shorthand and typing skills. And if she kept faithful to Aunt Judy's wishes, that's what she was destined to do.

The following day, when she'd decided to go to the library and see whether they could help – perhaps read some pamphlets about joining one of the Forces after all – she picked up the post. There was what looked like a bill for her father and, from the writing, a letter from her mother's English friend, whom Ursula had met when she first arrived in England. But the last item was an envelope with a typewritten address for Miss Katharina Valentine.

29

Her heart thumped when she saw the London postmark. This must be it. Could her future be contained in this one buff-coloured envelope? Tearing it open as she stood in the hall, she slid out the letter and read:

Dear Miss Valentine,

We are in receipt of your letter of 30th June 1940 and request you attend an interview at this department on Wednesday, 10th July 1940 at 10a.m. Please bring your secretarial certificate with you.

If you are unable to attend, kindly let us know.
Yours faithfully,
The War Office
Ref: V. W. L/cm

Whoever it was – this VWL – hadn't even bothered to sign his name and the tone of the letter struck her as quite curt. Then she shook herself.

Stop whining, for heaven's sake. He's granting you an interview so count yourself lucky. She couldn't wait.

Katie opened the curtains on the morning of her interview to a bright blue sky with a few trailing clouds. It was going to be another hot day.

Long may it last, Katie thought happily as she pulled her favourite cotton dress over her head. Her mother had designed it beautifully, as she had done with almost all of Katie's clothes. The dress was black and white checked, short sleeved and knee-length, the hem of the skirt swinging as she walked. It had a black patent belt emphasising her waist, and her mother had sewn a black and white bow on a band round the front of one of the many hats Aunt Judy had left her.

She glanced at herself in the mirror. Her blonde hair shone, her pink lipstick was freshly applied . . . She looked down at her shoes, polished and gleaming. Yes, she was ready for her interview at Whitehall – though she'd told her parents she was going to meet Daphne, because there might be a position in the place where she was working.

Katie took the train from Wimbledon Station to Vauxhall and walked the short distance to St James's Park. She crossed Horse Guards Road to the New Public Offices. Even though her head was full of how she was going to conduct herself in the interview – calmly and intelligently, she told herself – she couldn't help admiring such an elegant Baroque-inspired Edwardian building. Its outstanding features were the four decorative domes on the towers at each corner, the colonnade on the upper storey, and the Grecian-style pediments and cornices. Just a pity about the sandbag barricades – yet another sign that the country was at war, although so far there'd been no bombing in London as everyone had expected.

Taking a deep breath, Katie stiffened her spine. A sentry directed her to the west front where she would find the main entrance. Another sentry was on duty outside.

'Do you have an appointment?' he said curtly.

She showed him her letter.

'I see.' He gave her a cursory glance. 'Go in and ask at Reception.'

Inside, barely taking in the opulent surroundings, Katie walked up to the Reception desk and showed the same letter to one of the receptionists, a smartly dressed young man with dark Brylcreemed hair. He looked at a large open diary and glanced up.

'Someone will be along shortly to escort you,' he told her. 'If you'd take a seat . . . ' He gestured to a row of visitors' chairs.

Ten o'clock came and went. Katie repeatedly glanced at her watch. By the time it showed ten-thirty, she was lost in her irritation with the mysterious VWL who hadn't bothered to keep to the appointed time. Then she jumped as she heard her name.

'Please come this way, Miss Valentine.'

Katie followed the young receptionist up the wide, elegant staircase to a landing, and finally to a door with a sign bearing the same initials as on her letter. He knocked briskly and a voice from within said, 'Enter.'

'Miss Valentine for you, Mr Lester,' the receptionist said as he ushered her in.

A man with hair almost as fair as her own rose from his chair and stepped towards her. He was little more than average height, but somehow he had a presence. Instinctively, she stepped back as he thrust out his hand. She felt its pressure and, after a second or two, removed her own.

'Vernon Lester. Do sit down.' He gestured to a pair of chairs on the other side of his desk.

When she'd nervously arranged her skirt over her knees under his piercing blue gaze, he said, 'The reason I asked you to attend an interview is because we're expanding our office to cope with the extra work the war is causing.' He looked at her directly. 'Do you have your certificate to say you're qualified?'

'Yes.' She had it ready and handed it to him.

Katie sat silently while he bent his head and read it. She tried not to let him see her attempt to read some pencilled notes from upside down, but he abruptly looked up and caught her. Feeling the warmth colouring her cheeks she bit her lip.

'I see you've finished your secretarial course with a distinction at a well-regarded establishment,' he commented, 'but I'm interested to know why you approached us for a job at the War Office in particular.'

She told him it was her late aunt's suggestion only weeks before war was declared. And that she had had some kind of involvement with the War Office.

'And this sounded like an interesting place to work, now we're at war,' she finished lamely.

Mr Lester snapped open a gold cigarette case. He drew a cigarette half out and offered it to her. She shook her head, even though she was very tempted. It might calm her nerves. On the other hand, if she started to cough it would be too embarrassing for words.

He snapped the lighter and lit one for himself, inhaled deeply and stared at her.

'Is there anyone you're responsible for who could distract your attention from a position we might offer?'

'No.'

'What about boyfriends?'

She looked at him steadily, doubting he'd have asked that question of another man. It was so unfair.

'No one special.'

'Parents both in good health?'

'Yes.'

'What does your father do?'

'He's in the Home Guard.'

'And before the war?'

'He was a teacher at King's College.'

'Why is he not still there?'

The questions were coming thick and fast.

'He's quite a bit older than my mother and retired just before war was declared.'

'What can you add that would make me think you might be useful?' he said, casually leaning back in his chair and blowing the smoke out of the side of his well-shaped mouth. She had the feeling that if she hadn't been there, his polished shoes would be perched on the desk. Before she could answer he leaned forward. 'You mentioned in your letter that you spoke German fluently. How did that come about?'

'My mother is German. She's always spoken to me in German as much as English, so I've grown up with it.'

'Hmm.' He took another drag and tapped the trembling ash against his glass ashtray. 'That could prove most useful now we're at war with Germany.'

Her mother had often suggested she teach German to English children, but now there really was a war, wouldn't it be the last thing parents would want their children to learn? His next question took her by surprise.

'How did your parents meet – he being British and she being German?'

'She was studying English just after the Great War. He was one of the teachers. They got married and stayed in England.'

'Did they visit Germany at all?'

'I don't think so – not as far as I know, anyway.'

He nodded, his face expressionless.

'Hmm. Interesting.' He ground out his cigarette in the ashtray with the other stubs. 'Do you have any questions?'

She hesitated, aware that he was watching her. 'What would a job here entail?'

He raised a golden eyebrow.

'Anything I would tell you about the work would have to be preceded by your signing the Official Secrets Act. But first I want to reflect on where you might be most suited.'

It didn't sound as though he were turning her down. She felt a flicker of excitement.

'So does that mean you're offering me a job, Mr Lester?'

'It means I'll give it some thought.' His tone was impatient.

'I see.' Flushing with embarrassment, Katie rose from her chair. 'Well, thank you—'

For a moment his eyes narrowed in surprise. Then he said, 'Please sit down. I haven't finished.'

She did as she was told, confused as to where she stood

with this man, though she didn't want to upset him or it might backfire on her and she wouldn't be offered anything. Thank goodness she hadn't told her parents she was coming for this interview. She couldn't bear the thought of having to tell them she'd muffed this as well as the job at the secretarial school.

'I will discuss your credentials with my colleagues to see where we might possibly place you.' He gazed at her. 'I can see you're a bright young lady, Miss Valentine, but I couldn't guarantee we have a position to use your full potential. A lot of our work is very routine.' He gave what looked like an apologetic smile. 'However, as I said, I will give it some serious thought.' He came from behind his desk, shook her hand briefly, then opened the door to see her out.

'Thank you for your time, Mr Lester,' she said, determined to meet his eye, though she couldn't fathom his expression.

He nodded. With all the energy she could muster, Katie stood as tall as her petite figure allowed and walked out, hearing him close the door behind her.

When she was outside the Whitehall buildings she drew in a shaky breath. She'd bungled two job opportunities in less than a fortnight.

Please God, let there be a third and I promise I'll grab it with both hands, no matter what.

What now, she thought. She had nowhere in particular she wanted to go. She might as well make her way home – take Tanny for a walk. He never failed to cheer her. A bus was coming towards her and she ran to the nearest stop to catch it.

'Is Dad at the Home Guard?' Katie asked her mother when Tanny had given her his usual boisterous welcome.

'Yes, he was called in for extra duty and said he might be late for lunch.' Ursula stared at Katie. 'What did your friend Daphne have to say about a job, Katharina?'

'Oh, nothing much. It sounded too dull for words.'

'I hope you did not say that to your friend.'

'No, of course not. I just have to keep looking for something I'm really interested in.'

Ursula frowned. 'I hope you are not being fussy.'

Feeling a twinge of guilt that she'd deliberately fibbed about Daphne, Katie gave an inward sigh.

'No, Mutti. I just don't want to take something that doesn't appeal.'

Her mother didn't look convinced.

'*Ach, so.* I hope you will not be too long before you find something that *will* appeal.'

It might not be that simple, Mutti.

Chapter Five

Katie's heart plummeted every time she picked up the post from the mat and saw there was no official envelope for her from Whitehall. If only Mr Lester would just drop a line to say she wasn't suitable. At least she'd know.

There seemed only one thing left to do that Aunt Judy would understand and surely would have approved, now that they really were at war, and that was to join up. Several girls she knew had signed up for the WAAFs, the ATS or the WRNS. She had to admit that wearing the women's air force or navy uniform was quite tempting, and they'd likely be able to use her secretarial skills in one or other of them. But to her surprise she found working in one of the offices in Whitehall was more appealing. It was very near Number 10 Downing Street, so in a sense, she'd be closer to the war. She might even catch a glimpse of Mr Churchill, whom everyone was now behind.

It would be so good to talk this over with someone other than her parents. She'd ring Daphne this evening. Daphne had rung once to try to arrange a cinema trip but Mutti had had a sick headache and her father was out with the Home Guard.

'Mary Lorrimer speaking,' came the perfectly accented voice over the wire.

'It's Katie Valentine. I was wondering if I could have a word with Daphne.'

'I'm afraid she's out. May I have her telephone you when she's home? She shouldn't be long.'

Katie thanked her and then made her and her mother a tray of tea. Just as she was pouring it the phone rang and she jumped up to answer it in the hall.

'How nice to hear from you, Katie,' Daphne said. 'I was wondering if you've found a job yet – or maybe you've decided to join up.'

'Not yet. Have you?'

'Yes, I have. I started last week.'

'Oh, you've joined that aeroplane service.'

'Not yet, but the woman's promised to put me on the waiting list.'

She sounded exasperated and Katie couldn't blame her.

'So where've you ended up?'

''Fraid I can't say much,' Daphne said mysteriously. 'I've signed the Official Secrets Act.'

The same document Mr Lester mentioned.

'I'm working at Whitehall,' Daphne said. 'That's all I'm allowed to say.'

Katie fought down a spike of envy. How had Daphne managed to land a job there when her own interview had turned out to be so dismal? They chatted for another minute or two about how terrible it was to be at war, and Daphne's brother, who was an RAF pilot and had had no trouble being recruited.

'Because he's a man,' Daphne said. 'Women are still fighting to be accepted as pilots as good as the men. It's ridiculous. But they'll need us when things get tricky, I bet.' Unexpectedly, she added, 'By the way, I could put in a word for you. Tell them I have a friend who qualified from the same secretarial school as me with top marks.' She paused. 'If you want, that is.'

'That's kind of you but I recently had an interview for something I'd really like and I'm just waiting to hear back from them.' Katie paused. 'I'm really hopeful, but can I come back to you if it doesn't transpire into anything?'

'Of course. And do tell me more if you're successful.'

'Like you, I might not be able to say much, because the chap who interviewed me said I would have to sign the same document as you.'

'Oh. In that case we might be working in the same place.' Daphne chuckled. 'So keep me posted. And good luck that you'll soon hear something positive.' She rang off.

At noon that same day Katie, with Tanny rushing ahead, closed the front door behind her to pick up a few items at the grocer's. The dog gave a bark of delight at the postman.

'Yes, good boy.' The postman bent down to fondle the dog's ears. He looked up. 'Got one for you today, miss. Most official-looking.' He handed it to her.

Katie's heart jumped. 'Thank you. I've been waiting for this one.'

He grinned at her. 'Looks like it's important.'

'It might be,' Katie tossed over her shoulder as she went back inside. She rushed up to her bedroom and tore open the envelope. The letter was dated 24th July 1940.

Dear Miss Valentine,

I regret to say that at the present moment we do not have a vacancy for someone with your level of experience. However, this could change at any time and if so, I will be contacting you again.

Yours faithfully,
The War Office

Oh, no! Mr Lester had turned her down flat. Why? She must have left so little impression that he hadn't even bothered to sign his name. Katie bit back angry tears. Could it be to do with having a German mother? That they were suspicious of all Germans now? But of course she'd never know. It was just as well she hadn't mentioned the interview to her parents.

Tanny scratched at the door and she stood up to let him in. He pushed his nose into her hand, looking up at her with adoration.

'Thank goodness *you* still love me,' Katie said, patting his head. 'I can't keep moaning, Tanny. I have to find something else.'

But what?

Tanny gave what she interpreted as a woof of sympathy, and then another more urgent bark.

'All right. We'll go for the walk I promised you and pick up the bits Mutti needs.'

The following day brought her another letter – the envelope hand-written. She opened it and to her amazement saw that the signature was Vernon W. Lester! Her heart raced. He'd actually signed his name this time. She read:

Dear Miss Valentine,

Please accept my sincere apologies but somehow the letter we sent you yesterday got mixed up with another applicant.

We are pleased to offer you the position of stenographer at Whitehall starting Monday, 5th August. To that end, would you please come to Reception at 9.00 a.m. and you will be escorted to the correct office where you will sign the Official Secrets Act, and then shown the department you will be working in.

Please bring your Birth Certificate, your parents' Marriage Certificate and your passport if you have one.

If you have found an alternative position, please be so kind as to inform us.

Yours sincerely,
Vernon W. Lester

Goodness! She hadn't bungled it after all. But she'd only been offered a position as a stenographer when she was a qualified secretary. She'd learnt double-entry bookkeeping, studied basic business law, business English . . . oh, it was too bad. But there was a war on. She'd get her foot in the door. Then maybe when she'd proved herself she'd be promoted. She set her jaw. Yes, she'd accept. And she'd write the letter straightaway.

'You'll be pleased to know I've been offered a job today,' Katie said at supper that night.

'Oh, well done, Katie,' Oscar said. 'Your mother and I are proud of you for sticking at the school. Judy was right as she so often was. It's opened a door straightaway.'

Katie happened to glance at her mother at that moment and noticed her bright blue eyes momentarily close, as though trying to block out something unpleasant.

'Is it the one your friend, Daphne, had in mind for you? ' her father asked.

'Yes, it's at the War Office – in Whitehall.'

'The War Office?' Her father jerked his head up. 'You didn't mention that.'

'I didn't want to in case I didn't get it. But it was where Aunt Judy suggested I should apply.'

'Really.' He laid down his knife and fork. 'I wish I'd known.'

'Mutti knew because she read the letter,' Katie said tartly, staring at her mother, who flushed and looked down at her plate.

There was a strange silence. She couldn't make out why her father sounded perturbed. Why had he wished he'd known where she was applying? She finished her meal, suddenly remembering something.

'Oh, they said they want to see your Marriage Certificate and my Birth Certificate.'

Her mother instantly stopped her chatter, her fork frozen in the air, her jaw slack. Katie saw a glance pass between her and her father. What was going on? And then a dreadful thought sliced through her head. Maybe there wasn't any Marriage Certificate. Maybe they'd never got married. If that was the case then her mother would definitely be sent back to Germany – or at the very least interned – because she wouldn't be considered a British subject. Yet Dad had been quite definite that there was no need to worry about her on those grounds. Katie chewed her lip, trying to decide if she was imagining things that weren't actually there.

But just supposing they weren't legally married, she'd have been born out of wedlock. How could she bear such a shameful secret? She'd have to turn down Mr Lester's offer because she couldn't – mustn't – do anything that would endanger her mother. Oh, this was too awful for words. She looked at her parents. No, she hadn't imagined that glance between them. Dad was trying to catch her mother's eye but Mutti had directed her attention to the table again. Katie swallowed hard. The only thing for it was to ask them to show her their Marriage Certificate and she'd know one way or the other.

Her father cleared his throat, and her mother sent him a warning glance.

'Ursula, we haven't really thought this through, but if Katharina is set on working at the War Office, it's obvious her background will be scrutinised.'

'But we said—'

Katie shot to her feet and stared at them.

'I don't know what this is all about, but you're covering up something and I don't like it. Will you please tell me what's going on.' She stared at her father. 'Are you and Mutti legally married? Is that why you seem reluctant to show me your Marriage Certificate?'

There was a silence, only broken by the tick-tock of the clock in the dining room. Her father put his hand on her mother's arm.

'The time has come, Ursula.'

Katie, her eyes fixed on her mother, saw her face drain.

'I do not wish it, Oscar.'

'But we must – don't you see? We're not being fair to the girl.'

Ursula's jaw tightened.

'She is not yet a full adult of twenty-one.'

'For goodness' sake, Mutti, stop treating me like a child,' Katie interjected. 'What does a few more months matter?'

'We're at war,' her father continued as though there'd been no interruption. 'It's time. We did agree . . . and we should do this together.'

Agree to what? Do what together? What on earth is going on?

'No, Oscar, it is best if I clean the *Küche*. You know I cannot leave a dirty kitchen.'

Oscar hesitated, then slumped his shoulders. 'All right. I'll speak to her on my own. But can you bring that envelope first?'

With a deep sigh, her mother rose to her feet. Katie watched her disappear.

'All this secrecy is upsetting, Dad, especially as it seems to concern *me*.'

'Let's go into the drawing room,' he said. 'I'll pour you a sherry.'

A nervous tremor took hold of Katie's body. Something was up and it sounded serious. He rarely offered her a drink except on special occasions.

Just as they were settled into the easy armchairs, one beside the other, her father with a glass of whisky and Katie sipping a cream sherry, feeling as though she were bracing herself for something terrible, her mother came into the room, looking

43

almost fearful as she glanced at her daughter. She silently handed Oscar a brown envelope. Her father glanced up and nodded.

'Are you sure you won't stay, my dear?' he said.

Ursula mumbled something Katie couldn't hear and her father put his hand on his wife's arm for a moment before she moved out of reach and closed the door behind her. He pulled a sheet of paper from the envelope and handed it to his daughter. It was the Marriage Certificate. Her heart beating hard, she unfolded it, her eye going straight to the names in the columns:

Bachelor Oscar Henry Valentine

Spinster Ursula Inge Frankel

It was the first time she'd seen or heard Mutti's surname. But nothing seemed amiss. With relief she smiled at her father.

'Well, at least you made an honest woman out of her and I'm not illegitimate . . . so what was all the fuss about?'

Her father took another document from the brown envelope.

'This is your Birth Certificate,' he said gruffly, his hand trembling as he gave it to her.

With a strange sense of foreboding, Katie took the folded document, wondering why she'd never seen it before now. She supposed it was because she'd never needed it for anything. Slowly, she unfolded it. Yes, there she was. CHILD: Date of birth: Fifth April 1920, Katharina Ellen Valentine, the middle name the same as that of her aunt's; FATHER: *Oscar Henry Valentine*; MOTHER . . .

WHAT! She must be seeing things. She looked again, closely this time, certain her eyes were deceiving her. But it was as clear as could be. Her mother's name, Ursula Inge Frankel, did not appear on the Birth Certificate. But Aunt Judy's did.

44

Chapter Six

Katie's mind reeled. Her vision blurred. She tried to focus on her father but her head felt odd – as though it would float away. The room swam. She clutched the arms of the chair, fiercely pulling in her stomach.

I must get a hold on myself.

'Katie . . .'

She heard his voice from far away but she couldn't see him. She blinked.

'Katie, my dear . . .'

Suddenly her mind cleared as though she'd breathed in a lungful of mountain air. She'd been deceived in the worst way possible.

'Why wasn't I told this before? How could you have let me reach twenty and not told me something that affects me so much?' Her voice rose to an ugly screech. 'Don't you think I should have been told while my aunt . . . I mean my *real* mother was alive? I can't bear the thought that she died knowing she could never tell me I was her daughter. And I could never call her "Mother." She stared at her father as rage shook her. 'Don't you realise how much I loved her – how I would love to have known while she was alive? How *she* might have been happy to know she doesn't . . .' Her voice cracked on her use of the present tense. 'I mean she didn't have to keep such a secret any more.'

Tears streamed down her cheeks. She hurled the document

aside, her hand catching the stem of the sherry glass, knocking it off the table onto the carpet, the liquid spilling into a small puddle. Tanny raised his head from his basket and barked. Her father leapt from his chair and bent to put his arm round her. She flung it off. He picked up a pouffe and sat nearer to her.

'Darling, I'm so sorry. Your mother – who's been like a mother to you, you can't deny that – begged me not to say anything until the time was right.'

'What right has she got to decide what's best for me?' she flung at him. 'None. And when did she consider the time *would* be right?' She was shouting now. 'When I'm thirty, forty . . . on her deathbed?'

'Shhhh. You're working yourself up.'

'Working myself up? *Working myself up?*' she screeched. 'What do you expect me to do? I've been bearing a secret I had no idea about. My *real* identity. My *British* identity. And all the while I thought I was half German. With the war, Germans are not the most popular people in the world at the moment – in case you hadn't noticed. And I've been trying to protect who I thought was my *mother* from being sent back to Germany . . . or whatever they would do to her.' She paused for breath. 'I went on that interview and told them a pack of lies. But I didn't know it. How am I going to explain all that? Tell me, Dad, how will I explain this to Mr Lester? I've already told him I have a German mother and that's how I learnt to speak German. He'd have every right to change his mind because I can't be trusted.' She glared at him. 'I'll have to tell him – you do see that, don't you? And I'll lose my chance of a really interesting job that might even play a tiny part in the war effort.'

Fury lodged in her throat and she started coughing. Her father left the room and brought back a glass of water.

'And how is my dear *Mutti*?' Katie said, her voice coated with scorn, as she gulped some water.

'She's going to bed.' He paused, concern showing in his eyes but Katie ignored it. 'She's not been feeling very well lately and now she's upset.'

'*She's* upset. Has she any idea how upset *I* am?'

'Of course she does. She's not so insensitive as you're making out.'

Katie took in a deep breath, then finished the glass of water.

'This has answered some questions I've had since I was a child. Why she never told me she loved me. Rarely gave me a hug or a kiss like my friends' mothers did with their children. It was because there was no blood connection. Now I see why she never took me to Germany to visit my grandparents. Why they had nothing to do with me, their granddaughter. I wasn't of their blood.' She paused for breath. 'You owe me a full explanation.'

'Please don't be bitter,' her father said. 'Let me explain.' He sent her a direct look. 'And please don't interrupt. It's difficult enough and I feel disloyal by telling it, but this is what happened.'

'Don't leave anything out. I want the whole miserable truth.'

Katie rose and poured herself another glass of sherry. The glass was sticky where the liquid had spilt, but she was barely aware as she watched her father light his pipe. Normally, she found the odour of his tobacco pleasant but not this evening. It smelt cloying and threatened to choke her. Was he giving himself time to decide how and what to tell her? But maybe he was upset in his own way. No, don't excuse him, she told herself sternly. Don't feel sorry. He's been deceitful. They've *both* been deceitful. Forcing herself to calm her jerky breath, she waited, her heartbeat thrumming in her ears.

Her father took a puff on his pipe.

'I met Judy the year before I met your . . . Ursula,' he began. 'We fell in love almost instantly. Judy was a beauty when she was young . . . and still lovely when she died,' he added softly. 'She rather swept me off my feet. She was very intelligent, and enthusiastic, and loved her books, her music . . . she introduced me to opera, which I came to love as much as she did . . . but she was what you would call a free spirit. She didn't want to be tied down by marriage and children. At least she was quite clear about that so I was under no illusions.'

At this, he glanced at Katie.

'Sorry, Katharina, but that's how she was, whereas I wanted a family. Three or four children if possible, because I'm an only child and always wanted brothers and sisters. But she wanted to travel the world.' He stopped to take another puff on his pipe. 'She refused my proposal of marriage.'

Even though he'd gone back to his armchair a little distance away, Katie could see his eyes droop with sadness. He must have really loved her. She felt a twinge of remorse that she'd been so harsh, but brushed it away.

'I'm not ashamed to say that I was heartbroken.' Katie saw his Adam's apple rise and fall. 'I'd always imagined that when two people fell in love they married and had children. But it was *my* dream . . . not hers. And then she gave me the most wonderful news. She was going to have a baby. Naïvely, I thought that would seal our love and she'd be happy to get married and settle down. But it seemed it had the opposite effect.'

Katie thought her throat would close up for good. She licked her lips, trying to find some moisture in her dry mouth.

'You don't mean . . . you know . . . she didn't think of getting rid—'

'Never,' her father interrupted her. 'No, that wouldn't be Judy. But she said she'd put the baby up for adoption. I was devastated. There was no persuading her, and in fact we had a terrible row and I said I never wanted to set eyes on her again. It was then that I met Ursula, who was learning English and I was teaching it. She was blonde and pretty and from Germany.

I thought she had quite a bit of gumption coming to England when the war was only recently over.

'She didn't disguise her interest in me and we started going out together. She was quite frail and I felt she needed protection and that I was the one to give it to her. She knew I wanted children and she said she did, too. I found a flat and we married within a few weeks. I suppose you'd call it on the rebound. We just didn't give ourselves time to really know one another . . . if we were suited for a lifetime of being together. And on our honeymoon she gave me the most devastating news. She could never have a child. She'd had an operation when she was eighteen – a hysterectomy. She said we would have to adopt. I was furious that she hadn't told me before the wedding as I wouldn't have married her. She must have known that. She did it on purpose as she was terrified to go back to Germany.' He drew on his pipe again, not looking at Katie. 'Her parents were strict Roman Catholics, you see, and her father was worse, so I suspect Ursula was rather in awe of him.'

So *that* was why Ursula's mother was so upset: because her daughter had married a Protestant. Katie bit her lip. Her grandmother – no, her step-grandmother – had disowned her own daughter from the time of the marriage because she hadn't found a Catholic husband.

Her father continued. 'The solution was staring me in the face. I would be a father to my own child. So I met Judy and talked it over with her and she gladly agreed. I think she was pleased and relieved the baby would have its natural father at least. I put the plan to Ursula, who also agreed because I know she felt guilty for not telling me before we were married that she couldn't conceive. And also, it must be said, she genuinely wanted children.' He hesitated and looked directly at her. 'I hope you will believe that.'

For a few moments Katie felt a rush of sympathy. It must

have been dreadful to be told such news after the operation, and at such a young age. But Ursula had deceived her father. Oh, God, it was all so confusing.

'Go on,' she managed hoarsely.

'Judy did all the necessary planning and I sent Ursula away to my mother's in Bristol after explaining the situation. Mum was never that happy with my marrying a German woman but she went along with it because it meant her having her first grandchild. But she and Ursula never really got along. My mother was always suspicious of every German, having lost her sister, your aunt Mary, in the Great War. Anyway, Ursula finally came home armed with baby books and outfits she and my mother had knitted for the new baby. At least that was something they had in common that was practical.'

'Did Ursula –' Katie made herself say the name without stumbling '– ever meet Aunt Judy during that time?'

'Oh, yes. That was one of Judy's stipulations – to see for herself if Ursula would be a good mother. And to ask her if the baby was a girl that she would call her Judith. Ursula put her foot down at that – I don't blame her – and said she would allow Judy's middle name, Ellen, to be the baby's second name and Judy agreed. I think she could tell right away that you'd be in safe hands. And that's exactly how it turned out. Ursula took on the role of a mother immediately and did everything she could to bring you up in the right way.'

'Or what she deemed was the right way.' Katie couldn't stop a hint of bitterness. 'She forgot that love comes into being a mother as well. I never knew why she couldn't show her love, but now I do. I wasn't her flesh-and-blood daughter.'

'No, that wasn't anything to do with it,' her father said. 'Her own parents apparently never displayed any emotion and she thought that was the right way to bring up children.' He paused.

'But I can tell you with my hand on my heart that she loved you at first sight.'

Katie was silent. After a minute she said, 'Do you think Aunt . . . I mean Judy ever regretted giving me up?'

'Not in the way you mean. She just wouldn't be tied down. But as she saw you grow up I think she wished she'd been a different sort of person and kept you and married me. But of course it was too late for regrets.' He paused. 'Her other stipulation was that she would be part of your life as much as possible, but only as a doting aunt.'

And that's why I have more in common with my real mother than with Mutti.

As though her father had read her thoughts, he said:

'You remind me of Judy in so many ways. Not just your looks but even some of your traits, such as when you're reading a book and someone speaks, you stab your finger where you are on the page before looking up and responding.' He gave a wan smile. 'She used to do that.'

'So you never loved Ursula the way you loved Judy,' Katie dared to proffer.

Her father looked away. 'Let's just say it wasn't the same. But I grew to love her when I saw the way she took care of you.' He caught her eye. 'She does have her good points, you know, Katie, but sometimes they're buried. And maybe now you know the full story I'm hoping you might forgive us both, and indeed Judy, because all we wanted was to make sure you had a safe and happy childhood. And even if it wasn't idyllic, I think we had some success, and at least I had my wonderful daughter – and I still saw my darling Judy from time to time.'

So that was why Ursula was jealous of Judy, Katie thought. She hadn't imagined it. But no longer could she put the full blame onto her. She might have felt exactly the same in her position.

'And by the way,' her father went on, 'Judy wanted the anonymity as much as we did because she didn't want you hating her for giving you up. She was so proud of you. And she adored you. There was no question about that.'

An ache wound its way round Katie's insides.

'I don't know what to call Ursula now,' she said.

'Please continue calling her Mutti. She really likes it. And it's what you've always called her. I think she'd feel much happier if your heart is big enough to manage that.'

How she got through that night, Katie had no idea. She only knew that her head was buried in the pillows, first one way and then the other, furious one minute and sobbing the next. Why hadn't they told her when she was old enough to understand? But when would that have been? If the war hadn't started would they have left her still in ignorance?

One moment she blamed her father for getting himself into such a mess, the next she blamed Mutti for not being honest before she accepted her father's proposal, but to her shame Katie blamed her aunt – or rather her birth mother – more than anyone. Judy had insisted the baby would be adopted so she'd happily have given her daughter away to strangers. It was only good luck that Dad had married a woman who couldn't conceive – a German – who agreed to bring her up as her own. Judy didn't want to be saddled with a child. Didn't want the responsibility. Judy – her real mother – had outright rejected her before she'd even set eyes on her.

Katie tried to picture the scene – to resign herself to the thought that it was an awful situation that nobody had bargained for and could not now be changed. But she felt stuck in a web of lies and deception. Tears sprang into her eyes. Oh, why couldn't everything have been different? Why hadn't Judy's and her father's love for one another been stronger? Where was

Judy's natural maternal instinct? How could she hand over the baby she'd just given birth to?

A thought rushed into Katie's brain. Was she legally Dad's and Mutti's child? Had they legally adopted her? If not, would that make her illegitimate? And have to carry that shame for the rest of her life? But looming straightaway – how was she going to explain all of this to Mr Lester? And when?

One thing she knew for certain – *if* she was still accepted by the War Office – she was going to take that job whether her stepmother, as she now called her in her mind, was at risk or not. The three of them had landed her in this position and she would do her utmost not to allow it to have any detrimental effect on her life – especially now Britain was at war.

Chapter Seven

August 1940

Katie battled with the problem of Mr Lester right up until the weekend before the Monday when she was to start work at the War Office. Should she write and let him know or simply produce the papers on her first day and explain that this had all come to light after he'd offered her the job and asked for the two certificates? She only hoped they would accept her truthful explanation. If they didn't . . . well, she'd just have to look for something else where security wasn't at such a high level. It was too late to write a letter.

On the Monday she started her job, Katie gave a final glance in the mirror at her new two-piece navy-blue suit and crisp white blouse she'd bought with some of the money Judy had left her. Strange not to call her Aunt Judy. It also felt strange to be wearing something so tailored and so obviously smart for an office after the casual clothes she'd worn to the secretarial school, and even more so after working outside with the greyhounds in a pair of old trousers and one or the other of two old jumpers. That life seemed so far away now – her only reminder being her beloved Tanny.

'Whatever job you do in life, always dress the part,' she could hear Judy's voice in her ear. 'And if you have an eye for promotion, then dress as though you already hold that position. That way, someone will think of your name first. It's how it works.'

It was probably a good piece of advice, Katie thought. But thinking of Judy, her mind slid back to the fact that Judy was her real mother and had given her away. No matter how often she tried to tell herself, she still hadn't been able to take it all in – not wholly, anyway. How did Judy feel when she wrote that final letter, knowing that she could never disclose the fact that she was her mother? Katie remembered some of the words: *the daughter I never had*. It sounded as though she had been desperate to give some kind of hint but Katie had only felt sorry that her aunt hadn't married and had children. How wrong she'd been. And what a position her father had been in, caught between two very different women and an awkward child about to be born.

She shook herself.

Concentrate, Katie. With luck, you're about to do something interesting for the war effort. So stop going over old ground. Nothing can change, no matter how much you want it to.

At least by doing this job, she was carrying out Judy's wishes for her. Katie blinked hard and made herself smile. The smart young woman in the mirror smiled hesitantly back.

Katie stepped up to the same Reception desk, already feeling more confident than when she'd attended the interview, though her heart was beating hard in anticipation of the day and the man for whom she'd be working. Would it be Mr Vernon Lester himself? She wasn't sure if she wished it or not. He wasn't exactly intimidating, but he certainly wasn't the friendliest person. But then he had a position of responsibility. Though for what, exactly, she had no idea.

'This way, please, Miss Valentine.'

It was the same slim young man as before. This time he didn't approach the staircase but knocked on the door of one of the rooms leading off the foyer.

'Come in.'

He opened the door wide to let her through.

'Miss Valentine to see you.'

Katie gave a start as Daphne Lorrimer rose from her chair and grinned.

'Are you surprised it's me?' she said.

'Yes, I am, rather.'

'Come and sit down. Sorry about the mix-up of the letters. Stupid mistake the temp made. Thank goodness she's gone now.' She gazed at Katie. 'This isn't my usual role but I'm going to take you through the most important document we need on file before you start. Mr Lester, who would normally do this, has been called away. But if you have any question whatsoever that I can't answer, please say so. We don't want you to sign before you understand everything.'

Daphne took a cream document from a folder and handed it to Katie.

'Just take your time and read it carefully and I'll order a coffee for us.'

'You sound as though you have quite an important position here,' Katie said a little enviously.

'I was lucky. Initially, they put me in a filing room for a fortnight – on my own. Nearly drove me crazy with all those papers – I had no idea where to put them. But I somehow managed and actually tidied things up a bit. Then they became short in this department, but I won't be here much longer.'

Daphne didn't explain further and Katie didn't like to press her about what she would actually be doing, so she began reading the document. It was headed 'Official Secrets Act'. One of the headings was SECURITY. There followed a list of 'do's and don'ts' which mostly struck Katie as common sense, including not to mention any part of your job to *anyone*, including friends and family. She skimmed the rest of it twice, hoping she'd grasped all the instructions.

There was a knock at the door and a plump young woman brought in a tray of coffee. Without asking, Daphne put a sugar lump on each saucer and handed Katie's over.

But by the time Katie had finished reading, her coffee was cold and her brain felt addled; she couldn't take in another printed word. She had no idea whether she would be able to retain everything or even if she'd understood all of it in the first place, but she assumed it must be all right as everyone else who worked here must have signed as well. Daphne passed her a fountain pen.

'I must explain –' she flicked her eyes to Katie's signature '– that this is not just a contract – it's actual law. The most important document you will ever sign, but whether you sign or not makes no difference to the legality of the document. It has your name on it and we've given it to you to read and sign. Not understanding is no excuse for blabbing something you shouldn't. Nothing in your department must ever be discussed with anyone – that means both here at Whitehall and outside the building. Do you understand?'

'Yes.'

It was galling that Daphne, who had only just earned her qualification the same day, was already in a superior position and able to speak to her this way. Katie shrugged. She was being petty. Daphne was trying to tell her something for her own good.

'If you ever breach security, you will be severely punished,' Daphne went on. 'It could lead to imprisonment . . . or even worse.' She stared at Katie without blinking. 'That goes for your own family, friends, boyfriend, and absolutely everybody else.

If *anyone* asks where you work, you're allowed to say for the War Office as a clerk and leave it at that.'

For a few moments Katie wondered if Daphne was exaggerating by hinting an even worse punishment than imprisonment – until she looked at the woman's face, now dead serious. No, she was not exaggerating, she was warning her. A shiver ran across Katie's shoulders. Surely they wouldn't be allowed . . .

Wouldn't be allowed what? her inner voice whispered.

Put me in prison. She refused to think of anything more frightening.

Well, don't be too sure. Just keep your head down and do exactly what you're told.

'Do you have any questions?' Before Katie could answer, Daphne said, 'Oh, I nearly forgot – if you're placed in a job and you leave through indiscretion, you will be watched by the police – not only you, but your entire family.' She paused and looked directly at Katie. 'If you have any qualms at all, say so now.'

'I don't have any qualms. I'm ready to do what's required of me.'

Daphne leaned forward. 'Right, back to where we were. Any questions?'

'I don't think so,' Katie began. 'Well, not about the document I've just signed. But I'm sure I'll have plenty of questions when I begin working . . . though there is one thing.' She stopped. How much should she tell Daphne about her background? Probably nothing.

'Yes?' Daphne tilted her head.

'Mr Lester asked for a certificate.'

Maybe Daphne would think it was her secretarial one.

'Oh, yes,' Daphne said. 'Thanks for reminding me. He needs your Birth Certificate and your parents' Marriage Certificate.

58

And a passport if you have one.' She stared at Katie. 'Don't look so worried. We all have to produce these.'

'It's just that I don't have a passport,' Katie said, to cover up her anxiety.

'Not everyone does.' She looked towards Katie's handbag. 'Anyway, presumably you've brought the other two?'

'Yes.' Katie handed over the documents in the same envelope they'd been in.

'He won't keep them long. You'll have them back in a few days.' She smiled. 'Anything else? Now's your chance.'

Should she say anything to Daphne about her Birth Certificate? If Daphne opened the envelope she'd ask questions about what happened to the German mother. No, she'd wait until she could tell Mr Lester in person.

Katie cleared her throat as she thought of something else. May Stanley would have a fit if she heard what Kate was about to ask.

'Mr Lester didn't mention what I'll be earning, so are you able to tell me?'

Daphne seemed unperturbed by her question.

'You won't know until you open your first pay packet. It won't be anything wonderful. It should be around two pounds. But stick with it. It'll improve when you've gained some experience.'

Katie bit back the disappointment. 'Well, thanks for giving me a clue at least.' She paused. 'Can you tell me anything about the job?'

'They're expanding here in the War Office but haven't got the staff to fill the positions. And many people need training.' She glanced at Katie. 'I believe you'll be one of the stenographers – is that right?'

'Yes,' Katie said. 'I nearly didn't take it.'

Daphne threw her a glance. 'I imagine you felt it was a bit beneath you after being trained as a secretary. But this is the sort of place where you just need to get your foot in the door and it could open in an unexpected way, if you keep your eyes and ears open.'

'I'll be sure to do that,' Katie said.

'Then I think that's all.' Daphne rose. 'No need to shake hands. We're already friends. Come with me and I'll take you down the corridor to where you'll be working.' She looked at Katie. 'It will mainly be for Vernon Lester but don't be surprised if others nab you. There are never enough stenographers to go round.'

'What is Mr Lester's position exactly?'

'He's the head of MO – that's Military Operations.' She grinned. 'It's one of the most important positions. You've done well to get a job with him.'

Katie had never met so many new people in one day in her life. Thankfully, everyone seemed very friendly. Mr Lester was nowhere to be seen but perhaps that was just as well. If he didn't come in until tomorrow, she would have broken in her first day and be more ready to explain the certificates.

Her first morning was a mixture of putting files in alphabetical order and placing them in the correct drawer and making mugs of tea for at least a dozen members of staff. Not exactly what she'd envisioned. No one appeared to have a break but when one o'clock came, Daphne stopped by the filing cabinets where she was working with two other girls.

'What about a breath of air outside?' she said. 'And we can have a sandwich.'

Katie stretched her aching back. 'That would be lovely.'

'I wanted you to be the first to know,' Daphne said, when they were sitting at a table in the café, her cheeks colouring an attractive pink. 'I can't keep it to myself a minute longer.'

'Then spill it out.'

'They've accepted me!' Daphne's voice was bursting with excitement.

'Who has?'

'The ATA – the Air Transport Auxiliary.' A beam spread across her face. 'Oh, Katie, I'm finally going to finish my training as a pilot!'

'I can't tell you how glad I am for you,' Katie said. 'I know it's what you've wanted for some time.' She smiled back. 'When will you tell Mr Lester?'

'When he's back in the office. We don't always know in advance when he's going or when he's due back. I'll have to contain myself until then.' She grinned happily. 'But whatever happens, I leave in a week's time . . . and I can't wait!'

Katie chewed her lower lip. She hoped she didn't have to wait too long for Mr Lester to appear and in the meantime to worry about his reaction to those blasted certificates.

But Vernon Lester was at his desk that afternoon. Oh, thank goodness. She couldn't wait to get it over with.

'Mr Lester, may I have a word with you?' she said when she'd brought him a cup of tea.

He looked up, his forehead already creased.

'Can it wait?'

'Not really. It's about my Birth Certificate.'

His head jerked up. 'Didn't you bring both certificates?'

She felt her cheeks warm. 'Yes, but I wanted to explain something.'

'You'd better have a seat,' he threw over his shoulder as he went to his filing cabinet. 'Ah, here it is.' He took out an envelope and put it on his desk, then gazed at her. 'Nothing untoward in them, is there?' Without waiting for an answer, he removed the two documents and opened the first, then quickly scanned it.

'This looks in order for your parents' marriage,' he said, smiling as he then unfolded the second document. 'As you explained, your mother is German.' His smile faded as he read Katie's Birth Certificate. He frowned. Katie's heart began to beat in her eardrums. Finally, he looked up. 'So your German mother is *not* your mother, then. Your real mother is English – so who is she?'

'The aunt I told you about – who approached the War Office in the Great War.'

'And you didn't think to tell me this when I interviewed you – when I asked you to bring in the certificates?'

'I didn't know then. I only knew a few days before I was due to start here.' Katie stared at him, flushing at the unfairness of it all. She shouldn't have been put in such an embarrassing position. All three of them had betrayed her. 'I thought it better if I told you in person than wrote it in a letter.'

Mr Lester steepled his fingers together.

'Hmm. I wonder if you thought it would cost you your job if you'd written a letter.'

'That might be part of the reason,' Katie admitted. 'I want to do my bit in the war effort . . . prove myself, and it doesn't seem fair if—'

'Nothing's fair in this world.' Mr Lester's tone was abrupt. 'I just need to know you haven't lied to me about anything else because if so, I must remind you that you're here under the Official Secrets Act and—'

'Mr Lester, I haven't lied,' Katie burst out. 'I didn't know all this. Even when my aunt— when Judy,' she quickly corrected herself, 'left me some money and a letter with her last wishes, she didn't tell me she was my mother. I still wouldn't have known if I hadn't asked my parents for my Birth Certificate.'

'So what you now have is a German stepmother?'

She looked him squarely in the eye. 'She took on the role of my mother at the time I was born. I never knew any different. So I don't see the difference when you thought she was my mother.'

Oh, she hadn't meant to sound so rude. Mr Lester just raised an eyebrow.

'That's true,' he said. 'Being married to an Englishman, she's a British citizen with the same rights.' He sighed and leaned back in his swivel chair. 'Look, I'm going to take what you've told me at face value. But I would be cautious about telling anyone that you were misled about your parentage. It would be easy to let it leak out. I imagine it must have been quite a shock for you. That sort of thing doesn't need to get spread about, especially here in the War Office.' He took his glasses off. 'Do you understand?'

He wasn't going to get rid of her. Relief poured through her body.

'Yes. I won't let it go any further . . . I promise.'

'That'll be all, then.' He suddenly smiled. 'It's been quite a first day for you, I expect, hasn't it?'

Katie swallowed. 'Yes, but I've enjoyed it.' She rose to her feet, then said, 'Thank you, sir.'

Vernon Lester nodded. She was dismissed.

Katie approached her front door that evening with some trepidation. She was tired physically and mentally. And now she had to face something highly emotional that she still felt numb about, though nearly a week had passed. She gritted her teeth. She always prided herself on being strong – that her appearance as a petite young woman was deceptive. But now her insides constantly felt as if they were crumbling. She could tell her stepmother was putting on a brave face, trying to act naturally, but she'd found herself no longer able to be natural towards *her*. She shrugged. She'd just have to play each day by ear.

'Is that you, Katharina?' Ursula said as Katie came through the hallway.

'Yes.'

Her stepmother opened the kitchen door and an enticing smell of baking followed her.

'Come and have a cup of tea – and I've made your favourite *Käsekuchen* – the proper German cheesecake recipe – but you know I cannot make it perfectly without quark. But it is not possible to buy it in England so it never tastes exactly right.'

She knew immediately what Ursula was trying to do. Well, a cheesecake wasn't going to go any way at all towards making up for the bombshell she and Dad had hit her with. Feeling mean but not able to push it down, she bit her lip hard.

'Did you have a good first day?' Ursula said, when Katie sat at the kitchen table.

'A lot to take in,' Katie said, curtly.

Her stepmother sent her a woeful glance.

'Katharina, we have not had the opportunity to talk.'

Katie gave a start, not expecting Ursula would reopen the subject.

'I have tried.' Ursula continued, 'but you always turn away saying there is no need. Everything has been said.'

'Well, it's true.'

'No. You must hear what I have to say. Your father has explained his situation and perhaps some of mine, but not my feelings.'

Your feelings, Katie wanted to scream.

'This has been a shock for all of us,' Ursula began in a determined tone.

'I wouldn't call it a shock for you and Dad,' Katie's voice held a sarcastic edge, 'as you two have known all along.' She glared at Ursula. 'Or did you mean the shock you suddenly faced me with without your or Dad's planning?' Her mouth felt dry. She ran her tongue over her lips. 'Because I believe *I'm* the only one who's had a shock.'

'You know what I mean.' Ursula's blue eyes clouded. 'I take the blame for everything. But I was very young and fell in love with your father who was so handsome – and such a kind man. I should not have deceived him. But I was so worried if I told him before the wedding I could not have children, he would not marry me. I did not want to lose him. I would do anything . . . yes –' she held Katie's gaze '– even that.' She took in a breath, sounding more like a gasp. 'I wanted children desperately and I did hope Oscar would be prepared to adopt.'

When Katie remained silent, Ursula said:

'And then you came along, not even a week old – already part of the family. You were such a sweet baby, and so pretty . . . your blonde hair and fair skin, so like mine I felt you were my actual daughter. That is what helped me to believe. And your eyes were the colour of your father's – like the sea.' Ursula hesitated. 'I should not tell you this, but I must so you understand. Your father – although he tried – he never loved me the way he did Judith. And that made me insecure. So I put all my effort into becoming a mother. Doing the right thing. But he and I have grown closer over the years and I think perhaps he might love me a little more than he realises.'

It was the longest speech Katie had ever heard from her stepmother. She didn't know what to say. Tears threatened. She could feel them prick behind her eyes. Tanny, who was lying under the table, gave a small whine, as if he knew things weren't right. She reached out to pat his head and he thrust his wet nose into her hand.

'Katharina.'

Katie looked up.

'I know this is painful for you, but I would be so happy if you can forgive me.'

65

I can't, she wanted to scream. *Maybe in weeks or months – maybe never.* She swallowed hard and stared at her stepmother. Furiously, she brushed away a lone tear running down her cheek, for what might have been.

'I am so sorry, Katharina. I would not want to hurt you for the world.'

When Katie didn't respond, Ursula heaved a sigh and collected the dirty crockery and cutlery and put it in the sink, then quietly left the room.

Sick at heart, Katie washed up and put everything away neatly, as her stepmother always did. She wiped down the draining board and squeezed out the dishcloth Ursula had knitted when she'd once run out of wool and needed something to keep her hands busy. A lump formed in Katie's throat as she stared at it. That small domestic item seemed to sum up her stepmother's care for the home and family. Taking a jagged breath, she hung the cloth on the tap and stomped upstairs, knowing full well she was behaving badly but in no mood to put things on a better footing. Perhaps when she felt calmer she could look at the situation more dispassionately.

Chapter Eight

June 1941

It was hard to believe that she'd been working a whole year right through what the Londoners called the Blitz, Katie thought this morning as she made Vernon Lester his usual eleven o'clock mug of coffee. The bombing had been relentless for nine solid months, mostly at night, and not only in London. The worst attack so far had been Coventry last November, when the news came through that the beautiful medieval cathedral had been razed to the ground, the city left in ruins. That was heartbreaking. But at Winston Churchill's insistence that St Paul's Cathedral must be saved at all costs by sending fire-watchers on the roof night and day, to the joy of the Londoners, it still stood proudly amongst the wreckage. At least now the bombing had eased significantly. She felt herself lucky that although Whitehall had had some shelling, there'd been no serious damage to any of the departments, so far as she knew.

The good thing was that overall Mr Lester was a fair-minded boss, once she'd become used to him, and he'd never spoken again about her past. Yet something felt missing and she couldn't have put into words what it was. She'd apologised to her stepmother and there was now an agreed, though somewhat uneasy, truce between them.

With a sigh she set the mug on a tray and stirred a teaspoon of sugar into the mug, popped a couple of ginger nuts on a plate and knocked on his door before entering.

'Take a seat,' Mr Lester said. 'I need to talk to you about your position here.'

There was a serious note in his voice that made Katie's heart thump. She couldn't remember any complaints from him or anyone else she'd worked for. Her work had rarely been returned because of an inaccurate transcription. As far as she was aware, she hadn't said anything untoward – let out any secrets. So what was it?

She sat on the chair on the other side of Mr Lester's desk, stiff with worry that something must have turned up that she didn't know about. She wished she'd made herself a cup of coffee – tea – anything. Even a glass of water to sip.

Mr Lester took a couple of swallows of his coffee.

'Katie, I don't want to lose you but . . .' It was the first time he'd called her Katie. Was that to soften the blow that he was about to sack her? No! She was perfectly happy in her job. All right, it was a touch mundane, though she was always inundated with work, but she would rather have that. The people around her were pleasant and helpful, and working conditions were good. Sometimes she and one of the other stenographers would have a spot of lunch in a nearby café if she hadn't had time to prepare something for herself. She didn't want to start searching for another job.

'. . . so I've highly recommended you for the position.'

What was he saying? Whatever it was doesn't sound as though he's giving me the sack.

Mr Lester lit a cigarette. 'You're very quiet.'

'I'm awfully sorry, sir, but can you just go over it for me again.'

He took a puff on his cigarette. 'I've put your name forward in response to an urgent request. You'd be doing a similar job but you'd have even greater responsibility as far as security is concerned, since you'd be closer to the war and the powers that be.'

A prickle of excitement raced through her.

'It sounds interesting.' She kept her voice steady.

'I think it could be. But I must warn you that we will have to look even more closely at your family, any jobs you've already done, whom you've associated with, whom your parents have associated with etc., etc. . . . '

Katie swallowed hard. *Is this where it's all going to go wrong?*

She tried to sit calmly but her fingers dug into the underside of the chair.

'I'm sending you to see one of the private secretaries this afternoon. Bill Adams can be a bit curt but he's perfectly all right and will take you through some questions.' Mr Lester flicked his cigarette ash into the cut-glass ashtray on his desk, then cleared his throat. 'I'd better warn you that they might be a bit concerned about your German stepmother. But just answer everything to the best of your ability.'

In a way, Katie was relieved. He hadn't sounded particularly worried. So neither would *she* be. All she had to do was be truthful. She only hoped it would suffice.

Katie wondered for whom the private secretary worked. He was obviously high in the pecking order but he didn't appear to have his own office, as Mr Lester had told her to go to the general meeting room further along the corridor. Outside the door, she took a deep breath to steady her nervousness, knocked and walked in. Bill Adams was sitting at the head of a long oval meeting table. Her first impression was that even though he was short in stature, and wiry, with a thin, sandy moustache and hair to match, somehow he exuded authority. She swallowed as he half rose, unsmiling, and gestured to the nearest chair.

'Do sit down, Miss Valentine,' he said, without bothering to introduce himself. 'This shouldn't take long. I just need to ask you some questions, and then it will take a few days for us to check the facts.'

It was like being at school. She felt guilty before she'd even done anything and was sure Mr Adams would see right through her and form the wrong opinion.

'We knew a certain amount about you,' he began, all the time watching her, 'before we took you on in your present job, but I'd like to go over some points about your family.'

Here it comes.

Katie braced herself. She would deal with it in a practical, unflustered way. She would not let this strangely unprepossessing man disquiet her in any way.

'I gather you don't have siblings.'

She shook her head. 'No, I'm an only child.'

He gazed at her. 'With a German mother?'

Keep calm.

Katie sat up straighter. 'I think you'll see by my notes that she's actually my stepmother.'

'What happened to your birth mother?'

'I gather it didn't work out. They weren't married,' she added, feeling the warmth creeping up the back of her neck. 'My stepmother and father brought me up when I was just days old.'

'I see.' He looked directly at her. 'How did your stepmother and father meet?'

'She and my father met in England when she came over to study English. She was in his class. He taught English at King's College.' She forced herself to meet his eye. 'They married shortly after and she automatically became a British citizen.' She thought she'd say that to remind him, though of course he would know those sorts of details.

Mr Adams jotted down a few more notes.

'Do you know anything about your stepmother's background in Germany? Who your German grandparents are, for instance?'

'They'd be my *step*-grandparents,' Katie corrected him. The more distance she could put between them and her own family, the better. 'I've never met them. I only know they lived in Bavaria, somewhere rather remote, and ran a guesthouse. I've never even been to Germany. I do know my German step-grandfather was killed in the Great War, and I think my step-grandmother went to live with her other daughter in Munich. Ursula, that's my stepmother, never talks about her family. I don't think they approved of her marrying an Englishman.'

'Any idea why not?'

'I think it was because they were strict Catholics. She's never gone back to Germany to see any of her relatives. And with the war, she wouldn't be able to anyway at the moment.'

'Quite.' Mr Adams chewed his pen, regarding her with narrow eyes. 'Vernon Lester has a very high opinion of you and says you've done an excellent job and can be trusted not to gossip.'

'You can rely on that, sir.'

'Hmm.' His eyes pierced through her and she shifted in her chair. 'Just remember you've signed the Official Secrets Act and any gossip could lead you into serious trouble . . . very serious trouble.'

'Yes, I do understand.' Katie managed to keep her voice steady. Was he ever going to stop probing over nothing?

'Well, I think that will be all, Miss Valentine. If anything more needs to be investigated, we will let you know. If you don't hear in a week you can assume no more information is required.'

He half rose from his chair again.

Katie calmly rose to her feet, but her insides were trembling. She couldn't wait to make her escape.

71

'Thank you, sir.'

He nodded and showed her out.

Every day felt like a week to Katie as she mentally crossed another day off the calendar. Whenever Mr Lester called her into his office, she thought he was going to say they weren't happy about her background. Was it all about to fall apart over something she couldn't do anything about? A week to the day after her interview with Mr Adams, Mr Lester put his head round the door of his office.

'Please come in, Katie.'

She stared at him, her nerves prickling, not able to gauge what he was about to say.

'Seems they're quite satisfied with their investigations,' he began immediately.

With a sigh she felt her shoulders relax.

'So you'll be joining a team under a Mrs Goodman.'

'Will I be in the same building?' she asked.

'Yes, but on a different floor.' He looked downwards. 'It's in the basement under your feet.'

Katie startled. She hadn't even been aware there was a basement. It didn't sound like the best environment to work in.

'But I must warn you,' Mr Lester continued, 'you must not disclose where you'll be to anyone. Very few people on this floor are aware of its existence. It's a most secret location – the most secret location possible.' He stopped and looked at her. 'Are you still interested? Because if not, I need to know this minute.'

'Yes, sir, I am,' she said without hesitation. It sounded as though it was going to be an exciting challenge and she was more than ready for it.

'Good.' He leaned back in his chair and lit a cigarette. 'All you have to do is to report on Monday to Mrs Goodman. You'll use the same entrance as here and the guard will point out to you how you get to the floor below.'

He inhaled, then blew out a stream of smoke, not bothering to direct it away from her face. She tried to smother the tickle in her throat and her eyes began to water. It was no good. She had to cough. Mr Lester handed her his full glass of water and she sipped it gratefully.

'As I said, I hate to lose you. You've been an exceptionally efficient worker and very pleasant to have around the place. Also, you have the finest pair of pins. I shall miss seeing them as you tap-dance along the corridor in those heels.'

Katie pressed her legs more closely together at that last remark and simply gave a hint of a smile.

'Thank you for putting my name forward,' she said. 'I do appreciate it.'

He nodded in acknowledgement. 'In the meantime, I hope this works out well for you – you deserve it.' He looked at her. 'Believe me, this is a very important step up. You'll be responsible for keeping secrets that very few people in this country would have any idea about. But I expect you to rise to the occasion with honour.'

'I'll do my utmost, sir,' Katie said as she stood to leave.

'Good luck, then, Katie.'

'Thank you, Mr Lester. I've enjoyed working for you.'

She couldn't wait to begin the next phase of her wartime career.

Chapter Nine

June 1941

'Your pass, miss.' A tall sentry standing just inside the New Public Offices blocked Katie's way.

'Um, I'm new.' She flashed him a smile. 'It's my first day. I was told to report here . . . to work down below,' she added in an undertone.

'Sorry, miss. No going down without it.'

This was terrible. Then she remembered the letter telling her where she should report. Surely that would do the trick. She fiddled in her handbag and brought out the envelope and handed it to him. He removed the sheet of paper, read it, then peered at her.

'Very good, miss. That seems to be in order. They'll give you a proper pass by the end of the day.' He handed back the letter. 'But before you go, please sign the book.'

Katie quickly scribbled her name and the date and time, then looked at him.

'Do you know where I have to go?'

'Depends on what department, which I wouldn't know about.' His face was still impassive as he jerked his head towards the main door. 'Go inside the hall and up two steps. You'll see a door which leads to a staircase marked 15. Go down the stairs and knock on the first door on the right. Someone will escort you to where you will be working.'

Katie stepped into the hall, where a Royal Marine wearing a hat with a red band stood on guard. She wondered if he needed to see her letter from Mr Lester, but he didn't speak at all – didn't even blink – remaining as lifeless as a statue. She decided to walk past him and head for the stairs. He could easily stop her if she wasn't doing the right thing.

The staircase turned out to be one of those awkward spiral ones, but she twisted and turned until she reached the bottom. As she reached the last step, she could hear male voices, but they were behind closed doors and too muffled for her to catch what anyone was saying.

She knocked on the first door to the right.

'Come in,' a man's voice called.

She stepped in.

There were two men and a woman at their desks, which were necessarily pushed close together in the cramped, airless room. Both men, jacketless, their ties loosened at their throats, were smoking, which didn't help the stuffy atmosphere. The woman, smartly dressed in a fitted grey suit, was on the phone giving whoever it was on the other end curt directions to somewhere. One of the men, a stocky redhead, looked up and beamed at her. He was so full of *joie de vivre* that Katie couldn't help smiling back.

'Miss Valentine?'

'Yes, that's me.'

He nodded. 'Excellent. We're expecting you.' He picked up a large notebook. 'Would you sign here and then we'll get your pass made up.' Katie signed and he added the date and time. 'Right. You'll be seeing Mrs Goodman. She looks after the girls . . . ladies,' he added hastily. 'By the way, I'm Brian Lockstone.' He smiled. 'Come with me and I'll show you where she is.'

He stubbed out his cigarette and she followed him along a straight, wide, brightly lit corridor, the brickwork painted a pale mustard colour, with several tall mahogany cupboards and matching chests lining part of one wall. A rank smell filled her nostrils and a tickle started in her throat. She glanced up to see a fug of smoke wafting and clinging to a complex array of pipework running across the ceilings, from which came a constant droning.

Trying to suppress a cough, she slowed her pace a few seconds to read on the wall an eye-catching notice:

THERE IS TO BE NO WHISTLING
OR UNNECESSARY NOISE IN THIS
PASSAGE

Oh dear. What sort of a place had she come to? But there was no time to question. The red-haired man was hurrying along and she had to walk fast to keep up with him. Several doors had the sign QUIET PLEASE and she wondered who the people were in the rooms behind and what work they did. Whatever it was, it was bound to be secret. She shivered with anticipation as she thought what they might give her to do and what she might learn.

Her guide turned into a smaller corridor, then down another. How on earth would she manage not to get lost? Katie thought, as she hurried close behind. She couldn't bear the idea of becoming stuck in this rabbit warren overnight. Finally, the red-haired man opened a door numbered 15, which revealed a room accommodating six desks with swivel chairs, and four typists working although there was only a low, muffled thrumming sound coming from their machines. Strange. There ought to be quite a high-pitched clatter. Three of the girls briefly looked up without stopping their busy fingers, sending Katie a smile, then bowed their heads over their typewriters again. She glanced round. A telephone was hooked at a drunken angle onto a white-painted wooden pillar. On another pillar in a corner, a mirror had been fixed. Green lamps dangled from wires over each desk and a Gestetner copier was placed in the middle of the room on its own table, presumably for all typists to use. She noticed no one had a shorthand notepad propped up for transcription, though each typist had two trays bursting with paperwork.

A prematurely grey-haired woman was sitting at her desk facing the four girls. At Katie's and the red-haired man's entrance, she rose to her feet.

'I've brought Miss Valentine for you,' Brian Lockstone said.

'Help at last.' Mrs Goodman gave Katie a warm smile. 'I'm delighted to see you, my dear. I'm in charge of the typing pool – so welcome to the team.'

Typing pool? This was worse than being labelled a shorthand-typist.

She looked askance at Mrs Goodman who seemed not to notice.

'We're so grateful you've joined us, Miss Valentine. The work is coming at us like an avalanche. To make matters worse we have someone away on sick leave – possibly permanently – and someone who wasn't suitable, so we're very short.'

This was dreadful. How was she going to get out of it? She didn't want to spend her days, months – maybe years – underground in this gloomy place.

'Damn Vernon Lester,' she muttered under her breath. She tried to muster a well-mannered smile. Why hadn't he prepared her?

'I'll leave you to it then.' Brian Lockstone turned to her. 'We'll get your pass made up and delivered before you finish for the day.' He disappeared.

'Well, then, Miss Valentine, let's get you set up. I presume you've signed the Official Secrets Act?'

'Yes, at the War Office.'

Oh, should she have mentioned the War Office? But Mrs Goodman nodded.

'Excellent. You'll be reminded about our tight security every single day. Nothing we do in this building is ever to be disclosed to your family or friends. You will be found out and the punishment is of the most severe kind.'

'Oh, I won't ever say anything I shouldn't,' Katie said emphatically.

'Then let's get you settled.'

Mrs Goodman walked between the desks to an empty one by the wall.

'You may take this desk. Put your bag in this drawer, my dear, and I'll introduce you to everyone.'

Before Katie could protest that she hadn't come to fill a typing position, Mrs Goodman rapped on her desk.

'Ladies!'

All four stopped typing. In the sudden silence Katie was conscious of four pairs of eyes regarding her.

'We have Miss Katharina Valentine joining us today, so please give her all the help she needs.' She paused. 'But before we go any further I'd like to run through some points with all of you as it doesn't hurt to remind everyone.' She sent Katie another smile. 'You must all familiarise yourselves with the instructions telling you what to do in case of emergencies. You'll find the various alarm signals posted on the main corridor wall. There are different signals for different emergencies. We use bells, rattles, whistles and sirens to denote what is happening outside. For instance, if there's a rattle in the corridors it will be a gas attack. So keep your gas masks handy at all times.

'Please avoid reading newspapers. Sometimes the information for the public is not the same as what goes on here, and this is likely to cause confusion. Don't keep a diary – it's far too dangerous if it falls into the wrong hands. And don't *ever* remove any paperwork or other information from this building. That would be cause for instant dismissal.' She paused. 'Any questions?' She glanced round. 'No? Good.' Then she looked towards an auburn-haired young woman. 'Roz, I'd like you to show Katharina where everything is.' She turned to Katie. 'Roz is the person to come to when I'm not here.'

Roz was the one who hadn't looked up from her machine. Even standing several feet away, Katie felt the air cool as Roz's unwavering eyes met hers.

She forced a smile.

'I hope you're a fast typist,' Roz said. 'We can't do with another slowcoach like the last one. It was worse than not having anyone. And of course she didn't last.'

Katie drew back. This was not a good start.

'Now, now, Roz,' Mrs Goodman said. 'Katharina doesn't want to hear that.'

'Oh, please call me Katie.'

Mrs Goodman nodded and gestured to a glamorous-looking girl whose long dark hair formed a deep wave at the front and was gripped at the sides with combs. Her scarlet lips lifted in a smile. 'This is Amanda. She's new to the team, and then we have Martha . . . ' She looked towards a girl with steel-rimmed spectacles on a round face topped with mouse-brown curls. Martha nodded and gave a timid smile. 'And last, but definitely not least, we have Peggy.'

Peggy's smile was beaming as she stood and to Katie's delight, sent her a wink. Goodness, Peggy must be six feet tall and built like an Amazon. You wouldn't cross her, Katie thought, hiding a smile, but instinctively she knew she was going to like Peggy. That is, if she stayed.

But was she going to? If not, now was the time to say something. Tell Mrs Goodman – quietly, of course, so the others didn't hear – that she was a qualified secretary. Because if she'd just wanted to work in a typing pool she could have learnt to type in four weeks and achieve a reasonable speed in twelve. She swallowed. She didn't want to type all day long. But noticing in Mrs Goodman's clear grey eyes the sheer relief of finding someone who could make a real difference to the workload visible on every desk made her think again. And anyway, nothing was set in stone, as her father was fond of saying. If it was too awful – too boring – she'd have to look for another job. Though that might be difficult. She'd signed the Official Secrets Act and Daphne had warned her she couldn't chop and change after that commitment. No, that wasn't the answer at all. She set her jaw. She'd have to just get on with it. There was a war on.

Chapter Ten

'Roz, I'll be gone all morning,' Mrs Goodman continued, 'so show Katie her in-tray and what work we've got for her, and where we keep everything. Then take her to where she'll be sleeping when she does the overnight shift. We might as well get her over the worst straightaway.'

What did she mean – get the worst over with? And no one had mentioned an overnight shift.

'I'll take her to the Dock now.'

'Thank you, Roz. I'll be back later this afternoon.' Mrs Goodman gave Katie a smile of encouragement before she disappeared.

To Katie's astonishment, Roz led her to a concrete staircase going down. How could the sleeping quarters be even further below than they were already? She noticed how their heels clicked on every step until they reached the sub-basement floor.

'So this is the Dock,' Roz said as she opened a peeling, red-painted door with an overhead sign: MIND YOUR HEAD. 'Should probably be called the "Duck",' she threw over her shoulder as she bent low to pass through.

Katie was not so tall as Roz but she still had to stoop to pass through the steel-framed entrance. It couldn't be more than four feet high. She only hoped she'd remember that if she was ever in a hurry. Moments later she found herself in a room with bare brick walls and no windows. And what was that noise?

She cocked her ear to listen, then studied the ceiling. A deep-throated hum seemed to be coming from ducts overhead. Was it the ventilation? The ducts were so huge they reduced the ceiling height considerably and she wondered if Peggy slept down here as well. If so, she would have even a worse problem trying not to smash her head at every turn.

'There are two dormitories – one for women and the other for the men,' Roz said as Katie caught up with her. She led her to the first door and opened it carefully. Inside, cots lined two of the walls, several with figures huddled underneath army blankets. Only a weak night-light glowed in the dark space.

'You'll only know at the last minute where you'll lay your head,' Roz said, keeping her voice low 'You bring your own sheet and keep it in our room in the store cupboard. If you keep it down here, you'll find it will have disappeared next time you need it. Then nick whatever cot you find empty.'

Katie gulped. 'Do you mean we're not allocated our own bed?'

'Exactly what I mean.'

It sounded perfectly horrible. And sleeping in a room with all those girls. She counted fifteen cots on each side. Bad enough with that constant drone of whatever it was in the background. And there was a distinct and unpleasant lavatory smell that the stale cigarette smoke didn't disguise. But people were putting up with far worse conditions that this, she reminded herself sternly. They'd think they were in clover if they had a temporary cot down here, safe from the bombing.

And then she heard a scuffling noise.

'Did you hear that?' Roz said with a smirk. 'I hope you're not squeamish. There's mice and rats and all sorts of beetles running amok down here.'

She forced herself not to shudder in front of the woman. Instead, she asked:

'Where is the Ladies'?'

'We don't have one . . . or a Gents'. Nothing. Not on this floor nor on the floor where we work.' She grimaced. 'There's no plumbing in the basement or down here. We all have to go upstairs to the ground level for the bathroom and loos. And you have to get permission from the guard to even use it.' She paused. 'Well, His Nibs has his own lavatory next to the Map Room but we mere mortals are not so lucky.' She watched Katie's horrified expression. 'If you're desperate there are a couple of chemical toilets behind that screen. Any washing you do is in a bucket.' She pointed to a curtained-off cubicle in one corner, then turned to Katie. 'There's also nowhere in the basement or in here to make a cup of tea or coffee unless you make friends with someone in the so-called canteen down here. But it's not for general use – it's for the officers . . . and they rarely use it, it's so awful.' Her eyes narrowed. 'So, can you cope with the facilities – or lack of?'

This was getting worse by the minute.

One girl suddenly jerked up in bed and glared at them.

'Do you mind? Some of us are trying to get some kip.' She flopped down again.

'Oh, sorry,' Katie whispered.

No plumbing for all these people, she thought, as Roz shut the door behind them. So she'd have to go to the floor where she'd been working these past months. She shook herself. Somehow everyone managed. And so – dammit – would she.

'Well?' That smirk again. Roz was obviously delighting in her incredulity.

When they were outside in the dank corridor, Katie studied the older girl. Really, she'd be attractive if she didn't have such a supercilious attitude. She had a good skin and thick auburn hair coiled at her neck. Her lips were devoid of colour, but her deep-set eyes were a bright piercing blue and she was sure they missed nothing.

'Of course I'll cope,' Katie said. 'Just as everyone else has to.'

She wasn't going to let Roz know how the whole thing appalled her. Suddenly, she had a thought. 'Do *you* sleep here, Roz?'

'Good God, no. You wouldn't catch me down here for all the tea in China. I still go home even when I'm on the later shift. Thank the Lord I'm only in Vauxhall. I just get the Tube and I'm home in a jiffy.'

'What do you do after midnight when the Tube's closed?'

'I can walk it in half an hour.'

'And you're not worried in the early hours and in the blackout?'

'I've got my torch.'

'But what about the bombing?'

'If your time's up, there's nothing you can do about it.' Roz struck a match, lit a cigarette and inhaled deeply. She blew out a stream of smoke. 'Oh, that's better.' She threw the dead match on the concrete floor. 'I'd rather be blown up by a bomb than buried alive.' She gave an exaggerated shudder as she stared at Katie. 'Where do you live?'

'Wimbledon.'

'Hmm. It's not that far. You could easily go home every day.'

'I expect I will except when I'm on the overnight shift.' She hesitated, but she needed to know. 'How often is that?'

Roz grimaced. 'Usually one in three weeks. But it can vary. That day you'll come on at three and work until midnight, or it could be one, two, three in the morning . . . or right through the night if you're needed.'

Katie swallowed. It sounded gruelling. But if the others could do it, then so could she.

But it wouldn't be comfortable to sleep in one of those hard-looking cots. And the loud hum of the ventilation was already getting on her nerves. Did that carry on all through the night? She breathed in deeply, and wished she hadn't. Really, the odour from the chemical toilets was quite revolting. She couldn't wait to go back upstairs where it seemed slightly more civilised.

The next half-hour passed in a daze as Katie tried to follow everything Roz was telling her when they were back in the typing pool.

'Stationery is in here,' Roz said, opening a metal cupboard rising almost to the ceiling. 'Make a note of what you use so we don't run out of anything. All letters go on this headed paper – don't ever waste it, it's expensive –' she broke off to hand Katie half a dozen sheets '– envelopes in that box, large ones in that, Minutes on this foolscap size, carbon paper in those flat boxes, typewriter ribbon here – and there's the box of stencils. Do *not* waste those. They keep a close check on us and—'

'Yes, I do know about wastage and expense,' Katie said, getting tired of this pointless detail, 'and I'll probably find everything myself just by searching. It's more valuable to me if you tell me how people want their work presented.'

Roz threw her a cold glare.

'They want it presented to perfection,' she said, her tone coated with sarcasm. 'So you'll need to ask me until you've learnt the ropes.'

'May I ask something puzzling me?'

'Of course.' Roz placed her hand on her hip.

'The typewriters. You can hardly hear them and yet there are four in use.'

'They come from America – the Remington so-called noiseless typewriter. It's a special instruction from His Nibs. He can't stand any unnecessary noise.'

'Oh, that explains it.'

But it didn't. Katie had no idea who 'His Nibs' was, but she wasn't going to give Roz the satisfaction of asking. Instead, she said:

'What would you like me to do first?'

'There's a notice to be done and some urgent memos. They should be easy enough for you although they're quite long and have to go out today. You'll need to make carbon copies – it should tell you how many.' Roz stared at Katie. 'Do you think you can manage that?'

She asked the question as though she were speaking to a simpleton. Katie felt a bubble of irritation form in her throat, but she fought the impulse to give any kind of retort.

'I expect so,' she said, meeting Roz's eyes.

Katie hung her jacket on the coat rack in the corner. She went to the cupboard and helped herself to a flat box of carbon paper and some copy paper, then sat on her chair and picked up the first sheet in the in-tray. It was a notice requiring two copies. She took one piece of plain typing paper out of the desk drawer, added two sheets of flimsy and two carbon papers, then rolled the wodge into the typewriter. Her eyes fixed on the handwritten notice, she proceeded to type the day's date and snapped the carriage back twice to leave a double space.

'You don't have to do a double carriage space,' Roz said as she looked over Katie's shoulder. 'We have to cut down any noise we possibly can. You just pull this lever towards you once for a double space –' she demonstrated it '– and twice for a triple space.'

'Thank you, Roz.'

Katie would kill her with kindness if that was the last thing she did. Feeling the difference of the keys under her fingertips from those of her Corona typewriter at the secretarial school, she quietly tapped out:

IMPORTANT NOTICE
THE SOL-TAN BOX
Health Issues

It has come to our attention that there are various health issues associated with working long periods underground. This includes headaches, nausea and general lack of energy and motivation.

To assist in this matter we have ordered four ultra-violet lamps. Each lamp is a SOL-TAN box of high-pressure mercury. Once a week staff will be required to strip to their underwear—

What! Katie stopped typing. Stripping to your underwear? Was this some kind of joke?

—and put on a pair of goggles which will protect your eyes.

It is important to follow the operating instructions. Start with only one minute each side, and gradually work up to 8–10 minutes.

ALWAYS REMEMBER TO USE THE GOGGLES FOR EYE SAFETY.

G. Bates (Administrative Officer)

Katie sighed. Everything was so strange. Even the keyboard on the typewriter felt strange, and its odd low thrum didn't change even if she pounded the keys. She had an awful feeling she'd jumped into something she wasn't prepared for.

The rest of the day passed without incident. Katie rapidly typed the half-dozen memos as she began to get used to the machine.

'What happens to them now?' she asked Peggy, who was working at the nearest desk.

Roz looked up from her typewriter as though ready to answer but Peggy said: 'We take them to the various departments. Memos are nearly always urgent. Would you like me to come with you? I can show you where all the rooms are where you need to go. Get you used to the layout.'

It would be a nice change from the sour-faced Roz watching her every movement.

As the two girls walked along the corridor, Katie with her memos, Peggy said:

'Don't take any notice of Roz. I don't know what gets into her sometimes.'

'She doesn't know me – so why has she taken such a dislike to me? She was quite horrible this morning in the Dock.'

'She's jealous of anyone new. She can bully Martha, but she knows Amanda is more than a match, so she leaves her alone.' Peggy glanced down at Katie. 'And of course, you're a stunning blonde. You're competition. So she's going to see how far she can go.'

'That's ridiculous. She's not unattractive.'

'I think she has a sneaking feeling she's not quite so clever as she makes out, so she lashes out to boost herself.'

'What about you?' Katie said curious now. 'How does she treat you?'

'Me?' Peggy pointed to herself. 'Can you imagine her trying to bully *me*? I'd have her for breakfast.'

The two girls looked at one another and burst into a fit of giggles. Immediately, Katie felt better. If three out of the four were friendly, she doubted Roz would be too difficult to deal with.

Chapter Eleven

As Peggy was guiding Katie along several corridors, pointing out the various rooms, she mentioned that she regularly stayed overnight in the Dock, and also Amanda, but that Roz and Martha both lived close enough to go home and usually braved it in between air raids.

'How do you manage with such low ceilings?' Katie asked.

Peggy laughed. 'I've learnt to bend myself in two . . . and now I'm used to it.'

It had taken no time at all for the two girls to warm to one another. By the end of the day, Katie felt she'd made a real friend in Peggy. Martha was quiet but seemed very sweet and obliging, and Amanda brought her latest boyfriend into any conversation she possibly could. But they were all friendly and happy to help her and for that she was grateful.

By the time Katie reached her front door late that evening she was exhausted, mostly through having to absorb so much in a short space of time. Roz always spoke at breakneck speed, and Katie began to wonder if the woman did it on purpose so she didn't have a chance to take everything in. But all in all, it hadn't gone too badly, Katie thought. The comforting smell of red cabbage and apple and cloves rose to her nostrils when she opened the kitchen door

'How did you do on your first day?' Ursula asked, lifting the lid of the saucepan. She dipped in a teaspoon, then blew on the morsel of cabbage, tasted it and nodded. She turned to face Katie.

'It went quite well. They're a nice group of girls I'll be working with.' She wouldn't mention Roz.

'But you still cannot tell me where you are working or what you are doing?' Ursula said, frustration rising in her voice.

'You know I've signed the Official Secrets Act.'

Ursula heaved a long-suffering sigh.

'But it's in the War Office. I am allowed to say that. And I use my typing skills.'

'What about your shorthand?'

Katie hesitated. 'I'm not doing any – well, not at the moment anyway.'

'You worked very hard to get it. You will lose your speed if you do not practise it.'

She was right. It was something Katie was very aware of. She vowed to have a word with Mrs Goodman about it the very next day. If there were such piles of typing to be done, then surely the stenographers' in-trays were in just as bad a shape. Pleased that she'd made a decision, she'd see Mrs Goodman at the first opportunity they were alone. She didn't want to discuss it in front of the others – they might think she thought herself above them.

After a week, Katie was beginning to recognise a few of the corridors off the main one, but the atmosphere caused by working underground was still uncomfortable. She occasionally lit a cigarette, mainly to keep herself awake on the afternoon shift, but the others, with the exception of Martha, smoked incessantly and the room was always clouded with smoke. This afternoon was no different. Katie stole a glance at Amanda, who had a cigarette in one side of her scarlet mouth as she speedily typed away on her near-silent machine. What a different world she lived in now, Katie thought, as she turned to the next piece of work, a report that one of the government ministers was going to make. Katie rolled the last page out of her typewriter. She quickly scanned the half-dozen pages, thanking her lucky stars that her old teacher had been adamant that only one mistake could be made before the work was thrown into the waste-paper basket. It had made all the girls very conscious of accuracy in their work. She leaned across to Peggy.

'Peggy, would you have time to check this before I hand it in? It's only six pages.'

'Yes, of course.'

Fifteen minutes later Peggy handed it back. 'All present and correct,' she said.

'Oh, thank goodness.' Katie stretched her back that had been hunched for well over an hour. She smothered a yawn when she saw Mrs Goodman walking towards her desk, hoping she would announce the tea-break.

'I need to read the report.' Mrs Goodman put her glasses on her nose and took a few minutes before she looked up and smiled. 'Excellent, Katie. I'll just sign it off and you can take it to Major Morton – he's the Military Adviser – whose room is down the main corridor, and then second turning on the left. His name is on the third door on the right.'

She signed her name with a flourish, put a paperclip on the sheaf of paper and handed it back to Katie.

At least I can stretch my legs, Katie thought. She was beginning to get cramp.

She had just taken the second turning on the left when a plump, elderly gentleman with a purposeful walk came towards her. Katie halted in her tracks. It couldn't be. Of course it couldn't. This man was too short. But the cigar that was stuck in his mouth . . . She was about to slide by, hoping to be unnoticed, when he stopped her.

'You're new here, young lady.' He said it as a statement. There was no mistaking that gravelly voice.

Katie looked at him with awe. His expression was serious but his eyes were twinkling.

'Um, yes, sir.'

'Pray what is your position?'

'I'm in the typing pool.'

Oh, how she wished she could say she was a secretary to this great man.

'I thought so,' he said. 'Working under Mrs Goodman, no doubt.'

'Yes, sir.'

'I'm very pleased to hear it,' he told her with an elaborate wave of his hand as he hurried past.

Katie stood for a full thirty seconds looking after the short plump figure, her heart beating fast. Why hadn't she realised the Prime Minister would be working here? If an air raid was on, he and his aides and staff would be much safer down here than on ground level. This unknown underground maze was obviously extremely important when you looked at the responsibility of the three Chiefs of Staff of all three forces. And here she was, doing mountains of typing for the Joint Planning Committee, and they must have to send the reports to the Chiefs of Staff. And they in turn would presumably send them on to the Prime Minister, Mr Churchill himself. She drew in a sharp breath. Suddenly, everything slotted into place and she felt a frisson of pure excitement. She'd said she wanted to be closer to the war effort than simply joining up.

I couldn't be closer if I tried.

Well, she could if she was one of Mr Churchill's personal secretaries.

Berating herself for thinking such nonsense, she headed back to the typing pool. Somehow her role as a mere typist didn't seem so undignified now she saw how close she was to the Prime Minister and that the report she'd typed this morning might well be read by the great man himself an hour or so later. Imagine what Dad would say if she was able to tell him where she now worked and that it was on the very same underground floor as Mr Churchill.

And Judy. What would she have to say about her new job? Katie couldn't help an inward smile. Without doubt, she'd say that aiming to become a personal secretary to Winston Churchill was certainly not out of the question.

It was only when she entered the typing pool that she realised she still had Major Morton's report in her hand!

It had taken some time for Katie to become used to working underground, where there were no windows to let in fresh air, and the only exercise for her aching legs was to walk briskly along the corridors. But at least she felt she was fully contributing to the workload.

'You're on the graveyard shift tomorrow,' Roz told Katie at the end of her second week. 'So you come in at three and be prepared to work right through the night if necessary. The next shift will take over at eight that morning. If you're lucky you might get a few hours' kip from maybe one or two in the morning but only if you and everyone else have finished. And even then you could be called out of your bed.' She gave Katie what looked like a smirk. 'You'll go down to the Dock where I showed you and then you find who's left a vacant bed.'

This was what Katie had been dreading – going down another flight to that smelly room below. But she'd have to do it.

'Does it ever happen that there isn't one vacant?'

'Occasionally. Then you're out of luck.'

It sounded like musical chairs, the game she used to play with other children at her birthday party. Katie forced herself not to flinch.

'So bring an overnight case with you,' Roz was saying. She

paused and considered Katie. 'Have you gone under the sun lamp yet?'

Katie shook her head. 'What exactly does it do?'

'It tops up Vitamin D, which one normally gets through being in the sun. Well, as it's permanently airless down here they have to provide something else so they came up with this lamp. We're supposed to go once a week so I'd better put you down for it. In fact, why don't you go right away.' She paused and looked round the room. 'Martha, have you been under the lamp this week?'

Martha shook her head. 'I hate that lamp and the whole rigmarole. It's undignified parading about in your underwear.'

'Well, it's supposed to be for our benefit so we just have to grin and bear it, so go with Katie.' Roz put a fresh piece of paper into her typewriter as if to end the conversation.

Katie glanced across at Martha. 'Shall we go?'

Martha removed her glasses and set them on her desk. She gave Katie a weak smile as she stood up.

'I suppose we might as well get it over with.'

The outer door was marked Sol-Tan Room. There were three lamps, one of them in use by a plump girl wearing underclothes that looked a size too small for her. She nodded to Katie and Martha.

Martha removed her jacket and skirt. After a few seconds' pause, Katie set her mouth in a determined line until, like Martha, she was down to her underwear.

'You start off with a minute and after four or five visits you'll have worked up to ten,' Martha instructed. 'Make sure your goggles are firmly in position. And always wear them. One of the clerks forgot to put them on and she's almost gone blind.'

Dear God.

'Well, I hope it's done its job,' Katie said when the three of them were getting dressed.

'Gives you a healthy glow if nothing else,' Jean, the other girl, commented drily. 'See you in the Treasury.'

Martha broke into a rare grin. 'Yes, it's payday – everyone's favourite day.'

'Where do we go to collect it?' Katie asked.

'The Treasury – just above us.'

'Oh, the same as—' Katie stopped herself. No one in the basement was supposed to know who and what went on upstairs, and vice versa.

Martha gave her a glance as though wondering why she'd stopped in mid-sentence. 'We have to go outside and into the main entrance, then up the stairs,' she went on. 'Let's go now as it will get much busier soon.'

When the two women arrived upstairs, Martha pressed the button to enter the Treasury. Two Marines guarded the inside entrance. After showing their passes, the women joined a long queue, which thankfully moved swiftly. Then it was Katie's turn.

'Name?'

'Katharina Valentine.'

The young man rifled through some small brown envelopes then pulled one out.

'Here you are, miss. And just sign here.' He handed her a notebook where she wrote her name.

She still didn't know what her wages would be but she wasn't about to open it in front of Martha. She decided to take advantage of the Ladies' cloakroom before going back underground. Eagerly, she tore the envelope open. There were two folded pound notes and a florin – two guineas in total. She pulled a face. Only two shillings more than she'd had when working for Vernon. More than ever she was determined to secure a promotion as soon as she possibly could.

'Your mother has been worried to death,' Katie's father said when she finally stumbled through the front door that night. It was well after ten. 'We heard the air raid and I told her you'd probably taken shelter but she feared the worst.' He glanced at her. 'You look done in, love.'

'I am.'

'You weren't caught in it, were you?'

'No, but I stopped to help someone – an elderly lady who'd walked smack into a lamppost.'

Her father sighed. 'There are so many accidents like this since the blackout. Didn't she have a torch?'

'No. And she couldn't stop apologising that she didn't have it with her, but it's easily done.'

'Mind you always carry one,' he said as she hung up her coat. 'But now, go and see your mother. She's in bed with a headache.'

He still referred to her stepmother as her mother. Katie didn't know whether to be irritated or not. She supposed he could hardly change after all these years. She chewed her lip as she went upstairs, wondering if she would ever accept the situation.

But Ursula was fast asleep. Katie quietly shut the door behind her as she left the room.

When Katie had thankfully climbed into her bed that night she mused over the day. It had certainly been one of the most remarkable in her life but something told her this was only the beginning. With that thought in mind, along with the chubby-faced image of Mr Churchill and his famous cigar, she fell asleep.

Chapter Twelve

The following day, Katie packed an overnight case with soap and flannel and the rest of her toiletries, her bed sheet and pillowcase, a small towel, and clean underwear. She wasn't particularly looking forward to a week of working the graveyard shift but decided it would be another new experience.

'I do not like the idea that you are not home tonight,' Ursula said when Katie perfunctorily kissed her goodbye.

'I'll be safer where I'm sleeping than you will here in your own bed,' Katie said, trying to pacify her. 'And far more comfortable than sleeping in the Underground.'

All those people surrounded by noisy fractious children, head to head, toe to toe, squashed onto a station platform. Poor things. It didn't bear thinking about. At least she'd only be with other women.

'And I'll be home before you know it.'

At ten minutes before three, Katie showed her pass to the sentry as usual. Even though she knew he must now surely recognise her, he still scrutinised the small card, gave her a cursory glance, then nodded.

She hurried down the steps and along the corridor to her office, already familiar with the smell of stale cigarette smoke which hung from the walls and seeped through the doors after nearly a day of activity. When she entered the room she saw that Mrs Goodman, Roz and Peggy were already there.

'Good afternoon, Katie.' Mrs Goodman greeted her with a friendly but slightly distracted smile.

'Good afternoon, Mrs Goodman.'

Roz, busy typing, briefly looked up to see who it was, gave Katie a curt nod and continued the strange, almost noiseless tapping. Peggy was chatting to one of the girls on the earlier shift who was now packing up to go home. She looked round.

'Oh, hello, Katie. Are you prepared for a mammoth day and night?'

'I think so . . . I hope so.' She couldn't stop a note of anxiety creeping into her words.

Peggy grinned. 'You'll be okay, girl. You just need stamina in this job. It's the one thing that will see you through.'

Katie took in a deep breath and returned the smile. She was young and healthy. Surely that was enough to carry her through.

'Peggy's right, you know,' Mrs Goodman said. 'Mr Churchill expects us all to have the same level of energy on the same little sleep as he does himself.' She smiled, softening her words so that they seemed to Katie to be just a statement rather than any criticism.

At the sound of his name, Katie felt a tiny thrill that she was working on the same floor as the great man who would surely see the country through this evil war. She set her handbag in the desk drawer and adjusted her chair a little lower, then glanced at her in-tray. It was piled with a stack of reports and Minutes of meetings. She groaned inwardly as she picked up the top sheets, hardly blaming whoever the previous girl had been for leaving this one. It was in the tiniest writing, some of the letters hardly formed, as though the writer was in a perpetual hurry to be somewhere else. Well, it would be a challenge.

Martha arrived and murmured, 'Good afternoon', then slipped behind her desk and immediately got to work.

'Now where's Amanda?' Mrs Goodman said, looking at her watch.

It was five past three when Amanda sashayed into the office, perfectly made up and with not a hair out of place, holding a beautiful soft leather overnight case. Katie bit back a smile as she wondered how Amanda would cope with a night in what the girls called the dungeon, instead of the luxury of her own bedroom.

'Hello, all. I'm not late, am I?'

'Five minutes,' Mrs Goodman said, her tone a little sharper than usual. 'It's important we're all punctual so I know we're all safe from last night's bombing.' Her gaze fell on each girl. 'Right, now you're all here we have a long afternoon and evening ahead of us.' Her eyes fell on Katie.

'Katie, it's your first overnight shift though I'm sure you'll manage very well. So let's crack on, everyone. I'll be working in one of the other rooms until later this evening, so Roz will be in charge if there are any problems at all.' Her gaze fell on Roz. 'I'll leave you in her capable hands.'

'Thank you, Mrs Goodman,' Roz said, practically simpering.

Katie cringed as she rolled a stencil into her machine. It wasn't going to be the easiest afternoon with Roz and her barbed remarks. Well, she wouldn't take any notice of her. She had enough to do to peer through this report in front of her.

After what must have been a solid hour, Katie rubbed the back of her neck. There was still the final paragraph to decipher. This was taking three times longer than anyone else's work. Typing on a stencil was tricky. Mistakes were heavily frowned on. She could hear Mrs Stanley's voice from the secretarial school ringing in her ears when she gave one of her lectures warning about mistakes and waste of money.

Katie heaved a sigh. None of her colleagues she was now working with had mucked up a stencil. Well, if they had, she hadn't noticed. She read the last sentence.

Oh, no! Please don't let me have got it wrong.

Heart thumping, she read it over again, this time more slowly. But she'd read a whole word incorrectly. Instead of 'interrogation', she'd written 'interpretation'. Oh, it was too bad. She'd have to do the whole thing over again. Or could she get away with carefully using the bright pink corrector fluid on every letter? No, she'd be reprimanded as a careless typist. She glanced round the room. Everyone had their head bent. She sighed. There were strict orders that any mistakes in your work had to be put into the waste-paper basket in your office, then someone would empty it at the end of the day, and apparently the rubbish would all be sifted before being destroyed.

Quietly, she rose to her feet, deposited the offending stencil in the waste-paper basket, then went to the stationery cupboard. She carefully removed a fresh stencil from a flat box and closed the door. As she turned she saw Roz watching her and knew by the little smile on her lips that the woman had seen her throw away the stencil.

As soon as Katie was back at her desk and rolled the fresh stencil into her typewriter she realised she shouldn't have thrown away the stencil until she'd finished the fresh one. That way, she wouldn't have had decipher the practically illegible writing again. Oh, well. She'd have to remember what she'd already worked out so far. She certainly wasn't going to remove it from the rubbish under Roz's scrutiny.

This time, the report went without a hitch. With a sigh of relief Katie stretched her neck and rolled back her shoulders. She licked her lips. Her mouth was as dry as a prune. It must be time for a cup of tea. But first she needed to check the report before putting it into her out-tray.

'Like me to check your stencil?' Roz called over.

Just her luck that Roz was the only one who looked available. Katie held back a grimace.

'Thanks, Roz. This one's been a bit of a nightmare,' she said as she handed it over.

'Who's it from?'

Katie glanced at the reference at the top of the report.

'The initials are B.E.'

'Oh, our Mr Edwards. Yes, his writing is on the small side but personally I don't have a problem with it.' She gave one of her smirks.

She wouldn't. Katie forced herself to smile.

'I expect I'll soon get used to it,' was all she said, before starting to read aloud Mr Edwards's handwritten notes so that Roz could cross-check the stencil.

For the next ten minutes there was just the sound of Katie's voice, as low and quiet as possible so as not to disturb the others.

'Looks all right,' Roz finally said, seeming disappointed as she handed back the stencil.

Roz would love to have found another fault, Katie thought, relief flooding through her. She only knew she never wanted to type anything else again for Mr-blooming-Edwards. And whether it was teatime or not, she was going to have one. She'd go down to the makeshift canteen in the Dock to get one, whether it was for officers only or not!

If only she could just go upstairs and get some air. Katie's eyes were stinging from the claustrophobic atmosphere and the constant stream of smoke, particularly from the direction of Roz's desk, as she typed yet another set of Minutes. The air conditioning was a steady, noisy hum but there was no sign that it was bringing fresh air into the stuffy office. She glanced round at her colleagues. They all looked completely absorbed in their work, until Peggy looked up and sent her a sympathetic smile.

'You okay?' she mouthed.

Katie nodded.

'Do you want to pop upstairs for a breather?'

Katie could have hugged her. Roz twisted round.

'We need to get all this afternoon's stencils copied before anyone goes anywhere.' She stared at Katie. 'I've got a couple more here.' She rose and placed them on Katie's desk. 'Twenty copies each of mine. Anyone else have one?'

'Yes.' Martha passed hers over. 'Thirty copies, please, Katie.'

'Anyone else?' Roz said. 'Right.' She turned back to Katie. 'I presume you know how to use the Gestetner?'

'Of course.' Katie tried to quell her irritation at Roz's tone.

'You won't need my assistance then.'

'No, Roz, I don't suppose I will.'

Katie took the four stencils over to a table next to the machine in the middle of the room. She put Mr Edwards's stencil on the machine first. Get it over with, she thought grimly, as she carefully placed it round the ink-soaked roller, then filled the paper tray. Damn. Mr Edwards hadn't put the number he needed. Well, she'd better do thirty, just to make sure. Just as she was about to start she caught Roz staring at her. Was the woman going to watch her every move? Ignoring her, Katie began to turn the handle, mentally counting each copy.

She finished making copies from all four stencils and put the neat piles on Mrs Goodman's desk.

'They need delivering right away, Katie,' Roz said. 'Mine are both for the Cabinet Room, so you can drop them into the office next door.' She turned to Martha. 'Who's yours for?'

'Mr Jenkins.'

'Oh, he's also Cabinet. So it's just Edwards who's different. He's head of the Map Room Annexe – room 64, or in the Map Room itself – number 65. You'll see a row of coloured telephones they call the Beauty Chorus. But it's not the only beauty chorus. The Map Room is where the Wrens do the plotting so you can sometimes catch him there.' Roz looked at her, a mocking smile on her lips. 'You know where that is?'

Katie nodded. She wouldn't rise to Roz's gibes.

'It'll give you a chance to meet him. Tell him what difficulty you had trying to work out his writing, which is worse than a doctor's.'

'I doubt I'll do anything of the kind.'

Roz sent her a knowing smile.

What was that for? Katie wondered. Her only gripe was his minute handwriting, but Roz seemed to be implying something more. She shrugged. The sooner she got the copies delivered, the quicker she'd be able to get a breath of air upstairs.

It was good to stretch her legs, Katie thought, as she hurried along the corridors, hoping she might catch another glimpse of Mr Churchill, but no famous chubby figure complete with cigar came in sight. In fact, the corridor was unusually quiet except for the constant whine and hum of the air conditioning and a murmur of voices behind some of the closed doors.

She dropped off the three lots of copies for the Cabinet Room. Just Mr Edwards's pile now. A few yards along she came to a door with the sign 'Map Room Annexe'. By now, her exasperation had increased. Should she mention her difficulty in deciphering his writing? Hmm. She was the newcomer after all. Well, perhaps she should play it by ear. Hesitating for a few seconds to collect herself, she knocked on the door. There was no answer so she opened it.

Two men stood with their backs to her, the shorter one pointing to an enormous map of what she recognised as Russia. They both looked round.

'Sorry to disturb—'

'Come in, come in.' A tall, dark-haired man strode to the door. 'We were just discussing the latest news – Germany invaded Russia today.' At her horrified expression, he added,

103

'Don't worry, it's *good* news. Russia will now be on our side and they have a huge army we could well use. If you're around this evening the PM is making a speech to the nation about it at nine o'clock.'

Katie's eye caught a shelf with an array of clocks all giving different times. Someone must like collecting them – or mending them. She brought her attention back to the dark-haired man.

'I am. But I'll be working.'

'Then talk nicely to Mrs Goodman and she'll probably allow you to listen to it.' He gazed at her. 'I take it you're from the typing pool.'

It sounded so mundane. She nodded.

'Have you anything for us?' the shorter of the two said, nodding towards Katie's bundle of papers.

'Yes. Copies for Mr Edwards.'

'Oh, thanks for doing them.' The dark-haired man stretched out his hand. 'I'm sorry the writing's so difficult to fathom.'

Hmm. At least Mr Edwards admitted it. But he was rather dishy. Katie bit back a smile. Maybe she wouldn't grumble about it after all.

'You're new, aren't you?' he said, giving her an appreciative look.

'Yes. Katie Valentine.'

'I'm Barnaby. We're not formal around here so we'll probably take the liberty of calling you Katie, if that's all right with you.' He gave her a warm smile.

Barnaby. Nice name. It suits him.

'Of course,' she said, returning his smile.

'And this old chap is Mike.' Barnaby sent his colleague a grin. Mike was a man of middle age with a friendly open face.

'Less of the old,' he said, then turned to Katie and smiled. 'You'll have to get used to him, Katie, but welcome to the fold.'

'Come and see us anytime,' Barnaby told her, with a captivating smile that almost knocked her off her feet.

That's exactly what she *would* do. She'd already taken rather a shine to Barnaby Edwards. Pleased she'd met him and hadn't spoilt their first meeting by grumbling about his writing, she couldn't stop grinning as she went back to the office.

Chapter Thirteen

Katie rubbed her stinging eyes and yawned. She was sure if she looked in the mirror they'd be bloodshot. She stared at her watch. It couldn't be twenty-five to one. No wonder she felt so drained. The only break she'd had from typing was when Mr Churchill made his speech on the invasion of Russia. She and Amanda had sat mesmerised by the voice of the man who was responsible for the whole of the British Empire's safety. Amanda told her he was speaking from an office just along the corridor.

'All this was no surprise to me,' came the gravelly tones. 'In fact, I gave clear and precise warnings to Stalin of what was coming. I gave him warnings, as I have given warnings to others before. I can only hope that these warnings did not fall unheeded.'

He finished by saying, 'Germany's invasion of Russia is no more than a prelude to an attempted invasion of the British Isles. Let us redouble our exertions and strike with united strength while life and power remain.'

The two girls sat in silence for a few moments. Then Amanda blew out her cheeks.

'We're so damned lucky to have him.' She looked at Katie. 'If anyone can get us through all this, *he* will, there's no doubt.'

'Well, he has our support to the bitter end,' Katie said. 'We can't say more than that.'

* * *

She stretched her arms above her head, looking towards the ceiling, a headache starting. The green lampshade with its fierce light shone straight into her eyes causing them to water. Every typist sat under one and complained – even Roz. Katie was sure that part of the problem was having such a bright light constantly fixed on her desk, watching the words appear on the paper in front of her as she typed, then peering at the various reports and Minutes every few seconds to keep the flow going.

She looked across at Amanda, who caught her eye and smiled wanly, then gave a wide yawn without bothering to hide it.

'It's a bit of a pig, isn't it,' Amanda said, 'working this late?'

'Yes, it is. But I wouldn't have missed that speech for anything. I just hope my parents listened.' Katie glanced up at the ceiling. 'But this awful overhead light doesn't help and I'm going to find something to wrap round it to stop the glare.'

'Good idea. What will you use?'

'I don't know . . . yes, I do.' Katie switched off the light and retrieved a sheet of paper from the waste-paper basket, then stood on her desk. 'Can you cut me some Sellotape, Amanda? About three inches.'

Amanda handed her a piece and Katie wound the paper round the inside of the lamp and taped it. With a few more pieces of Sellotape, the paper was firmly in place.

'Can you switch the light back on while I'm up here?'

There was a click. Katie's overhead lamp was nicely dimmed but she was sure she'd still be able to do her work perfectly happily – unless she had something else from Mr Edwards, she thought with a grimace. She climbed off the desk.

'I think I might do mine,' Amanda said, 'but not now. I'm too tired.' She glanced at her watch. 'It's quarter to one.' She looked at Katie. 'Have you anything important that still needs doing?'

107

Katie flicked through the almost empty tray.

'A couple of reports,' she said. 'Not very long – one's four pages, the other's six. I was going to leave them for the morning shift. I don't think they're terribly important.'

'Any report needs to be on the Joint Planning Officers' desks by eight o'clock sharp,' Amanda said, 'so give one to me, and you do the other, then we'll pack up.'

How kind she was, Katie thought, handing over the shorter report.

Forty minutes later they had both finished and had checked one another's work.

'Thanks so much, Amanda,' Katie said as she put the cover over her machine. 'I don't think I could have typed another word.'

'Then let's make our way down to those comfortable feather beds in our own private bedrooms with bathrooms attached,' Amanda said, picking up her handbag and overnight case.

'I wish,' Katie said, grinning at her colleague's sarcasm.

Katie didn't relish the night at all, knowing there were no washing facilities and she'd have to go up two floors to ground level to have a bath in the morning – that is, if she was lucky. She'd need to be really early to beat the others. She wondered how everyone coped as she clambered down the stairs to the floor below to find three others getting undressed and putting on their nightwear. One girl, with her cascade of golden hair and pale-blue negligee, was sitting on the edge of her cot looking in her powder compact to remove her mascara. Katie was thankful she didn't bother with eye make-up at work. Powder and lipstick had to suffice.

But her straight hair was the problem. Since she'd left the kennels she'd smartened up for office work, which meant she'd put her hair in pipe-cleaners every night. But could she do this without a proper mirror? And if she managed it, would the others think her vain? She shrugged.

We're all girls here. We're used to this sort of thing. They won't take any notice of what I'm doing.

Disappointed there weren't two vacant cots together, she walked to the far end of the dormitory and took the last one. The girls on either side of her were asleep. One was snoring – making a kind of growl. She wouldn't get a wink next to that racket. Well, short of poking her in the ribs, she'd have to get on with it and hope tomorrow night the girl would be on a different shift.

Katie bent the last pipe-cleaner to put in her hair. She'd been right. No one raised an eyebrow – the only two girls nearby who were still awake, that is. Amanda, several beds away, was putting pin curls in the front of her hair. She waved to Katie and mouthed 'Okay?' Katie nodded and waved back, then unscrewed her jar of Pond's Cold Cream and quickly smoothed a blob into her face. She'd been so tired she'd forgotten to clean her teeth before she'd come down the two flights of stairs from the bathroom. Oh, well, she'd know tomorrow what to do. They wouldn't fall out just because she'd neglected them for one night.

Katie slept uninterrupted on the lumpy narrow cot out of sheer exhaustion. She'd told herself she must be up before six so she could beat any rush for the bathroom upstairs. But it was twenty past when she peered at her watch through eyes that were bleary. Her mouth tasted dry and stale. Through not doing her teeth last night, she remembered, pulling a face. She glanced round the dormitory. It seemed she was in luck. No one was stirring. She hopped out of bed, shoved her feet into her slippers, threw on her dressing gown, snatched her sponge bag, then rushed up the first flight of concrete steps.

But a Royal Marine guard stopped her on the first landing.

'Where are you off to, miss?'

Oh, it was so embarrassing to be caught in her dressing gown.

'Miss?'

'Um, to the bathroom.'

'Oh, not to the office then?' He gave a twist of a smile.

'No. As you can see,' Katie said sharply, irritated with what he must think was a witty remark.

He straightened his neck to maintain his posture.

'Right. You may go.'

She had just put her foot on the second step of the spiral staircase that would take her up to ground level, where the blessed bathroom was, when a man, hatless but immaculately dressed in RAF officer's uniform, appeared at the top and proceeded to take each twist of the spiral staircase in one leap. Instinctively, she stepped down backwards to give him room and almost lost her balance.

'Hey, steady on,' he said, as he reached the basement floor and grabbed her arm, righting her.

She looked up into a pair of hazel eyes set into a craggy face under a thatch of nut-brown hair. His grin almost split his face in two. Already annoyed with the guard, her hand flew to her head, taking only a split second to feel the pipe-cleaners that she'd forgotten she still had in, and now realising that her face would be shiny from the cold cream.

And don't forget your eyes are probably bloodshot, her inner voice reminded her. Oh, why couldn't she have been wearing one of those glamorous peignoirs that the actresses always wore in films as soon as they emerged, fully made-up, from their beds?

Oh, it was too bad.

'Are you all right?' he said when she pulled away from his hand, which had been encircling her arm.

'Yes, but no thanks to you.'

110

His eyes widened. Then he threw his head back and laughed.

'I've not seen you before,' he said, still chuckling. 'You'll soon get used to being caught in all kinds of undress – happens to all of us – but just remember we're in this together.'

His voice was warm and refined but he'd made the words sound more personal than simply assuring her that no one took any notice of what you looked like here – that there was an important job to do which took precedence over everything. Instead, his self-confident manner increased her irritation with him. She could so easily have had an accident because of his lack of etiquette in not letting a woman go first when he'd plainly seen her, even though her inner voice told her the spiral staircase was narrow and difficult, making it impossible for him to suddenly stop and turn around.

In as dignified a manner as she could muster, she said in a cool tone, 'Would you please allow me to pass?'

'Oh, be my guest.' His grin only faded a fraction as he stepped aside.

Cheeky devil!

She swept by but caught the underside of her ankle-length dressing gown on the edge of the rail. He immediately bent to unhook it. Not bothering to turn and thank him, and feeling her face grow hot with his burst of laughter ringing in her ears, she reached ground level, where she breathed out her relief. Thank goodness the bathroom was just a few feet away, clearly marked. And thank the Lord it was vacant!

She ran the bath up to the five-inch line – all anyone was allowed since war was declared – and tried to calm down from her unwelcome encounter. Was this how it would be every morning on the graveyard shift – running into guards and beautifully dressed officers? She vowed she would be in the bathroom tomorrow morning by six sharp. Furthermore, she never wanted to risk running into that cocksure officer again.

111

In her fury she hadn't noticed how many gold rings he had on his sleeves. She was sure there'd been a few, which would make him quite high up in the ranks. But as for doing any typing for him and having to deliver it, she would find out his name and make sure she passed any work of his onto one of the others. Let them deal with him.

By the time she'd towelled herself dry, Katie had calmed down but she was still determined to find out who he was. He obviously worked on her floor. She'd mention him to Amanda at the first opportunity.

Amanda was yawning and stretching her arms above her head when Katie returned to the dormitory, her hair now free of curlers and settling in blonde waves on her shoulders.

'You were early this morning,' Amanda said.

'Not as early as I'd have liked, or needed to be,' Katie returned with a rueful smile as she hurriedly dressed.

'Oh, what was the problem?'

'I ran into an officer who didn't have the courtesy to step back while we were both on the stairs. I was just going up and he was at the top, saw me, but came flying down anyway and knocked me off balance.' Katie bit her lip. That wasn't quite accurate but it was near enough.

'Oh, dear. Who on earth was that?'

'I don't know but I'm going to find out.'

'What did he look like?'

'Tall, broad-shouldered, nut-brown hair, immaculately dressed at that time of the morning in RAF officer's uniform. And there was I, the great unwashed, in a dressing gown with curlers in my hair and a shiny face.'

'Oh, I think I've seen him, but I couldn't tell you his name. But then I've only been here a fortnight longer than you.' She grinned. 'He sounds rather intriguing.'

'Well, he's not,' Katie said crisply, then immediately felt

contrite. 'Sorry, Amanda, I didn't mean to snap at you. But when I told him off for his bad manners he just laughed at me and I knew it was because I looked such a sight.'

'Well, I have to sympathise. I'd hate to bump into someone dishy without my hair and make-up done.'

'He isn't dishy. That's the point. He's not good-looking enough to get away with such arrogance.'

That's not quite true, her inner voice whispered. *If it was, you wouldn't have reacted in such a way.*

'Anyway, I want to forget it and start the day afresh.'

'I'd better get up then,' Amanda sighed. 'The others are stirring. I need to beat them to the bathroom. But wait for me – I'll be ready in a jiffy and we'll go out and get some breakfast when the next shift comes in. Then we're free until three o'clock.'

Amanda, now perfectly groomed, knew of a café not far away from the entrance of the War Rooms. Katie drew in deep breaths of damp air, almost choking with fumes as a bus passed them, but it felt so good after sixteen hours or so in a stuffy atmosphere beneath the pavements.

Inside, the café was packed with both military men and women, the women mostly Wrens, and a sprinkling of civilians. Katie found a table by the window. What bliss it was to look out onto the world – see mothers wearily pushing prams, businessmen in bowler hats striding along carrying briefcases, some hailing taxis, young lovers out early in the morning, not noticing anything except one another . . . everything was ordinary, and yet to Katie it seemed endlessly fascinating.

Amanda immediately lit a cigarette and inhaled deeply.

'Oh, that's better.' She leaned back on the chair, blowing out the smoke in a steady stream. 'I was going mad for one.' She stared at Katie. 'I haven't seen you light up lately.'

'There's so much smoke in the basement and sometimes

I feel quite suffocated. I don't suppose it does our lungs much good either.' Katie grimaced. 'So I've decided not to light up at work. Maybe just have the odd one when I'm off-duty.'

'Good for you. I should probably do the same but I haven't got the discipline.' Amanda studied the menu as the waitress came to take their order. 'Sorry, Katie. Here.' She passed the menu over.

'Good morning, ladies. What can I get you?'

Amanda didn't hesitate. 'Fried egg, fried bread, tomato and bacon, please.'

'Sorry, no bacon with the shortage,' the waitress said, then looked enquiringly at Katie.

'I'll have scrambled egg on toast, please.' Katie glanced at Amanda. 'Tea?' Amanda nodded. Katie turned to the waitress. 'And tea for two.'

'Coming up.' The waitress sped away.

She soon reappeared with two steaming plates. 'Tea on its way,' she told them as she rushed off.

'How do you like the work so far in the dungeon?' Amanda asked, immediately tucking in. 'Gosh, I'm hungry.'

'It was rather a shock but I'm getting used to it.'

'What did you do before?'

Katie hesitated as she buttered a piece of toast. She mustn't say she worked close by in the War Office. Perhaps the job before that would be a safer bet.

'It was in huge contrast to what I'm doing now. I was a kennel maid, looking after forty greyhounds.'

'Oh, my goodness. You are a dark horse . . . excuse the joke,' Amanda chuckled. 'So what made you decide to be a secretary?'

'A relative died and left me a legacy to be used for going to a secretarial school. And conditions at work were getting bad so I thought I'd better carry out her dying wishes.'

'But you weren't so enthusiastic?'

'You're right. But now there's a war on everything's changed, hasn't it?' Katie looked across at her friend, who suddenly put her knife and fork down even though she hadn't finished.

'Yes, it has.' A tear started in the corner of Amanda's eye.

Something's happened, Katie thought. She shouldn't pry but Amanda was lighting another cigarette. She was obviously upset about something. Putting her hand over Amanda's slim white one, Katie said:

'What is it?'

Amanda hesitated. 'I've finally met someone I really like and who seems to like me. But I've just found out he's married. He didn't tell me because he didn't want to lose me.' She took a furious puff of her cigarette. 'Well, he's lost me, and I shall tell him so.'

'Oh, Amanda, I'm sorry.'

'Don't be.' She squeezed Katie's hand before drawing her own away. 'Just don't make such a silly mistake as I have and fall for the wrong man. Most of them aren't worth it.'

Without warning, the RAF officer whose name Katie didn't even know floated in front of her. Yes, she thought, the job we have to do is more important than any man right now.

Chapter Fourteen

July 1941

The dreaded week of the graveyard shift seemed to go on for an eternity. Katie's body felt battered as well as brain-fogged when she was unable to get to bed before 3 a.m. on most nights. She was typing reports, memos and Minutes automatically, only gaining a fuzzy hint of the contents when she and Amanda and Peggy checked their work with one another.

It was her last day on the shift. Tomorrow was her complete day off and then she'd be returning to the daytime shift. She couldn't wait. Thankfully, she hadn't bumped into that craggy-faced, arrogant officer again who had blatantly laughed at her. Her cheeks warmed at the very thought of her confrontation with him in her curlers. How embarrassed she'd been. A vision of how he must have seen her dangled in front of her – this crazy woman in a dressing gown, hair tightly wrapped in pipe-cleaners, shiny face, no lipstick . . . And then it suddenly struck her as funny. She couldn't help chuckling as she reached for the next report that required a stencil.

'What's so amusing?' Amanda said, breaking off from her typing and smiling across from a nearby desk.

'That officer I bumped into on my first morning.'

'I thought you were annoyed with him.'

'I was. But now I see the funny side.'

'Did you ever find out who he was?'

'Not yet – but I will.'

'Well, let me know when you do. I want to look out for him. He sounds my sort of chap – since I dumped that one I was telling you about.'

Katie grinned. 'You're welcome to him.'

'Mmm. I'm not sure you really mean that,' Amanda said, sending her a cheeky wink.

Katie's grin faded when she glanced at the next piece of work to do. Oh, not Barnaby Edwards again. This time she must not make a mistake with Roz's sharp eyes on the lookout for anyone who slipped up. The tip of her tongue showing between her teeth, she rolled a stencil into her machine. She would watch the letters before she struck the keys so there was no way possible she could make a mistake.

Twenty minutes rolled by. She'd been painstakingly peering down at every letter and pressing the key, instead of typing automatically at her usual rapid speed.

'Is anything the matter, Katie?' Mrs Goodman said, walking towards her a few minutes later.

Katie jerked her head up, warmth rushing up the back of her neck. She'd been acting like a nervous beginner.

'I don't think so, Mrs Goodman.'

'You seem to be typing very slowly today. I wondered if you didn't feel well.'

'No, I'm all right, really. It's just another of Mr Edwards's reports again. It takes me a while to work out his writing – it's so tiny.'

'Why don't you give it to Roz to type? She's used to him.'

Roz looked round at the sound of her name, the usual supercilious smile playing on her lips.

'Hand it over, Katie. I'll do it.'

'No, it's all right, thank you,' Katie said firmly. 'I'm over halfway.'

But she wasn't. She'd only just struggled through the first two paragraphs. She couldn't keep this up. She must have faith in her usual ability to type accurately without peering at the letters or she'd never get the damned thing done. She drew in a breath and, keeping her eye on the report instead of the keys, typed the next sentence, then looked at the stencil to check all was well. She gave a sharp intake of breath. To her horror she'd had her fingers on the wrong home keys. She'd typed a whole sentence of complete gobbledygook.

Oh, no! Roz was now on the alert.

Surreptitiously, Katie glanced round. Everyone was hard at work. At that moment Roz got up and removed the work from her out-tray.

'Anyone want anything delivered?' she said. No one answered. 'Okay, I shan't be long.'

Good, Katie thought. She could roll out the stencil and put in a fresh one without her or anyone else noticing. She took out the offending stencil but what could she do with it? Roz was bound to see the second ruined stencil in the waste-paper basket and would have no compunction in reporting her. The only thing would be to sneak it into her overnight case and then get it into the waste-paper basket after Roz left for home that night. That way the cleaners would empty it and Roz would be none the wiser.

From her drawer she took out an elastic band. Her overnight case was under her desk, ready to be taken down to the Dock. She bent low to pull it forward and undid it. Keeping her head down she rolled the stencil, put the elastic band round it and carefully placed it inside the case. She snapped the locks and pushed the case back under the desk. Putting in a new stencil, she returned to her touch-typing and when she and Martha checked the report it was letter-perfect. Phew! She was saved!

She'd make the thirty copies and get it over to Barnaby Edwards right away, and, handsome or not, this time she would ask him – politely – if he wouldn't mind making his writing more legible.

'Anyone got anything to deliver?' she asked, as she glanced round the room. 'Nothing? Well, I'm going to give Mr Edwards a piece of my mind. If he thinks he can get away with his writing that needs a microscope to read it, he has another think coming.'

Roz looked up and gave one of her smirks. 'Rather you than me.' She bent her head over her typewriter again.

How strange. Roz made it sound as though he was an ogre. But the one time Katie had spoken to him he was charm itself. This was obviously going to be interesting.

Katie carefully squared the thirty copies and secured them with a piece of string, together with the original on the top, and marched along to the Map Room Annexe. She knocked and someone called out but when she opened the door she saw that only Mike was at his desk. No sign of Barnaby.

'Hello there, Katie,' Mike said when she entered. 'What can we do for you?'

'I was hoping Barnaby would be here. I wanted a word with him.' She put the stack of copies on the nearest desk.

'Anything I can do to help?'

'Not really.' She looked at Mike's friendly face. He'd probably be sympathetic. 'I just wanted to have a word with him about his writing. It's so small I can hardly read it and I've mucked up two of his stencils already because of it.'

Mike's eyes flew wide. '*Barnaby's* writing? No one's ever complained about his writing before.'

That's because he's so damned good-looking half the girls are probably in love with him and don't want to upset him.

'Now, Baxter's—'

'Do I hear my name being mentioned?' a voice, more of a drawl, came from the doorway.

Katie wheeled round. She'd heard that voice before. Even before her eyes lifted to his face she knew who it was. He came towards her. The very man she never wanted to set eyes on again. She drew in a shaky breath. But he wouldn't recognise her now she was properly dressed, surely.

'Baxter,' Mike said, 'Katie here needs to speak to you about something someone should have told you weeks ago.'

'What's that?' He turned to look at her, his tone sounding calm and reasonable.

Katie's brain was working furiously. So it was *Baxter*, not Barnaby – whose surname likely wasn't even Edwards. Oh, how could she have made such a silly mistake. She felt the heat rise to her cheeks, this time not in embarrassment but in fury that once again he had the better of her – or thought he did. But this time she was going to take control. From the three rings on his sleeve she worked out his rank.

'Wing Commander Edwards—'

'Oh, we don't go in for that sort of formality around here,' he interrupted.

'Mr Edwards, then, would—'

'No, no, call me "Baxter". Everyone else does,' he said. His smile made his uneven features look even more attractive.

She caught herself.

'Mr Edwards,' she repeated deliberately, trying not to be influenced by that smile, 'would you mind telling me if the original report on that desk –' she jerked her head towards the offending papers '– is from you.'

He frowned and strode over to the desk.

'Yes, it is. Did you type it?'

'Yes.' She waited for him to apologise.

'Thanks. How many copies?'

'Thirty.' She kept her voice cool.

He looked at her. 'I need forty-five.'

'You didn't say,' she retorted. 'I had to guess, just as I had to guess practically every word you wrote. Your writing is so small that some of the letters are just a line. It takes me three times as long to do something from you as it does from anyone else . . . which doesn't look good to the rest of my colleagues and certainly won't help me to keep my job.'

Baxter Edwards reared back, lifting his hand as if to ward off her attack. Good. He deserved it.

'Hmm. I certainly wouldn't want you to lose your job. They're short-staffed in the typing pool as it is.' He regarded her as though she were an insect under a microscope that he had a mild interest in. 'You're new here, aren't you?' He took a step towards her.

Oh, please don't come any nearer. I don't want you to recognise me.

'No, I've been here quite a while,' she lied, noticing out of the corner of her eye that Mike was watching them with an amused expression.

'I'm not sure that's true,' he said, coming another step closer and studying her. He was no more than three feet away. 'Aren't you the girl I bumped into the other morning on the stairs?' He paused and grinned. 'Don't deny it – I'd recognise those incredible eyes anywhere.'

Katie squirmed, waiting for him to spill the full details of her state of undress in front of Mike. When he didn't, just stood there looking at her, his mouth still quirked in a smile, he gave her the smallest wink, as though they had a secret between them. This only infuriated her further. How dare he. Pulling herself up to her full five foot two and a half inches, she faced him squarely.

'I don't remember bumping into anyone on the stairs,' she told him, which seemed to amuse him even further, judging by his widening smile, 'but what I *do* know is that you're getting me into trouble for taking so long with your work and messing up expensive stencils.' He opened his mouth to speak, but she quickly carried on. 'I'm used to people's individual writing but yours is so minute, I'm peering at the letters and making mistakes – and that adds extra work to our already overloaded trays.'

'Mmm. I see.' He fingered his chin. 'I'm sorry it's been so difficult for you. You know, Roz usually does my work and she's never complained.'

'Well, there's your answer. Put a note on your work in the future that you only want Roz to type it. I'm sure she'll be more than delighted and that way we're all happy.'

Without waiting for any reply, she spun round and flounced to the door. Mike was quick to open it, giving her a sympathetic smile as she marched through, sure she'd hear another shout of laughter from Mr-bloody-Edwards.

But all she heard was Mike saying to him, 'Katie's right, old chap. You do need to make your writing clearer. It really isn't sporting to her or the others.'

She didn't hear his reply as the door closed behind her.

Katie tried to shut Baxter Edwards from her mind as she ploughed through her in-tray, but it was a relief when she and Peggy wrapped up for the night. Quarter to two. She yawned. Amanda was still typing.

'Sure we can't help, Amanda?' Peggy said.

'I'm all right – I'll be down in half an hour. I just want to finish this.'

After a short, restless sleep, Katie practically fell out of the cot and shot up the stairs well before six. No one was about except the usual guard at that time who wished her good morning. Quite honestly, she'd be glad to escape for twenty-four hours. After a quick wash, she dressed and picked up her overnight case and handbag. She was off!

It was a different guard now, standing on the ground floor to the entrance.

With merely a nod, he said, 'Would you please open your case.'

'Oh, yes, of course.' She placed it on the small table beside him.

And then she felt the blood drain from her. She put a hand out to touch the wall, afraid she might topple over with fear. Dear God. She'd forgotten the stencil! Mrs Goodman's warning rang in her brain.

'Oh, I've just remembered . . . my mother asked me to bring my dirty bed sheet home to wash.' He raised an eyebrow. 'I won't be a minute,' she added quickly, and snatching her case, dashed out of his sight and ran down the stairs to the basement.

In the typing pool, Katie noticed the new shift hadn't yet arrived; only the cleaning ladies were there, chatting away as they polished and swept.

'How's your Eric these days?' one of them was saying.

''E's not too good,' was the reply. ''E's never been the same since 'e 'ad that accident at work.'

'That were terrible,' came the first one.

They both looked up as Katie came into the room.

'Don't let me disturb you, ladies,' she said. 'I've forgotten something.'

'You go ahead, miss,' the second cleaner said. 'Don't mind us.'

Katie glanced at the waste-paper basket. Thankfully, they hadn't got round to emptying it yet. While their backs were turned, she pulled out the offending stencil and pushed it in amongst the rubbish. Her bedsheet neatly folded and now on top of the overnight case, she snapped back the locks.

'Thank you, ladies,' she said, but neither of them looked up.

Phew!

But still her heart beat faster as she stepped onto the ground floor where the same guard was. This time, however, several people were leaving. She joined the queue and when it was her turn to show her identity card she made to unlock her case but he glanced at her, nodded, and waved her through.

Once outside, her racing heart calmed down.

You will never do anything so stupid as that again, she scolded herself. *You would have lost your job and any future prospects with any other employer.*

But she couldn't help thinking that this fright had stemmed from the fact that it was all Baxter Edwards's fault.

Chapter Fifteen

'Why am I suddenly getting all Baxter Edwards's work?' Roz demanded a fortnight later on another graveyard shift.

'Probably because he knows you never complain about him,' Katie said, not being very successful in hiding a tiny but malicious streak.

Roz sent her a cold glare.

'How would he know unless someone told him – you, for instance?'

'Me?' Katie pointed to herself. Thankfully, it wasn't a fib. Mr Baxter Edwards had told her himself that Roz never complained. 'Why should I discuss with anyone how you deal with your work?'

'Well, someone must have,' Roz muttered. 'He even puts "Only for Roz's attention". He never used to put any names on.'

Katie barely supressed a smile. So Mr Edwards had actually taken notice of her. It served Roz right. She'd been so cocky the way she'd said she never had a problem with his writing. Funny how the woman was so annoyed to receive his work now.

Roz studied the latest report from him and frowned. 'I tell you what – I'll do this one, but you can take the other two.' She stood and dropped them into Katie's in-tray.

'Aren't you being a bit unfair to Katie, Roz?' Martha said mildly. 'Pass me one – I'll do it.'

'I'm sure I'll cope,' Katie said, not wanting to see Roz's smug expression if she said anything different, but Martha retrieved it, giving her a sympathetic smile.

There was no more mention of Baxter Edwards until later that afternoon when the out-trays were piled up with the day's work.

'I'll do the deliveries today,' Roz said, rising from her chair. She picked up her own pile. 'Anyone got anything ready to go?'

'Are you going to ask Baxter Edwards why he's picked you to do all his work?' Amanda said, with a surreptitious wink at Katie. 'Although you're really good at deciphering his writing. Probably better than any of us.'

Katie choked back a giggle. Eyes glinting, Roz looked as though she could cheerfully throttle Amanda.

'It's none of your business, or anyone's,' she snapped. 'Just get on with your own work, Amanda. And that goes for all of you.'

Really, Katie thought, the minute Mrs Goodman was out of the office, Roz was beginning to sound more and more cantankerous.

'I don't know what gets into Roz sometimes,' Peggy said when Roz had slammed the door behind her. 'She lets her self-importance go to her head, if you ask me.'

Katie bent her head and for a short time there was the quiet clicking of the four typewriters.

'Well, did you give him a piece of your mind?' Amanda asked when Roz returned twenty minutes' later.

'If you must know, he was on the phone all the time I was there,' Roz said. 'I couldn't wait any longer.' She looked around the office at everyone who had stopped typing to listen to her answer, then caught Katie's eye. 'Oh, he did point to an envelope on his desk.' She paused. 'He said it was for you but it doesn't have your name on the envelope.'

'How do you know it was for me?' Katie said, aware of everyone watching her. Peggy and Amanda were grinning. Even Martha's eyes were twinkling.

'Well, he said it was for the girl who bumped into him on the stairs the other morning.' She looked at Katie. 'He mentioned your strange turquoise eyes so it must be meant for you.' She put the envelope on Katie's desk. 'What's he talking about – you bumping into him?'

'Oh, nothing,' Katie said through gritted teeth, acutely aware of Roz standing over her obviously wanting to know what Baxter had written. She deliberately put the envelope into her handbag and reached for the next piece of work.

She had to wait until Roz left the room again before she opened the envelope and took out a small piece of notepaper.

TO THE GIRL WITH THE SEA-GREEN EYES – I'M TRULY SORRY YOU HAVE HAD SUCH TROUBLE READING MY REPORTS. WOULD YOU COME TO DINNER WITH ME ONE EVENING AS AN APOLOGY. ANY NIGHT THIS WEEK IS FINE IF ONE WOULD SUIT YOU. JUST PUT A NOTE IN SAME ENVELOPE WITH MY NAME AND LEAVE ON MY DESK IF I'M NOT THERE.

B.E.

P.S. I'LL FIND SOMEWHERE THAT ISN'T NORMALLY TARGETED BY OUR NIGHT-TIME FRIENDS!

What a cheek! He was being sarcastic, she was sure, writing it all in capital letters. So why would she want to spend any time in his company, let alone go through a whole evening's dinner with him? And he'd written it as though it were a foregone conclusion. No, she wouldn't dream of it. But should she simply write a note saying, 'No, thank you'? Or should she tell him in person? But that would be humiliating for him if his two colleagues were there. Though why should she care about that? Her eyes picked over the words again. He wanted to say sorry. Well, she wasn't interested.

'What's he say?' Amanda said, leaning from her desk, a wide smile on her face.

'He wants to apologise over dinner one evening.'

Just her luck, Roz appeared at that moment and threw her a contemptible look, then walked to her own desk.

'Oooh, lucky you,' Peggy said with a chuckle. 'To be invited by Baxter Edwards is quite something.'

'What do you mean?'

'He's one of the most attractive men here.'

'Do you think so?' Katie said. 'I think Barnaby beats him hands down on looks.'

'And doesn't he know it,' Amanda put in. 'No, I agree with Peggy – I'd much rather spend an evening with Baxter Edwards. He's just got . . . well, I don't know . . . charisma, I suppose you'd call it.'

Hmm. Is that what you'd call it?

'Do you think you'll go?' Martha said.

'Would you please all get on with your work,' Roz cut in. 'I'm getting fed up with hearing all this nonsense.'

Katie was almost relieved that Roz had stopped the conversation. If she told the girls she wasn't going they might think she was being unfair not to give him a chance to explain.

During the early evening, Katie decided she had to give Baxter Edwards an answer. Taking a moment's break from her typing, she took out her fountain pen and, in her best handwriting, wrote a note on the bottom of the page he'd written on:

128

Dear Mr Edwards,

Thank you for your invitation but I am not available in the evenings.

Katie Valentine

She knew she was being churlish – maybe even rude – but she didn't want him to pursue any other time for a dinner date. Quite frankly, she had more on her mind than to discuss Baxter Edwards's handwriting!

Once or twice while she stood and stretched her aching back, she caught herself wondering if she was being mean not to have given Baxter the chance to defend himself.

For goodness' sake, she told herself, *there's no need to make it into a court case.*

You don't need to, her inner voice reprimanded. *It's only good manners to allow him to make amends. Give the poor bloke the benefit of the doubt.*

'No, I'm definitely not going to,' Katie said aloud without realising.

'Did you say something, Katie?'

Damn! Roz was looking straight at her.

'Er, no. Just thinking out loud.'

'Well, keep your thoughts to yourself and let us get on in peace.'

Katie bit her lip to stop herself from giving a snappy answer. If only Mrs Goodman wasn't out of the office so much and could see Roz in action.

As though she'd conjured up her superior, Mrs Goodman entered the room. Katie looked up from her typewriter, noting the woman's drawn face, the heavy bags under her eyes, the brows knitted together.

'Is everything all right, Mrs Goodman?' Roz simpered.

'What?' Mrs Goodman seemed vague as she gazed in Roz's direction. 'Oh, yes . . . well, not exactly – Louise didn't turn up this afternoon – apparently, she's had to go home – so I stayed on to do extra time. I just hope she's not coming down with something.'

'Anything I can do?' Roz said.

'Not really, Roz,' Mrs Goodman said. 'But thank you for asking.'

She reached for the telephone on her desk and Katie heard her say: 'Could you tell me what's the matter with Louise?' There was a pause. 'Oh, dear, what a nuisance.' Another pause. 'A *month*?' Mrs Goodman's voice rose. 'That's going to be difficult.' She heaved a sigh. 'Oh, well, thank you for letting me know.' She put the receiver down, looking even more worried.

As Katie reached for the next report, she wondered what Louise's position was. She'd never met her or even heard about her until just now. As far as that went, she didn't know what Mrs Goodman did when she mysteriously left the typing pool – as she did most days, and often for long spells.

An hour later she bumped into Mrs Goodman in the upstairs cloakroom. Katie hesitated. Would this be the time to ask about Louise's position? If she let a possible opportunity slip by, she'd be so cross with herself. But how to begin the conversation? The cloakroom wasn't the most private place. She took a deep breath, still undecided, but before she knew it she'd opened her mouth to speak.

'If I may say so, you do look rather tired, Mrs Goodman,' she said, hoping it wouldn't sound out of turn.

'I am, Katie. I don't know how we'll manage with Louise gone a whole month – possibly longer. She's broken her wrist so that's what the doctor has ordered.'

'What does Louise do?'

'She's one of our best stenographers.' Mrs Goodman blew

out her cheeks as she wiped her hands on the roller towel. 'We have a rota and we're already another one down so we're going to be really short.'

Katie felt her heart speed at what seemed double rate. Finally, this is where she could use her skills.

'I believe I might be able to help.'

Mrs Goodman looked puzzled. 'I'm sorry, my dear. The job requires shorthand – someone who's both extremely accurate and fast at the same time. But thank you for the offer.'

Just what she'd dreaded. Someone needing shorthand and she'd probably lost half her speed.

You can soon recover it, girl.

Katie drew in a breath.

'Mrs Goodman, I did a secretarial course at May Stanley's Secretarial School. I was the fastest and most accurate of the class in shorthand and typing.'

The supervisor's eyes flew wide.

'That's one of London's best secretarial schools so whatever are you doing in a typing pool?'

'When I was interviewed for the job I was told I would be a stenographer. I nearly turned it down as I wanted a secretarial position but was told it was in a very important setting – and then when you said I'd be in the typing pool, I was ready to leave there and then. But I knew with signing all those security documents it might not be easy.' Katie lowered her voice. 'Then I nearly fainted when I spotted Mr Churchill coming down the corridor towards me a few days after I started the job. He was very kind, telling me I was new – as if I didn't know it.' She grinned. 'But it did cheer me up to think he might even be reading one of the endless reports we all type every day.'

When Katie mentioned Mr Churchill, Mrs Goodman's eyebrows shot almost into her hairline. Then her face relaxed and she smiled back.

'So you've already had a chat with the PM,' she said.

'Not exactly a chat, but enough to make me realise how lucky I am to be working on the same floor as our Prime Minister,' Katie said fervently. 'I decided not to grumble ever again about any job I'm given.'

Mrs Goodman seemed to be wondering if it really was possible that Katie could stand in for Louise for a short period.

'May I ask your shorthand speed?' Mrs Goodman finally said.

'It was a hundred and thirty when I was last checked.'

Mrs Goodman nodded. 'Hmm. Louise is about that. But you must have dropped down quite a bit since working here, though I doubt it would take much practice for you to get it back up again.' She looked at Katie directly. 'If you can get to at least a hundred and twenty words a minute I think we may be able to put you somewhere you'd find very interesting indeed.'

Chapter Sixteen

The problem was, Katie thought, when she'd calmed down a little, she had no one to test her as she practised. Mrs Goodman had warned her there wasn't much time to lose and unfortunately she was too busy to help, or she would have been only too happy to do so. Katie couldn't exactly ask any of her colleagues – she gave a wry smile at the thought of asking Roz. But she would have to practise every spare moment – tea-breaks and lunch-breaks, maybe staying an extra hour and going somewhere quietly where she'd be able to time herself. She'd need a stopwatch but where to get one? She heaved a sigh. Right this minute she had to go round with the day's deliveries.

She collected everyone's output together with her own and had just stepped into the corridor when a man, his face half-hidden by a huge pile of outsized maps he was carrying, banged into her.

'Mind where you're going, miss,' he said, in an irritable tone.

She knew that voice. Oh, not again!

'Goodness me, it's you!' His tone now softened as he lowered the bundle. 'The very person I was looking for – the girl with the sea-green eyes.' She saw his mouth quirk at the corners. 'Do you make a habit of bumping into people?'

He was mocking her – just like the last time. He really was the most annoying character.

'Actually, let's get this straight,' Katie said. 'I believe it was *you* just now who not only bumped into me but *banged* into me. You probably couldn't see me under all your maps.'

He looked at her for an instant as though surprised she'd argued with him. Then he threw his head back, just like he had last time, and gave a hoot of laughter.

Swallowing her indignation, she waited for him to stop.

He gazed down at her, still chuckling.

'I'm sorry. Perhaps it was my fault this time. So what can I do for you to forgive me?'

Her mind flying, she suddenly remembered that shelf full of clocks. Before she could stop herself, she said:

'Actually, there *is* something.'

He raised an eyebrow. 'Oh, what's that?'

'I have a problem. Maybe you can help me.'

'Come with me to my office. I'm on my own at the moment. Then you can tell all.'

He made it sound as though she had some kind of confession to make. Biting her lip and calling herself a complete idiot for getting herself into a position she might regret, she hurried along, trying to keep up with his long strides.

When they were in the office, he said, 'Have a seat. Now, what's the problem.'

Tentatively, she said, 'Do you know a woman called Louise?'

'Louise Chalmers?'

She nodded. 'Yes, that's probably her.'

'She's one of the stenographers – possibly our best one.'

'Well, Mrs Goodman says she's not able to come into work for a few weeks and if I could get my shorthand speed up to scratch, she'd put my name forward to take her place – on a temporary basis, of course,' she added hastily.

Baxter Edwards regarded her with what looked like renewed interest.

'Well, this is a chance you can't miss, but I'm not sure I understand where I fit in.'

'I know I'll have lost my speed so I need to practise every minute I'm not working to be considered.' She showed him her wrist. 'I have a second hand on my watch but it would be almost impossible to look at it and write at the same time. I really need a stopwatch.'

'I'm afraid I don't have one.'

She glanced towards the shelf. 'It looks as though someone likes clocks—'

'Yes, me. Tinkering with them is a hobby of mine.'

'Well, if there's an alarm clock that's working, I wonder if I could borrow it for a few days.'

'Hmm.' He drew his eyebrows together. 'You know, I can probably do one better than that. How about if I sort one of the alarm clocks and find a quiet corner and read from something and you take it down. I'll be timing you on how many words you've written and how long it's taken. We can do very short quick bursts so no one will miss you – ten minutes here and there when you're delivering work. If you haven't anything for us in here, you can usually track me down here or in the Map Room next door. If I'm about, I'll help.' He looked directly at her. 'What do you think?'

She was taken aback. This was more than she expected. But did she want him to be involved in that way? Would he think he had some kind of hold over her? Some obligation such that she would now have to have dinner with him?

As though he were reading her thoughts, he said, 'And no need to worry. You've turned me down on my dinner invitation and you certainly don't have to feel under any pressure to change your mind, though I hope you might. But if I can't help a colleague go after a promotion, then it's a poor show.' He glanced at her. 'So I'll be more than happy to help out – so long as you don't keep calling me "Mr Edwards".'

'All right . . . and thank you for offering . . . Baxter.'

He smiled. Gone was the mocking smile – the ironic, sardonic, cynical smile. This one looked absolutely genuine. And it had the power to encourage her to smile back.

'That's better,' he said. 'I knew you had it in you to smile at me. And what a gorgeous smile you have, too.'

He thinks he still has the upper hand by flattering me – no, flirting with me is more like it.

What an infuriating man. But if he'd help her to get this job, then that was all that mattered.

'Thank you,' she said, managing to hold on to the 'gorgeous smile'.

As if he knew what she was up to, he grinned back. And this time she was sure she detected a hint of mockery.

'When can you start?' he said.

'I need to deliver these reports first.'

'Okay. I need to get these maps to the Old Man, as he's commonly known – not to his face, of course,' he added with a wink.

It must be the name they used for the Prime Minister. She couldn't help a little thrill at how close she was to the war.

'Just go in the Map Room Annexe,' Baxter went on. 'Don't take any notice if the other chaps are there. There's a small room at the back we can use.'

'I think I should clear it with Mrs Goodman first,' Katie said, a little worried that she might be reprimanded for being too long with her deliveries.

'I'm sure she'll be delighted you're taking this seriously,' Baxter said.

Katie had made sure Roz was out of the room before she approached Mrs Goodman. Roz's ears were sharp and no matter how absorbed she appeared when she was typing, she still seemed to hear and see everything around her. The last thing she needed was for Roz to start kicking up a fuss. Instinct told her that if Roz found out she was being considered for even a temporary promotion, she would be even more disagreeable than she already was.

'What a very nice man he is,' Mrs Goodman said when Katie told her how Mr Edwards had offered to help her get back to her speed. 'I'm not sure whether you know, but he's the Chief Cartographer – one of the most valuable members of the team as far as the Prime Minister is concerned. The PM's Map Room is very precious to him and he insists it's kept up to date minute by minute – which is the job of the plotters – they're mostly Wrens. But it's Baxter Edwards who oversees everything to do with the maps – maintenance, creating new ones . . . everything.'

'Oh, dear, I didn't realise he was so important,' Katie said, feeling a tinge of nerves, 'but I just couldn't think of anyone else to ask.' Remembering their conversation, she added, 'Besides, he offered.'

Mrs Goodman nodded. 'He would. But we all have to lend a hand when necessary.' She gave her tentative smile. 'So let me know when you've got to a hundred and twenty or near enough, my dear, and I can put your name forward. But be prepared for a formal test.'

Katie inwardly groaned. Not another test! And it wouldn't be Baxter reading at a reasonable pace this time.

Mrs Goodman looked at her watch. 'Would you like to go off now for ten minutes?'

But when Katie knocked and entered the Map Room Annexe, Baxter Edwards was nowhere in sight. Neither was he next door in the Map Room itself.

She sighed. Back at her desk she reached in her in-tray and pulled out the first report. It was only a coincidence, surely, that it was written by Baxter Edwards.

* * *

'Another note for you, Katie, from our lovely Mr Edwards,' Peggy said with a wide grin, as she plonked some more work round the desks. 'I was strictly instructed to deliver it to you in person.' She put a pile of letters on Katie's desk and dangled an envelope in front of her. 'Come on, this is the second love letter he's sent so you have to promise to tell all – at least the juicy bits.'

As usual, whenever there was the slightest hint of gossip, everyone stopped typing. Thankfully, Roz had just taken a telephone call on Mrs Goodman's desk.

'You know jolly well it's nothing of the kind,' Katie said, feeling her face become warm as she snatched the envelope – with her name on it this time.

Peggy giggled. 'We shouldn't tease you, but what's this all about?'

'Well, I turned him down on the dinner invitation. Maybe this is to try to persuade me to go.'

Peggy's mouth fell open. 'Why did you do that?'

'Because I'm not interested. He's more or less apologised so it doesn't need a dinner date to confirm it.'

'Hmm. Most girls would jump at the chance.'

'Well, I'm not most girls,' Katie said brusquely. She looked up. 'Sorry, Peggy, I'm not in a very good mood. I've got a bit of a headache.'

It was true, she did. It was the third time lately and she rarely suffered from headaches.

'Is it your monthlies?' Peggy said, looking concerned.

'No. But I've had one or two lately.'

'Most of us suffer from them at some time or another,' Peggy said. 'It's such a stuffy atmosphere – no air, everyone smoking. In fact, I think I'm going to give up as I'm just adding to it.' She glanced at Katie. 'You don't seem to smoke much.'

138

'Not when I'm working. If I'm honest I don't enjoy it that much. But socially it seems to be the thing to do.'

'Well, if you want a breath of air, I should go now, Katie.'

'It's not for you to say when we go on a break,' Roz broke in, glaring at Peggy. She looked across at Katie. 'Have you finished everything, Katie?'

'No,' Katie said, 'but I've been sitting in this position since half-past three and it's now nearly eight o'clock, so I hope it's all right with you that I take ten minutes.' She stared at Roz. 'I do believe you've had the chance along with the others to have a breather.'

'Ten minutes, then. No more.'

'Thank you *so* much, Roz.' Quite honestly, she couldn't care less if Roz noticed the sarcasm in her tone.

Before she got up, she decided to open the envelope or it might look to the others as though she really was concealing something more. She read:

KATIE, THIS IS A GOOD TIME FOR YOU TO NIP OUT. I'VE GOT A FEW SPARE MINUTES. B.E.

Perfect timing. She wouldn't get any air but she'd be doing what was necessary to get a break from Roz, if only for a few weeks.

Chapter Seventeen

Katie tried not to look as though she was in a hurry as she stepped briskly along the corridor to the Map Room Annexe, her shorthand pad and a book tucked in her handbag.

Baxter grinned as she knocked and opened the door.

'Good, you've made it. Sorry I wasn't here earlier. I was called away.' He paused, his hazel eyes looking at her. 'Let's sit over there.' He pointed. 'Do you have the text you're going to use?'

'Yes.' She handed him Thackeray's *Vanity Fair*, her latest library book, which she was really enjoying

'Isn't this said to be a novel without a hero?'

'Well, as long as there's a heroine, that's all that matters,' Katie quipped, hiding a smile as she opened her notepad and took up her sharpened pencil.

'Hmm. I'm not so sure about that.' She quickly glanced at him, pleased to see his mouth quirking. He caught her eye. 'Anyway, let's get on. Is there any particular passage?'

'No, you choose or you'll think I've cheated.'

'As if I would – or as if *you* would.' He grinned. 'Okay –' he flipped open the book about a quarter of the way through '– I'll time you.' He picked up a small travel clock and fiddled with the knobs at the back. 'Right. Off we go.'

'*She promised acquiescence and tried to obey.*'

Katie's pencil stumbled on the third word and by the time she'd made the logical marks, she'd lost the thread. Baxter's voice was carrying on, not at a more rapid pace than she'd been used to, but too fast now that she was out of practice.

'Can you slow down, please?' she said, trying to catch her breath.

'What?' He stopped abruptly. 'Oh . . . yes, of course. But we'll have to reset the alarm.'

Damn! Katie bit her lip to stop herself from saying it out loud.

'Right, I'll start again.' He glanced at her. 'Ready?'

'Yes.'

'*That effort was too much for her; she placed them back in her bosom again . . .*'

The tip of her tongue protruding between her teeth in concentration, Katie took down the words Baxter said, only hearing them phonetically as she'd been taught. But although he'd slowed down a little, she struggled to keep pace. The alarm bell made her jump.

'Pencil down, please,' Baxter said. 'Right, you'd better read it back so I know you've taken it down accurately.'

She looked at the marks on her notepad and brought the pad a little nearer to her eyes.

'The effort was too much for her. She placed the . . . um,' she stuttered, not being able to read the next word. She'd have to guess. '. . . the letters back in her bosom again—'

'She placed *them* back in her bosom,' he corrected. 'And it's *that* effort.' He glanced at her. 'Carry on.'

She wouldn't – she just wouldn't let a flush creep to her cheeks. Him see her embarrassment at all this 'bosom talk'. She managed to finish reading the extract and looked up.

'Well?'

'A few minor things but not anything to change the content. I'll just count the words and work it out.'

She waited a minute or two and then he said: 'I'm not sure what you were aiming for . . .'

For heaven's sake, just tell me, Baxter.

' . . . but you were a fraction under ninety.'

'Less than ninety! Are you sure?'

'Yes, of course I'm sure.' Hazel eyes penetrated hers. 'What were you expecting?'

'I was hoping for at least a hundred. I need to be a hundred and twenty – minimum – a hundred and thirty better. So that's quite a jump to get there.' She gave a sigh. 'Well, I've got a bit more work to do on it, then.'

'It looks like it. But I'll help you. Just tell yourself you'll be there within the next three days.'

She looked at him. Why was he being so nice when they'd got off to such a bad start? He did have the most lovely eyes: hazel with gold flecks, twinkling down at her. His nose was too large, but his mouth was wide and smiling, showing a dimple at one side that she hadn't noticed before. She supposed he was rather attractive in his own way, but nothing like as handsome as Barnaby. Yet Baxter was beginning to intrigue her a little. She wished she could demand to know why he was being so helpful but she'd just have to accept his offer and be grateful. All this was running through her mind when he said:

'Do you think a few practices each day for three days will do it?'

'I don't know.' Katie desperately tried to weigh it up. She'd needed a lot more time than that in the secretarial school. But maybe this was different. She'd already achieved a very good speed. It was simply that she was rusty. 'But it's no good taking longer as Mrs Goodman looks at her wits' end, and if she goes under then whatever department she works in will be even more short-handed.' She chewed her bottom lip. 'She looks so drawn these days.'

'Hmm.' He frowned. 'You're obviously on the graveyard

shift . . .?' She nodded. 'I am, too. So what about having another go tonight? Maybe a bit longer this time.'

He made the words sound warm, intimate. She felt her face heat, then berated herself for being ridiculous.

'Yes, I should be able to get away then.' She tried to quell the tremor in her voice.

'I'll see you in my office then,' he said, matter-of-factly, which made her feel a little better about any possible motive she'd imagined.

At precisely eleven o'clock that night, Katie hurried along the corridor. She had no idea why her heart thumped. All she could put it down to was nerves. He'd be testing her again and she'd had no time in between to look at her Pitman's shorthand book, which she'd brought with her, just in case. She knocked and let herself in. Baxter was poring over an enormous map.

'May I have a look?' she asked tentatively.

'Be my guest.' He moved slightly to one side to give her some space. 'It's a good blown-up one of the Sussex coast.' His hand brushed her arm as he pointed. 'See how close France is from here – too close for comfort, I'm afraid.'

She moved away a few inches to the left of him to let him see she wasn't trying to get close, although from that angle she couldn't see the town names so clearly.

'Trouble is,' he went on, his eyes still on the map, 'the Boche don't worry about running out of fuel any more as they no longer need to return to Germany. Now they've invaded France, the Luftwaffe simply uses their airports – and their shipping ports, too, of course.'

Katie swallowed. Baxter was right. France's coast was very close.

'Enough of that,' he said briskly. 'Let's get on with the matter in hand.' He looked at her. 'Are you going to use the same book?'

143

'No, the words are too outdated. I've brought a newspaper article.'

'Have you looked at it to give yourself a head start?'

'No, of course I haven't.'

'Well, that's all right then.' He gave that same mocking smile he'd given her that first morning by the stairs.

She bit her tongue. She would not make any retort. It would only amuse him.

He laughed. 'Sorry, I'm teasing you again. I shouldn't. I know it makes you very cross with me and I don't want you to be cross. I want to see that smile again.'

'Baxter, I'm quite tired. Could we please get on with it, so I can get back to the office? I do have more work to do.'

'Of course. Take a seat.'

He read steadily and at a fair speed but not so fast this time and she just about kept up. She formed the shapes in her notepad automatically as she listened to his voice, rich and full of inflection as the passage became alive. It was about a bomb that had taken out the side of a cinema in London the night before. The audience had helped strangers on the way out and thankfully only one person had been injured, but she was recovering. The alarm bell rang on the clock and she immediately stopped.

'No mistakes at all,' Baxter said when she'd finished reading it back.

Katie breathed out her relief.

'That was quite a moving piece, don't you think?' he said.

'Yes, it was. Thank goodness there weren't more injuries, or worse.'

'It's because people didn't panic and scramble over each other.' He let out a sigh. 'Bloody Boche – excuse my French.'

'You're excused. I say worse than that if I'm on my own.'

'Oh, really?' He grinned at her. 'I'd love to be around when you do.' He took his pen. 'Right, let me work out what you did this time.' He glanced at the travel clock, bent his head over his calculations for a few moments, then looked up.

'Is it better?' She tried to keep the anxiety out of her voice.

He grimaced. 'Not enough to make much difference.'

'What is it then?'

He's playing a game – pretending, just to aggravate me. It's his warped sense of humour.

'You're about ninety-seven words a minute.' He glanced down at the newspaper, then back to her.

She blinked. It was only marginally better. Oh, how disappointing.

'Do you want me to read a bit more?'

Her head had started to throb.

'Thank you, but I should go back to the office. I have several letters and a report to do before tomorrow –' she met his eye '– and the report is from you!'

He pulled his eyebrows together. 'Oh, dear. I'm sorry. But I've done my best to make my writing clearer. It's just that when I'm in a hurry, my writing seems to get smaller and smaller.'

She gave a half smile. 'I don't think I can grumble this time as I really appreciate what you're trying to do. But I feel an opportunity will slip away if I don't make the grade.'

Baxter frowned. 'Is there anyone at home who could help?'

'Not really. I'd rather keep my work separate from home.'

'You'd only be reading from newspapers, like I am.'

She shook her head. 'No, it wouldn't work.'

'Well, then, let's try to fit in at least three practices tomorrow.' Baxter looked at his watch. 'Shall we say half-past two for the first one? That'll give us half an hour before our shift starts.'

Katie smiled her thanks. 'That would be a great help.'

'Any time, Katie.' He stared down at her. 'What's Katie short for?'

'Katharina.'

'With a "C"?'

'No, a "K". K-a-t-h-a-r-i-n-a.'

He raised a dark brow. 'Ah, the German way.'

Heat flooded her cheeks. Oh, why had she blurted that out? She didn't want anyone to know she had a German in the family. If anyone here found out, and with all the tight security, Ursula would be more closely investigated – married to Dad or not.

'Er, yes, I believe it is.' To hide her mortification, she quickly bent to gather her pad and pencil and the newspaper, then turned to him. 'I do appreciate what you're doing, Baxter.'

'Because you refuse to have dinner with me, it's the only way I can apologise to you.'

His mouth twitched at the corners as if he found the situation amusing. 'What about if . . . no, not if, *when* you get up to your speed, we go out and celebrate with supper?'

'Baxter, you're being very kind but—'

He held up his hand. 'I know, I know. You've turned me down more than once. Well, just to be clear, "supper" is obviously completely different from "dinner", so you won't have changed your mind. It will be a totally different invitation.'

She couldn't help a wry smile at what he obviously thought was his nimble wit. But much as she would have liked to accept his so-called new supper invitation, she couldn't. He already knew her name was unusual in that it was spelt the German way and might question her further. She was terrified that in the course of ordinary conversation over a meal she'd blurt out something about her stepmother being German. Even if he didn't raise the subject, as far as he or anybody else was concerned, it would only mean one thing – one or both of her parents was German. Besides, she wasn't about to divulge the secret of Judy – her real mother. No, it was safer not to see him outside the office – much as she was tempted.

She was about to tell him she had a headache, when he added quite seriously:

'I think we'd both deserve it . . . don't you?'

If she hadn't known him better she'd have thought he was almost imploring her to accept. When she couldn't think of a reply, he gave a shrug.

'Anyway, no need to answer. It's late. I'll see you tomorrow.'

He wasn't the kind of person to take no for an answer, Katie thought, on her way back to the office. Maybe when she was less tired and this latest headache went, she might feel differently. All she could think of at the moment was not wasting the opportunity Mrs Goodman had presented her with.

'Ah, there you are, Katie,' Mrs Goodman said as Katie stepped into the office. 'There's been a change to the schedule. You don't have to finish the week on the overnight shift. Tomorrow you'll be working from two until nine.' She looked at Katie and frowned. 'You don't seem very happy. Don't tell me you like the last shift.'

Darn it! It was going to mess up her shorthand practice.

'I don't mind it.'

'Well, I'm sure you'll be glad to get into your own bed at home,' Mrs Goodman said firmly. 'I expect your mother worries about you all the time.'

Katie murmured in agreement.

'I think we've all had enough for the day. You and Peggy need to go down below to make sure there's a bed free for you both.' She disappeared.

'Where does Mrs Goodman go at this time of the night?' Katie asked Peggy.

'She has her own bedroom upstairs. I think she works quite closely to the PM so needs to be on hand.'

Katie's eyes widened. 'Oh, is Mrs Goodman one of Mr Churchill's personal secretaries then?'

'Something like that,' Peggy said cheerfully.

Katie couldn't help a flutter of excitement.

'Peggy, can you manage to bag me a bed? I need to give someone a note.'

'Would that someone be a certain Mr Baxter Edwards?' Peggy's mouth curved in amusement.

'Yes, if you must know.'

'Oh, I must,' Peggy giggled. 'This is starting to get serious.'

'Only in your imagination,' Katie said as she grinned back.

He'd probably be gone by now, she thought, as she sprinted down the deserted corridor. She was about to knock when the door opened and Baxter came out, barging straight into her. She wobbled on her heels and he grasped her, pulling her towards him to steady her. For a few seconds she was in his arms, feeling his heart beat against hers, wishing she could stay there for ever. Somehow she managed to draw away, breathless.

'Katie! I'm so sorry!' He appeared caught off-guard; his voice didn't sound quite so assured. Then, as if to collect himself, he said, 'This time I take *all* the blame!' Even his smile seemed forced. Then he dropped his hands from her arms and gazed down at her, now looking serious. 'What's wrong, Katharina?'

Why had he called her 'Katharina' at that particular moment? He never had before. Did it mean he'd felt something, the way she had when he'd held her close? Had he, too, felt her heart beat in unison against his chest? She put her hand to her burning cheek. He was waiting, watching her. For a blank moment she forgot why she'd gone to see him in the first place. She blinked, then looked up at him. 'I was just coming to tell you that I won't be continuing the graveyard shift this week, so I can't do my practice as I'll be on from two 'til nine tomorrow.'

He didn't even hesitate. 'Yes, you can. I'll come in early and we can run through it at half-past one.'

'Are you sure?'

'Of course. I'll see you then. Now get to bed. You look tired out.'

In her hard cot that night she gave a sigh of relief. He wasn't going to abandon the project even though she hadn't agreed to go out with him for supper. It wasn't that she didn't find him attractive. She did. In fact, the more time they'd spent together, even though the intervals were brief, the more she liked him. His voice – he spoke beautifully, but not exaggeratedly clipped like some upper-crust people. She liked the shape of his hands. He had one ear that stuck out a little. She liked that, too. And she liked . . .

But she never had the chance to put into words what else she liked about him. She was fast asleep.

Chapter Eighteen

'One hundred and fourteen words a minute,' Baxter said triumphantly two evenings later in the Map Room Annexe.

Katie had managed to squeeze in several short practice sessions. He'd taken her into the back room of the annexe because Barnaby and Mike were working in the Map Room itself. The small, dimly lit space felt . . . well, not exactly clandestine, but their relationship had definitely shifted to something more personal. She'd had to force herself not to be so acutely aware of his presence – not remember how it had felt to be in his arms – and concentrate on what he was dictating from this morning's newspaper.

Before she could comment on her new shorthand speed – which still needed at least another session – Baxter continued, 'Well done – it's as near as dammit to your hundred and twenty. If it were me I'd tell Mrs Goodman I'd recovered my speed and when can I start.' His eyes danced with merriment.

She laughed. 'Well, it's four days since she told me about Louise and she's looking more and more harassed so I don't want to leave it much longer.' She looked up at Baxter, meeting his eyes. 'You don't think I'd be fibbing if I tell her I'm ready?'

'Not at all. By the time you start taking down whatever you're asked to do, you'll be there – no trouble at all.'

'I can't thank you enough.' She repressed the disappointment that this would be their last time together on their own.

He held up his hand. 'No need for that. It was a pleasure. Just go and see Mrs Goodman and let me know what happens.'

'I will.'

But as luck would have it, Mrs Goodman was nowhere around. Katie's mouth was dry but she didn't want to stop for a drink in case she missed her. By nine o'clock, when it was time for her to pack up, she decided to mention it to Roz.

'Do you know where Mrs Goodman is, Roz?' she said, looking across at the next desk.

'No,' Roz answered curtly. 'Why are you enquiring?'

'Concern,' Katie kept her tone mild. 'She normally pops her head in, even if she can't stay.'

'There's no need to concern yourself,' Roz said. 'I'm sure *I'll* hear if there's any problem.'

An hour later Katie looked up as a familiar redhead poked in the doorway. It was Brian Lockstone from the admin office.

'Oh, Miss Valentine, Mrs Goodman is asking for you.'

Katie rose to her feet, aware of Roz's curious eyes on her, wondering what this was all about. Brian moved swiftly along the main corridor and Katie had to take little running steps to keep up. When they came to the weather sign, which poked out at right angles to let the staff know throughout the day what the weather was like – cloudy today – he turned right into another corridor, and then down a third where Katie had never been.

It's like a maze down here, she thought, trying to look out for any landmarks to remind her how to get back again. But one corridor looked much like another.

He rapped on one of the doors.

'Enter.'

'Miss Valentine, sir,' Brian said, then smiled at Katie and disappeared.

She stepped into a smallish office where there were only

two desks and no window and the usual ugly air-conditioning pipe. At one of the desks sat an officer in RAF uniform who immediately stood and held out his hand, and at the other desk was Mrs Goodman. She looked over at Katie and smiled.

'Katie, this is Flight Lieutenant David Sinclair – David, this is Katharina Valentine, the person I was telling you about.'

'Pleased to meet you.' He dropped her hand. 'Your ears should be burning.' He smiled. 'Do take a seat.' When she sat down, he went on: 'We're desperate for another stenographer to be on hand for dictation as a result of our daily meetings. Obviously you wouldn't be attending the meetings themselves, but we might call you in afterwards to take down any lengthy telegrams, action reports – that sort of thing. In between times, you'd still help with the work from the typing pool.' He looked at her. 'How does that sound?'

'I'd be honoured to be chosen, sir.'

'Good. In that case, I'll leave you with Mrs Goodman, who'll give you a short piece of dictation.' He left the room.

'Are you ready, Katie?' Mrs Goodman said.

'I hope so.' If only she didn't feel so tired from working so many hours with no fresh air. Her head was beginning to feel muggy. She opened her pad and took her newly sharpened pencil, her mouth tight with nerves. She must take it down accurately and rapidly.

Mrs Goodman spoke clearly and briskly. For the first two minutes or so it was going well – then suddenly, to Katie's horror, the lead in her pencil snapped.

'Oh, Mrs Goodman—'

'Don't worry, my dear. Just read back what you have.'

When Katie had finished, Mrs Goodman nodded. 'No mistakes at all.' She smiled. 'I'm not going to start calculating your speed because I was reading at the sort of rate anyone might and didn't pause as they will every so often when they need to collect their thoughts. You don't need to worry.' She rose from her chair. 'Now let me find David.'

Katie could have thrown her arms around dear Mrs Goodman when she came back with David Sinclair, who was smiling at her.

'Mrs Goodman says you're going to fit in perfectly,' he said.

Was it Katie's imagination or did Mrs Goodman give her a surreptitious wink before she turned to David Sinclair.

He looked straight at Katie. 'We'd like you to start tomorrow.'

It was more than she had expected. Katie left the room feeling like one of the floating barrage balloons that helped to thwart enemy planes over London. She mustn't let herself become too excited. Louise would be back in a month. But meanwhile she would be demonstrating her skills and improving her speed, and, best of all, it sounded as though she'd be closer to the war itself. She had to stop herself from skipping along the corridor.

She suddenly came abruptly to a stop. Where was she? Nothing looked familiar. Had she taken a wrong turning? Should she go back and start again? She went to the end of what was a short corridor and turned left, and to her relief saw the weather sign. Good. She was in the main corridor. The sign had turned from CLOUDY to WINDY but a few gusts of wind weren't going to stop her going home tonight.

Baxter's image floated in front of her. If it wasn't for him, she probably wouldn't have been offered this position. She should try his office and see if he was there, and if he was on his own she could tell him they'd offered her the job. She wondered if he'd bring up the subject of dinner again. If he did, she thought she just might accept. She knocked and someone called out to come in, but it wasn't Baxter's voice.

'How nice to see you,' Mike said, his friendly face split into a smile, gesturing her in. 'I expect you've come to see Baxter.'

Oh, why did her face have to flush?

'Um, yes. I had a message for him.'

'I don't think he'll be back today,' Mike said. 'He had to do some errands.'

'Oh.'

'Do you want me to pass anything on when he comes in tomorrow?'

'N-no. Maybe just tell him I stopped by. I'm just about ready to pack up and go home myself.'

'Right-o. But mind how you go. It's supposed to be windy tonight.'

'So I noticed.' She smiled. 'Anyway, thanks, Mike.'

'No trouble at all.' He paused. 'Be careful on your way home.'

'I will.'

Back in the typing pool, Peggy had already left. Katie put the cover over her machine and picked up her handbag and shrugged on her raincoat. It had been a rather marvellous day and she couldn't wait to get home, have a cup of tea, and then slip between the sheets of her lovely comfortable bed.

She showed her pass to the Marine at the top of the spiral staircase and he nodded that she could leave. When she stepped out of the building onto Great George Street, she was surprised to find it virtually empty. Usually, at this time of night, it was busy, as it had consistently been ever since Hitler appeared to have given up trying to break Londoners' morale by blasting the city off the map. Now, as he only sent the occasional Messerschmitt across the Channel, Londoners were beginning to behave more normally. She opened her handbag for her torch but her fingers couldn't feel it.

Oh, no. Where was it? She must have left it at home. And after her father had warned her. She'd have to be extra careful where she trod, as it was already dark and there were no streetlights on because of the blackout. But at least it was only a ten-minute walk to Westminster Underground Station. She began fumbling her way, her arms outstretched like a blind person, knocking into a lamppost, now missing the kerb and tripping into the road, when a blood-curdling wail made her freeze. Dear God, the air-raid warning! It sailed up to a crescendo, dropped down and then shrieked up the scale again, finishing in a terrible scream. She looked round frantically, her heart thudding in her chest. Where was the nearest shelter? Where was the ARP warden? Where should she go?

The alarm sounded again and again. She must take shelter immediately. There would only be a few minutes – maybe not even that – before the Luftwaffe came. Another sound, like a thousand angry bees. Katie's head jerked up at the sky but it was just dark cloud. The noise was getting closer. She began to run but her legs felt weak and she couldn't see what or where she was running towards. Pounding footsteps ran after her. What was happening? Who was it? Was someone about to rob her? The pounding came closer . . . then stopped. With a sickening lurch, she realised whoever it was had caught her up. As though in a nightmare she felt a strong arm encircle her waist and run with her . . . rushing her along Westminster Street. A stitch began to stab her side as she was about to tell whoever it was to stop. She couldn't go on any further. She was panting now. The man, for it must be a man, slowed. Gasping for breath, she stole a glance at him but all she could make out was the dark shadow of his hat. Moments later she found herself hurrying down some concrete steps.

Thank God, it was an air-raid shelter. She could hear people talking and children crying. What a kind person to help her. Obviously someone who knew the way and where the nearest shelter was. As she got to the bottom of the stairs, she could sense it was already packed with people by the strong odour of sweat and fear.

'Is there a space anywhere for my girl to sit?'

Her heart somersaulted. She didn't have to see him.

'There's a seat for your young lady over here, mate,' called an old man through the darkness.

She heard the scrape of a match and someone flicked on a cigarette lighter.

'Thank you, sir.'

Baxter removed his hat and looked down at her.

'Are you all right, Katie?' His grin was broad.

She blinked. 'Where on earth did you appear from?'

'I followed you. I'll explain why later. But for now, let's just wait it out until Jerry decides he's had enough.'

A woman with her two children took the younger one, who was crying, onto her lap to make a space for Baxter. He thanked her and sat down beside Katie, his shoulder pressed against hers. His nearness made her blood sing. She felt her cheeks flush but put it down to the stuffy atmosphere and forced herself to focus on her surroundings.

She'd never been in an air-raid shelter before. This one was larger than she expected, and the few old rugs that seemed to have been carelessly flung down anyhow exuded damp. *There must be a hundred or more people here*, she thought, and more were rushing down the concrete steps to claim any small space left. There were dozens of hard-backed chairs, mostly occupied by children and the elderly, and thirty or forty people, mostly couples, were standing. Her eyes fell on a few books and magazines scattered around, presumably for when there was a long wait before the All Clear. Keeping his arms tight to his sides because of the cramped space, Baxter opened a packet of cigarettes and offered her one.

'It might help to calm you,' he said when she shook her head.

He took one out of the packet and lit it, then handed it to her. She hesitated and he nodded. With a trembling hand she put it between her lips, acutely aware that his lips had just touched it. He lit one for himself, looking for all the world as though he were perfectly at home in such a strange situation as he eased his long legs and turned and smiled at her.

She took a puff or two on the cigarette but it was no good. She didn't want it. He took it from her and ground it under his shoe on the concrete floor.

The dank smell permeated the shelter. People began murmured conversations as they patiently waited. A baby wailed and the mother tried to comfort it. Baxter chatted about how he loved walking on the South Downs. He'd grown up in Lewes in East Sussex. Katie, trying to come to terms with the muffled booms of explosions only a few feet above her, knew he was trying to divert her attention. She tried to focus on what he was saying.

'It's just so beautiful even on a cloudy day. Few people around and those that are usually have a smile and a word. When I was a boy I was always up on the Downs. I wasn't a sporty type at school, except cricket, and being an only child in a strict household, I wasn't used to chatting to people, but my dog always opened up the conversation.'

She gave a start. 'Oh, I have a dog at home.'

'You do? Any special breed?'

'Yes, a greyhound. I rescued him.'

'Hmm. Was he a retired racing dog?'

'Yes.' Katie briefly closed her eyes as she recalled the image of her darling Tanny when he was caught on the wire fence and thrown into the air. 'He had an accident on the racetrack. I saw it happen.'

Baxter's eyebrows shot up. 'Oh, what a shame – but at least he has a good home now.' He paused. 'You know, I didn't have you down as a betting girl.'

'I'm not. I used to work there . . . when I left school. I was a kennel-maid looking after forty greyhounds. But as soon as Tanny was injured the owner had no more use for him.'

'I'm afraid that's typical. They're just used for making money.' He looked at her. 'I can't quite see you as a kennel-maid. You always look so fresh and glamorous with that Cinderella-colour hair – except the first time we met,' he added, grinning.

'Well, I *was* a kennel-maid until that incident,' she went on, trying to get his mind off that first painful scene. 'And then I realised I hated the whole set-up behind the racetrack. Having to feed some dogs extra so they can't run as fast – not feeding them so they can run faster. I was so naïve – only seventeen when I was introduced to such a corrupt world.'

Baxter gave her a sympathetic glance.

'Well, Tanny – was that his name?'

She nodded. 'Yes. It was Tan Pet, but "Tanny" sounds more friendly.'

'You saved his life because he would definitely have been put down, so you can be happy some good came out of a not very pleasant experience.' He smiled. 'I bet he couldn't believe his luck when you took him home.'

'Well, he doesn't like it that I'm away so much now and Mu—' She stopped herself, feeling her face grow warm. Would she ever stop thinking of Ursula as Mutti? 'Mother wasn't so keen at first,' she continued, 'though she's begun to enjoy taking him for his walk and seeing what great company he is.'

He chuckled. 'Sounds like it's good for both of them.' He inhaled the last of his cigarette and stubbed it out, then turned to her. 'I'm so glad you like dogs, Katie. I love all animals.'

'Me, too.'

'And talking of walks – when our time off coincides next time, would you join me?' The flecks in his eyes sparked with mischief. 'Don't turn me down again.'

A walk in broad daylight wouldn't be anywhere near as intimate as a dinner for two at night in a restaurant. If she could just trust that he wouldn't start asking personal questions.

The words leapt to her throat without any further thinking.

'I'd like that.'

'Good. We'll fix up a time.'

Then, just when her heart seemed to have resumed its normal beat, there was a tremendous thunderclap overhead. Katie startled, beads of clammy sweat forming above her lips as a series of explosions shook the walls. The shelter was closing in on her! She felt her head swim. She tried to swallow but her mouth was dry.

'Mamma!' a child screamed.

'Please, Baxter, let's get out. I don't want to be buried down here.' Her voice was jerky but low so only he could hear her. She made to rise.

Baxter immediately pulled her back. 'Don't be afraid,' he said above the noise of people shuffling around and arguing. He took her hand. 'We're safer here . . . and you're with me.'

She closed her eyes for a few seconds, silently thanking him for being so calm, and grateful that he kept hold of her hand, chatting to her about nothing, distracting her from the terrible image of being buried alive.

It was a full half-hour before the All Clear sounded and people began to gather their belongings, muttering about 'bloody Hitler', and mount the steps up to street level again.

'Right,' Baxter said, buttoning his raincoat, 'you need to get home and I'm coming with you to make sure you're safely inside your own front door.'

She wouldn't let him know how her insides felt they had been shaken like one of those snowmen locked forever into a little glass ball. She jumped up, and immediately her knees buckled. He put out a steadying hand.

'Careful.'

She gave him a wan smile.

'Just a bit of cramp.' She looked up at him. 'I'm sorry to have been so pathetic down there but I'm fine now so there's no need to come with me. The Underground's only a few minutes away. Or I can get a bus. In fact I'd rather get the bus. I don't fancy being underground any more today.'

Baxter frowned. 'You can get yourself into all sorts of trouble in just those few minutes. Besides, there's bound to be a walk at the other end.' He caught her eye. 'I'm sorry, Katie, there's no argument this time. I'm seeing you home and that's the end of it.'

Chapter Nineteen

By the time they'd walked to the bus-stop a crowd had already gathered, including a few Katie recognised from the shelter. Within minutes a double-decker came to a halt and one couple alighted. Everyone surged forward. Baxter steered Katie towards the front but as she was about to step onto the platform the conductor stopped her.

'Sorry, miss. It's completely full now. You'll have to wait for the next one. It might be awhile, what with the detours we've had to make tonight because of bloody Jerry – excuse my French.'

She could see there were people standing inside from end to end but surely there was room for just two more.

'Are you sure you can't squeeze us on?' Baxter said from behind. 'My girl needs to get home.'

'Sorry, mate. I'm over the legal limit as it is.' He rang the bell and the bus moved off. The people left behind began muttering and a few of them broke away from the queue and walked off.

'Seems like we don't have any choice,' Baxter said. 'We'll have to do the Tube.'

Trafalgar Square Station was packed with bodies spread out along the whole length of the platform. It was difficult to pick their way through the hundreds of people, body to body, who had already settled down for the night, cocooned in blankets and sleeping bags. There was a steady hum of conversation. Someone had brought a wireless set and turned it on at full blast playing marching tunes. It didn't seem quite the soothing music to prepare people for a night's sleep on a hard platform, Katie thought. From the look of several mothers nursing crying babies, and others glaring at the culprit, the wireless was clearly annoying people nearby. Some were eating sandwiches as a late supper and tipping up Thermos flasks of steaming liquid; children were howling, their mothers doing their best to comfort them, or they were playing tag in and out of all the obstacles on the platform. One woman was stepping deftly between sleeping bags and blankets with a cardboard tray on a cord round her neck selling cold drinks and packets of crisps, and Katie saw several hands go up for her to stop.

Announcements came at regular intervals over the tannoy.

'The next train will be delayed for twelve minutes.' Then it was twenty, and finally it was half an hour before a train came along that they were allowed to board. It was standing room only. Strangers were pressed so closely together, Katie felt trapped. But it was Baxter's proximity that made her catch her breath. She told herself it was the same for everybody – trying to breathe in the stuffy carriage, which held an odour of stale human sweat and of smoke, both from the train and from the many people around her smoking. But then she felt his arm around her shoulders as the train juddered and swayed. She was almost disappointed when it came to a halt in Wimbledon.

'My stop,' she said as people scrambled for the door.

Baxter sprang onto the platform before her, his hand ready to help her down. After her feet had touched the ground, she attempted to draw it away but he held it a little more firmly.

'I think I'd better keep hold of you,' he said as they were swept along by the scuffle to the escalator. 'I don't want to lose you now we're nearly there.'

She didn't argue. There was no point. After such a night it

was a relief to let someone take charge. Outside, she said: 'I just need to stop a moment. It was so awful down there.'

She took in a few deep breaths. Every vehicle had its headlights shielded against the radiance, so there wasn't anywhere near enough light to make it safe to walk without bumping into lampposts, pillarboxes and shadowy figures. People seemed to be edging their way along the pavements, most of them carrying a torch covered with the regulation piece of tissue paper to dim the light. The one Baxter held was no better. And then it happened. Someone missed the kerb and fell into the road right in front of them. There was a shout as the figure tried to struggle up. Katie rushed forward but Baxter was already there, helping the person to their feet.

'Are you hurt?' she heard him say.

'No. I'm all right. I missed my footing. It's lethal out here at night.'

It was the voice of a woman.

'Do you have far to go?'

'No. Just down the road.' The woman paused. 'Thank you for your help. Goodnight to you.'

'Goodnight and good luck,' he answered, then turned to Katie. 'Now for the next patient.'

She felt rather than saw his smile of amusement.

'Are *you* all right?' he asked.

She wouldn't admit that she'd felt a little dizzy. He'd take it as a sign of weakness.

'I am now. I just feel I'm spending my life down under the pavements.' She paused. 'And then running to a shelter, which is the same thing.'

'Hmm. You'll get used to it. You have to. Both shelters and jobs.'

'I know that,' she said, a little irritated. 'It just seems a strange life at the moment, not seeing or knowing what's going on above you.'

163

They walked the few minutes' distance to her house. Baxter didn't attempt to take her hand again. She didn't know whether she was disappointed or relieved that he'd broken the contact with her. Thankfully, there didn't appear to be any sign of bomb damage where they were but it was still a relief when she picked out a shadowy but familiar house.

'This one's me,' she said, gesturing towards it.

Even though the blackout curtains had blocked the light, she knew her father would still be up. Should she invite Baxter in? It would be rude not to, and yet all she wanted was to get to bed – not even stop for a cup of tea. Just slip between the sheets and hope that sleep wouldn't elude her. But she had to at least make an offer.

'Would you—'

'No, I won't come in,' he interrupted her. 'It's far too late.' He grinned in the darkness. 'That was what you were going to say, wasn't it?'

'Yes, but—'

'But you're tired. And you've got a big day tomorrow starting your new job so I'll say goodnight.'

He bent down to her. He was going to kiss her. She was sure. She didn't know if she wanted him to. But before she could decide, she felt a peck on her cheek.

'Night night, Katharina. I'll probably see you tomorrow.'

She liked the sound of her full name on his lips. For some reason, she didn't want him to go quite so soon. She swallowed. He'd said he would explain something and he hadn't.

'There's something I want to ask you . . . you never did say why you followed me.'

'Oh, that. I suddenly had the feeling you might not have understood the sign for the weather this evening.'

What was he on about?

'It said "cloudy" – oh, and then later it was changed to "windy".' She looked up at him. 'What's wrong with that?'

'The chap who changes the weather sign has rather a twisted sense of humour. When he puts the "windy" sign up it means there's an air raid going on above us, or they've had *wind* that there's going to be one.'

Katie gasped. 'You were right – I didn't know,' she said in a low voice. 'Thank you for coming after me. It was really thoughtful of you.'

'I'm livid you weren't told because not long ago a bomb fell on Whitehall – actually on the War Office. One of our switchboard girls finished her shift, walked outside into Great George Street and was instantly killed by shrapnel.' She heard him sigh. 'We have to take this seriously.'

Katie swallowed hard. 'Oh, that's dreadful.'

He nodded. 'But at least my instinct gave me the opportunity to see you outside the office and talk more naturally, even though it wasn't in the best of circumstances.'

When she didn't answer, he added, 'I can't help thinking I'm glad I was around.'

With that, he lightly brushed her jaw with his fingertip. Then he turned and she watched as the night swallowed him up.

She put her finger to her jaw where he'd touched it. Sighing deeply, she inserted her key into the front door.

'Is that you, love?' her father called out from the sitting room.

'Yes, Dad.' She opened the sitting-room door. 'Sorry I'm so late. Did you hear the raid?'

'We did. Your mother's been worried to death that you were caught in it. I assured her you'd been held up and made her take a sleeping tablet. For once she did what I suggested.'

Katie sat on the chair opposite and gave him a wan smile.

'What happened, love? You look done in.'

'I started for home and then heard the alarm so I went to the nearest shelter.'

'Good thing you knew where it was.'

'I didn't. But I followed someone who seemed to know.' Should she mention it was someone from work? Maybe not. It wasn't necessary. 'And then the bus wouldn't take all the people at the stop, and the Tube was packed with people staying the night on the platform, and the trains were delayed or so full you couldn't get on them. And just now a woman fell over into the road.'

'Oh, dear. Was she hurt?'

'I don't think so. Someone helped her up.'

He shook his head. 'Well, don't tell your mother all this. She'll have a fit.' He glanced across. 'Why don't I make a cup of tea for both of us and let you calm down a bit? I'll put a teaspoon of sugar in it – that's always good for shock.'

'I'm over it now, Dad. But I'll make *you* one.'

'Have one with me. We don't often have a chance to have a chat.'

'All right, as long as you let me do it.'

She went to the kitchen and put the kettle on, all the while trying to work out the relationship between her and Baxter – if there *was* a relationship, that is. She set the tea-tray with her father's favourite mug and a cup for herself and filled the teapot, then carried it into the sitting room, where he was reading his newspaper.

'All bad news,' he said, putting it aside when he saw her, 'but at least Russia is now on our side. The trouble is, their soldiers are no match for the German Army in training and discipline.' He gave a deep sigh. 'How's work going, love?'

'It's very routine at the moment. But tomorrow I'm taking someone's place on a temporary basis because she's on sick leave, and I'm told it will be more interesting.' She couldn't keep the little thrill of excitement from her voice. 'I think I'll be closer to the war this time.'

'Good for you. I just wish you were allowed to tell me what you're doing.'

'You know I can't, Dad.'

'I do understand.' Her father took a swallow of tea and pulled a face. 'Oh, there's no sugar in it.'

'Sorry, Dad. Not thinking.' She jumped up but he held up his hand.

'No, don't bother. I can manage for once. I've probably used up my ration anyway. And I can see you're tired out. You go off to bed when you've finished your tea. Get a good night's sleep. You'll be right as rain in the morning for the new job.'

She drained her cup. 'Thanks, Dad. I think I'll take your advice.' She walked over to his chair and kissed his cheek.

'Night night, love. Sleep tight.'

Oh, the relief to slip into bed, Tanny contentedly in his basket by her side. But she tossed and turned, trying to get comfortable as she relived the last hour with Baxter. She couldn't really make him out but she had to admit she was beginning to like him, and had the feeling that he liked her too, if his comment that he was glad he'd been around to help her was anything to go by. And calling her 'my girl' – once when they were in the shelter and the second time to the bus conductor. For a fleeting moment she wondered what it would be like if she really was 'his girl'. If he'd actually kissed her instead of just that peck on the cheek. If she'd turned her head and met his lips. If . . . Tanny suddenly gave a grunt and then began a loud rumbling snore, putting paid to any further analysis. Grinning at how Tanny had brought her down to earth from being completely ridiculous, she turned her pillow over to help cool her hot cheeks.

But it was almost midnight before she finally gave in and fell asleep.

Chapter Twenty

Katie had set her alarm for six o'clock as she had to be back in the War Rooms by eight. The sudden piercing bell made her shoot up in bed. She grimaced. Her eyes stung as if she'd barely slept a wink. Tanny was already butting her and licking her arm as she tried to pull on her dressing gown.

'Yes, I know, you want your breakfast,' she told him. 'I'll be lucky if I get some this morning.'

Tanny gave her a woof that she took as one of sympathy and trotted down the stairs after her. Ursula was already up and in the kitchen stirring porridge. She turned as she heard Katie come through the door, her eyes anxious

'Good morning, Katharina. I have hardly slept because I was so worried. But I have made you porridge.'

'I'm sorry.' That twinge of guilt again. Her stepmother was trying so hard to keep their relationship normal though it felt anything but. 'Thank you for getting up early to do it.'

'I wanted to make sure you had something warm inside you because your father told me you work an early shift today. Why is that when you were so late last night?'

'It's because I have a new job starting today . . . only for a month but apparently it's quite important.'

'You will be using your shorthand?' Ursula questioned as she ladled out the porridge.

'Yes, every day.'

'*Das ist gut.* You must not lose your skills.' She put a bowl in front of Katie. 'And what is the new job?'

'Even if I was allowed to tell you, I couldn't, because I don't have a clue myself.'

Ursula heaved a sigh. 'When you find out, I hope you will tell me. Please do not forget I am still your mother.'

Stepmother, she wanted to scream.

Don't argue with her. Just get on with eating your porridge.

'That was very nice, thank you,' Katie said, scraping the bowl.

'I would give you an egg but your father has asked for an omelette for supper, so I do not have a spare. We are only allowed one egg a week now.'

Katie suppressed another twinge of guilt. Ursula looked as though she was losing some weight and could have done with an omelette herself but she'd unselfishly reserved the eggs for her husband.

'I didn't want an egg. The porridge was just right.' She glanced at her watch and jumped to her feet. 'I'll go and feed Tanny and then I need to get ready or I'll be late.'

She gave her stepmother a peck on her cheek and, to her astonishment, Ursula ran her fingertips down the side of Katie's face.

'Good luck, Katharina.'

It was ten past seven when Katie pulled the front door behind her and ran to the bus-stop. Her heart sank at the long queue as she hurriedly joined it.

'Have I missed the 76?' The breathless tones made Katie twist round to see a woman, not much older than herself, carrying a basket with one hand and holding on to a toddler with the other.

'I don't know,' Katie answered. 'I've only been here a minute or two, but that's the one I want.'

'I must get my little girl to the doctor's.' The woman sounded frantic. 'She's got a sore throat and shouldn't even be out here. I'm frightened it will turn into pneumonia.'

'Oh, dear, I am sorry.' Katie looked down at the child, whose cheeks were too red. 'I do hope it won't be long coming.' After what seemed to Katie like an hour, but was only ten minutes when she looked at her watch, the 76 finally rumbled towards them and stopped. Four people alighted. The conductor held up his hand. 'No more than nine,' he said, 'and only upstairs.'

The people surged forward and now Katie was at the front.

'Just one more,' the conductor said, looking at Katie and nodding.

Impulsively, Katie whirled round to the mother and child standing behind.

'You go ahead with the little one,' she said, grasping them both to go in front of her.

'Oh, I can't thank you enough,' the young woman threw over her shoulder as the conductor helped her and her little girl onto the platform and saw them safely in.

'Hold tight.' He rang the bell and the bus pulled away from the kerb.

Katie looked at her watch. This was a disaster. If she didn't get one in the next five minutes, she was going to be late on her very first day.

Miraculously, another bus came along almost immediately, and with relief she got on, taking an inside sideways seat. But they hadn't gone more than a few minutes when the driver called the conductor to go to the front of the bus. After a short exchange, the conductor came down the aisle, his forehead creased with concern.

'We must make a diversion, I'm afraid, due to last night's bombing, so it's going to take us out of our way. The driver will do his best to make up some of the twenty minutes he expects to take extra to the usual journey.' He glanced at everyone. 'If you look to your right, that gives you a good idea of last night's damage.'

Katie half stood to look over and gasped. What was once a row of shops was now unrecognisable. The individual shops were crumpled skeletons of themselves amongst the smoke and smouldering embers. Mountains of rubble and the buildings' contents were strewn all over the road. People were wandering around looking dazed and children were hopping over it, shouting to one another, making it a game and grabbing anything that caught their fancy – a toy here, a tin of something there. A cat, once loved, judging by the size of its rounded body, was carefully picking its way through the debris. Workmen using enormous brushes were sweeping up the piles of glass, and she could hear, even in the bus, the sound of clinking and tinkling and finally shattering as the men tipped the shards into enormous sacks.

There was a general murmur of sympathy. Katie suddenly felt ashamed of herself. She was definitely going to be late now, but those people had lost their livelihoods. And if anyone lived above, they'd lost their home and maybe even family members – and possibly their own life. A shudder ran across her shoulders.

But late on her first day. She told herself it couldn't be helped – that there was a war on – and there was nothing she could do. No amount of worrying would alter anything. She took in a couple of deep breaths and closed her eyes, letting the bus sway her into a fitful doze.

If the conductor hadn't called out 'Whitehall', Katie would have gone past her stop. As it was, she scrambled to her feet, and ran all the way to Horse Guards Road and the entrance to the War Rooms, not daring to look at her watch to see how late she was.

Hurriedly, she showed her pass to the armed guard, then

rushed down the spiral staircase. At the bottom she suddenly realised she wasn't sure where she was supposed to go. She couldn't wander about. She could go either to the room where she'd had that brief interview with Flight Lieutenant David Sinclair or back to the typing pool to see if Mrs Goodman was there. No, that would be the last resort.

She half ran along the main corridor when she heard a voice from some way behind.

'Not so fast, young lady.'

Oh, no. Why did it have to be him of all people? She stopped, heart thudding, and jerked round to see the Prime Minister hurrying along, with a young boy trotting after him carrying a red box under his arm. When Mr Churchill got close enough, he said, 'Ah. It's one of Mrs Goodman's typists.' He studied her. 'I've met you once before, haven't I? You're new.'

'Yes, sir,' Katie faltered. 'Although I'm not quite so new now.'

A big grin slowly spread across Winston Churchill's face.

'No, I don't suppose you are. But you're going in the wrong direction. The typing pool is the other way.'

'Yes, I know. But I'm starting a new job today in place of one of the stenographers.'

The grin faded and a frown took its place. 'Who would that be?'

'Miss Chalmers.'

'Ah, yes, Miss Chalmers. She's broken her wrist.'

Goodness. How on earth was he able to keep up with those sorts of details?

When she couldn't think of an answer he said, 'Jimmy, give the box to Miss—?' He turned to Katie.

'Valentine.'

The Prime Minister nodded and Jimmy handed the red box over to Katie. 'Deposit Miss Valentine in room 69. She should find Mrs Goodman there.'

'Yes, sir.' The boy bowed his head in deference.

172

Mr Churchill glowered at Katie, although she fancied there was the hint of a twinkle in his pale-blue eyes.

'And you, young lady, no more running down here!' he growled.

'Yes, sir – I mean no, sir.'

He'd disappeared.

Trembling with a mixture of nerves and excitement, she felt her cheeks must be as scarlet as the box she was holding so carefully, its obvious importance weighing heavily on her mind as well as in her arms until she could hand it over – to whom, she had no idea. She hastened along the main corridor with Jimmy to a door with a sign pinned to the overhead pipes: '69'. A guard stood outside and Katie showed her pass. The guard scanned it and nodded.

'I'll leave you to it.' Jimmy scurried away.

Should she knock or wait for someone to come along? While she hesitated Mrs Goodman herself appeared.

'There you are, Katie. I've been looking for you.' She took the red box. 'We were worried when we heard you'd braved it home last night and there was a raid on.'

'I managed to get to the shelter,' Katie said, embarrassed that she'd caused concern. 'But the bus had to make a wide detour this morning because one of the streets was badly damaged last night.' She drew in a breath. 'I'm terribly sorry to be late.'

She felt sick inside just mentioning that street with those poor bewildered people. Mrs Goodman nodded sympathetically.

'You're all right – they don't start yet.' She nodded towards the door. 'This is the Cabinet Room, which of course you've not yet been in. You won't be allowed to stay, for obvious reasons, but we have to set it up ready. Let's go in and I'll show you what we do.'

A few men had already gathered and set briefcases and folders on some of the chairs at the U-shaped row of tables. Mrs Goodman placed the red box on the table in front of the central

173

chair, which Katie guessed was for the great man himself. Facing it was a central well of three chairs.

'They're for the Chiefs of Staff – Navy, Air Force and Army – so they can't escape the PM's eagle eye.' Mrs Goodman gave her half smile. 'Now, first we set up the table with a large notebook and pencils and blotting paper that you'll find in the stationery cupboard. Make sure the pencils are well sharpened. There's a sharpener on the table. You place the pencil in upright and turn the wheel.' She looked at her watch. 'Let's get on with that now.'

Katie did as she was instructed, working fast to get it all set out in time. More people, all men, were arriving and taking their places, some throwing approving looks at her.

'Then make sure every third setting has an ashtray – that's most important. And make sure those two brown bottles labelled "Writing Ink" are nice and full.' She gestured to a shelf.

Katie flew round the two tables with the box of clean glass ashtrays, gently shook both bottles, which felt half full, and then went over to Mrs Goodman, who was preparing the stationery for two desks with typewriters.

'These are for two of the private secretaries,' she explained. 'We don't get involved in any of this unless the meeting has finished.'

The door opened again. She turned her head to see three smartly dressed officers enter, representing the Navy, Army and Air Force. Her heart missed a beat when she saw Baxter in full dress behind them. As though he was aware she was in the room watching him, he turned and met her gaze. He held it for several seconds, then without further acknowledgement, made way for the three Chiefs of Staff to take their places opposite Winston Churchill's special seat.

'Right, Katie, I think that's it,' Mrs Goodman said, quickly scanning the room. 'We need to go. The PM will be here at any moment.'

Chapter Twenty-One

Katie rolled three sheets of paper with two pieces of carbon in between into her typewriter. She took no notice of Roz's curious glances, although the other girl hadn't questioned her as to where she'd been, as Katie had feared.

As she peered at her shorthand pad, Katie felt another of her headaches beginning. She was getting too many of them. It must be the stuffy, smoky atmosphere. It couldn't be healthy or they wouldn't make the staff, who hardly saw daylight, go under the lamp. Wishing she had a couple of aspirins in her handbag, she put her fingers on the home keys and began to type. Her rhythm was broken by Roz.

'Where were you anyway all morning? We thought you must be ill.'

Katie bit her lip. She hadn't got away without Roz's questioning after all.

'I wasn't ill. I just did a job for Mrs Goodman.'

'Why *you*?'

Here it was.

'Roz, I don't think you have any right to question Katie any more than any of us,' Peggy put in sharply.

'I most certainly do. I'm in charge when Mrs Goodman isn't here.'

'I understand you put yourself in charge,' Peggy retorted. 'I don't think Mrs G had anything to do with it.'

'Think what you like,' Roz said. 'I need to know where everyone is. We're short enough already.'

'You don't need to know anything of the kind, Roz,' Katie said, suddenly fed up with Roz's superior manner. 'If you insist in knowing, then speak to Mrs Goodman.'

There was a silence from every desk. Then a few moments later came the gentle thrum of Martha's machine joined by Amanda's. Peggy threw a final glare at Roz before she picked up her next piece of work to type.

'I say we all get on with our own work and stop poking our noses into others', Peggy said, having the last word before sending Katie a wink.

Katie was almost glad that she didn't set eyes on Baxter for the rest of the day. At three o'clock, when she'd finished the other pieces in her tray, she stood up and stretched. It had been quite a day and now she was ready to go home, thankfully in broad daylight.

'See you all tomorrow,' she said as she picked up her handbag.

'If you appear at all,' Roz said, looking up, a sardonic smile hovering over her lips.

Katie ignored her. There really was no point in arguing and she wasn't going to be the one to explain where she was for the next few weeks. This was obviously how it was going to be during that time. And now that she might be needed for special confidential telegrams and action reports, she didn't want to risk bringing Cabinet Room work into the office. The only solution was to work somewhere else, away from Roz's prying eyes. She brought her lips together in a firm line. She'd speak to Mrs Goodman.

As she was delivering the day's work from the typing pool to the various offices, she saw the very person coming towards her.

'Oh, Mrs Goodman, may I have a word?'

'Of course.'

176

'I was wondering if there's a quiet place I can work in rather than the typing pool.'

Mrs Goodman gave her a sharp look. 'Any particular reason?'

Katie felt a flush. 'I think I could concentrate better.'

'Ah. Has a certain person enquired where you've been this morning?'

'Yes,' Katie admitted. 'But that's just part of it. I think I'd work better on my own, especially as you say there could be some confidential typing to do as a result of the meetings. Of course, I'd still collect my share of work from the typing pool,' she added quickly.

Mrs Goodman drew her eyebrows together.

'We're bursting at the seams here,' she said. 'There's no spare office.'

'What about in one of these alcoves?' Katie pointed to the nearest one. 'It's easily big enough to get a desk and chair in.'

'This is the main corridor and it's always busy with people going to and fro. Are you sure they wouldn't disturb you?'

Not half as much as Roz. But she wouldn't say that to Mrs Goodman even though she suspected she was well aware of Roz's prickly personality.

'I don't think they'll disturb me in the least because they'll just pass by to wherever they're going and I'll be very careful not to leave any sensitive paperwork unattended.' She caught Mrs Goodman's eye. 'Could we at least try it?'

Mrs Goodman nodded. 'I can't see any real objection, even with the PM going up and down. He probably wouldn't even notice, he's always so wrapped up in his thoughts, and you'd be pretty much tucked out of the way.' She looked thoughtful. 'You'll need a desk and we're short already but I'll see what I can do for tomorrow.'

Roz would have a fit when she saw her working on her

own, out of her clutches. Katie couldn't help feeling a twinge of satisfaction.

Mrs Goodman was true to her word, and when Katie arrived just before eight the following morning, there was a table that would double as a desk, with a typewriter and a typist's chair, set up facing the wall in a large alcove only a few feet from the Cabinet Room itself.

And nearer to Baxter's office.

Crossly, Katie brushed the thought away and was pleased when Mrs Goodman came hurrying along, ready for the morning's meeting. She smiled as she spotted Katie.

'Do you think you'll be all right in here?' she said, nodding towards the alcove. 'I thought it better if you faced the wall so you wouldn't get distracted by anyone.'

'I think it will work perfectly, so thank you for arranging it.'

'I'm so pleased, my dear. Now, why don't you go and clear your things from the office.' She glanced at the table. 'And I'll keep a look out for a proper desk . . . oh, and Katie, I want you to set up the Cabinet Room on your own this time.'

In two minds about Roz being there or not, Katie opened the typing pool door.

'Hey, look who's come in to pay us lowly lot a visit?' Peggy said, her eyes twinkling.

Amanda turned from the mirror pinned onto one of the pillars, where she'd been reapplying her lipstick. 'Oh, it's our lovely Katie.' She gave a wide smile. 'We've missed you.'

Katie felt Roz's eyes penetrate hers.

'I'm just filling in for someone on a temporary basis,' she said.

'Louise Chalmers?' Roz's tone was almost belligerent.

'That's right.'

'But you're not a stenographer so how can *you* be of any help?'

'But that's where you're wrong, Roz,' Katie shot back. 'I'm a fully qualified secretary with a certificate to prove it – and with a distinction.' She managed to hold back a chortle at Roz's stricken expression. 'So apparently I *am* of some help.'

Amanda and Peggy broke into peals of laughter. Even Martha put her hand in front of her face to smother a giggle.

'So if it's all right with you, I'm going to clear out my desk.'

Roz blinked. 'Why?'

'I'm moving.' She'd spin it out as long as possible. It was worth it just to watch Roz.

'Where? There aren't any spare offices that *I* know of.'

'It'll be a surprise then.' Katie smiled sweetly as she went to her old desk she shared with two other typists on different shifts. She wondered if she should take her bed sheet out of the cupboard but decided against it. There wouldn't be anywhere to put it out of sight in an alcove.

'Do you need any help?' Martha said.

'Thanks, Martha, but I can manage. I know you're busy. I'll come back for the rest.'

Martha jumped up. 'No, let me help. We can get it all in one go.'

The girl's tone was so determined and it was so out of character that Katie agreed.

The two of them armed themselves with Sellotape, paper clips, carbon paper, copy paper, envelopes, and anything else Katie thought she would need to set up her new alcove office. She found a couple of cardboard boxes in the stationery cupboard and handed one to Martha.

'Would there be a couple of spare trays for the in and out work?' she asked Roz.

Roz gave her a glare. 'No, there aren't. You'll have to find some more cardboard boxes and cut them down.'

'Thanks for *all* your help, Roz,' Katie said before turning to Martha. 'Are we ready?'

'We are,' Martha said, holding the filled box. 'And don't worry, I'll find some *proper* trays for you.'

They both grinned as Roz, her mouth unattractively turned down at the corners, furiously rolled a sheet of paper into her typewriter and stabbed at the keys.

When Katie showed Martha her new alcove with desk and chair, she said, 'Goodness, Katie, what a strange place to do your work. Whose idea was this?'

'Mine, actually,' Katie said. 'I think it's going to be far more satisfactory than Roz questioning me every minute as to what I'm doing.'

'Oh, I see.' Martha smiled. 'Well, good for you.' Then she hesitated and bit her lip.

'What is it, Martha?'

'Well, I'm not sure if I should say anything after all. It's such a cheek.'

Katie waited, suddenly feeling a wave of apprehension. When Martha didn't go on, she said, 'Well, come on. You have to tell me now.'

Martha cleared her throat. 'Roz has been trying to snoop into your background.'

Katie's mouth fell open. 'What! How?'

'Amanda and Peggy told me she'd been pressing them.'

'What makes her think I have something in my background that would interest her?'

Dear God, all I need is for someone like Roz to start poking her nose in and find out I've got a German stepmother. She'd make a meal of that piece of information.

Katie swallowed. It wouldn't take much probing to find out her stepmother was German, but, as her father had reassured her, Mutti had become a British citizen on the day she married him. There was no need at all for her to be alarmed yet she couldn't help a frisson of uneasiness. Then she scolded herself

180

for overreacting. She must put it to one side. Get on with the job in hand. Show she was capable of doing first-class work. Only then would she have a chance of being used as a stenographer elsewhere once the month was up and Louise Chalmers took back her old position. All this was going through her head when Martha said:

'Amanda and Peggy had no idea what she was on about so they gave her short shrift and told her to mind her own business – as she's always telling *us*. I shouldn't worry about it.' She looked up from setting out the table. 'You don't have anything to hide, do you?'

Martha's question was innocent. She must think her parentage was like anyone else's.

'No, of course not,' Katie said briskly. 'But thanks for tipping me off. I'll have to make sure I stop my shenanigans and keep squeaky clean from now on so Roz doesn't have any excuse to ferret out anything on me.' She chuckled to make light of it, but deep down she was unnerved. Nothing must come out in the open that could affect her job. It was too important.

Chapter Twenty-Two

The following afternoon Katie prepared her typewriter for some work she'd collected from the typing pool.

She'd barely begun when a shadow fell over her.

'Good morning, Miss—'

That gravelly voice. Katie swung round, then shot to her feet.

'Miss Valentine, sir,' she said. 'Katie Valentine.'

'Ah, Miss Valentine – so this is where they've relegated you.'

There in front of her, close enough to touch her arm, stood the plump-cheeked, sharp-eyed Prime Minister, an unlit cigar in his mouth.

Katie felt her cheeks flush.

'I asked if I could be somewhere where I won't be disturbed.'

'And here am I doing just that.' Mr Churchill gave a sly grin without removing his cigar.

'Oh, no, Prime Minister. Not at all. But when you're working with several people in the same room, it can sometimes be distracting.'

'Very sensible.' He hurried away.

Katie bit back a chuckle – she'd passed the test as mistress of her own alcove with the great man himself!

It wasn't more than an hour later when another voice spoke.

'Is that Katie?'

Baxter!

When she pretended she hadn't heard him, he added, 'I'm sure I recognise that blonde hair.'

She tried to compose herself before turning round but her heart wouldn't cooperate. Instead, it beat harder. Warmth creeping into her cheeks, she mumbled, still with her back to him, 'I'm just finishing something.'

'Oh, don't let me stop you. But I must say this set-up looks quite original.'

'I asked if I could use it,' she said irritably as she looked at the letter she'd just typed.

What was the matter? Why were the words blurring?

'Do you have a minute?' Baxter said, after a long silence.

She swung round to face him. He threw her a quizzical look.

'Not really,' she said, his nearness unnerving her. If only they weren't so exposed to everyone – particularly those who loved spreading gossip.

'Shall I come back later?'

'No, you'd better not. I've got a lot to get through by the end of the day.'

'I see. Well, I've got to deliver some paperwork and give an update to the PM, but I'll see if you can spare a few moments on the way back.'

Katie reluctantly nodded and turned back to her typewriter, placing her fingers on the keys, her eyes on a report.

She worked through a handful of memos and had dropped a report from Baxter that she'd just typed into the out-tray when he stopped by again. She handed it to him and he put it in a folder without even glancing at it. Instead, he gazed at her.

'By the way, I've noticed you hold things you're about to type very close to your eyes.' He hesitated as though wondering if he should continue. 'Do you have regular eye checks?'

What was he on about?

'Yes,' she said. 'Why?'

'When was the last time?'

'Oh, I don't know – two or maybe three years.' She hadn't been entirely truthful. The last time she'd had them tested she'd been a schoolgirl. Not allowing her gaze to meet his, she said, 'But there's nothing wrong with my eyes – they're perfectly fine, thank you.'

'I would book an appointment to have them checked,' Baxter said. Then his face broke into a grin. 'You never know – it might not be anything to do with my writing at all.' With that he marched past her desk towards the Map Room Annexe.

Katie stared after him, her head starting to throb and irritation bubbling up in her throat. So he was implying the fault lay with her when she had difficulty transcribing his reports. He wouldn't admit it might just be his own style that was causing the trouble. Well, she'd show him. She'd get them tested. It was about time. But one thing she was sure of – it would be many a year before she'd need to wear glasses.

'Could you please cover your right eye,' Mr Blake, the optician, said, when Katie sat in the chair facing the large card a few yards in front of her. It began with an enormous 'E' and she picked out various other letters of the alphabet as the lines became smaller.

'E, S, R, B . . . '

'Next line.'

'X, L, J, C.'

'Next.'

Katie didn't hesitate – until she came to the last three lines. And then she faltered and started from the beginning of the line again. She stumbled again. She'd have to admit it.

'I'm sorry but I can't read any more.'

'No need to apologise – it's what we're here for.' He switched something on his machine and glanced up at her. 'Now cover your other eye.'

When she'd finished, Mr Blake remained silent for a few moments. Then he said:

'Do you get headaches?'

'Yes, I have lately. But I put it down to where I work.'

'Which is—?'

Careful, Katie. You mustn't even hint.

'I'm a stenographer doing long hours every day with not a lot of fresh air.'

'Hmm. Sounds rather unhealthy.' He put his light down and looked directly at her. 'I'll tell you what your trouble is. You're short-sighted in one eye and long-sighted in the other. For years they've tried to compensate for each other.' He paused. 'Do you find yourself holding the work closely to your face? Or are you able to type if it's by the side of you on the desk?'

'Bit of both, I think.'

'When would you need to hold the work up close?'

When I get a report from Baxter.

'Usually when the writing is quite small.'

Mr Blake nodded. 'You need glasses.'

Katie gave a start. She hadn't imagined this would be the outcome although it seemed Baxter had.

'Are you sure . . . ?

'I'm absolutely certain. We'd better get you fixed up right away. Come with me and I'll try some frames on you.'

Reluctantly, Katie followed him into the reception area where there were a few plain-looking frames on a revolving stand. They all looked much of a muchness to her. The optician gazed at her, then tapped the side of his jaw as he pondered the display.

'I think these will do an adequate job,' he said, removing a pair. He deftly put them on her. 'Go and look in the mirror.'

Katie, very aware of something on her nose, walked over to the mirror. A plain-faced girl she barely recognised stared

185

back at her. She couldn't believe how different she looked – how different she felt.

'Do they feel comfortable?'

She wanted to tell him that they looked hideous. But he'd think her vain and he'd probably be right.

'I think so,' she said.

'Good. We'll get the prescription lenses sorted and you can come in and collect them at the end of next week. I think you'll find they'll make a big difference to your efficiency at work and you'll find your headaches will subside.'

Chapter Twenty-Three

August gave way to September. It was still warm and had been dry for several weeks. Sometimes Katie felt she simply bypassed the weather, only glancing at the sign in the passage to have a clue as to what was going on outside, but paying particular attention when it stated it was windy. Roz had been her usual bossy self, but Katie decided that was the woman's way and she wasn't going to change. Best let it wash over her as Martha, Amanda and usually Peggy did.

Apart from two hurried coffee breaks where they'd just chatted casually, she hadn't been aware of Baxter at all this past week and even wondered whether he'd gone on leave. She missed seeing his tall figure rushing from one room to another with a bundle of enormous maps under his arm or stopping by her desk for a quick chat. The War Rooms certainly didn't hold the same little thrill of anticipation they once did.

'The optician left you a message,' Ursula said one evening when Katie arrived home from the day shift. 'He said your glasses are ready to collect.'

Katie pulled a face. 'Oh, I'd forgotten about them.' She sighed. 'All right. Thanks. I'll get them on my next graveyard shift when I'm off in the morning.'

It was another week before Katie was able to pick up her

glasses. Immediately she put them on and looked around the Reception area she felt dizzy.

'You'll soon get used to them,' the receptionist said with a sympathetic smile. 'You won't even notice they're there but you *will* notice how much clearer things are.'

'They'd better be,' Katie grunted.

She'd wear them for work, but she certainly wasn't going to wear them all the time.

That afternoon, when Katie arrived at her makeshift desk, she took the glasses out of the case and self-consciously put them on, then glanced at her in-tray. Ah, just one file with a report inside and half-a-dozen memos. She'd get the report done first and out of the way. Pulling the sheaf of papers from the tray, she glanced at the initials: BE. Hmm.

But it couldn't be Baxter who'd written it. This writing wasn't nearly so tiny. In fact, she could read it fairly well. But she knew his way of forming the capital letters and this was identical. So how could that be possible? Something itched on her nose and she put her hand to the bridge to scratch it. Of course . . . her new glasses. So Baxter's handwriting wasn't that difficult to read after all; her eyes simply hadn't been able to cope. Now they had help.

Still not feeling very stable peering through her new glasses, Katie wasn't looking forward to seeing Baxter but she knew it wouldn't be long before he came by. She braced herself, determined to keep her dignity while he pointed out he'd been right all along. With a sigh she removed her jacket and slipped it onto the back of her chair, then took up the first few sheets of paper.

Three hours later, with people coming and going and handing her more papers and taking some away, she was still pushing through the never-ending pile. There'd been no Baxter in sight to get under her skin. Just as well. She could do without his burst of laughter at her expense.

Yet as the minutes and then the hours ticked by, she felt disappointed that he didn't seem to be around. Maybe he'd already left on the day shift, yet mostly their shifts appeared to coincide. Katie reprimanded herself. She was becoming quite silly. First she dreaded him seeing her bespectacled, making her look so plain, and now she'd started to wonder if something had happened to him when he went home . . . to wherever that was. But as far as she knew, there'd been no sign saying WINDY today. Her thoughts were interrupted by Amanda.

'Katie!' Her friend stared at her when she turned round. 'Oh, you're wearing glasses. Gosh, you do look different. Kind of intellectual.' She gave her tinkly laugh.

'Well spotted,' Katie said, returning it with a wan smile. 'But you know those headaches I've been getting?'

'Yes.' Amanda suddenly looked alarmed.

'I didn't do very well on the eye test. And that's what's causing them.'

Amanda visibly relaxed. 'Oh, is that all? I thought for a moment you were going to say something serious.'

'It *is* serious,' Katie said. 'I don't recognise myself.'

'Not your normal glamorous self then?' Amanda grinned.

'Nothing to do with glamour. It just doesn't look like me. I look as stern as a schoolmarm.'

Amanda studied her for a few moments.

'I know exactly what you need to do.' She went up to Katie and took a chunk of her hair, then twisted it up and nodded. 'Yes, I thought so.' She let Katie's hair fall back to her shoulders. 'All you have to do is sweep this gorgeous blonde hair up, brush on a ton of mascara and wear the brightest lipstick you can lay your hands on. You'll be the epitome of sophistication.'

'I don't use mascara or a bright lipstick.'

Amanda didn't even hesitate. 'You need to from now on. And I've got a range of Max Factor, so come in half an hour earlier tomorrow afternoon and I'll do your transformation.' Her face beamed. 'You'll knock Baxter Edwards off his feet.'

'Don't say such things,' Katie said. 'I'm not interested in him in that way.'

'Hmm. I'm not so sure.' Amanda lowered her tone. 'You've been seen together on more than one occasion.'

Katie's cheeks glowed. 'Who's told you that?'

'I believe Roz mentioned it.'

Katie bristled.

'I'm getting fed up with Roz. She's stirring as usual.' She paused and looked directly at Amanda. She must convince her.

Or am I trying to convince myself?

She ploughed on. 'A walk along the corridor doesn't mean I'm interested in him. He's all right . . . nicer than I'd first thought. He gave me a bit of advice about something. But that's all.'

'Methinks the lady doth protest too much.' Amanda grinned mischievously as Katie rolled her eyes.

'Sorry, Amanda, I've got a pile of work to transcribe.'

'Then I'd better leave you to it. But take my word – there's some gossip going on about the two of you.'

Oh, for heaven's sake, not more gossip. How could anyone have found out about Baxter helping me improve my shorthand speed? And even if someone saw us together, there's nothing whatsoever going on between us that they could make something of.

'I refuse to listen to gossip,' she said. 'But thanks for the offer of glamorising me. I'll be here at half-past two. But don't go mad, will you?'

''Course I won't. I'm practically a pro. I was just starting training in film make-up when the war started. That's how I got my supply of cosmetics.' She grimaced. 'And that was the end of my new and exciting career.'

Katie blinked. 'Oh, I'm sorry, Amanda. But you'll be able to take it up again when the war's over, won't you?'

'Hmm. I doubt it. There's so much competition. I can't tell you how thrilled I was to beat all the others. It was a dream come true.' Amanda's eyes suddenly misted. 'This damn war affects everyone.' Then she brightened. 'But if I can transform you into this efficient, gorgeous-looking lady, then at least I get a bit of practice.'

'If that's supposed to be a compliment –' Katie couldn't help laughing '– it was rather backhanded, to say the least.'

'Oh, you know what I mean,' Amanda said, joining in the laughter. Then she looked past Katie's shoulder. 'Mmm. Who's that?'

Katie turned to see a fair-haired man in civilian clothes, maybe thirty or so, striding along the corridor, his eyes on some paperwork. Just as he was passing he looked up.

'My, my. If it isn't Katie Valentine. I almost didn't recognise you with your glasses.'

Katie jerked up her head, her hand automatically going to the bridge of her nose.

'Mr Lester!' She blurted his name without thinking. Oh, dear. But he didn't show any alarm.

'*C'est moi*,' he said, giving her a broad smile.

Amanda looked curiously from one to the other.

'Thanks, Amanda,' Katie said pointedly. 'I'll certainly come earlier tomorrow as you suggest.'

'Your colleague, I presume,' Mr Lester said, watching Amanda swiftly leave them.

'Yes.' She wasn't going to elaborate in case she got reprimanded for saying something unnecessary about where Amanda worked, though it was likely Mr Lester knew anyway. Then something struck her. 'Mr Lester, did you realise I was only going to do typing down here?' She watched his expression.

Mr Lester pulled his brows together. 'No, I didn't. They said they needed a stenographer. Why? Is that what you do all day?'

'I did, although I'm now filling in for a stenographer while she recuperates, but I lost my speed, and if it hadn't been—' She stopped herself short.

'If it hadn't been for what?'

'Well, if I'd gone below their minimum, I wouldn't have been offered the job,' she said lamely, seeing Vernon Lester more clearly through the new glasses. She hadn't noticed his eyes were so deep-set.

'So you're much happier now, then?'

'Yes, but in a month I'll be back to the typing pool.'

'Well, it's up to you to make yourself indispensable.' He paused. 'Anyway, I'm here because I wanted to talk to you about something.'

'Oh.'

'Yes – Judith Ellen Baker.'

Katie held her breath. Mr Lester looked so serious. Surely Judy hadn't done anything wrong.

'Don't look like that,' he said. 'It's nothing bad – *au contraire*, she was a pretty special person at Whitehall.'

Katie took an inward sigh of relief.

'What did she do?'

'I thought we might discuss it over dinner one night.'

Baxter had invited her to dinner and she'd turned him down. She couldn't quite remember now why she had. Maybe it wouldn't hurt to go out with Vernon Lester – just this once. There must be quite a bit for him to tell and she so badly wanted to know as Judy had never hinted anything until Katie had read that snippet in her final letter.

He tapped his fingers on the desk, as though impatient for her to accept.

'Thank you. That would be a nice change.'

He nodded. ' 'Shall we say Monday?'

'All right.'

192

'Good. What time do you leave work?'

'Usually around seven.'

'Then I'll wait for you in Great George Street at seven-thirty in case you're held up.' He looked at her directly. 'And please drop the "Mr Lester" and call me Vernon.'

He ambled away whistling. Didn't he know that whistling was not allowed in the corridors? Mrs Goodman had told her the Prime Minister couldn't bear to hear whistling as it disturbed his train of thought. Katie was just about to settle at her desk when Baxter suddenly shot out of the Map Room. It was the first time she'd seen him for several days but he didn't even glance at her as in a few swift strides he caught up with Vernon. Intrigued, she watched as he put a hand on Vernon's arm. Vernon swung round and she heard him say, 'What's up, old chap?'

'I don't know who you are but no whistling down here.'

'What?'

Baxter pointed to one of the many 'no whistling' notices:

'And if you don't know where that came from, you shouldn't be down here anyway,' he said firmly.

'Ah. I get it.' Katie saw Vernon lift his eyes skywards. 'Well, thanks for the warning, old chap,' he threw over his shoulder as he strolled off.

Baxter caught her gaze as he came back to her desk.

'Did you see that?' he demanded.

'Yes, I couldn't help it.'

'Damned idiot. I've never seen him here before. He certainly didn't seem to know the rules. If the PM had heard him, he'd have given him a tongue-lashing.' He frowned. 'Was he talking to *you* just now?'

Katie felt the warmth rush to her cheeks. There'd be no point in lying to him with his hazel eyes staring at her.

'Yes, he did stop by for a few moments.'

'What for?' Baxter's tone was coated with suspicion.

'He ... um ... he wanted to tell me something.'

'Oh. What was that?'

'Nothing important,' she said vaguely.

Baxter frowned. 'Who is he? Do you know him?'

This was dreadful. She shouldn't be discussing members of the staff, nor should he, especially when Vernon didn't even work down here. Irritation curled in Katie's stomach.

'There's no need to interrogate me, Baxter.'

'I'm not interrogating, I'm asking. Security is extremely tight down here and I don't like the look of him at all. Too cocky for my liking. If you don't tell me who he is, I'm afraid I'll have to report him.'

Oh, no.

'I wouldn't do that if I were you,' Katie said, keeping her eyes fixed on him. She wasn't going to let him intimidate her. 'He works above us where I used to work. In fact, he recommended me for this job.'

Baxter's eyebrows rose in surprise.

'Really? Well, that throws another light on him. And I suppose he fancies you as well.' He stared at her. 'Does he?'

'I'm sure he doesn't,' Katie said.

A few seconds hung between them.

'Has he asked you out?'

Katie stood silent.

'He has, hasn't he? And you're going. That's it, isn't it? You turned down my dinner offer but accepted his.' The gold flecks in his eyes sparked with anger. 'Fine. At least I know where I stand.'

He turned on his heel and marched off, leaving Katie dumbfounded and, for some reason she couldn't pinpoint, more upset than the situation warranted.

Chapter Twenty-Four

Katie changed her mind more than once about having dinner with Vernon, but there was no way she could let him know without drawing attention to herself. And anyway, she longed to know more about how Judy had been involved at Whitehall during the Great War.

Amanda had kept her promise and they'd gone down into the Dock in the dormitory where the only girls there were asleep. She'd sat Katie on the edge of a vacant bed and applied mascara and a coat of bright red lipstick, then pinned up her hair with kirby grips and combs. She studied Katie, then nodded happily.

'It's quite a transformation,' she whispered. 'You look like a film star.' She whipped out a pocket mirror and handed it to Katie. 'Here, have a look at yourself.'

Katie peered at the reflection.

'Goodness, I *do* look different. I'm not sure it's me but at least the glasses don't *completely* hide my eyes now.'

'I think they actually enhance them,' Amanda said, grinning.

'You've done a very professional job,' Katie said, turning to her. 'I don't think you'll have any problem taking up your career again.'

'We'll see. We've got a war to win first.'

Katie had felt surprisingly self-conscious when Amanda left. She almost never wore her hair up – it was too thick to stay in tidily, but Amanda seemed to have the knack because it felt quite secure and she'd shown her how to use the grips to hold it firm. She wondered what Baxter would say when he saw her. He'd not mentioned her glasses at all on the afternoon when he'd stopped Vernon whistling. She couldn't help smiling as she recalled the sight of the two of them, Baxter not allowing him to go until he'd read him the riot act. Her smile faded at the second image. He'd prised from her that she'd agreed to have a date with Vernon yet refused to accept *his* dinner invitation. Then he'd stalked off in a huff.

Baxter didn't pass by her desk again and she saw him only once, in the distance, completely engrossed in conversation with the Prime Minister. She decided it was for the best.

Ursula had taken a step back when she saw Katie's new look. She grimaced.

'What *have* you done to your face and lovely hair?'

'It's just a bit of make-up. Someone at work did it and put my hair up.'

'It doesn't suit you. It reminds me too much of Judith. She was always painted up.'

Katie flinched.

'I used to love seeing her in the latest fashion,' she protested. 'And those fabulous hats she made.'

'*Doch*, there is more to worry about in life than what hat to wear.' Ursula regarded Katie with a flash of her blue eyes. 'So you will not be putting that stuff on tomorrow.'

'Oh, but I will. I'm twenty-one. I have the key of the door, remember,' she added as she hung her jacket on the hall stand.

'As you so often wish to remind me,' Ursula said through pursed lips.

On Monday morning, back at work in her alcove, Katie found herself actually looking forward to the evening. Vernon was certainly not as volatile as Baxter and she was sure they would have a pleasant evening. So long as there were no strings attached, Katie thought. He was a nice-looking chap with an affable manner but she wasn't in the least attracted to him. Besides, it was only a dinner.

Early in the afternoon, when she was back from a few gulps of air and a hurried sandwich, Katie found a folded piece of paper with her name by her typewriter.

Would you come to the typing pool asap to help out. Roz.

Katie grimaced. No 'please', no 'thank you' – just an order. She rifled through the last papers in her in-tray. Nothing desperately urgent except a couple of short reports. She'd finish them first.

'So where's Roz?' she asked when she was back at her old desk.

'Don't ask me,' Amanda said. 'She up and left just before you came, saying she didn't know what time she'd be back.'

That evening, when Amanda had checked Katie's last piece of typing, Peggy leaned back in her chair and stretched her arms.

'Oh, I need some fresh air. This place has got me down lately. No time for a cuppa this afternoon and the noise of an air conditioner that actually does nothing.' She yawned. 'It must be time to pack up.' She glanced at Katie. 'Thanks for helping us out this afternoon, Katie. I know you have plenty of your own to get through but we were snowed under with Martha away.'

'Luckily, I'd just about caught up,' Katie said. 'So please always ask. I'll tell you if I can't.' She echoed Peggy's yawn.

'You sound as tired as I feel,' Peggy commented.

'You're right. It's the lack of air. And it's so smoky in here today.'

'You probably notice it more in here now you're out in the corridor,' Amanda said, 'with just a whiff when anyone passes by smoking a fag . . . or a Cuban cigar,' she added with a grin. 'I don't suppose you'd make a complaint then.'

Katie chuckled. 'No, I probably wouldn't.' She looked at her watch. Nearly quarter past. 'I'd better be going.'

'Heavy date then?' Amanda said, sending her a wink.

'Not exactly.'

'Oh, so there is someone,' Amanda pounced.

'Leave the poor girl alone,' Peggy put in. 'I'm sure she'll tell us all about it tomorrow, won't you, Katie?'

'I'm sure I'll do nothing of the kind,' Katie said, laughing and realising she missed their banter. They were super girls. She only wished she had time to get to know them better.

Vernon was waiting for her in Great George Street.

'Hello, Katie.' He put both hands on her arms. 'My, my, you look fabulous with that new hairstyle and . . . well, everything.' He took her arm. 'It's a ten-minute brisk walk to the restaurant. It's Italian. The owner, a decent chap – as most of them are – was released from internment last December though he'll be monitored by the British authorities.' He looked at her. 'Does that worry you at all?'

Katie shook her head. 'Not really. From the little I know about Italians, I can never quite believe they're the enemy. And I've never eaten Italian food so it will make a nice change.'

Thankfully, there was only one street with visible bomb damage in the area, which looked as though it might have been part of the recent bombing when she and Baxter had sheltered. The rubble and debris still hadn't been cleared away, and windows had been blown out of several of the buildings. She swallowed hard as she and Vernon passed by the end of the street, but although he glanced at it, he didn't make any remark.

Mario's was a small, insignificant-looking restaurant, located just before the turquoise-coloured façade of Fortnum & Mason's in Jermyn Street. Vernon held the restaurant door open for Katie and a dapper waiter with a white cloth over his arm stepped forward.

'Good evening, *signore* –' he nodded towards Katie '– *signorina*,' he said. 'May I have the name?'

'Lester. I've booked a table for two.'

The waiter checked off the name on his list. 'Thank you, *signore*. Come this way.' He led them to a table near the side wall.

'This do, Katie?' Vernon said, and she nodded.

The waiter took her jacket and hat and another waiter placed a white linen napkin on her lap and did the same for Vernon. He handed Vernon the wine list and menu.

'I am sorry but we do not have the veal this evening,' he said with a soulful expression. 'Or the beef. They are very difficult to buy.'

'Hmm.' Vernon studied the menu for a few moments, then handed it to Katie. 'I'd suggest a pasta dish if you've not tried Italian.'

'We make our pasta here,' the waiter told them. 'Our special one is spaghetti puttanesca.'

Katie glanced across at Vernon.

'I don't know what that is.'

'It's one of their traditional pasta dishes,' he said. 'The sauce has tomatoes and capers – all sorts of herbs—' Vernon looked up at the waiter.

'Also anchovies, onions, garlic,' the waiter responded with a beaming smile. 'It is very delicious. I think you will like it, *signorina*.'

'I'll try it then on your recommendation.' Katie smiled up at him.

'*Grazie, signorina.*'

'I'll join you.' Vernon snapped the menu closed. 'And some bread rolls and a green salad.'

'Certainly, sir.' The waiter paused. 'We recommend a bottle of our house red to accompany it.'

'Yes, keep it all Italian,' Vernon said, looking up at him. 'We'd like that straightaway.'

'But of course, *signore*. It is coming.'

As if by magic the bottle appeared. After Vernon had sniffed the sample, rolled a mouthful around, swallowed and nodded his acceptance to the waiter, and Katie was enjoying the first sips, he looked closely at her.

'Where are your spectacles?' he said.

'I don't have to wear them all the time,' she said. 'They're mainly for work.'

'I'm glad. They don't do anything for you.'

Katie raised her chin. *Oh, thanks, Vernon.*

'Sorry, that sounded rather abrupt. I didn't mean it quite like that. But you can't see your pretty face so well when you're wearing them.' He threw her a rueful smile. 'I see I've upset you.'

'Not at all,' she said, not quite truthfully. 'But I'm not here to talk about my glasses. I want to know about Judy.'

'Who we now know is your mother.'

It sounded strange to hear those words on his lips. And did his tone have a hint of a reprimand that she hadn't told him when he first interviewed her – when she didn't even know herself?

'She didn't exactly work in Whitehall, but she came to the War Office with a proposal.'

'Oh. What was it?'

Before he had a chance to answer, the waiter set their bowls of steaming pasta in front of them, and a large salad in between.

'Can I get you something more, *signorina*, *signore*?' he said, looking from one to the other.

Vernon shook his head. 'No, I think that'll be all.'

'*Thank you*,' Katie emphasised, looking up at the waiter with a smile. He gave her a slight bow. She turned back to Vernon. 'You were saying . . .'

'Yes. This was 1915, the second year of the Great War. Apparently, Judith Ellen Baker came to the War Office to discuss setting up a new charity.'

Katie wasn't expecting something like this. Judy had often mentioned she had some favourite charities but she'd no idea she'd actually started one up.

'Apparently, she was deeply concerned about the animals – what was happening to them now the Great War had begun.' Vernon continued.

'I knew she loved animals because she once rescued a dog that had been terribly mistreated,' Katie said, her heart leaping at the thought that her aunt hadn't forgotten the animals at such a crucial time. 'Weren't there any animal charities in those days?'

'Oh, yes. The main one was the Blue Cross Fund, which was like a Red Cross for animals, treating the sick and injured, but Miss Baker realised the charity wasn't really able to help traumatised animals such as horses and dogs who played quite a part in that war. She discovered they would end up being slaughtered because they were considered too far gone to be anyone's pet, so she and a group of volunteers did some fundraising and set up a charity just for this purpose.'

'Why did she have to go to the War Office for permission?'

Vernon paused to take a forkful of spaghetti.

'Any kind of charity for the war effort was under the aegis of the War Office,' he said, 'although from the notes on the file they rejected her idea. But Miss Baker wouldn't let anything stand in her way and wouldn't take no for an answer.'

'That sounds just like her,' Katie said with a chuckle. 'Do you know what the charity was called?'

'Yes . . . Home for Distressed War Horses and Dogs.'

'Does it still exist?'

'No, but it did carry on right through the war, which was what was intended. And apparently the people thought very highly of it. Many of the animals recovered enough to either be adopted or finish their lives in peace in one of the rescue centres.'

Then why was Judy so against her working with the greyhounds, insisting she did a secretarial course? But of course it wasn't working with the dogs that her aunt was against, Katie remembered, it was because she didn't approve of her daughter working in a gambling atmosphere.

'You've gone quiet,' Vernon remarked. 'What are you thinking?'

'I absolutely adored my aunt,' Katie said. 'I mean Judy,' she hastily corrected herself, 'but she didn't ever mention this.'

'The Great War – the war to end all wars, so they said – was terrible.' Vernon sighed. 'Most people wanted to get on with their lives. So many of their men were killed in the trenches and people tried to put it behind them, but it was very difficult for young girls to find a husband.' He looked at her and smiled. 'Let's talk about something more cheerful.'

'Not easy now we're in the middle of another war,' Katie said crisply. She took a sip of wine, trying to work out the kind of man Vernon was. He was obviously intelligent but rather offhand when talking to those he seemed to consider beneath him. Was she being unfair? No. He hadn't once said a 'please' or 'thank you' to either of the waiters.

'What do you like to do in your spare time?' Vernon cut through her thoughts.

'Oh, the usual. Reading, music, dancing . . . my dog, Tanny.'

'Ah, like Judith, then?'

'Not on quite her scale, though I did rescue him.' She regarded him. 'Do you like dogs?'

'I do, as working dogs. But the British are far too sentimental over their animals.'

As far as Katie was concerned, the conversation went flat at that point. Vernon talked mostly about books he'd read and was reading – none that she had read or recognised, and plays he'd been to, and had she seen them? No, she hadn't. They sounded too dull for words. Not her sort of evening's entertainment at all. She smothered a yawn.

'Am I boring you that much?' Vernon said, his expression amused, as though that was the last thing he thought he could possibly do.

'I'm so sorry,' Katie said politely, but letting him see her glance at her watch. 'I'm quite tired though.'

'I'll ask for the bill.'

When they were outside he said, 'How are you getting home?'

She gave a start. 'Oh, um, the bus or the Tube, whichever comes along first.'

'I'd better come with you.'

He didn't sound that enthusiastic. Well, she certainly wouldn't put him out.

'No, no. I'm perfectly all right.'

'If you're sure, then, I'll say goodnight.' He paused. 'May I kiss you?'

No, Vernon. Not now and not ever.

Was this because she'd met Baxter and he was the only man she would ever want to kiss? But no, Vernon just wasn't her type. She gave what she hoped was an apologetic smile.

'I'm sorry, Vernon. I'm not really in the mood.'

Ignoring her, he held her arm while he attempted to kiss her mouth but she turned her face and his lips landed on her cheek.

'I've really enjoyed myself,' he said, not seeming to take any notice of her rejection but simply giving her arm a brief squeeze, 'so I hope we can do this again.' He gazed down at her. 'And I really like the new hairstyle and lipstick – it made the evening even more special to see you across the table looking so lovely. I never realised how very pretty you were until tonight.'

'It was a lovely supper,' Katie said, fighting down her irritation at his tactless remark. So it was only the make-up that had enhanced his interest. 'I'd better be getting home,' she said, not quite managing to hide the cooler tone, 'but thank you for inviting me and telling me about my . . . mother.'

That was the best bit, she so badly wanted to add. But what was the point? All she could think of now was her nice comfortable bed.

Chapter Twenty-Five

October 1941

A fortnight passed. It was already autumn but the weather remained mild. Katie decided to angle her desk so she could catch sight of anyone who passed by, but still feel a little private and detached from the comings and goings along the main corridor. She was beginning to get used to the loud thrum of the air conditioning and able to block out most of the noise when she was immersed in her work. During the second week, Mrs Goodman had telephoned in to say she couldn't get out of her bed. The doctor had been and diagnosed influenza and told her to stay there for at least a week, so Katie had taken over some of Mrs Goodman's responsibilities. Thankfully, all was going well, but even when she occasionally caught Baxter's eye, he gave no sign that they were anything more than work colleagues.

Each time it happened, Katie was disappointed. She enjoyed their bantering and hadn't forgotten his kindness in giving his time to help her win this job, even though she mustn't forget it was only temporary. *Was our friendship still the same?* she asked herself, because he seemed to have forgotten she'd agreed to go for a walk with him on the South Downs. Maybe he thought she was caught up with Vernon so wouldn't be interested now. It wasn't true. She wasn't going to accept any more of Vernon's invitations – if indeed he asked her. She'd enjoyed working for him for those months and he'd proven a decent and fair boss whom she'd respected. Also, he was the one who'd given her the chance of a more prominent position. But out of the office, she'd realised quite quickly, he simply wasn't her type.

She decided at the first opportunity to come straight out with it and ask Baxter if his invitation was still open. Pleased with herself for making this decision, she was deep in a report when she felt the presence of someone. She looked up into the eyes of one of the most striking creatures she'd ever seen. The brunette, maybe three or four years older than herself, standing tall, smiled down at her, showing dimpled cheeks and enormous deep-blue soulful eyes fringed with black lashes under dark winged eyebrows. Her generous mouth was tinted red. The mouth was smiling, showing perfect white teeth.

'Hello,' she said. 'Louise Chalmers.' She threw out her arm. 'You must be Katharina. Sorry, I don't know your last name. I just wanted to introduce myself.'

Katie stood up and shook hands. The woman's hand was cool to the touch.

'Katie Valentine,' Katie said, then added, 'How's your wrist?'

'The fracture's all welded together,' Louise laughed delightedly, waving her arm and shaking the wrist. 'I'm ready to take back my old job.' She paused. 'I must say, I've missed everyone but I've heard you've held the reins beautifully.'

Katie felt her heart plummet. She hadn't at all discarded her friends in the typing pool but she was sorry to have to go back to simply typing. Her work associated with the Cabinet Room had made her feel much closer to what was going on in the war, even though it was a worry when she gleaned that much of it was not going the Allies' way at the moment.

Katie was caught up in her own thoughts, almost forgetting the young woman who was about to snatch her job back. She put on her best smile.

'I've enjoyed it very much, Miss Chalmers. I'd like to have carried on but Mrs Goodman will soon be back so you'll be a full team again.'

'Oh, do call me Louise,' she said, smiling back. 'Yes, it must be awful for you to go back to the typing pool.'

Katie raised her eyebrows. Was Louise deliberately putting her in her place? It was difficult to tell if the woman genuinely felt any sympathy.

'Um, excuse me, but how did you know that's where I was working before now?'

Louise chuckled – a throaty laugh.

'It doesn't take much for gossip to fly up and down these corridors,' she said. 'I've heard quite a bit about you . . . *and* our delightful Baxter Edwards.'

Katie startled. Louise had emphasised the 'and' as though putting her and Baxter together. Or was she just imagining it?

'Oh, don't worry, your secret's safe with me.'

'I don't have a secret,' Katie said firmly.

Louise stared at her. 'We all have secrets. And it's wise to keep your cards close to your chest down here. But I hope we can be friends.' She looked at her watch. 'I'd better be going. You'll probably see me tomorrow as Mrs Goodman's not coming back until after the weekend. But I do know one thing –' Louise broke off and glanced into the alcove '– I'm not going to be pushed into one of those. I can't think of anything more ghastly, getting interrupted dozens of times a day.'

'I quite like it,' Katie said, smiling.

'Good for you. But I'll be going back to the office I used to work in.'

'Oh, where's that then?' If Louise could ask those sort of questions, then so could she, Katie decided. And if there was a better office, why hadn't Mrs Goodman allowed her to use it while Louise was recovering?

'In the Map Room Annexe . . . with the cartographers, Mike and Barnaby . . . and your Baxter, of course.'

Katie felt a rush of blood to her cheeks.

'Louise, let's get the record straight – he's *not* my Baxter.'

'That's not what everybody here thinks,' Louise chortled. 'Didn't he help you with your shorthand or something – and you both made a big secret of it? Because things like that always get out.'

Katie put her hand to her face, which felt as though it were on fire.

'I'm sorry but I don't want to discuss such nonsense.'

'Then why are you blushing?' Louise said. 'Because it's giving you away.' She put a hand on Katie's arm. 'Don't be cross. It's all round the War Rooms that there's romance in the air.' She gave Katie a mischievous smile. 'And with a name like yours – how romantic is that?'

'There's no romance between us as far as *I'm* concerned,' Katie snapped. 'And I'm sure that goes for Baxter as well. He'd be horrified if he thought that was what people were saying.'

He'd probably think I *was the one to put it about.* She moved away from Louise's hand. 'I must get on with my work but it was very nice to meet you.'

'Oh, the pleasure's all mine,' Louise said. 'Anyway, see you tomorrow.' With a cheerful wave of her newly mended wrist, she strode off, her high heels echoing along the main corridor.

Katie stared after her. Louise had such a clear, innocent face – but some of the things she'd said . . .

She shook her head, not at all sure what to make of Miss Louise Chalmers.

Thankfully, Katie was soon absorbed in her work but every time she put one of Baxter's newly typed sheets into her out-tray, Louise's ridiculous claim that there was some sort of romance going on between Katie and him floated to the surface. Should she warn him what people were saying? No, she couldn't. It would be too embarrassing for words, especially as he was not at all pleased with her.

Bang goes my asking him if we're still going for that walk on the South Downs.

If she mentioned that, he would think she had designs on him. No, better for him to believe that she had her eye on Vernon and so squash the gossip.

But that thought depressed her. She didn't want to have that kind of a relationship with either of them – pretending to Vernon she was interested in him and pretending to Baxter that she wasn't in the least interested in *him*. Which she had to admit wasn't true. She wondered now if that was the reason he'd avoided her lately. Maybe it wasn't that he was annoyed about the dinner invitation, but he wanted to put a stop to anyone thinking there was something special between them, when there was nothing. She nodded, even though there was no one to see it. Yes, that would be it. He'd heard the rumours too and was deeply embarrassed. Well, she'd keep up the pretence as well. The pretence that he wasn't special. But just that thought made her feel as though she'd stabbed herself in the heart. Because much as she'd tried to smother, ignore, disown any emotional feeling towards him, her heart told her different.

She might as well admit it, even if it was only to herself – she'd fallen in love with him. But she must never let him suspect it.

Chapter Twenty-Six

It was only a few days before Mrs Goodman returned.

'So you've met our Louise,' she said to Katie late one morning.

'Yes, I have,' Katie said. Mrs Goodman waited as though she should add something more. 'She seems very nice.'

'She is a lovely young woman,' Mrs Goodman said, smiling. 'All the men are in love with her.'

'I'm not surprised,' Katie said, feeling a tug on her heart. Was Baxter one of them?

'I don't suppose you're much looking forward to going back into the typing pool, are you?' Mrs Goodman cocked her head on one side.

'It will feel strange,' Katie admitted. 'But I know it's an important job we're all doing.'

'That's the spirit, my dear.'

Katie bit her lip. Maybe this was the time to say something. She simply didn't relish going back to the typing pool under Roz's watchful eye.

'Mrs Goodman, is there any chance I could be transferred to another department so I can keep my shorthand speed up? I really feel I could be more use. I've loved standing in for Louise but I've always known it was coming to an end. Would there possibly be any chance of a secretarial position?'

Mrs Goodman paused. 'Yes, I can see why you're rather wasted just typing all day, Katie.' She drew her brows together.

'Leave it with me. I'll go through all the staff and have a word with the powers that be.' She looked around the alcove. 'In the meantime, would you like to stay here in the alcove?'

Katie hesitated. She enjoyed the camaraderie of the typing pool, if you didn't count Roz, but she did feel more part of the hustle and bustle of what she called the 'high-ups' – the three Chiefs of Staff and the three men in the Joint Planning Committee who always greeted her with a smile and occasionally stopped to have a quick chat with her. She wouldn't put into words that she was more likely to see Baxter if she was in the corridor rather than if she was behind the closed door of the typing pool.

'Actually, Mrs Goodman, I think I *would* like to stay here. I've got used to it. I even had a brief chat again with the Prime Minister the other day.'

'Ah. Good. Has he seen you with your new hairstyle?'

'Yes, but I wouldn't expect him to notice.'

'He notices everything. And I mention it because it does make you look very different. Rather bookish, yet glamorous. It suits you.'

Katie grinned. 'Thank you. It's all because Amanda said she couldn't see my eyes when I first put my glasses on, so she made me wear some make-up and change my hairstyle.'

Mrs Goodman looked thoughtful. 'Yes, Amanda's career has been cut short like so many others. But one day this'll all be over and we'll all be proud that we played our part.' She sighed. 'It can't come quick enough for me. I was on the verge of retiring. My plan was to spend more time in the garden. But instead of flowers I've got vegetables – not nearly so pretty, but vital with all the rationing.' She smiled. 'Well, I'll leave you to it,' then added, 'Ah, here's that nice young man coming your way.' She hurried off.

Katie twisted her neck. Baxter was striding towards the

211

alcove. Confusion flooded her. What should she say? What shouldn't she say? Oh, why had she told Mrs Goodman she'd like to stay out here in the corridor? She'd be far safer with the others in their room.

'Katie, could we have a word?'

Here it comes.

She managed to compose herself.

'Of course.'

'In private,' he said.

Katie glanced up and down the corridor. 'There's nobody around.'

'It won't stay that way. Are you able to have a break in one of the cafés?'

She might as well get it over with.

'All right. I'll make it my lunch-break.'

'Good. So what about if I meet you in The Copper Kettle,' Baxter went on. 'That's the second café in—'

'Yes, I know where it is.'

'Say, twenty minutes.'

She nodded. Someone came out of the Map Room Annexe. Mike.

'Baxter, you're wanted on the blower.'

'I'll try not to be any later,' he said in an undertone as he put a report into her in-tray.

'Won't Louise be dealing with your work now?' Katie couldn't help saying.

He raised an eyebrow. 'What's Louise got to do with it? Of course if you're too busy, I can—'

'Baxter, it's the PM,' Mike called.

'I'd better go.'

By the time Katie took her seat at one of the tables in The Copper Kettle, a quarter of an hour had gone by and there was still no sign of Baxter. And they only had half an hour for lunch at the most. Well, she was here and her mouth was like parchment. She'd order two coffees and hope he would turn up. Just as the waitress brought them over, the door flew open and Baxter stormed in. For a few seconds their eyes locked and then the spell was broken as he made his way through the crowded tables to where she was sitting.

'Oh, good, you've ordered one for me as well.' He glanced at his watch. 'I'm sorry, we won't have much time, but I have something important to talk to you about.'

Katie braced herself.

'There's some gossip going on about us.' Baxter looked at her directly. 'Have you heard?'

She swallowed. She couldn't feign ignorance. He'd know immediately.

'Yes, just recently.'

He nodded. 'May I ask who told you?'

She wasn't expecting this. Should she tell him it was Louise? *All the men are in love with her.* That's what Mrs Goodman had said. Maybe Baxter was as well and wouldn't like it if he heard her name mentioned in that context.

'I'd prefer not to say,' she said lamely.

'I'd prefer you did.' He kept his gaze fixed on her. When she remained silent he said, 'Was it our charming Louise?'

She gave a start. 'Yes, as a matter of fact it was.'

'Hmm. I thought as much. Tell me, Katie, what did you think when she said that?'

She lowered her eyes. 'I said it wasn't true – that there was nothing going on between us.'

He leaned forward over the table, his eyes imploring her . . . to say what, she couldn't tell. 'Did she believe you?' he asked quietly.

'I don't think so.' Katie twisted a strand of her hair around her finger. 'But I was worried you'd heard and be mortified.'

213

'You thought that?'

'Yes.'

'But we *are* friends?' Baxter pressed, not taking his eyes off hers.

'I hope so.' Katie answered, starting to feel warmth creeping up her neck. What was coming now?

His face lit up with a wide, triumphant grin.

'Then if we're friends, will you come on that walk with me that we talked about?'

Her eyes widened. 'Oh, I'd like to. I thought you might have forgotten about it.'

'No, I hadn't forgotten.' His smile faded. He cleared his throat as if giving himself time to put his thoughts into words. 'If you must know, Katie, I didn't want to step on Lester's toes.'

He sounded jealous. She was about to put him straight on her non-existent relationship with Vernon when he suddenly sprang up.

'I'm sorry, but I must rush. I said I'd only be gone ten minutes and it's more than that now. Will you excuse me?'

He put a hand on her arm and even though she was wearing a jacket, she felt the touch as intensely as though her skin were bare.

'We'll find a day when we're both free. I'll contact you.'

Katie watched him until he closed the café door behind him. After a minute she followed, a new spring to her step and a glow around her heart. He hadn't seemed annoyed about the rumours and instead had reminded her that they were friends. But he still wanted to spend the day with her. It was enough. She would just enjoy his company, and he would never have to be embarrassed to learn that she loved him.

That afternoon, after she'd unwrapped an egg sandwich she'd brought from home and eaten at her desk, she noticed Mrs Goodman walking in her direction.

'Oh, Mrs Goodman . . . '

Mrs Goodman stopped. 'Yes, my dear.'

'I was wondering – are you able to tell me when my next day off might be?'

Mrs Goodman hesitated. 'I'm not sure which specific day. But ask Roz. She has the new timetable. She'll tell you.'

And with that, her boss hurried off.

Damn! It *would* have to be Roz she'd have to see. Katie rose from her chair. She might as well go and find out now so she could let Baxter know.

Roz was immersed in her typing and only glanced at her, then dropped her eyes to her paperwork again.

'Roz?'

'What is it?' Roz said without looking up.

'I just need to check my next day off.'

'Oh, doing something special?' Roz's smile was more akin to a smirk.

None of your damn business.

'I just want to know the day, that's all,' Katie returned in as cool a voice as she could muster.

'I need to finish this first. I'll let you know later when I have a minute – though when that will be, I have no idea.' She jerked her head to her in-tray which was piled high.

'Can I help with that?' Katie said.

'No, no, I'll do it. I'm sure you have *much* more important things to do than a pile of memos and letters.'

'Everything's important that we prepare,' Katie said mildly.

'If you say so.'

What was the matter with the woman?

'Well, if you change your mind, I'll be glad to help, so you know where I am.'

'Yes, I know where you are,' Roz said, a sarcastic edge to her voice as she carried on typing.

215

Katie sighed as she walked back to her desk. Roz was so prickly. Whatever you said never pleased her. She saw some more work had been put into her in-tray while she'd been gone. She sat at her desk and removed the top layer, whereupon a small brown envelope fell to the floor. She bent to pick it up and turned it over. It was addressed to Miss Valentine in Baxter's inimitable writing. She sat at her desk and opened it.

Katie, I can take either Tuesday or Thursday as my day off next week. Would either coincide? When I go by tomorrow, if I'm with anyone, just nod for yes on Tuesday, two nods for Thursday, or shake your head if neither and I'll try for another day. B.

She'd have to wait for Roz to confirm. And Roz would probably hold out as long as possible just to annoy her.

Chapter Twenty-Seven

Roz came nowhere near that afternoon. At five minutes to three, Katie tidied her desk ready to go home and called into the typing pool. One glance told her that everyone was there except Roz.

'Where's Roz?' she said.

'She went about ten minutes ago,' Peggy said.

'Oh, she is too bad.' Katie went to Roz's desk in case she'd left the schedule ready for her to look at, but it was nowhere in sight. She'd have to speak to Mrs Goodman again. 'Is Mrs Goodman still here?' she asked Peggy.

'She's in the building but I think she's been called on an emergency job.'

'Oh. Any idea where she might have gone?'

'She mentioned the Chiefs of Staff office.'

'I'd better see if I can find her.'

Katie hurried along the corridor away from the Cabinet Room. The Chiefs of Staff conference room was next to Mrs Churchill's bedroom, though she'd never caught any glimpse of the lady herself. She knocked. There was a murmuring of voices and then a tall man with dark, close-cut hair and moustache, dressed in Army officer's uniform, opened the door. She recognised him as one of Mr Churchill's close advisers but had never typed anything for him as far as she knew.

'Are you Miss Valentine?'

'Yes,' Katie said, wondering how he knew her name. 'I'm looking for Mrs Goodman and was told she'd probably be here.'

'Yes, of course. Won't you come in?' He stepped aside and waved her in front of him.

She stepped into a vast room, brightly lit and modestly furnished. It was clearly a male-occupied office, from the lack of any frills. There were four desks, all with the usual green glass shaded desk lamps, and Mrs Goodman was sitting at one of them, studying her notepad. She looked up and smiled.

'Am I interrupting anything?' Katie asked.

'No, not at all,' the Army officer said. 'In fact we were just talking about you.'

'Oh.' Katie waited, wondering what on earth about.

'Do sit down.' He pointed to a chair near Mrs Goodman. When she was seated, he said, 'I'm Alan Brooke, Chairman of the Chiefs of Staff. I was just telling Mrs Goodman that one of my secretaries had to give in her notice this morning. She's had an emergency at home and has already left. It seems she will not be returning.' He paused and looked at her directly. 'Mrs Goodman said she had just the person who would suit the position and mentioned your name. Normally, I would want to interview a few young women but you've been highly recommended by David Sinclair and one of the other officers as well. And as time is of the essence I'd like to offer you the job. You will be on a month's trial but I'm sure there won't be a problem with it becoming permanent – at least until we win the war.' He appeared to allow himself a wry smile.

Katie gripped the sides of her chair. Goodness. She hadn't been expecting anything like this. Or so quickly. She could feel her heart beating faster. She looked at Mrs Goodman, who smiled and nodded.

'Oh, yes, please,' she said. 'If you think I'd be right.'

'I think you'd fit the post admirably,' Mrs Goodman said.

'You're fast and accurate with your shorthand and typing and proved yourself when Louise was away, and you're a sensible and efficient worker. I think Sir Alan will be more than happy. He does have a personal secretary, Miss Nicholson, and you would be her assistant.'

'I'd love it and I can't thank you both enough,' Katie said, blushing with the compliments.

They sat and chatted for a few more minutes, Mrs Goodman telling her she should see some extra in her pay packet, which felt to Katie like confirmation that it was a definite step up. Sir Alan closed it by saying, 'I'd like you to start next week. Miss Nicholson will show you the ropes.'

She only hoped that she and this Miss Nicholson would get along well if they had to spend much time together. She shook herself for feeling doubts about a wonderful opportunity of real promotion. Of course they would get along. She would make sure of that.

The only blight on the new arrangement was that she couldn't possibly ask for a day off next week, when she would only just have started, to go to the South Downs with Baxter. It was a shame but duty had to come before anything.

'Now Louise is back,' Sir Alan said, turning to Mrs Goodman, 'would it be convenient for you if Miss Valentine starts this Wednesday? I'll be in the office that day.'

Oh, that would work beautifully. She might be able to have Tuesday off after all. She held her breath.

'Yes, I think we can let her go by then,' Mrs Goodman said, smiling, 'as we're hoping for a new typist to join us. It's been difficult lately with sickness but it should all work out well now.'

'Thank you again, sir.' Katie stood to shake hands with him.

'I shall look forward to seeing you Wednesday at eight-thirty,' he said. 'Mrs Goodman will show you Miss Nicholson's office.'

Katie walked out of the office on air. If Mrs Goodman would allow her to have just this Tuesday free – after all, she hadn't had any time off at all for more than a fortnight with no let-up because Mrs Goodman herself had been off sick – she would pour every ounce of energy into her new role.

Half an hour later Mrs Goodman stopped by her desk.

'I'm glad you got on well with Sir Alan,' she said, catching Katie's eye. 'He's a real gentleman and never gets in a flap like –' she hesitated '– well, like some, but he's extremely clever and has just been promoted to the Chairman of the Chiefs of Staff, which is the highest position in the PM's gift. But he doesn't let his human side show much because he has such important things on his mind, so don't worry if he comes across as a little abrupt – his attention is absolutely focused on the war and all its challenges. But he's a good balance for the PM, who can get riled if things don't go the way he expects. But thankfully, the PM is no dictator like Hitler. He does at least listen . . . particularly to Sir Alan . . . and can often be persuaded.' She paused. 'I think that's what makes him so lovable. He might be a grumpy bear at times but most of us would do anything in the world for him.'

It was interesting to catch a glimpse of the relationship between two such outstanding men, especially from someone like Mrs Goodman whom Katie admired and respected.

'It's good that Mr Churchill has someone steady to talk things over with,' she remarked, not knowing quite what else to say. 'I only hope I'll measure up.'

'I know you'll do a good job or I wouldn't have recommended you.' Mrs Goodman paused. 'By the way, did Roz show you the updated schedule?'

'No, she was finishing off some typing and would do it later, but when I looked in just before packing-up time, she wasn't around.'

Mrs Goodman frowned. 'I told her you hadn't had a day off for getting on three weeks and to make sure she slotted you in for one day this weekend.' She looked at Katie with concern.

'Oh, I can work this weekend,' Katie said quickly, 'but I'd love it if I could have Tuesday off instead. Then I'll be starting work with Sir Alan the next day.' She glanced up at Mrs Goodman. 'Would that be all right?'

'I'm going to say it is, even if it isn't,' Mrs Goodman said firmly. 'Someone else can change if it's not. So have a lovely day and you'll feel fresh and ready for Wednesday. Come to the typing pool first thing Wednesday and I'll take you to Miss Nicholson's office and introduce you.'

'Thank you for being so thoughtful to me, Mrs Goodman,' Katie said. 'And for recommending me for such a prestigious position. I'm absolutely thrilled.'

After Mrs Goodman disappeared, Katie returned to her typing, hugging herself that Tuesday was now to be hers. She couldn't wait to give her nod to Baxter when he passed by tomorrow. It suddenly dawned on her that Sir Alan had mentioned David Sinclair and also another unnamed officer who'd highly recommended her. Her heart gave a little flutter – could that person be Baxter?

Baxter was by himself the following day when she spotted him leaving his office, but there were several people coming and going along the main corridor, so Katie thought it best to stick to their codes. He casually glanced at her as he walked by and she gave a small nod. He smiled and strode on. On his way back an hour later he casually tossed an envelope into her tray.

She tore it open to read:

Excellent! I'll come and pick you up at your house on Tuesday at 10 a.m. We might as well make a day of it! B.E.

I'm not sure I can wait that long, Katie thought happily.

Tuesday had seemed a long way off, but eventually the day dawned. Katie sprang out of bed to open the curtains, then looked out in dismay to sheets of rain. She glanced up at the sky – the little she could see in between and over the buildings. Nothing but grey cloud. She bit her lip. It *would* be. Did that mean Baxter would cancel the walk? It wouldn't be much fun trailing around in pouring rain but somehow she didn't think it would put him off. She'd just have to brace herself, wear her heavy raincoat with a serviceable hat and hope it was enough for her not to get drenched.

She'd had her bath the night before so she had a quick rinse at the wash basin in her room and swiftly dressed. She'd bought a pair of dark brown trousers on her last visit home, much to Ursula's disgust, and now took great delight in wearing them.

'Trousers do not sit well on women,' her stepmother had said. 'It takes away their femininity.'

Well, if she didn't look feminine enough for Baxter it was too bad, Katie thought, as she pulled a Fair Isle jumper over her head, then looked in the full-length mirror. There was no point in putting her hair up today in this weather. Besides, it was her day off. She'd leave it loose and wavy, thanks to the pipe-cleaners she'd used last night. She applied her now daily bright-red lipstick Annabel had generously given her from her Max Factor assortment and grinned in the mirror. No horrible glasses today. She gave a nod of satisfaction.

Ursula was making the porridge as usual and turned when she heard Katie come into the kitchen.

'I hope you are not going out in those trousers,' was the first thing she said.

Katie's mouth tightened. 'Yes, I am. They're perfect for this weather. All my friends are wearing them.'

222

It wasn't quite true. But one woman she slightly knew, Ruth, a postwoman, wore them, and it was Ruth who'd inspired Katie to buy a pair.

'Well, *I* have not seen this,' Ursula said, placing a bowl of porridge at Katie's place. 'You are going out today with a nice young man. Whatever will he think?'

'If he's really a nice young man, as you call it, he won't mind at all. Probably think how sensible I am.'

Her stepmother pursed her lips.

'I am sure you know best.' She hesitated. 'I hope you will introduce me to him.'

Oh, no. She hadn't thought of that. She'd imagined she'd just rush out when Baxter rang the bell. She didn't want Ursula to start questioning him but more to the point, she didn't want him to notice her German accent.

Immediately, she felt disloyal to the woman who'd brought her up. But nothing must stop her from doing her secret work in the War Rooms. The way everyone warned you about the Official Secrets Act, and the severe punishments if you ever divulged the slightest thing, sent a shiver through her. But Baxter was different. She didn't think he would blab about her German connection if he ever found out about it. But she didn't want to take the chance.

'We'll probably go off straightaway,' was all she said, trying not to notice Ursula's sudden frown.

At precisely ten o'clock the doorbell rang. Tanny barked and leapt out of his basket to follow Katie, who hurried into the hall, grabbing her raincoat from the stand.

'Woof!' He sat by the side of her thumping his tail as if to say he'd be perfectly happy sharing his mistress with anyone if it meant his going for another walk.

'Tanny, I've already taken you for your walk this morning. And you were lucky it wasn't raining.'

She couldn't stop her heart giving a little flutter. Damn the weather, but she wasn't going to let it spoil the day she'd been looking forward to so much. She opened the door and there he was, standing in the pouring rain under an enormous black umbrella.

'Not exactly the weather I'd planned,' he said, smiling as he folded his umbrella.

'Come in,' she said. 'I *am* ready ... just got to put my raincoat on.'

For goodness' sake stand aside and allow him to pass, now you've invited him in.

'Tanny, back!' she ordered the excited greyhound.

'Hello, Tanny.' Baxter bent and patted the top of his head, ruffling his ears. He looked up. 'What a splendid-looking boy. We should be taking him with us.'

'I would have suggested it if we'd been going to the Downs,' Katie said, her heart warming with the attention he'd given Tanny, 'but I doubt we'll be going for our walk now.'

'No, it's not looking good but it seems a shame to leave him behind,' Baxter said, putting his umbrella in the stand and looking at the excitable dog. 'We'll definitely take you next time, Tanny.' He took Katie's raincoat from her and held it out.

But in her hurry and his proximity, she couldn't get her arms into the sleeves.

'Shall we start again?' Baxter said, amusement in his voice. He shook out the raincoat. 'Now, put your right arm in here.'

Has he guessed what's the matter with me?

Katie gritted her teeth and tried to concentrate. As she got her arms safely into her raincoat, wrapped her scarf round her neck and adjusted her hat, she heard her mother's footsteps hurrying along the narrow hall.

'Did I hear the doorbell?' Ursula said.

'Yes, we're just leaving.'

'You will introduce me to your friend.'

Katie's heart plummeted.

'This is Baxter Edwards – Baxter, Ursula Valentine.'

'I'm very pleased to meet you, Mrs Valentine.'

Ursula put out her hand and Baxter shook it.

'My daughter is reluctant that I meet you,' she said. 'This is because I am a German.'

Chapter Twenty-Eight

Katie wished she were anywhere else than in the hall when Baxter raised his brows in surprise. She couldn't tell whether it was because Ursula had told him her daughter didn't want to introduce them, or because she was German.

'Mother, we have to go.'

'You see, Mr Edwards, that I am right. Katharina always calls me "Mutti", but not today – not in front of you. She is ashamed of me so I am now "Mother".'

Katie felt the heat rush to her cheeks.

'I'm sure she didn't mean anything by it, Mrs Valentine,' Baxter said, non-committally.

'*Doch*, I assure you she does.'

Katie stared at Ursula.

Doesn't she realise I'm trying to protect her by not advertising the fact that she's German?

If Ursula blurted this out to someone she'd never laid eyes on before, then who else was she going to tell? And now Baxter knew her German connection. Katie swallowed hard. She *had* to bring this awkward conversation to a halt.

'I won't be too late, *Mutti*,' she said, emphasising the last word as she brushed past Baxter to open the door. Immediately, gushing rain and a squall of wind swept in.

'And you are going for a walk in this weather?' Ursula said.

'We'll go somewhere inside first,' Baxter said, 'and hope it clears later.' He glanced at Ursula. 'It was very nice to meet you, Mrs Valentine.'

Ursula gave a gracious nod. 'I hope to see you again,' she said as she shut the door behind them.

Oh, the relief to be outside, away from Ursula's wounded expression.

'I'm sorry about my . . . mother,' Katie began, the word sticking in her throat.

'All families have their ups and downs,' he said, opening his umbrella. 'Here, come under before you get soaked.'

Katie shifted closer as he held it over her. She was intensely aware of his nearness, the raindrops seeming to rattle on the umbrella in time with her heartbeat.

'Now take my arm,' Baxter said, looking down at her. 'I don't want any accidents and to have to report to your mother that I wasn't looking after you.'

She put her hand in the crook of his arm and he glanced at her.

'Shall we have coffee first? Somewhere local so we don't get completely drenched. Do you know anywhere?'

'Yes. There's a very nice café near the Town Hall.'

'Right – let's get going. We can discuss what to do in the dry.'

Baron's Café was located in one of the elegant Regency buildings in a long parade of shops. Inside, echoing the Regency period, the room bustled with uniformed waitresses flying from table to table.

'It looks packed,' Baxter said as they stood dripping just inside the entrance.

'Someone will soon leave,' Katie told him. 'They can't all have arrived at the same time.'

Miraculously, an elderly waitress broke away from some customers and hastened up to them, smiling.

'I'm just about to clear a table,' she said, then nodded towards the coat rack. 'Why don't you hang those wet coats up and I'll be there in a tick.'

Baxter took her raincoat and put it with his on the rack and their hats and Katie's scarf on the shelf above.

The same waitress came back two minutes later and showed them to a table by the window, beautifully laid with a white linen cloth. She handed them a menu and promised to be back right away to take their order.

'This is charming,' Baxter said, looking around.

Katie followed his gaze at the glittering chandeliers, the moulded ceiling and the framed watercolours, now noticing details that she'd never given much consideration to before. She had simply accepted it as a café offering a gracious, relaxing space to be alone with her thoughts. .

'I come here occasionally to give myself a special treat,' she said.

'I'm glad you viewed today with me as special,' Baxter said, giving her one of his disarming smiles, which sent a quiver through her.

Was he just teasing her – or did he really mean it? If only she could see what was going on in that dark head of his. And what had he *really* thought when Ursula had announced she was German? She had to admit that he hadn't looked shocked at all.

'This is actually a very good lunch menu,' he said, 'but I think we should stick to coffee . . . and a cake, of course,' he added with a grin. 'Maybe by then the rain will have let off.' He gazed at her. 'Is it coffee for two and then something to go with it?'

'Do you know, I'd love a round of hot buttered toast,' Katie said.

'Nothing sweet?'

'No, thanks. Plain toast is just what I fancy right now.'

'I'll have the same,' Baxter said.

Soon they were drinking good strong coffee with hot milk and sharing a plate of hot buttered toast. Somehow this small act of eating and drinking together seemed strangely intimate. Katie scolded herself. She was becoming quite irrational lately.

'By the way, I like your new sophisticated look at work, but I prefer you now with your hair on your shoulders—'

'Gone dead straight in the wet,' she finished, wryly. She must look a sight but somehow she didn't care, because Baxter was gazing at her with what looked like approval rather than horror.

'You look charming from the rain,' he said. 'Almost as charming as when I first set eyes on you and you were in your dressing gown and curlers,' he chuckled. 'Although I'll never forget the look you gave me when you pushed past.' This time he burst into full laughter.

'Don't remind me.' But his laughter was infectious and she laughed, too. 'I just never expected to see anyone at that hour, and especially not a man immaculately dressed in full wing commander's uniform.'

'You have to expect anything in wartime,' Baxter said, still grinning, 'but I wouldn't have missed that vision for anything.' He took her hand across the table. 'What would you like to do for the rest of the day?'

Katie took her last swallow of coffee and set her cup down.

'That was delicious,' she murmured.

'Apart from having another cup of coffee,' he said.

'How did you know?'

'Because you licked your lips like cats do when they've really enjoyed something and wish it hadn't stopped there. And talking about cats, it's still raining cats and dogs.'

Katie glanced out of the window where sheets of rain fell, making the street look almost like an Impressionist painting. It was rather lovely, even if they would get soaking wet again.

'Are *you* going to have another?' she asked.

'Yes, I'll join you.' Baxter waved their waitress over and ordered. 'Tell me what you'd like to do today now the weather's not fit for the walk.'

'Maybe go to a museum or art gallery,' she said.

His face lit up by his smile. 'I'm so glad you like those kinds of things, because there's not much I'd rather do than mooch around a museum or gallery.' He paused for a few seconds, then tapped his knee. 'I've got it! Do you like classical music?'

'I love it,' she beamed. 'I have some records at home though there's nothing like a live concert.'

'I completely agree,' he said. 'Have you ever heard Myra Hess play the piano?'

Katie shook her head. 'No. I've read about her and keep meaning to go. She plays at one of the galleries, doesn't she?'

'Yes, she gives lunchtime concerts at the National Gallery and all she charges is a shilling. There's nowhere in London you could attend a concert at that standard for such a pittance. But it's done on purpose. She wants everyone to be able to attend, particularly working people who can't usually afford such luxuries or think they're only for the elite. Do you know, she played right through the Blitz, even when the bombs came down. She stayed at her piano so the audience stayed with her.' He shook his head as though in awe. 'She's not only a wonderful pianist but she's also a wonderful person.'

'Oh, I'd love to hear her,' Katie said.

'Right. Why don't we look round the National Gallery first and have a snack there, so we're in good time for the concert. It starts at one-thirty and there's always a queue. Then after the concert we'll have a think about what to do for the rest of the afternoon depending on the weather.' He glanced at her. 'Would that suit you?'

'Very much,' Katie said. It sounded absolutely wonderful.

'Good. I'll get the bill.'

Once outside on the shiny wet pavements, still splattered with raindrops, Baxter tilted his head towards the sky.

'By the looks of those clouds this is what we're in for for the rest of the day, so we'll do the Downs another time.'

Mmm. So he wanted to see her again.

'Let's sprint before the next deluge.' He tucked her hand firmly through his crooked arm. Not minding in the least, she had to half run to keep up with his long strides as they hurried towards Wimbledon Park Station. 'Right, we'll change at Earls Court,' Baxter said, as they boarded the train.. 'It shouldn't take much longer than half an hour if there're no hold-ups.'

Katie noticed sad little piles of belongings from people sheltering on the platform from the night before. She gulped. The owners obviously trusted the day passengers not to remove anything before they returned this evening.

After changing trains, it was only a short ride to Charing Cross.

'Presumably you've been to the National Gallery,' Baxter said, unfolding his umbrella yet again as they hurried along towards Trafalgar Square.

'Not for years,' Katie said. 'My father took me when I was sixteen. But I do go to the Portrait Gallery every year or so. I just love portraits.'

'Do you paint them?'

'Oh, no. I'm not talented in that way. But I suppose I like looking at people's faces. They're all so different. It's fascinating.'

'I like looking at faces too,' he said, his mouth quirking with humour as he looked round at her. 'You could show me your favourites one day.'

Katie felt a warm glow. They were getting on so well. Different from lately when he'd gone off in a huff. She still hadn't had the opportunity of explaining about Vernon but she'd have to pick the appropriate time. Nothing must spoil today – she was enjoying herself far too much.

The National Gallery stood like a beacon of the best of British architecture with its Grecian columns and colonnaded portico – a wonderful combination of Ancient Greek and Roman elements. Katie never tired of looking at it with a feeling of pride.

'We're soaked,' Baxter said with a grimace. 'Even with the umbrella.'

'It'll be a good place to dry off,' Katie said, chuckling. 'I bet loads of people have come here just to be out of the rain.'

'I'm sure they have.' He glanced at her. 'By the way, the majority of the most valuable paintings have been whisked away to some secret location as a precaution against any invasion—' He broke off. 'Don't look so alarmed, Katie. The PM seems to think that's been put on the back burner.'

A shiver ran across Katie's shoulders. That terrible word – invasion. It had such an ominous ring. It mustn't happen. Surely it wouldn't. But if it did . . . No, she mustn't think of it. Concentrate on today.

'We might discover some gems amongst those they've considered inferior and left,' Baxter added. 'So where would you like to start?'

'You lead. You know it better than I do.'

They spent an hour wandering around. Katie had been right. There was a fair crowd in every room. But somehow, with her hand in Baxter's, it didn't matter a jot as they stopped to look at paintings by artists she'd never heard of, and read descriptions of those she had, which were now mere rectangles of faded wall paint.

After an hour Baxter looked at his watch. 'I can't believe the time. It's already quarter to one. We've just got time to have a quick cup of tea. I'm afraid lunch will have to wait until after the concert because if we're any later than quarter-past, we won't get a seat.'

'That's fine. I'm not hungry yet after all that toast,' Katie said, smiling.

After their snatched cup of tea and biscuits, they had to go outside and join the queue which grew behind them. Thankfully, the rain had dropped to a drizzle but Baxter kept the umbrella up and made sure she was completely under by pulling her a little closer. Katie felt a warm glow. He liked her – she was sure of it – though he might be somewhat disconcerted if she admitted to him the strength of her own feelings.

Inside, they found two seats on the end of a central row. When they'd settled, Katie gazed around the enormous, opulent room, admiring the marble Corinthian columns, the sculptured reliefs in the semi-circular arches on either side of the main arched walkway, and the more modest marble fireplace, which she noticed was blocked up. She turned to Baxter.

'It's a beautiful room, isn't it?'

'Mmm. Beautiful.' But he wasn't looking at the architecture – he was looking directly into her eyes.

She smiled to hide her confusion.

Very quickly the room filled up with what must have been eight hundred or more people, the majority of them sitting on the floor, having brought their own cushions. At exactly half-past one, a pleasant-faced middle-aged woman, her dark shining hair elegantly coiffed, stepped onto the stage, briefly nodded at the applause, and settled herself at the piano. She turned to the audience.

'I would like to play for you Chopin's Piano Concerto Number One in E Minor – my special arrangement *without* an orchestra,' she added, smiling.

There was a soft chuckle amongst the audience. And then a hush of anticipation.

At the first notes, Katie closed her eyes. All she was aware of was the music washing over her, transporting her to somewhere magical. When it finished she turned to Baxter at the same time he looked round at her.

'I've never heard anything so beautiful,' she murmured. 'Chopin really is my favourite composer of all.'

He nodded as Myra Hess faced the audience, who were loudly clapping. She waited a few moments for it to die down.

'I love that piece,' she said. 'He wrote it when he was only twenty. I only wish we had time for me to play it for you again. But I'll finish with a slightly shorter piece from the great composer.'

'Brava,' someone called from the back of the room.

'Oh, Baxter,' Katie said, her face shining with happiness. 'Aren't we lucky?'

'Yes, we are,' he agreed. 'Incredibly so.' There was no mistaking the warmth in his eyes. He took her hand, giving it a light squeeze, then kept it firmly in his. She drew in a shaky breath. The way he was looking at her told her it wasn't only the music that he found incredible.

Then that same hush.

Myra Hess began and there was a chuckle from the audience. She caught Baxter's eye.

'The Minute Waltz,' she mouthed, and he nodded and smiled.

Taking a little longer than the title suggested, the music came to an end and the audience clapped even louder than before.

'Well, I wouldn't have missed that for anything,' Katie said as she stood up and wound her scarf round her neck. 'I'll never forget her . . . and that beautiful Chopin concerto.'

'We'll try to come again soon,' Baxter said. 'That is, if you'd like to.'

She tilted her head up and gazed at his face, taking everything in. The way his mouth quirked at one corner as though about to break into a smile. Those unusual flashes of gold in his eyes, under dark curling lashes that most girls could only dream of. The way one ear stuck out – just enough to look endearing.

'I'd love to,' she said, hearing herself sound unsteady 'She's wonderful. I simply drifted along, enjoying every single note.'

'That was exactly her intention,' Baxter said. 'I felt the same way.'

Without taking his gaze from her face, he touched her cheek lightly.

'Katie – Katharina . . . ' His voice was thick.

The air stilled between them.

'Excuse me, you two lovebirds, but some of us have to get back to work.' A woman's voice behind Katie penetrated into the precious moment as she squeezed her plump figure in front of her and Baxter.

He must have heard. Oh, how embarrassing, ran through Katie's head as she joined the queue for the exit. She could only hope he wouldn't mention it once they were outside.

But Baxter merely scanned the clouds.

'It's almost stopped raining.' He glanced at her. 'You must be starving. I know I am.'

'I could eat something,' she said honestly.

'Look, there's a Lyons' Corner House over there.' He pointed. 'And then I have another idea what to do, provided it's to your liking.'

'What is it?'

'Tell you when we're in the teashop.'

'Do you like second-hand bookshops?' Baxter asked when they were tucking into two generous slices of cheese and onion pie.

'I'm not sure I've ever been in one, but I do belong to the library.'

'Then I have a treat for you. There's a quirky little bookshop along Charing Cross Road which takes you back to Dickens's time. It's one of my favourite places.'

They quickly finished their lunch and stepped outside.

'We could do the Tube,' Baxter said, 'but now the rain's cleared we can easily walk.' He glanced down at her feet. 'You should be all right in those flat shoes.'

'As opposed to my high heels,' Katie chuckled. 'I thought I'd give them a break after wearing them all day for work.'

'Yes, I've noticed . . . and admired them.' He paused. 'And by the way, I like you in your trousers. Somehow they make you look even more feminine – if that's possible.' He grinned.

Katie basked in the compliment. It was so good to see the gold specks in his eyes no longer flashing with anger at her. In fact, he seemed to have forgotten his temper with Vernon.

At that last thought, the sun came out.

'You'd better hold my arm – just in case.' Baxter's eyes twinkled as he crooked his arm and happily she took it. 'We're looking for number 84.'

Eighty-four Charing Cross Road lived up to Baxter's description. A clanging bell announced their entrance and a smartly dressed gentleman, wrapping a parcel of books, looked up and his face creased in smiles.

'Ah, Mr Edwards. It's been quite some time since you last came to see us.'

'Yes, it must be a year at least – and this time I've brought my friend, Miss Valentine.' Baxter turned to Katie. 'Katie, this is Frank. He's in charge of this little gem of a shop.'

'I don't know about being in charge, Mr Edwards, but it's nice of you to say so.' He beamed at Katie. 'Was there anything in particular you'd like me to help you with?'

'We'll just have a browse. I wanted to introduce Katie to the shop, but I'm sure one of us will find something.'

Katie wandered to the shelves on a different wall to where Baxter was looking. This one displayed classics by authors such as Jane Austen and Samuel Pepys. She decided she'd like something a little more modern. She walked to the next section and the title of a book caught her eye: *The Enchanted April* by Elizabeth von Arnim. She sounded German. Intrigued, Katie lifted it off the shelf and looked at the frontispiece. Apparently, Miss von Arnim was a British novelist and had married a Prussian aristocrat but now lived in America. The book was about a group of friends who were bored with their lives, dying to have an adventure, and ended up in an old villa in Italy. It sounded perfect.

'Found anything?' Baxter was looking over her shoulder.

'I rather like the look of this.'

He took it from her hands.

'Oh, *The Enchanted April.* It was written in the Twenties but it's still a best-seller. Let me see this copy.' He flipped a few pages. 'It seems to have been very carefully read and I don't see any damage.' He looked at her. 'I'd like to buy it for you.'

'Oh, no, I didn't say it for you to—'

He held up his hand.

'Please, Katie. I'd like to. And what's more, I haven't read it so I'd like to borrow it after you.'

'It's very kind but—'

It was too late – he'd already gone up to the counter.

Frank, the manager, took his time packing the book in a half sheet of bright green paper, carefully tucking the ends in, then fixing them in place with a thin piece of string.

'There you are, Mr Edwards. That'll be three and six.'

Baxter fished out some coins, then put the small parcel in Katie's hand.

'A small memento to remind you of our special day in the rain,' he said, his eyes twinkling.

237

'Thank you, Baxter.' She glanced up at him, loving him, wishing she had the nerve to tell him. 'I won't ever forget.' Hiding her flushed face, she tucked the book into her shoulder bag.

They spent another twenty minutes or so in the bookshop until Katie said, 'I think we should go as I need to give Tanny his walk when we get back. '

'That's probably a good idea,' Baxter said, 'though I hate to see it end.' He smiled. 'Can we do this again?'

'Only if it pours with rain,' Katie chuckled, 'because if it's fine, it wouldn't be the same.'

'You're right.' He grinned. 'It wouldn't be nearly so challenging.'

The trains were even more crowded, with people starting to head for home before the blackout took hold. The light was going by the time they reached Wimbledon. Katie unlocked the front door to the sound of Tanny rushing towards her, his tail wagging. He barked as he caught sight of Baxter behind her, then gave his hand a good lick.

'He's showing his approval,' Katie laughed.

'I won't ask his mistress to do the same to show *her* approval,' Baxter chuckled. He glanced down at her. 'May I accompany you on your walk with Tanny?'

'Yes, we'd like that, wouldn't we, Tanny?' Katie said to the excited dog as she put his lead on. 'I'd better just go and tell them I'm back.' She handed him the lead. 'Can you wait here a moment?'

Ursula was in the drawing room reading a magazine. She looked up when she saw Katie.

'Ah, you are back,' she said. She patted a space on the sofa. 'Sit down and I will make you a cup of tea and you can tell me about your day.'

'I'm just going to take Tanny for a walk in South Park Gardens,' Katie said. 'Baxter's coming with me.'

'You have spent a long time with this young man today,' Ursula said, putting down her magazine. 'Do you not think it looks forward?'

'We're not in the Edwardian age. People don't think anything of spending a day with friends.' She paused. 'And by the way, he said he liked me in my trousers.'

'He was being polite,' Ursula said, her blue eyes gleaming. 'And I am not so sure he is only a friend.'

'Well, he is,' Katie said firmly. 'So don't make him out to be anything else.'

Baxter grinned as Tanny gave a joyous bark at being with his beloved mistress and a new friend, almost pulling her arm out of its socket as he trotted in front on the pavement.

'May I take the lead for a while?' Baxter said.

'Gladly. He's making my arm ache. You'd think the last time he went for a walk was a month ago instead of only this morning.'

'I like to see enthusiasm,' Baxter said, taking the lead and glancing down at the happy dog.

They walked along chatting about nothing in particular, then falling into companionable silence. All too soon they were back outside Katie's front door.

'I've enjoyed our day so much,' Baxter said, gazing at her. 'Pity about the weather but it turned out well in the end, didn't it?'

'Yes, it did. I enjoyed every minute.'

'Katie, I *do* like you – very much.'

'I like you, too.'

'We didn't get off to the best start, did we?' His eyes held a question.

'No, but . . .' She hesitated, wondering what was coming.

'But we're all right now, aren't we?' he said.

'Yes, we are. And I value your friendship.'

'You do?'

'Of course I do . . . very much,' she dared to add.

She watched him closely. He didn't seem quite his usual confident self. Would he kiss her? The thought swept over her so powerfully that even in the cold damp air she felt her cheeks must be pink. She looked up at him, her eyes fixed on his mouth. Those lips. How would they feel on hers? A spark flared between them. He bent towards her and took her in his arms. Her heart began to beat out of control. It was going to happen. She knew it. She felt her own lips part and her insides tingled with anticipation.

But he simply kissed her cheek and the spell was broken.

'I'd better go,' he said a little gruffly. 'Your mother will be wondering where on earth you are.'

Katie sighed as she went through to the drawing room. Maybe she was wrong – maybe Baxter liked her just as a friend. But his voice when he said he'd better go – it was as though he'd had to tear himself away. It had taken all her willpower not to blurt out that she loved him. She tried to picture his face. Would he have looked surprised or merely concerned that he didn't feel the same way? Or would he have responded in the way she longed for?

Chapter Twenty-Nine

Katie arrived at the War Rooms the following morning at quarter-past eight, not feeling her best. The curse had arrived three days early.

Typical, when it's the first day of my new job.

But it was no use grumbling. She just wished she didn't have to meet Mrs Goodman in the typing room, though she knew the girls would be pleased for her. Roz was a different matter.

'Morning, Katie,' Peggy greeted her as she stepped into the room. 'We wondered where you'd got to. Then Martha remembered you'd decided to keep your desk in the alcove, which we couldn't blame you.' She sent a pointed look in Roz's direction.

Roz didn't bother to look up, but Katie was sure she was giving her full attention to the conversation. There was no sign of Mrs Goodman and she didn't feel like hanging around while everyone else was working.

'So have you decided you missed us and are coming back to the typing pool?' Amanda said, grinning.

Darn it – no one knows I've been promoted.

Katie bit her lip. 'I'm not actually back here,' she said. 'I'm starting work for someone.'

Roz's head shot up.

'Oh. That's the first *I've* heard. Who might that be?'

'Roz, you're not in charge of this office.' Amanda didn't

241

bother to hide her irritation. 'And maybe if you stopped that accusing tone we might hear where Katie's going – if she's allowed to tell us.'

'I'll leave that to Mrs Goodman,' Katie said, not prepared to get into any trouble over any indiscretion.

'So cagey Katie is going to bigger and better places than the likes of us.' Roz's lips curled.

If you put it like that, then yes, Roz. Katie badly wanted to voice the words but she managed to hold them back. She was determined not to say anything that Roz could accuse her of.

Roz's mouth took a sulky downturn. She went back to her typing but stopped when Mrs Goodman entered.

'Good morning, girls.' Her glance fell on Katie and she smiled, then turned to the others. 'I'm sure you'll all be pleased to learn that Katie has just been offered a very prestigious position with Sir Alan Brooke as assistant to his personal secretary, Miss Nicholson.'

'Oh, well done, Katie,' Martha said, beaming. 'You deserve it.'

'Congratulations,' Peggy and Amanda said in unison. 'Nice to know you've been spotted,' Peggy added.

Mrs Goodman glanced at her watch. 'We should go, Katie. Sir Alan is always punctual and it's just coming up to eight-thirty.'

'Good luck, Katie,' her friends chorused. 'Don't forget us.'

'Good luck with the ogre,' Katie heard Roz mutter as she closed the door on them.

What was Roz on about? Who was the ogre? Sir Alan or Miss Nicholson? She hoped to goodness it wasn't the latter.

Katie's heels tapped a smart pace on the concrete floor to keep up with Mrs Goodman's sensible brogues. Mrs Goodman knocked on a door on the other side of the Chiefs of Staff room and it opened immediately. To Katie's consternation a tall, middle-aged woman stood there, erect and grim-faced.

The woman consulted her watch. 'Four minutes late. This

242

really must not become a habit. I require a hundred per cent punctuality.' Her voice was clipped as she stared at Katie. 'Miss Valentine, I presume.'

Please don't let her be Miss Nicholson. But I know she will be.

'Yes,' Katie said, 'and I'm sorry—'

'I think you'll find you're a few minutes fast, Jocelyn,' Mrs Goodman broke in mildly. 'And yes, I've brought Katharina to assist you. She's a very experienced stenographer.'

'She needs to be able to do more than simply take shorthand and type,' Jocelyn Nicholson said, still fixing her eye on Katie. 'I hope you'll be able to keep up with the vast amount of work and be accurate because Sir Alan is very particular.'

Before Katie could reply, Mrs Goodman said, 'I think you'll find her an excellent addition to the team – she is a qualified secretary.'

'I'm pleased to hear it.' Miss Nicholson jerked her head to an empty desk on a blank wall. 'You may take that desk, Miss Valentine. Set your things down, put your bedsheet up there –' she gestured to an overhead cupboard '– and we'll get cracking straightaway. We have a lot to get through and can't waste time.'

'Good. I like being busy. So please show me exactly what you'd like me to do.'

Miss Nicholson's eyes widened. Katie hid a smile. She'd bet most people were in awe of her but she was determined not to be bullied in any way. She had to work with the woman and if they didn't get on it wouldn't be *her* fault. And at least she had some experience of dealing with Roz, which would surely hold her in good stead.

'I'll leave you to it, then,' Mrs Goodman said and gave a surreptitious wink to Katie. Just that little sign cheered Katie up. It said: *Don't worry, Katie, Jocelyn's bark is worse than her bite.*

* * *

The hours flew by. Katie couldn't believe it when she looked at the time and it was already gone two. No wonder her stomach was making such a row. But Miss Nicholson, thin as a stick, seemed to live on nothing except water. Thank goodness she'd had the foresight to pack a hurried cheese sandwich this morning. She swallowed it quickly, then continued to work through a pile of typing, mostly detailed reports from the Chiefs of Staff. She'd answered Sir Alan's telephone to the best of her ability under Miss Nicholson's watchful eye and had been shown his appointment book and how to keep it, and how Sir Alan liked each appointment noted in a memo placed on his desk and not in the in-tray. There'd been no sign of him this morning but Katie felt that with all she had to take in and remember, it was just as well.

However, he appeared that afternoon. Although he was quietly spoken, and seemingly modest, Katie had the distinct feeling, as he welcomed her, of being in the presence of a very important man.

'I trust our Miss Nicholson is looking after you.'

'Yes, she's been very helpful,' Katie said blandly, aware of Miss Nicholson's ears pricking up as the woman covered a page in her notebook, her spiky handwriting matching her physique and tone of voice.

'Very good.' He paused and Katie felt his mind was thousands of miles away. Then he turned to her. 'I'm sure you'll soon get used to us.' He disappeared.

An hour later the telephone rang on Katie's desk.

'Brooke here,' he said. 'Would one of you come and take some dictation, please.'

'Yes, of course, sir.' She put the receiver down and glanced over at Miss Nicholson.

'What did he want?' Miss Nicholson demanded.

'He'd like you or me to take dictation.'

'Then you should go. He's just next door – outside and next door on the right. We're lucky that we have our own office. Most secretaries have to share with the officers they're working for.'

Katie stood and picked up her pad and pencil and knocked on his door. She waited until he called, 'Enter', and stepped in. Sir Alan was sitting at his desk rifling through some paperwork.

'Take a seat, Miss Valentine.'

'Oh, please call me Katie.'

'Right you are, Katie. I have a dozen short pieces to be dispersed in the Cabinet Room tomorrow.'

His dictation was faultless. There was very little hesitation, not too fast, and he had a clear, well-modulated voice. She had no trouble at all keeping up with him and forming her strokes so that when she came to transcribe them, there'd been no difficulty.

It was now four o'clock. She needed the Ladies'.

'Miss Nicholson, could I just nip upstairs to the lavatory?'

'Have you finished Sir Alan's work?'

'Almost.'

'Don't be long. We have plenty more to go through.'

I need to be as long as it takes to change my sanitary towel, Katie thought, as a griping pain pulled at her stomach. She snatched her handbag. Honestly, Roz hadn't been wrong – the woman was a bit of an ogre. And then the vision of Mrs Goodman giving her that unexpected wink made her smile. Her old boss would never have made light with that gesture if Miss Nicholson was that bad.

Miss Nicholson turned out to be extremely efficient and hardworking and suspicious of anyone new who might not come up to her exacting standards. *When she sees she can trust me to take on some of her heavy workload, she'll be fine*, Katie told herself each time Miss Nicholson spoke to her in an abrupt tone and scrutinised every piece of her work – even a short memo – giving a brief nod that she'd approved it. And Sir Alan was a gentleman from the top of his dark head to his highly polished shoes.

If only Aunt Judy could see me now, Katie thought, a few days later after she'd taken dictation from Sir Alan. Angrily, she bit her lip. Was she *ever* going to get out of the habit of calling her real mother her aunt? And then the thought flashed through her mind: she wasn't just angry with herself, but she was still angry with Ursula, with her father – but most of all with Judy for giving her away in the first place. How different her life would have been with her own mother and father, who must have truly loved one another once upon a time – but Judy hadn't wanted the commitment, the responsibility of bringing up a child. And Ursula had used Katie's father for convenience. Katie swallowed hard. She mustn't indulge in this misery. Glancing at her notepad, she rolled a sheet of paper into her machine to transcribe Sir Alan's message, but the marks on her shorthand pad blurred with unshed tears.

'Katie.'

Not hearing anyone come in, she started and raised her head to find Baxter staring down at her, looking so damned attractive. She tried to steady her breath. They'd not had time for more than a brief word since the concert. Thankfully Miss Nicholson wasn't due in until after lunch.

'I heard you've been promoted and I wanted to congratulate you. But you don't look very happy.' He paused and she saw concern in his eyes. 'Katie, what's the matter?'

'Oh, nothing. Families . . . you know,' she said vaguely.

'Yes, they can be difficult.' He paused. 'Do you want to tell me about it? Sometimes it's easier if you share a problem.'

'This is a problem that can never be resolved,' she said miserably.

'You might think that because you're immersed in it. I'll look at it from a different angle.'

'You don't want to hear it.'

'Yes, I do. It concerns you, so it concerns me.' He frowned. 'Tell you what – let's go out tonight – have a meal after we finish. And before you argue, this won't be a formal dinner as I know you've already turned that one down. So it'll just be a casual supper, okay?'

'You're never going to let me forget it, are you?' Katie said with a wan smile.

'No, I'm not – until you say yes. But this evening I know I'll be glad to relax a bit.' He caught her eye. 'And by the looks of things it would do you good, too. And then you can dump all your problems on me. And don't worry. My shoulders are broad – I can take it,' he finished with a grin.

She couldn't help smiling back.

'I'd like that but I'll have to ring to let them know at home.'

'There's a telephone kiosk on the way,' Baxter said. 'You can phone from there.' He glanced at his watch. 'Well, I'd better be going and get some work done if I'm off out tonight with a gorgeous blonde.' He blew her a kiss. 'Meet you outside just after seven.'

Chapter Thirty

Katie was too busy to look forward to her evening. But when it came time to pack up for the day and a frisson of anticipation shot through her that she was going to spend an evening with Baxter, Miss Nicholson, who'd been rather quiet all afternoon, suddenly said:

'Katharina, would you kindly stay and redo this report. Ben Grant, one of the Joint Intelligence chaps, needs to present it first thing tomorrow morning to Mr Churchill.' She handed Katie two foolscap sheets covered top to bottom in typing. 'The girl who did it hadn't realised it was to go on a stencil – and he needs twenty-five copies.'

Oh, not on a stencil. It would take much longer and she'd have to roll off the copies on the Gestetner as well – a messy job. She glanced at the top sheet and blinked at the typist's initials: RM. Unless she was very much mistaken it was Roz's report: Rosalind Mason. Good gracious, Roz hadn't read the instructions properly. She couldn't help a small smile as she separated the two pages. Pity Roz wouldn't know her work had had to be redone and that it was Katie who did it. She stopped herself.

You're sounding petty. Just get on with it so you can be out of here.

But she wouldn't be able to knock it out in fifteen minutes. She glanced at her watch. Already five minutes to. By the time

248

she'd finished, it would be much later than 'just after seven'. How long could she expect Baxter to wait?

'I'll stay until you finish, Katharina,' Miss Nicholson said, 'so I can check it with you before you run them off, but I've got something I need to do this very minute.' She made for the door. 'I'll be back shortly.'

'Don't worry, I'm not going anywhere,' Katie said, forcing a tired smile. It had already been a long day but it was no use grumbling. Everyone had to muck in at any time of the day or night in the War Rooms.

The tip of her tongue showing between her teeth, she concentrated on the job in front of her, pushing all thoughts of relaxing evenings to the back of her mind.

By the time Katie had finished the stencil and Miss Nicholson had checked it, and she'd run off the copies, it was quarter to eight. Katie looked down at her ink-stained fingers, from the damned Gestetner. She seized the jug of water standing by a bowl to scrub her hands, but to her dismay only a dribble came out. Wondering for the umpteenth time why no one had thought to install plumbing on the lower ground floors, she'd have to wait until she was in the restaurant. That is, if Baxter was still outside.

Almost in tears, she buttoned her coat, plonked on her hat without bothering to check it in the mirror, and ran up the spiral staircase. Stopping for vital seconds, she shoved her pass under the guard's nose, then rushed out of the building. Damn. A mist was swirling, giving a surreal look to the few people still out.

There was no sign of Baxter.

Should she wait at least five minutes? But that was pointless. He must have given up ages ago. Trying to catch her breath, she wondered what she should do. It looked as though the mist might get worse so maybe she'd better head for home. Luckily, the telephone kiosk wasn't far away so she'd ring home first and tell them she was running late. Disappointment that the evening she'd so looked forward to had literally vanished into the mist, she crossed the road and hurried towards the kiosk. Blast! Someone was already in there, making a call. She waited a couple of minutes, tapping her foot. Was he *ever* going to come out? He had his back to her so he wouldn't even know she was outside waiting. Another minute passed. She took her glove off and rapped irritably on the glass pane. The man swung round, his frown breaking into a beaming smile as he flung the receiver down and pushed open the door and stepped out of the kiosk.

'Baxter! I thought you'd given up and gone back to your digs.' A quiver of delight that they might still have an hour or two together pulsed through her, and her smile was wide as she took his arm.

'I was ringing the office to find out where you'd got to.'

'I was held up and I couldn't let you know.' She glanced up at him. 'Do you think it's too late to go out for supper?'

'No, I don't. We're both hungry and you've had a long day.' He gestured towards the kiosk. 'But should you phone your parents?'

'Yes, I think I'd better.'

Ursula answered. 'It's getting foggy so you must come home before it gets worse.'

'It's only misty here and if it gets too bad I'll go back to the office to sleep,' Katie said. At least there was always that option. 'So don't worry if I don't turn up. I'll be perfectly safe.' She hesitated. 'I'm with Baxter and we're going to have some supper first.'

'Then I will not worry if you are with him,' Ursula replied and Katie heard the receiver go down.

'Everything all right at home?' Baxter asked, when she emerged. Katie nodded. 'We'll talk as we walk.' He took her arm. 'Did Miss Nicholson keep you?'

She explained about the sudden extra work without mentioning names and he nodded.

'Yep. We can never tell from hour to hour – sometimes minute to minute – what's on the agenda. I thought it would be something like that. But I did start to get worried when it was nearly eight. I couldn't get through to the office so I was on the point of going back to see whether you'd actually left.'

A warm glow found its way round Katie's heart. He'd been worried. He'd bothered enough to try to find out where she was.

'Do you think this mist will get any worse tonight?' Katie said anxiously.

'Could do. But we need to eat. We'll go to my club. They're usually reasonably quick at serving.' He looked along the road and suddenly darted off. 'I think I've spotted a cab,' he called.

She caught up with him as the taxi stopped.

'The Royal Air Force Club,' she heard him say.

'Hop in then,' the driver said cheerfully.

Inside the dark interior, Katie was overcome by shyness. But Baxter took her hand as though it were the most natural thing in the world and she relaxed into the comfort of the leather seat.

The taxi drew outside the magnificent Regency building that was Baxter's club. A doorman stood by the entrance and Baxter gently steered her in.

She drew in a gasp of pleasure when she stepped into the long, elegant hall with its high moulded ceiling and sequence of lighted chandeliers, and a double row of aviation paintings and photographs adorning the walls. He led her through to the warmth of the carpeted reception area with its scattering of leather armchairs and a uniformed man behind the mahogany desk looked up with a welcoming smile.

'Wing Commander Edwards! Good evening.' He glanced at Katie and nodded.

'Evening, Fisher. I'm sorry I had no time to book, but can we dine?'

'You're in luck, sir. There should be a couple of spare tables but I would suggest you go straight in as the kitchen closes in twenty minutes.'

As if by magic Katie's coat and hat were whisked away with Baxter's and she was sitting opposite him in a quiet corner of the dining room. A kaleidoscope of colours from the flickering candlelight on their table danced over the silver cutlery and crystal glasses, completing the fairylike atmosphere. Momentarily, she wished she'd been able to change into an evening dress, more appropriate for the occasion, judging by the handful of women with their elaborate hairstyles, sparkling earrings and glittering necklaces at their throats.

But Baxter didn't appear to be paying them any attention. His eyes were fixed firmly on her.

'Women have only recently been allowed to come here,' he said, 'so I thought it would be a good place to bring you.'

'I'm glad you did. It's such a contrast to our daily lives at the moment where we can barely get a cup of tea from that poor little specimen of a canteen.' Her smile faded. 'It's just so wonderful to have an escape now and then.'

'An escape with *me*, I hope you mean,' Baxter chuckled.

'You must interpret it how you see fit.' She smiled back, looking at him from under her lashes.

I'm flirting with him – and it's fun.

'We'd better order before I get too carried away.' Baxter handed her a menu. 'Do you like curry?'

'I haven't ever tried it.'

'It'll be the quickest to serve. And the Old Man is a real fan of curries.' Baxter winked.

'Well, if it's good enough for whom I think you mean, then

it's definitely good enough for me.' Katie grinned, her stomach making embarrassing noises.

'We'll report to him tomorrow. I'm sure he'll be interested in our opinion.'

'I imagine he has *slightly* more important things on his mind,' Katie chuckled.

Oh, it was such fun to have silly banter instead of everything being so serious and important in the claustrophobic atmosphere of the War Rooms. Katie loved her new position and to know she was involved in something she could put her heart into, but this was heaven, relaxing and joking with Baxter in such wonderful surroundings.

'We'll have a glass of champagne while we're waiting as wine is not really the thing with a curry.'

Katie watched as the waiter poured the golden liquid into the engraved champagne saucers, the bubbles rushing to the surface.

'Good health,' Baxter said, raising his glass.

She raised her glass to his. And then she saw the state of her fingers. She put her glass down and held up her hands.

'Look at these.'

'Yes, I noticed but I didn't like to say anything in case you bit my head off.' Baxter's eyes danced with merriment.

'Well, I'm going to the Ladies' to try to wash it off,' she said.

A few minutes later she was back.

'Let me see.' Baxter took one of her hands and examined it, turning it over. 'Hmm.' He let it go and reached for the other, then looked at her, his face straight. 'Well, the stain's faded a bit, but it will take a few more scrubs and my close examination before we can say they're back to their normal loveliness.'

'At least it's proof I really *was* working,' Katie laughed, both hands now tingling from his touch.

'As opposed to meeting another bloke.' He clinked his glass with hers. 'Anyway, good luck with your new position.'

'Thank you . . . and to our victory – it can't come too soon.'

'It won't be soon,' Baxter said soberly. 'I suspect it has a few years yet left to run. The Nazis aren't going to give in.' He lowered his voice and glanced round but no one was anywhere near them. 'Trouble is, it's going too much their way at the moment and the PM is desperately trying to persuade the Americans to come in on a formal footing and not just assist from afar – valuable though that is.'

'Do you think they will?'

Baxter sighed. 'Unfortunately, Roosevelt has promised the public he won't lead them into a war in Europe which they consider has nothing to do with them. He's also suspicious about the PM's love of the British Empire, so why should he risk his soldiers' lives for something so far away that he doesn't even believe in?'

Katie felt a flutter of fear.

If the Germans keep winning more battles, maybe we'll lose the war.

She shook herself. This was *not* the way to think.

Baxter put his hand over hers. 'Let's talk about something nicer. You haven't even tried your champagne yet.'

Katie took a sip, letting the gold liquid effervesce around the inside of her mouth. Mmm. Delicious. She took another.

'It's good, isn't it?' he remarked.

'It's lovely. I'm feeling better already.'

He took a swallow, then said, 'Now, what's this family problem you mentioned?'

'Do you know, I've forgotten it.' It was true. Her stomach pains had gone and she couldn't have been happier at this moment, with the man she loved in such beautiful surroundings, being pampered.

Baxter grinned. 'That's champagne for you.'

But it isn't just the champagne, she badly wanted to say, beaming back at him.

He looked up as the waiter came forward with their curry and all the accompaniments. 'Oh, that smells wonderful . . . thank you.'

'I hope it will be to your liking, sir . . . madam.' He vanished.

'What did you do before you worked where we do now?' Katie asked when they were casually chatting.

'I was working for a map publisher. It's what I trained to do, as I've been mad about maps ever since I was a boy. And when the war started, I joined up, then was asked to work where we are today.'

'Do you ever feel hemmed in there?'

He speared a cauliflower floret on his fork.

'I do manage to get out occasionally, and in fact I'll be doing just that in a couple of weeks' time – not that it's pleasure . . . I'm off up north to a conference.'

She looked down at her bowl so he wouldn't see the disappointment on her face.

The curry was the tastiest meal she'd had since the war started. It was served with rice and yoghurt mixed with grated cucumber – 'raita', Baxter called it – together with mango chutney. Taking Baxter's cue, she mopped up the last of the spicy tamarind sauce with a warm piece of flat bread and placed her spoon in the now empty bowl. Baxter had finished several minutes ago. She looked across the table, wanting to pinch herself for being here with him in his club, able to speak without worrying about people like Roz and Louise watching and gossiping.

'Oh, I did enjoy that.'

'You really *were* hungry,' he said, giving her hand a little squeeze. He looked into her eyes. 'We needed somewhere private. Pity it got so late. We won't have as much time together as I'd have liked.'

Shame we're not here in this beautiful building for the night.

She pushed down such a dangerous thought – brazen, too. He just looked so downright attractive only three feet away. But he still hadn't even kissed her. Was it possible that he had a girlfriend already . . . or even a wife? She gulped. She knew so little about him.

'Now, Katie, tell me what the optician said.'

The question was so unexpected, Katie laughed.

'I didn't think you'd noticed.'

'Of course I noticed. I notice everything. You looked like a different woman – rather splendid. The first time I saw you in glasses I was quite in awe of you.'

'*You?* In awe of *me*?' She tapped her chest, laughing.

His mouth quirked. 'Not that the awestruck feeling lasted long,' he chuckled. 'But you only seem to need them for work. Is that right?'

'Yes, thank goodness.'

Baxter leaned over the table.

'With or without, you have the most wonderful eyes. I've never seen such a colour. You know, I call them sea-green.'

Katie held her breath. He was so near she could have bent towards him and kissed those lips. Whatever would he say if she did? She tilted a few more inches towards him and saw the gold flecks in his eyes spark.

'Katie,' he said, his voice sounding a little rough, 'I don't know if you're thinking what I'm thinking, but I want to kiss you more than anything in the world.' She blinked. He ran his fingertip along her jaw. 'What do you say to that?'

She didn't hesitate. 'I was thinking exactly the same.'

He stood up. 'Then shall we go?'

She nodded. She couldn't trust herself to speak another word.

He put the bill on his account and in moments they were on their way out, Baxter's arm around her waist, whisking her to the foyer.

'Did you and the young lady enjoy your meal, Wing Commander Edwards?' the same receptionist said as they passed his desk.

'Excellent, thank you, Fisher,' Baxter said, 'but we've just realised the time and we're due to be somewhere and have left it rather late.' He gave Katie a surreptitious wink and she tried to smother her giggles.

'I'll get your coats right away, sir.'

The receptionist was back in a trice. 'Be careful as you go,' he said, helping Katie with her coat. 'It's getting very foggy out there.' He paused. 'Would you like me to call a cab?'

'Thanks, Fisher, but it'll be quicker by Tube.'

Baxter held open the entrance door for her and Katie, letting her laughter gush out after Baxter's remark about being late, stepped outside. She stopped and gasped. The mist had turned to thick, swirling, yellow smog.

'Dear me, we've got a real peasouper,' Baxter said as he stood beside her, his shoulder brushing hers.

'What will we do?'

'Find our way to the Underground,' Baxter said. 'It's the only method of transport that won't be affected.' He crooked his arm. 'Hold on to me. I don't want to lose you now I've found you.' There was a pause. Then he added, 'Our first kiss will have to wait that bit longer but . . . '

She felt rather than saw his grin.

'. . . it will be all the sweeter for it.'

Chapter Thirty-One

It was almost midnight when Katie rang the doorbell after fumbling in her bag unsuccessfully for her keys, conscious of the nearness of Baxter on the doorstep and wondering whether they might manage their first kiss in private.

Please let Dad be the one to open the door.

She heard his heavy footsteps along the hall and then the sound of the door unbolting. Her father's head peered round the door, then opened it wide.

'Dear God, we didn't expect you to even attempt coming home in this,' he said, waving them in. 'Your mother's gone to bed saying you were staying at your office.'

'I wanted to see your daughter safely home,' Baxter said.

Her father nodded. 'Come through. I expect you could do with a drink.' He glanced at Baxter with raised brows.

'I won't, thank you, sir. I'd best be going before it gets even worse.'

'Where do you live, my boy?'

'Kensington.'

'Hmm. It's not far but you could so easily come a cropper. Bad enough with the blackout but this on top of it . . . ' He shook his head. 'No, dear boy, you go through to the sitting room . . . you'll see it . . . door's open –' he gestured vaguely down the hall '– and I'll bring you a whisky – if that's to your taste.'

'It certainly is,' Baxter began, 'but—'

'No buts.' He turned to his daughter. 'Katie, would you like something?'

'I'll make myself a cup of tea, thanks, Dad.'

She went to the kitchen and put the kettle on, all the while wondering why her father hadn't let Baxter go right away. Maybe he thought a whisky would warm him to face that ominous yellow smog again.

She took her cup of tea through to the drawing room in time to hear Baxter's voice.

'I really couldn't take advantage of your hospitality but thank you for the offer.'

Katie stopped in her tracks. She didn't realise she was holding her breath.

'Not a bit,' she heard her father say. 'I wouldn't dream of sending you out in this. My wife would never forgive me. No, we have spare rooms here and she always keeps the beds aired.'

Katie pushed the already half-open door.

Baxter turned. 'Katie, your father's insisting I stay the night. Would you be all right with that?'

She felt the warmth rise to her neck. Attempting indifference, she said, 'That might be wise with the weather like it is.'

'There you are,' Oscar said. 'You have my daughter's permission.' He stood up and took Baxter's empty glass. 'I'll get you a top-up.'

'In that case, I accept,' Baxter said, throwing Katie a look almost of apology.

Her father sat with them, seeming to enjoy another man's company. One moment Katie wanted him to go, the next she inwardly begged him not to leave Baxter alone with her. But after a while, he gave a deep yawn and looked at his watch.

'I'll be going then. Switch off the lamps, love, won't you? I've locked up already.' He kissed the top of her head as he passed her chair.

When he'd disappeared, Baxter said, 'Are you sure you don't mind, Katie?'

She feigned surprise. 'Of course I don't. I'm glad he invited you to stay. I would have worried if you'd gone out in that.'

'Would you really?' Baxter's expression was unfathomable.

Katie looked at him directly.

'Yes. I would.' She couldn't take her eyes off his face. 'You know I would.'

'Then come over here.'

He stood and held out his arms. She walked straight into them as though it were the most natural occurrence in the world. He folded her to him, kissing her cheek, her hair, her forehead. She drank in the scent of him – musky, the not unpleasant odour of his last cigarette, the maleness of him.

She inched away and looked up at him, an ache of longing for him – all of him.

'You said you wanted to kiss me in the restaurant – so will you please do so right now.' The tone of her voice sounded strange to her ears: half pleading, half demanding.

'You mean like this?' he murmured against her lips.

She closed her eyes. Felt the firmness of his lips on hers, then softening with the fullness of his mouth . . . she parted her lips . . . his kiss deepened . . . she felt his tongue. Her senses reeled. She heard him groan.

'Just like that,' she said, breathless, when they finally drew apart. 'In fact, you did it so well, I'd like a repeat . . . if that's all right with you, of course,' she added with a grin.

His answer was in his next kiss.

He guided her to the sofa and sat her down, then pulled her to his chest. She put her hand up to let her fingers wander over his face, hardly believing this was happening.

'You know I've fallen in love with you, don't you?' he said.

She hadn't prepared herself for this moment in case she

tempted fate. Gazing at him, she saw the pupils of his eyes were dilated.

'You *do* know, don't you?' he persisted.

'I wasn't sure.'

'Are you now?'

'Yes . . . I think so.'

'I want you to *know* so.'

He held her gaze, his eyes feeling to her as though he were looking into her soul.

'When did you know for certain?' She kept her eyes fixed to his.

'When I saw you in your dressing gown and those ridiculous pipe-cleaners, with a shiny face and the most captivating eyes I'd ever seen.'

'Now you're being silly.' She nudged his arm to emphasise her words.

'I'm not . . . it's true. I thought you looked adorable. And you were so cross with me, those eyes were flashing daggers.'

'Well, you irritated me. I thought you were the most bad-mannered, arrogant, cocky—'

'Hang on,' he interrupted, showing the palm of his hand. 'I know all those good traits so tell me now what my bad ones are.'

He chuckled and Katie burst into giggles.

'And now, Miss Valentine, perhaps you'd like to let me in on *your* feelings.'

'I'll have to think about it . . .' She let the moments drip away. 'All right, you want to know the truth.' She felt his body tense. 'Well, I happen to have fallen in love with you, too.'

'That's what I was waiting to hear.' He kissed her swiftly on the lips. 'But it sounds so wonderful now you're saying it.' He gazed at her. 'So when did you know for sure, my darling?'

She felt a quiver of joy at his endearment.

'Katie?'

She frowned, pretending to think back. 'Let me see . . . was it . . . no . . . it must have been—'

'You know *exactly* when it was – same as me – when I appeared at the top of the stairs and you realised you'd met the man of your dreams – same moment as I knew I'd met the woman of my dreams . . . once she'd got her curlers out, that is.'

She laughed. 'That's not how it was with me at all. It was quite a bit later. I think it was when you were so kind and helped me with my shorthand speed and I began to know you better.'

'Ah, the slow burn that can suddenly turn to passion.' He swept her into his arms again and this time his lips were burning with desire, and she kissed him back with the same fierce intensity.

'It's nearly one o'clock,' Baxter said, glancing at his watch, which glowed greenly in the dark. 'Your father will be wondering what's happened to us, so I think we should go to our separate rooms before I start thinking things I shouldn't.' He kissed her forehead. 'And talking about your father, what's your mother going to say when she comes down in the morning and finds me in the house?' He looked directly at her. 'Will she think the worst?'

Her nerve endings tingled at the implication. *If only* . . . She moistened her lips. Tried to make herself come back to the real world. She took a breath.

'I have no idea, but the good thing is that they both like you.'

A smile split Baxter's face in two.

'Then we're halfway there,' he murmured.

She didn't want to part from him on the landing.

'You don't *have* to go to your room,' he whispered.

'You know I do.'

'If you get scared in the night you can knock on the wall. That's all there is between us.'

'And it's going to stay right where it is,' she said, giving him a little shake, then dragging herself out of his arms.

Baxter gave a deep sigh. 'All right, my love, you win.' He kissed the top of her head. 'Night night, my darling.'

'Night night, Baxter. Sleep tight.'

The second she opened her bedroom door and stepped inside, she missed him. Missed his strong arms around her. Missed his slightly crooked smile. Missed that mouth that made her feel hungry for more. For a mad moment she wondered if he might knock softly on the door when he thought she was in bed.

If he did, what would she do?

She mustn't think like that. He was in her parents' house. And anyway, Baxter was too much of a gentleman. Tanny broke her thoughts by leaping out of his basket. He licked her hand, giving whimpers of pleasure at seeing his mistress.

'Yes, Tanny, I know you want my attention,' she laughed as she bent to kiss the top of his head and ruffle his ears.

He would certainly have something to say if Baxter suddenly marched into the room and climbed into her bed.

Smiling at the image, Katie splashed her face with water in her bedroom sink, dabbing it with her flannel. She quickly brushed her teeth and without bothering to cream her face or curl her hair, she pulled on her pyjamas and slid under the covers. Ursula had changed her bed that morning and Katie relished the feel of the crisp sheets. Whatever her stepmother's faults, she was a marvellous housekeeper, Katie admitted, as she sank her head into the pillow. Breathing rhythmically, her body calmed as she thought of Baxter so very near, telling her he was in love with her. She couldn't help grinning in a ridiculous way because she'd never felt so happy. For the first time in weeks she immediately fell asleep.

A gentle tap on the door and Tanny's answering bark jolted Katie awake. She glanced at the clock. Twenty to eight! It couldn't be. She never slept this late. This time the tap was firmer. Ursula telling her she was getting late. Katie threw on her dressing gown and opened the door, whereby Tanny shot past, nearly knocking her over, and flew downstairs.

Instead of Ursula it was Baxter who stood there holding a large tray. The smell of toast wafted into her nostrils and she was suddenly hungry.

'Your breakfast, madam.' He grinned, walking over to her bedside table and making space for the tray. He gave her a swift kiss on her lips. 'If you want breakfast in bed you'll have to get back in.'

'What a treat,' she said, hopping back into bed. 'I think the last time this happened was when I was a child with tonsillitis.' She glanced at the tea-tray. It was all there. Pot of tea, two cups and saucers, milk, sugar cubes, two plates of buttered toast spread thinly with marmalade. 'Is Mother up already?'

'No, your father. He'd just made the tea and asked if I'd like to join him. But I asked if I could take you a cup of tea first and he made the tray up for both of us, so it seems I've gained his permission to enter your room.' He sent her a mischievous wink. 'Am I allowed to sit on the bed?'

'If you can balance.'

She watched as he poured their tea, loving the shape of his hands, remembering how they felt when he'd caressed her. Her stomach fluttered.

'Sugar?' Baxter asked her.

'No, I gave it up when it was rationed last year.'

'Forgive me if I indulge.' He dropped two cubes in his cup and stirred.

'Did you sleep all right?' she asked.

'On and off. I kept thinking how close you were, but not close enough.'

She felt herself flush and bent her head to her cup so he wouldn't notice.

'What about you?'

She glanced up. He was looking at her intently. Then he grinned and took a handkerchief from his pocket.

'Allow me,' he said, wiping a crumb from the corner of her mouth.

'I should have a bib,' she laughed, hoping he'd forget what he'd asked. But he didn't.

'Did *you* sleep?'

He was watching her expression. She couldn't fib.

'I did at first. Then an hour later I woke up.'

He raised a dark eyebrow. 'Any particular reason?'

'Probably not much different from yours.'

He took her empty cup and saucer, brushing her hand before he set them back on the tray, then placed his own with hers.

'You should have joined me.'

'It would have been too dangerous,' she retorted, half joking, half serious.

'We're living dangerously already, Katharina.' He was still gazing at her.

She loved how he sometimes used her full name. Then he gave that lopsided smile that turned her to liquid.

'And now, my darling, I want to do one of my favourite things . . . are you ready?'

'For you to kiss me?'

He nodded.

'Yes, I'm always ready for that.'

His kiss tasted of oranges. Ursula's homemade marmalade.

'I suppose I must let you go.' Baxter's tone was heavy with reluctance. He kissed the tip of her nose.

'What's the time?'

'Just gone eight.'

She shot up.

'Goodness. I'm never this late getting up. Good job I'm not on until two o'clock.'

'Me, too. But I have an appointment at No. 10, which is just as well. It would start the gossips again if we made an appearance together.' He gave her a rueful smile, kissed her forehead and picked up the tray.

'Will you be back at the office later?'

'Yes, but I don't know exactly when.'

She hesitated. 'Baxter, if Mother starts to—'

'Don't worry – your father has made me more than welcome and I'm sure your mother will be fine about my staying.' He grinned. 'It was an emergency, after all, but for the first time ever I'm thanking that peasouper. It gave us the chance to be alone together.'

Katie was singing the first verse of a popular song of the moment, as she hurried down the spiral staircase to the Cabinet War Rooms.

'*You made me love you, I didn't wanna do it, I didn't wanna do it . . . You made me—*'

Just as she turned into the main corridor she ran smack into the Prime Minister, who took a step back, his forehead heavily creasing.

'*No* whistling, humming or *singing* down here, Miss whoever-you-are. I need absolute quiet when I'm thinking. Pray do not let it happen again.'

His stern tone took her by surprise.

'I'm sorry, sir, I forgot.'

Oh, why did it have to be him of all people?

'There are plenty of signs to remind you.' He pointed to one with his stick.

'I know, sir. It won't happen again.'

'Make sure it doesn't.'

She bit her lip. Oh, dear, one black mark against her. She wouldn't forget Mr Churchill's irritable expression in a hurry.

Chapter Thirty-Two

Damp November nudged its way into cold December. Every day was colder than the one before. Few trees had kept their leaves – not that Katie kept an eye on the changes as there were no windows to look out on, buried as she was in the bunker, as she'd heard Baxter call it. And when she did emerge into the outside world yawning and blinking from the artificial lights and the strain of typing hour upon hour, she hardly had time to notice her surroundings. All she could think of was getting home in the warm and into her lovely bed. Nowadays, she was typing reports from several of the most senior members of the Cabinet and so far – touch wood – she hadn't had to redo any of her work. Sometimes she worried it was going too well. Miss Nicholson had stopped looking over her shoulder and had even complimented her on her neat work from time to time. High praise indeed, Katie thought, a wry smile touching her lips.

She and Baxter had managed to go out to dinner twice and even squeezed in another lunchtime concert to hear Myra Hess play Mozart this time. And last night, a Saturday, Baxter had booked tickets for *Me And My Girl* at the theatre. Katie had laughed at him for half dancing and singing one of the tunes on their way to the Underground but had joined in, thinking how well their voices blended. She'd told him so.

He'd roared with laughter.

'I can't hold a note in tune,' he said. 'I wasn't even allowed to sing in the school choir.'

'I thought you were harmonising,' she chuckled. 'That's what it sounded like anyway.'

He caught her to him and kissed her right there in the middle of the pavement.

'Oh, how I love you,' he said, stepping into the road to avoid two women taking up most of the path.

'Look where yer goin', mister,' bawled a young lad, swerving his bike so as not to run him over.

'Sorry, mate,' Baxter had called after him.

Katie's mouth curved in amusement as she remembered Baxter's exuberance. For once the phone had been quiet and there had been few interruptions. Sir Alan was away for the day on meetings with the Chiefs of Staff, even though it was a Sunday, leaving her and Miss Nicholson to carry on with their work almost undisturbed.

Katie was conscious her fingers were flying over the keys more rapidly than her new boss, and that the pile in her out-tray grew faster. It wasn't that she was being competitive, but it did give her a sense of satisfaction that she could keep up with the flow of work.

She was relieved at the thought of spending a quiet evening at home and then in her own bed with a comfortable mattress for a change after so many nights on those dreadful cots.

She put the key in her front door hoping it wouldn't be another awkward evening of conversation. But before she could step inside, Tanny rushed through the hallway and stood up on his hind legs almost knocking her over. Immediately, her tension ebbed away at her dear dog's enthusiastic greeting and she couldn't help smiling as she patted his head.

'Have you been a good boy today?'

Her answer was the dog's rough tongue giving her a good lick on her hand. He followed her through to the dining room where Ursula had laid out the supper and her father was already tucking in.

'How's work going?' her father asked.

'I think they're quite happy with me – I hope so anyway.'

'I'm sure they are.'

Ursula was silent as she ate her supper, looking up now and again to glance at her stepdaughter. Katie knew she should chat to her but ever since the 'great deception' as she called it to herself, she found it difficult to be natural. She heaved a sigh. What a mess it all was.

'We'll listen to the nine o'clock news,' Oscar said when she and Ursula had cleared the table and washed up and the three of them were in the sitting room.

'I do not want to hear any more news,' Ursula said emphatically. 'It is all terrible.'

'We must keep up with it,' Oscar said, 'though I imagine Katharina knows far more about what's happening than us, being closer to the war effort.' He glanced at Katie. 'Is that right, love?'

'I can't say. We're warned not to even read newspapers because they can sometimes get their facts wrong.'

Ursula left the room just before the news was about to come on. Oscar switched on the wireless. On the stroke of nine came the velvet voice of the newsreader.

'This is Frank Phillips at BBC London. Here is the nine o'clock news.' He paused a second or two and proceeded to describe some of the happenings on the Russian front and on the British front in Libya. He then went on to mention that the Japanese had attacked the American shipping at Hawaii and also British ships in the Dutch East Indies.

Her father jerked his head up, with a sharp intake of breath,

270

but didn't say anything. When the news bulletin was finished he got up and switched off the wireless.

'Well, we expected the Japs to give *us* a run sooner or later, but they've gone for America at the same time. I just hope the Americans were ready for them and gave them a flea in the ear.' He took a few puffs on his pipe. 'Fighting on two fronts is dangerous and the Japs are going to use up a vast number of troops.' He looked thoughtful. 'But going for America –' he turned to Katie '– might be the answer to Churchill's prayers – depending, that is, on how much of a surprise it was for the US Navy and how much damage they inflicted. If the US Navy was caught napping, they'll be furious. And that might well bring America into the war on our side.' He looked at her with a wry smile. 'You're bound to be one of the first to hear more details about it tomorrow.'

Her father's comments were still running through Katie's mind at noon the following day when she was setting out everyone's places in the Cabinet Room, later than usual since one of the junior members of staff had stopped by her desk to tell her the meeting would be delayed until 12.30 p.m. It must be because of the Japanese attack on an American island. There was definitely a strange atmosphere of expectancy now the room was starting to fill up. She hurried round checking the usual notepads and sharpened pencils and ashtrays were in place, and a number of square red tins bearing the words: Cigarette Ends.

All of a sudden the murmuring of chatter stopped. Everyone looked towards the door as Mr Churchill entered with Sir Alan and two others she didn't recognise. Dear God, she should have left the room by now. It was too late. But it was a private meeting so how could she push past everyone without causing a scene? Mr Churchill would be furious. Her knees buckled. She couldn't have moved even if she'd wanted to. The Prime Minister nodded for everyone to be seated as he sat down himself. She was still standing and directly in his sight. She had to escape. But just as she gathered her courage, Mr Churchill shot up from his chair. She was trapped! He caught her eye and held up his hand, flapping it down, motioning for her to sit. With relief, she drew in a jerky breath as she felt the hard seat under her bottom.

She stole a glance at the Prime Minister. His features looked drawn with exhaustion, yet his expression was jubilant as he began pacing up and down. There wasn't a sound, not even a murmur. No one fidgeted. All eyes were on him. Her scalp tingled as she listened to his words.

'I have come from Downing Street,' he began, 'to tell those who may not yet have heard the news that last night Japan attacked the United States port of Pearl Harbor in Hawaii.' He paused and his eyes swept round the room, seeming to alight on every single person. 'Last night I spoke to President Roosevelt on the Atlantic telephone when I heard this news and asked if it were true. The President assured me it was and said: "We are all in the same boat now." I told him that the Japanese High Command had at the same time declared a state of war on Great Britain. And that tomorrow morning – that is, this morning in the Cabinet – I said I would authorise an immediate declaration of war on Japan.' He took a puff on his cigar. 'This next bit is not to be included in any written report –' to her consternation, his glance fell on Katie '– but you can all imagine how grateful I am to the Japanese, because at last it will bring the Americans into the war – making victory a certainty with their resources and manpower.'

There was a unanimous roar of delight. The Prime Minister's chubby face broke into a triumphant grin.

It was strange being grateful to the Japanese considering they were very much the enemy, Katie thought, though she wondered why Mr Churchill hadn't seen fit to mention the Japanese attacking the British ships in the Dutch East Indies. She supposed it was far less significant.

Thankfully, at an appropriate pause she made her escape as quickly and quietly as she could to her office. To her relief, no one was there. Good. She'd had enough excitement for one morning.

It was the afternoon by the time Miss Nicholson appeared, her expression stern. Katie's heart beat faster. *Here it comes.* She gave Katie a searching look.

'Apparently, you didn't leave the Cabinet Room before the PM arrived.' Her eyes remained fixed on Katie. 'You know that's against the rules.'

'I do know and I'm sorry.'

'Why on earth did you leave it so late?'

Katie's heart thumped.

'They said the meeting wouldn't start until 12.30 and Mr Churchill arrived at ten past. I just wasn't expecting him and he suddenly turned up.' She tried to appeal to her boss. 'He's usually late, if anything.'

Miss Nicholson snorted. 'Well, he wants a secretary. He asked for Louise but before I could tell him she was on an early shift today and has already gone home, he'd put the phone down. So I'm sending *you* in her place.' She blew out her breath through pursed lips, shaking her head. 'I can't say I'd want to be in your shoes right now, Katharina,' she added, as though for good measure.

Katie nervously bit her lip. This was getting worse by the minute. She'd heard many rumours about how difficult it was to take dictation from him. And he was bound to pull her over the coals for not leaving the Cabinet Room in time. Not only that, but her last encounter with him had also been a disaster.

He'd told her off in no uncertain terms about her singing and disturbing him. Maybe she'd be dismissed. Oh, she couldn't. It would be too awful . . . to embarrassing . . . too humiliating . . .

Then she gathered her wits. *It's what I've been aiming for right from when I started here. To do some secretarial work for Mr Churchill. For goodness' sake don't muff this opportunity when it's been handed to you on a plate, girl!*

'Katharina! The PM wants you *right away*.'

She leapt to her feet and snatched her shorthand notepad.

'Sorry, Miss Nicholson. Yes, of course. I'll go now.' She glanced at her boss. 'Where will I find him?'

'In his bedroom,' Miss Nicholson said with a tight smile.

Chapter Thirty-Three

Katie had always assumed the Prime Minister went to his quarters at No. 10 at night – or more likely the early hours of the morning. But of course he'd have a bedroom down here, she thought, her heart fluttering as she walked swiftly along the main corridor. After all, she'd spotted Mrs Churchill's bedroom. When she arrived outside what she hoped was the right door, there was only a notice stating: STRICTLY PRIVATE. She'd passed it dozens of times, on the other side of his private lavatory, but she'd never known until now that it was Mr Churchill's bedroom and not merely another office. Taking a deep breath, she gave a sharp knock.

'Come in,' came the gravelly voice.

She opened the door and immediately took a step back. Her eyes widened in disbelief. Mr Churchill was sitting upright in a single bed wearing a bright-red piece of shiny material draped around his shoulders, looking perfectly relaxed. His usual red box of the day's important documents and messages was open on the bedspread, papers scattered around him, a tray pushed to one side holding an empty tumbler and a champagne flute, and an unlit cigar clenched between his teeth. His outfit was the only colour in the dull, grey room. When he caught sight of Katie his expression tightened.

'Where's Miss Chalmers?'

Katie swallowed. 'She's on the early shift, so she's gone home, sir.'

'That's who I requested.' He flapped an arm. 'I don't like new faces.' His expression was that of a sulky schoolboy as he poured himself a drink from a bottle of whisky on his bedside table.

'Oh, I'm not really new, sir.' It was useless to pretend otherwise. 'You've spoken to me two or three times.'

Surely, he must recognise her. She waited, hardly daring to take a breath.

'Have I?' He glared at her, then thrust his head forward. 'Remove your spectacles.'

She did as she was told.

'Ah, yes,' he said with a note of triumph. '*Now* I recognise you. You were causing a disturbance by singing in the corridor the other day, contrary to my orders which are clearly marked all over the place.'

'I'm sorry, sir. I told you it wouldn't happen again. I was just happy and forgot myself.'

'Hmm. It sounds as though there's a man involved.'

Immediately, she felt her face redden. He was more insightful than she would have imagined – or liked.

'And I believe it was *you* who left it too late to leave this morning.'

Katie gulped. 'I'm sorry, sir, I—'

'No matter. You'll make yourself scarce the next time.'

'Yes, of course.'

He suddenly changed direction.

'What experience have you?'

'I'm assisting Miss Nicholson and sometimes I take dictation directly from Sir Alan.'

'Ah.' He grunted as he sank back into the abundance of pillows. 'We'd better try you out, then. But I warn you, I don't allow any mistakes.' He ran his hand over his thinning crown.

It was all very well taking down shorthand for any of the higher-ranking officers, but for Winston Churchill himself . . . was she good enough? She'd heard rumours that his dictation was nowhere near as smooth as Sir Alan's. She drew in a deep breath, set her jaw. Of course she was good enough.

'I'll do my very best, sir.'

'Let us both hope your best is good enough.' He flapped his arm. 'Come and sit over here on this chair.'

She must be in a dream. How could this possibly be Katie Valentine, trying to look as though she took dictation from the most important man in the country in his bedroom every day as part of her routine. She stepped over to the Prime Minister's bed, which was beneath a wall map of the world, and took the upholstered dining-room chair he'd indicated, then sat and crossed her legs. As she flipped open her notepad, she stole a glance at him. His spectacles had slipped down his nose, the shiny red material was parted at the edges showing his striped pyjamas and a few grey hairs poking out at the base of his neck. His hair was standing up in spikes since he'd raked it through, and he wore an expression of mild irritation – such a different picture from his performance just a few hours ago in the Cabinet Room, when exuberance oozed from every pore and she'd never been aware of someone so alive.

'You've caught me after my nap,' he said, eerily reading her thoughts. His tone was as though she'd been the one to interrupt him.

'I'm sorry, sir.'

'No, no, I need to get through my work. Vital work.' He threw her a glare. 'Shorthand!' he barked.

Katie thanked the stars that he stopped to light his cigar, grumbling when it didn't take first time. But it gave her time to compose herself. To stop her hand holding the pencil from trembling with . . . was it excitement – or fear?

277

'Letter to the King . . . letter to the King,' he announced in a voice quivering with exhilaration.

Kitty's heart somersaulted. The King himself would read something she'd typed. It was almost too much to take in that she was privy to something the two most important people in Britain would discuss. Probably she'd be almost the only one in the War Rooms to know about this letter. A burden she wasn't used to descended upon her shoulders like a cloak and she prayed she wouldn't make any errors. She mustn't. By the look of him he would never give her another opportunity.

Finally, Mr Churchill was satisfied with his cigar. He cleared his throat and looked at her, a crafty smile on his lips.

'I have to ask the King's permission to leave the country.'

Did that smile mean that whether the King gave his permission or not, there'd be no stopping him? Mrs Goodman had once hinted how the PM loved travelling, but to fly in the face of the King's orders – literally, well, really . . .

Without warning, Mr Churchill flung back the bedcovers, causing some papers to flutter to the floor as he hauled his bulky torso to the edge of the bed and placed his feet into a pair of velvet slippers. He stood and pulled his arms impatiently through the red silky material that she saw now was an oriental dressing gown. When he turned his back towards her, she had to smile at the outrageous green and gold dragon embroidered there.

She bent to pick up the papers and put them neatly back on the bed. Mr Churchill took no notice and began muttering as he paced the floor, the cords of his extravagant dressing gown trailing behind him. She startled. Was he actually dictating? Dear God, she was just sitting there poised ready. She hadn't written a thing.

'Excuse me, sir, but—'

He lurched to a stop and frowned.

'What is it, Miss Valentine?'

'I was wondering if you were already dictating.'

'No. I will tell you when I'm ready.'

His abrupt tone made her sit up straight. He'd think she wasn't up to the job if she interrupted again.

'Well, Miss Valentine, we will start.' More throat-clearing. 'Your Majesty, I have formed the conviction that it is my duty to visit Washington without delay, provided such a course is agreeable to President Roosevelt as I have little doubt it will be, and I must ask for your royal approval to cross the Atlantic immediately in light of the attack on the American port, Pearl Harbor, in Hawaii yesterday.'

She swallowed hard. Was she the first person to learn that the PM was secretly planning to go to America to visit President Roosevelt? A quiver of excitement prickled her spine. She pulled her lips tightly together as though to guard the precious secret right here in Mr Churchill's bedroom. She'd pretend to herself that it was all a dream when she was back at her desk.

'Read it back!'

The Prime Minister's bark made her jump. She collected herself and read the sentence back. He nodded. 'I should arrive . . . let me see . . .' Katie waited. 'I am prepared to leave the day after tomorrow and should arrive –' he chewed on his cigar '– well, I don't know at the moment when that will be – it's according to whether I sail or fly,' he mumbled. 'And I don't know at this stage how long I'll be gone – maybe a fortnight, maybe longer. I'll be as long as it takes . . . who knows.'

Was she supposed to take all that down? She just hoped she'd be able to work it out when she started typing what he was muttering to himself and what he wanted to relate to the King.

'I await your reply.' He glanced at Katie. 'Then the usual valediction.'

Dear God, how was she supposed to know what that was?

Katie squeezed her eyes shut for a second, ready to ask him, but he'd already started talking again.

'We must write a memo to Ismay with instructions as to who will be travelling with me and to make arrangements to put this into operation without delay.'

Katie took down the dictation, which stopped and started while Mr Churchill paused to consider who would accompany him. She didn't always recognise the names but hoped her outlines would give her clue enough to ask Miss Nicholson. She certainly wasn't going to ask the Prime Minister.

When he'd finished, he jerked his head towards a large office desk on the other side of the room stacked with several telephones, a brass lamp with a movable green shade and a typewriter.

'You may type it all while you're here and I can then have it without delay.'

'Excuse me, Mr Churchill . . .'

He looked at her. 'Well?'

'I'm not sure how you like to sign off a letter to the King.'

'Your Majesty's faithful and devoted servant, Winston Churchill,' he replied irritably.

'Thank you, sir.'

She'd be even more nervous if he did what she suspected and looked over her shoulder. To her surprise he sat on the edge of his bed and continued to read his paperwork. She gave a sigh of relief when she'd finished and read them both through, hoping against hope she'd spelt those names correctly, and handed them to him.

With a fleshy hand he took them. She waited for his smile of approval. But to her horror his face contorted with anger.

'Double spacing!' he bellowed at her. 'I always have everything *double-spaced*.'

Katie's chest constricted.

'I-I'm awfully sorry, sir. No one told me. I didn't—'

'Type them again,' he roared. 'Double-spaced.'

He didn't need to repeat it. She'd got the message loud and clear.

'Yes, sir. And I promise I'll remember next time.'

'And the "and" in "faithful and devoted" should be an ampersand.'

'I'll put that right, sir.'

'And you've spelt "harbour" wrong in Pearl Harbor.'

She glanced at the carbon copy. No, it was correct.

'H-a-r-b-o-u-r,' she spelt out.

'No "u",' he barked. 'That's the way the Americans spell it.'

Katie inwardly groaned. How was she supposed to know that? What more was he going to spot?

'I'll remove it, sir.'

Sick to her stomach, Katie went back to the typewriter, blinking back the tears. No, she would *not* break down in front of him of all people. He'd assume it was women's tears just to get round him. She gritted her teeth as she pulled the carriage sideways to set it for double spacing. If only Miss Nicholson had warned her that he liked even personal letters to be double-spaced. He certainly had a temper but she supposed with all that was on his mind, it wasn't surprising when something didn't go right. What she had to do now was concentrate on retyping the letters without making a single mistake and escape from his bedroom as soon as she possibly could.

'On second thoughts,' Mr Churchill's voice made her jump, 'leave it like it is. That's how we British spell "harbour".'

For the next hour, as Katie amended the errors, all that she could hear was Mr Churchill drawing on his cigar, quietly muttering as he strode up and down the room. And after what seemed like an eternity of being in the Prime Minister's private bedroom, she was finished. Rolling out the last sheet she scanned it for any errors, heart beating hard. Nothing there that shouldn't be. For an instant she forgot who was in the room and heaved a sigh.

Immediately, a gruff voice floated over.

'What was that for?'

She twisted her head round.

'Oh, nothing, sir.' She rose to her feet and handed him the papers, then waited.

'Hmm. All seems to be in order.' He reached for a beautiful gold pen and signed, then handed them back. 'Get these off straightaway. Miss Nicholson will tell you where to send them.' He gave her a fierce look. 'That will be all.'

'Thank you, Prime Minister.'

He couldn't have made himself clearer that he wanted to be rid of her.

Still smarting, Katie shot out of the room, quietly closing the door behind her. If only there was a proper cloakroom she could visit. Just to sit for a while to compose herself. But there was no private space unless she went upstairs, and she was in enough trouble as it was, without aggravating the situation by not getting these important letters and memo off immediately, as Mr Churchill had instructed.

'You look rather flushed,' Miss Nicholson said when Katie was back in the office to report to her. 'I suppose he gave you a good dressing down.'

Katie shook her head. 'No, he just warned me to make myself scarce the next time.'

'Oh, I'm surprised.'

She looks almost sorry I got off lightly, Katie thought, amused, when at one time she knew she would have been irritated.

'But he did say he'd asked for Louise to take dictation.'

'Yes, he would,' Miss Nicholson said knowingly. 'He hates new faces and is never happy about it.'

'But even people he's familiar with had to start off as fresh faces the first time they did any work for him.'

'That's true, of course. But I should have warned you not to take any notice. He can get very grumpy and even fly into a temper over the smallest thing, but we all make allowances because of his enormous responsibilities.' She paused. 'Well, at least we'll have America on our side now. That was what he's always longed for.'

'He's asked me to give you this telegram to send to the King and says it's urgent.'

Miss Nicholson scanned it and nodded.

'Yes, I'll get that sent right away.' She disappeared.

Katie went to her desk and thankfully for the rest of the afternoon there were no further demands from a certain bedroom for a stenographer.

Chapter Thirty-Four

The following morning Sir Alan stepped into Miss Nicholson's office.

'How did everything go with the PM?' He glanced at Katie, his expression one of concern.

Has Mr Churchill told him not to send me ever again?

Katie swallowed and crossed her fingers behind her back, grateful that Miss Nicholson was out of the office.

'Yes, I think everything was all right.'

'He didn't say anything about you not leaving the Cabinet Room on time?'

This was what she was dreading.

'Um, he mentioned it, but just told me not to let it happen again.'

Sir Alan nodded. 'He can be extremely brusque when any small detail goes wrong, but when something is much more important, he tends to play it down.' He gave a rueful smile. 'At any rate, he wants to see you and I couldn't tell from his tone if that was a good or a bad sign, but I warn you he's not dressed yet.'

She didn't bother to tell him he'd been in bed yesterday so at least this morning she was prepared.

Filled with trepidation, Katie knocked on Mr Churchill's door. When she'd been told to enter, she opened the door to find him sitting on the edge of the bed, this time enveloped in an enormous towel. To her surprise his cherub face was lit by an appealing smile like a contrite schoolboy who's not done his homework.

'Sorry I was cross yesterday. Had a lot on my mind.'

His apology was so unexpected that she was startled.

'We'll have another go, shall we?' he said before she could answer. 'I have an important message to send and it has to go by wire.'

She opened her shorthand pad and held her pencil in readiness.

He glanced at her. 'Pray do not forget to double-space.'

'In my notepad as well, sir?' Keeping her face straight, she raised the pad a few inches for him to see.

There was a silence.

Dear God, that silly quip had slipped out from nowhere. She'd gone too far. Her cheeks felt they were on fire. He'd think she was being sarcastic and he wouldn't like it one bit.

'Maybe not,' he grunted. 'We're short of paper as it is with the war on. Just be sure you remember when you're typing it.' Then he grinned and his small eyes twinkled.

'Oh, I will, sir.' She smiled back at him, her heart lighter.

'Now, where were we? Oh, yes. To the President. We're sending a telegram to the President. Mark it in capitals: MOST SECRET. My dear Mr President . . .'

He stopped and puffed on his cigar. It wasn't an unpleasant smell. He shifted his position. She prayed he wouldn't suddenly stand up and his towel fall . . . What on earth would she do? Pretend she hadn't noticed anything out of the ordinary?

'Now that we are, as you say, in the same boat, would it not be wise for us to have another conference? We could review the whole war plan in the light of reality and new facts, as well as the problems of production and distribution.'

285

He paused to chew on his cigar and half stood. Katie froze. *Dear God, please make Mr Churchill sit down.*

Katie bit back a grin. He must have heard the godly voice from above and felt the towel slip because he hitched it up and said most politely:

'Will you please pass me my dressing gown?'

Relieved, she rushed over and picked up the red silky bundle.

'Thank you, Miss Valentine. Now you must look the other way.' Seconds later, he said, 'It's all right. I'm decent.' And in the same breath, 'Where were we? Oh, yes, reviewing new facts.' He muttered to himself as he walked up and down, then nodded to Katie that he was about to start dictating again. 'I feel that all these matters, some of which are causing me concern, can best be settled on the highest executive level. It would also be a great pleasure for me to meet you again, and the sooner the better.' More puffs. 'I propose to leave in a day or two and come by warship and to bring certain members of staff with me.' He looked round at Katie. 'No need to waste money asking for his reply. Just sign off "Former Naval Person, WSC".' His smile was more of a smirk. 'That should do it.'

But he hadn't actually asked the President if it would be all right if he descended upon him and his family just before Christmas. She wondered what Mrs Roosevelt would have to say about the sudden group of guests sprung upon her. Katie gave an inward shrug. It seemed these sorts of aristocratic people went about things in a very different way from anyone else.

'How was the PM this morning?' Miss Nicholson said, when Katie returned to the office, still bemused by Mr Churchill's nerve in inviting himself to be President and Mrs Roosevelt's guest without any notice. She tried not to think of it as plain cheeky.

'He apologised for being cross with me yesterday,' she said.

Miss Nicholson raised her eyebrows. 'Oh, why was he cross?'

Drat! She'd left herself wide open.

'Oh, I didn't double-space his letter to the King. I didn't think you would when it was a personal letter.'

'I should have warned you that *everything* you do for him has to be double-spaced.' She paused. 'People do say he apologises when he's been particularly angry with someone.'

'Do you ever work for him?' Katie asked.

'No, I'm Sir Alan's personal secretary and that's as close to the PM as I ever want to be.' She looked at Katie. 'Sir Alan would never raise his voice to me – he's always a perfect gentleman. Not that Mr Churchill isn't . . . in his way,' she added hastily, 'but he's too eccentric for me. I couldn't handle him.'

Somehow that little snippet of information cheered her up.

'Telephone for you, Katharina,' Miss Nicholson said a few days later when Katie was just about to ask if she could go for a quick cup of tea.

'Katharina, will you step into my office.' It was Sir Alan.

As usual he sounded very serious. You could never tell by the tone of his voice or his facial expressions what he was thinking. Judy would say he played his cards close to his chest. Bracing herself, though for what for she couldn't imagine, she knocked on his door and entered.

'Have you a passport, Katharina?' Sir Alan plunged in straightaway.

The question took her aback.

'Um, no, Sir Alan, I don't.'

A frown creased his forehead.

'That's a pity. There's a good opportunity for you but you'll need a passport.'

Katie's heart began to thump in her chest. They must be

debating whether to send her abroad. Oh, she must go. Even Sir Alan had said it was a good opportunity and she couldn't let it slip away.

'Does this mean you're thinking of sending me overseas?'

'Precisely.'

'How long would it take to get one?'

'If it's processed immediately there's a chance they'd have it ready in twenty-four hours, but if it's longer, we've had it.'

Everything rested on the passport. Suppose it didn't get back in time. Suppose— She must stop this . . . focus on what Sir Alan was saying.

'Where would I be going?'

'The PM proposes to travel to America on Thursday.'

Katie jerked upright, adrenaline rushing through her body.

'And we've just heard that one of his personal secretaries has had to attend to her parents, who were caught in a bombing raid last night,' Sir Alan continued, 'so I've suggested that you go instead.'

Oh, my goodness, it could only be Washington.

Her mind reeled. The letter Mr Churchill had dictated to be sent to President Roosevelt at the White House, saying he considered it imperative to meet him without delay, and without even asking if it would be all right. He must have had a telegram already from the President to say yes.

'Oh, Sir Alan, I would very much like to go.' Her voice, though shaky to her ears, was decisive. She lowered her tone. 'Though I'm very sorry about those parents. I hope they'll be all right.'

Sir Alan nodded. 'Dreadful business.' He regarded her. 'But it's a temporary position for you and will give you the chance to do some travelling . . . that's if we can get your passport promptly. So speak to Miss Nicholson right away, who will arrange it. You need to emphasise that it must be done by this time tomorrow, as the following day you'll be leaving.'

'Do you know how long we'll be gone, sir?'

'You never know with the PM. You might be back before Christmas . . . but you might not.'

Katie came out of Sir Alan's office dazed. She stood for a moment trying to get her breath. It wasn't possible. She was going to America with Winston Churchill himself!

'Ah, just the person I was looking for.'

She blinked as Baxter hurried towards her.

'Are you okay?' he said.

'Y-yes.'

'You look like a schoolgirl who's been given a medal and doesn't deserve it.' He regarded her closely. 'What's the matter?'

'Nothing.' She mustn't say anything about the conversation.

He sighed. 'Well, something's up, and I can't tell whether it's good or bad.'

'Oh, it's good,' she said quickly. 'Sir Alan seems pleased with me.'

'He'd better be or he'll have *me* to contend with.' When she chuckled, he said, 'Can you tell me what you've done that he's so pleased about?'

'Baxter, I have to see Miss Nicholson to give her an urgent message.'

'Okay. I guess it's something you can't mention – but is there any chance of us having a quick cup of tea this afternoon? Say four-thirty?'

Aware of her insides shaking from her interview with Sir Alan, she tried to steady herself. She must appear professional in case anyone else came along and saw her trembling like a blancmange.

She glanced at her watch. 'I should be allowed to escape for a few minutes as I've had no lunch break today.'

'I'll be waiting outside in the usual place.'

A warm sensation stealing round her heart at the thought of

an hour or two in private with Baxter, Katie opened the door to Miss Nicholson's office. She was on the telephone.

'Yes, I'll get onto it right away, Sir Alan,' Katie heard her say before putting down the receiver. She looked at Katie.

'It seems you've been given a wonderful chance to go abroad,' she said.

Immediately, a rush of guilt caused Katie to swallow hard. Why hadn't they asked Miss Nicholson? She was far more senior.

'It's perfectly in order, Katharina,' Miss Nicholson said, as though reading her mind. 'You've proved yourself. Even to the PM, after a few ups and downs, and believe me, he doesn't take to everyone. Sir Alan's asked me to deal with the paperwork. And remember – the fewer people who know about any forthcoming trip the better.' She allowed a smile. 'I'll get your passport arranged immediately – that is, if you have a copy of your Birth Certificate and your ID card handy.'

Oh, no! She'd taken it home after Vernon had returned it to her. It was in her bedroom dressing-table drawer. Katie bit her lip. At least she was going home this evening and could bring it back in the morning. But that would lose several hours. And every hour would count.

'I've got my ID but my Birth Certificate's at home,' she said. 'I can't get it to you until tomorrow morning.'

Miss Nicholson pursed her lips as though thinking. 'I shouldn't worry too much.' She went to the filing cabinet, pulled out a file headed 'Passport Applications' and handed Katie a form. 'Fill this in and we'll get it off first thing in the morning.'

'But it won't arrive until Thursday – and that's when we're leaving.'

'It will be sent by courier,' Miss Nicholson said, 'and returned by tomorrow evening.'

She glanced at Katie. 'Oh, I'll need a recent photograph.'

Katie swallowed. 'I don't have one.'

'Well, go down to the admin office and someone will take it. You can do that right away. And come in early tomorrow. You'll have a lot to do before you go.'

For once it was a bright afternoon when Katie stepped outside, blinking in the sunlight. True to his word, Baxter was waiting and immediately came to her, swept her into his arms and soundly kissed her.

'And I don't care who sees us – rumours or not,' he said, smiling down at her. 'It's been far too long since I've kissed those lips.'

Her lips still tingling, she said:

'Yes, it has . . . and I've missed it.'

'But have you missed *me*?'

'Only your kiss,' she teased.

He took her arm. 'Come on, you minx, let's go and have some tea – you're probably dying for one.'

'I am.' She hurried to keep up with his strides. 'But the worst of being in the bunker is no air.'

'Are you keeping up with the sunlamp routine?'

Katie pulled a face. 'Not always. There's rarely time with all the workload we have. Every single report and memo and letter is urgent nowadays.'

He nodded. 'Yes, things are hotting up since the Japs' attack on Pearl Harbor.'

Oh, if only she could tell him where she'd be going in a day or two's time. If she received her passport, that is. It was so frustrating keeping such momentous news from those closest to her.

'Penny for your thoughts,' Baxter said when they were seated at a window table in the café and he was pouring the tea.

She shook her head. 'Just everything. The war, my work . . . you.'

'Me?' He pointed to himself. 'I'm not a problem, am I?'

'No, of course not, but you do seem to sneak into my thoughts quite a lot.'

'I should hope so.' He looked at her directly. 'Oh, Katie, darling, I do love you . . . so much.'

'I love you, too.' She hesitated. When she thought about him, she realised she didn't know much about him at all. This wasn't the place but she had to say it. 'Baxter, can I ask you something personal?'

'Go ahead.'

'Are you married?' She held her breath.

'No.' He paused a moment. 'Next question.'

She swallowed and looked directly at him. 'Before you met me, did you have a serious girlfriend?' Keeping her eyes fixed on him, she added, 'I don't mean over the years, but more recently.'

'Yes.' His mouth tightened.

Her heart seemed to miss a beat.

'Did something happen?'

'You could say that. I don't really want to talk about it.' He made quite a performance of taking a packet of cigarettes from his pocket, lighting one, then inhaling deeply, all the while not meeting her eyes.

She could tell her questioning was making him feel uncomfortable. Did that mean he was still in love with her? Was that the reason he didn't want to talk about her?

Wishing she hadn't mentioned any girlfriend but knowing it was too late, she said, 'How long ago was it?'

'Oh, well before the war. She was Australian. That's where I met her.'

'What were you doing in Australia?' Once again, Katie realised how little she knew this man she was in love with.

292

'I had a bout of TB that winter and the doctor said I should go to a warmer climate for at least six months so I took his advice. I'd always wanted to go to Australia but it was very expensive so I sailed on a cargo ship. It took nearly two months and I wouldn't have missed it for the world. It opened my eyes to all aspects of life on that ship.' He chuckled. 'Then in Melbourne I worked my way to Sydney doing odd jobs. That's where I met her when I was a waiter in a posh restaurant and she was a customer – well, we had to call them clients. Anyway, I wanted to bring her back to England and she agreed, but at the last minute before we were to sail, she changed her mind and said she couldn't be stuck on a tiny island.' He heaved a sigh. 'So I came back on my own.'

'Would you have married her?'

She held her breath, waiting for his answer.

'Probably not. It was all very rushed – I didn't get to know her properly but even *I* realised we were too far apart socially and our values weren't the same.'

'Were you very upset?'

'Not so much as I thought I'd be. It was more the case that I didn't like being rejected.' He gave a rueful smile. 'Bit of a male thing, I suppose.'

'How do I fit in then?'

He took hold of her hand. 'You're different. When I met you it was like a thunderbolt. I realised I'd never felt like this before and I was determined you were the girl I wanted to spend the rest of my days with – even though you didn't like me at all,' he added with a grin.

'I would call that rushed as well,' Katie said seriously.

'It's not the same. There's a war on. We don't want to waste a moment. We love each other and there's no time for playing games.' He stroked her jaw lightly with his fingertip. 'How about you, Katie? Do you agree? And before you answer, I'm not going

293

to ask you about any of your previous boyfriends, only to presume you're not married or engaged as I see no sign of any rings.' He paused. 'So do you agree that we shouldn't waste a moment?'

Katie felt her shoulders relax. She smiled at him.

'Yes, I agree, because I feel exactly the same.'

'I'm glad.' His voice was warm. 'By the way, I'm off to that conference shortly – the one I mentioned the other day . . . though I'm not particularly looking forward to it as it's scheduled for ten days with a weekend in between.'

'I don't suppose you can tell me which city or town.'

'No, it's all hush-hush as usual.' He gazed at her. 'Don't look so serious, darling. We'll miss each other but I'll be back before you know it.'

'It's not that, it's—' She bit her lip.

I daren't tell him I'm going away, too, because he might question me. Best he knows nothing and then no one can accuse me of blabbing.

'Well, however long it is, it's *too* long,' she added lightly and smiled. She mustn't breathe a word about her plans. But she'd write if she was allowed to from wherever she was going.

Baxter drained his cup.

'Do you know whether you'll be able to have a few days off to be with your family over Christmas.'

'I'm not sure yet about the schedule,' Katie said, 'but if there's work to do – and I'm sure there won't be any let-up – that's fine, too.'

'The war changes everything, doesn't it?' He glanced at his watch. 'We'd better go, darling.'

'What day do you leave?'

'Thursday.'

Katie blinked. *Both of us leaving on the same day but going in different directions and neither of us is allowed to tell the other where we'll be. Almost like we're dangling in space.*

Chapter Thirty-Five

The following day, the tenth, Mr Churchill appeared almost every hour, rushing along one corridor or another, his face animated. He was obviously looking forward to his trip but Katie couldn't help wondering if the President had accepted the fact that he might have such a prestigious visitor and his entourage over Christmas whether he wanted them or not. Or what his wife would have to say about it.

She'd duly given Miss Nicholson her Birth Certificate early that morning. It was coming up to five o'clock and there'd been no news yet about her passport – and they'd probably close at half-past. It wouldn't arrive until tomorrow now. But that was when they were supposed to travel. Normally, she would have cleared her desk by now and gone home, but her in-tray was still half full. She'd stay late and get it done – at least she'd know if her passport had come through or not.

But five-thirty came and went and by six o'clock Katie had long ago sipped the last of her water. Her throat was parched. She stood and rolled her aching shoulders, then stretched her back.

'I don't suppose there's any news of my passport,' she said to Miss Nicholson.

'No. It'll be tomorrow morning now. But I haven't seen anything to say the PM is leaving tomorrow so I doubt he will. His plans are often delayed.' She looked at Katie. 'Go home – but if I were you, I'd do some packing so you're ready at a moment's notice. And if you want my advice, where you're going will be very cold, so take warm clothes.'

'Should I bring my suitcase in tomorrow?'

Miss Nicholson shook her head. 'No, because if you do travel tomorrow, it will be later in the day and you'll go straight from home to meet the party at the station.'

That evening, when Katie walked through the front door at home, exhaustion overcame her. She'd worked eleven hours solid, which wasn't unusual, but maybe it was the strain of wondering if she would be going to America within the next couple of days or not. And what she should take? She had no formal evening dresses and she'd need a dozen coupons even if she had time to buy something suitable.

After saying hello to her father and Ursula, she went upstairs, Tanny following, and looked in her wardrobe, then grimaced. There was a black jersey dress which possibly could be brightened with a contrasting belt and scarf, or a necklace, but anything else was too summery. If only she'd had a bit more notice, so as to get her passport without worry and perhaps to find something in a department store for the evening.

'I'm not prepared for a grand trip to America, Tanny.'

Tanny gave a short bark.

'That's right. I might be off to Washington in a day or two.'

The dog wagged his tail with enthusiasm. Katie couldn't help chuckling.

'You won't be so happy if I do go, Tanny, because it might be for a fortnight or more. Then what would you do?'

'We are ready to eat, Katharina,' Ursula called up the stairs.

'I'll be down in a minute.'

As usual, her stepmother had laid the table in her precise manner with a flowered tablecloth, beautifully ironed, and the cutlery sparkling. Katie sniffed the air. The dish of red cabbage emitted an enticing spicy smell.

'These sausages are very good, dear,' her husband remarked at the supper table, spearing another mouthful.

'I made them.' Ursula smiled at him. 'I stood a long time for the butcher but there were no more left when it became my turn. I made them with vegetable and Spam.'

'You can't tell,' Oscar said. 'What do you think, Katie?'

She knew her father was desperate to heal the rift between her and his wife.

'I'm sure Tanny could.'

Immediately she'd said it, she reprimanded herself. She was being mean. This kept happening. Quickly, she added, 'But you're right, Dad, they're very good.'

She could almost see the relief filtering over Ursula's face.

'Did you have a nice day at work?' her stepmother asked.

'Yes, it was all right.' Katie hesitated. She had to tell them something of what she was doing. She cleared her throat. 'There is something – I might not be here for Christmas.'

She noticed Ursula throw her father a quick glance.

'Is it personal or to do with work?' her father said mildly.

'Oh, work. But I won't know until the last minute. And then I can't tell you where I'm going or when exactly I'll be back.'

'Why is this so mysterious?' Ursula said.

'It's because she's not allowed to say,' her father cut in. 'We have to take everything our daughter says at face value. If she wants or needs to tell us something, I'm sure she will.'

'I will, Dad. But it's all very hush-hush where I am.'

'We know, love.' He studied her. 'Can you tell us if you will be right away, or still in Britain?'

'It will be "right away",' she said, feeling safer in using his careful choice of words.

He nodded.

'How long might you be away?' Ursula said a little timidly.

'It could be two or three weeks – possibly longer.'

'Will there be other people – other girls – with you?' Ursula said.

'Oh, yes, I'm sure there will.'

'And you will go out in this new country in the evening?'

'I suppose so.'

'Are you wondering if you have the right clothes?' Ursula said, unexpectedly.

Katie gave a start. How was it that she'd hit on exactly the problem?

'I'm probably all right in the daytime, but I only have that black jersey dress for the evenings.'

'Yes, I know it.' Ursula hesitated. 'If you have time I could make you a nice winter evening dress.'

'I don't have time,' Katie said. 'We're supposed to be going tomorrow or possibly the day after.'

'They should inform you in a proper manner,' Ursula said, frowning. Then her expression cleared. 'You are the same colour . . . colouring with the hair as I am – and not far away from my size except you are a few inches shorter. I have a beautiful dress that would be perfect for the evening and I only wore it once. I could adopt . . . adapt it for you perhaps.'

Oh, no. She really didn't want to wear one of her stepmother's old-fashioned evening gowns. Being reminded each time she wore it of her stepmother's part in the betrayal. But curiosity got the better of her and Katie thought she might as well just have a glance at it.

'I will fetch it.'

Ursula was back in two minutes, her arms full of a gorgeous silky material. She gathered up a section, placing it under Katie's chin.

'I knew it,' she said. 'The colour of the Mediterranean when

298

it is more green than blue – just like the colour of your eyes.' She held it out to Katie. 'Try it on and if you like it, I will alter this evening ready for tomorrow.'

'It's lovely material.'

At least that was true. Heaven knew what the out-of-date style would be. Well, she could easily make an excuse that it was too tight but that meant she mustn't let her Ursula see it.

'I'll try it on upstairs.' She took it, ignoring the disappointment on her stepmother's face as she realised she was not invited to the fitting.

'Come down and show me,' was Ursula's response.

Katie whipped off her office suit and pulled the silky dress over her head. She spread it down her body with the palms of her hands. It fitted perfectly but fell nearly to her ankles, and a glance in the mirror confirmed that she looked frumpy. The shot silk shimmered the colours of greens and blues, but it wasn't going to be suitable at all. Pulling a face, she went downstairs.

'It should be halfway at your calf,' Ursula said, ready with the pincushion. 'I can easily cut a few inches off to show more of your lovely legs.' She bent down and put a few pins in to show the new hemline then stood back. 'Go up and look in the mirror again.'

Katie was stunned by the difference the shorter dress made. A classic design, it had a deep boat neck and showed the outline of her bust, then skimmed to a neat waistline to fit snugly over the hips. All at once she looked glamorous and sophisticated. She went back downstairs.

'Why did you only wear it once?'

A tinge of pink rushed to Ursula's face. Katie noticed for the first time how blue her eyes were, her hair still blonde with a little ash here and there. But it was her cheekbones that made her innate beauty shine through. Though was her face a little thinner? Maybe her stepmother was just tired.

'I made it for a special occasion and it is not for me to wear again, but it is almost made for you.'

Katie was about to question her further, then decided against it. It was obviously something deeply personal.

'Do you like it?' Ursula asked tentatively.

'It's truly beautiful,' Katie said. 'And if you could do the alteration, I would be honoured to wear it.'

'I am so glad.'

Ursula looked at her as though about to say something more. Then she clamped her lips together and finished pinning the hem.

Katie couldn't believe the change in the Prime Minister as he came out of the Cabinet Room next morning. His whole demeanour exuded despair in the bowing of his head and the slump of his shoulders, and he shuffled rather than practically marched as he usually did along the corridors. His cigar hung unlit from the side of his mouth as he muttered under his breath. When she saw everyone else's serious expression as they filed out behind him, she knew something dreadful had happened. She couldn't even catch Baxter's eye; he was talking quietly to Barnaby.

Miss Nicholson told her later in the morning that Japanese aircraft had sunk the old warship *Repulse* and, worse, the new battleship *Prince of Wales* off the east coast of Malaya, both causing a huge loss of life. Apparently, the Prime Minister had been on the *Prince of Wales* as recently as August, when he met President Roosevelt for the first time in Newfoundland.

It must have been a terrible blow to him, Katie thought, her blood running cold that he could easily meet disaster from the enemy when travelling so much. Everyone said that if something happened to him, no one would be able to take his place. Well, it wasn't a scrap of good dwelling on these possibilities. Resolutely, she fed another sheet of paper into the Remington.

The phone rang. Miss Nicholson answered it.

'Thank you.' Pause. 'Yes.' Another pause. Miss Nicholson nodded. 'I will let her know straightaway.' She put the receiver down and turned to Katie. 'A new date has been decided upon. You will be leaving tomorrow evening. And your passport has just arrived,' she added.

Katie drew in a breath.

'Oh, that *is* good news.' She glanced at Miss Nicholson. 'Will any other girls be travelling with us, do you know?'

'The PM doesn't usually decide who to take with him until the last minute . . . but I do know Louise is going so you'll have some female company.' She glanced at Katie. 'I believe you've already met her.'

'Yes, I have,' Katie said. 'She seems very pleasant.'

'Hmm.' Miss Nicolson wrinkled her nose. 'I'm not sure that's exactly how I'd describe her.'

Really? Then you must be the only person here who feels like that.

'Oh, don't get me wrong,' Miss Nicholson said hurriedly. 'I'm told she's very good at her job. It's just that "pleasant" isn't the first word that springs to mind.' She hesitated. 'I'd call her charming – by name and by nature.'

It sounded as though Miss Nicholson didn't have much truck with charm. As though she thought it was superficial. Hmm. Katie wondered. This trip might prove even more eventful than she'd at first imagined.

Chapter Thirty-Six

Katie wanted to pinch herself to make sure she wasn't dreaming. It was Friday night and she was standing on a platform at Euston Station, where the train was hissing and emitting bursts of impatient steam against the roar of the engine. Disappointingly, there was nothing on the livery to denote it was Mr Churchill's special train.

Of course there wouldn't be, she told herself crossly. The Prime Minister advertising that he was on board would attract most unwelcome attention, to say nothing of the delight of any lurking enemy agents. She was only feet away from Mr Churchill himself, who suddenly bustled off with his three Chiefs of Staff. It looked as though they were about to board the train, but where to, she had no idea.

'Oh, there you are, Katie-Katharina,' a female voice behind her said. 'I've been looking for you.'

Katie swung round to make out the glamorous figure of Louise, wearing a light-coloured coat trimmed with fur and a hat to match, her smile wide.

'Louise!' Katie returned her smile. 'I was told you'd be coming.'

'Wouldn't miss it for the world,' Louise said. 'Even though I don't know all the parts of the world I don't want to miss.' She gave a tinkling laugh.

'I think that makes it even more exciting.'

'I only hope we'll get our own sleeping quarters and not have to bunk together,' Louise said. 'Nothing personal,' she added quickly.

She'd only voiced exactly what Katie was thinking.

'It would be nice, but we can't take anything for granted,' was all Katie said in answer.

The crowd began to queue to enter through the various doors.

'We need to find our carriage,' Katie said. 'I'll go and ask one of the secretaries.'

'Oh, I know which carriage,' Louise said with a grin of triumph. 'It's actually the one facing us right now. Come on, let's go and find out the worst.'

They were out of luck. Behind one of the partly glazed partitions was a hand-written notice informing them that this was the sleeping compartment for Louise Chalmers and Katharina Valentine.

'Oh, well, we'll have to put up with one another,' Louise said, momentarily letting her mouth slide into a sulk before she added, 'I just hope you don't snore.'

'I don't think I do,' Katie answered, a little annoyed at this one-sided conversation in which Louise was taking her to be the interloper.

'I'll take the bottom bunk.'

It was as though the woman had a right. Katie bit her lip.

'Or we could toss a coin,' she said.

'Oh, don't let's bother with all that.' Louise gave her ready smile. 'It's only for one night, after all, but I get vertigo if I'm higher than two feet off the ground.'

Katie sighed. Louise was rather a selfish person when you got to know her better. And if they were going to sail to America rather than fly, they might be thrown together in the same cabin for several nights.

For heaven's sake stop moaning, she told herself. *You're incredibly lucky to be picked to even go on this tour, let alone grumbling about conditions. You're accusing Louise of being a spoilt brat but you're sounding just like her.*

She forced a smile at Louise.

'Let's be determined to have the best time on this adventure,' she said.

'I'll drink to that.' Louise removed a beautiful lacy nightdress from the top of her case, then a sponge bag. 'Well, I would if we were offered one, though I doubt it at this time of night.'

There was a knock on the partition door and one of the private secretaries whom Katie knew by sight slid open the door.

'Hello, ladies. Which one of you is Katharina?'

'That's me,' Katie said, putting her case on the rack opposite.

'The PM wants you for dictation . . . right away.'

Katie's heart jumped. She could feel Louise's eyes on her, saw her lips part with astonishment.

She suppressed a giggle. 'Can you tell me where he is on the train?'

'He's in the last compartment before the restaurant car.'

'Thank you . . . I'll go straightaway.'

The secretary disappeared. Katie reached in her bag for her shorthand notebook, which fortunately she'd had the foresight to pack at the top, ready to grab at any minute.

'Rather you than me at this time of night,' Louise said, opening her sponge bag and pondering the contents. Not looking up, she said, 'So you're His Nibs' personal secretary, are you? That's certainly a big step up,' she added before Katie could answer.

'I'm not sure of any title. But I'm covering for one of his secretaries – a bit like when I stepped in when you broke your wrist.'

Louise glanced at her wrist, now adorned with a watch encrusted with what looked very much like real diamonds.

'Well, I'm glad I can forget about work and have an early night.' She paused. 'Don't wake me when you come back.'

Biting back a snappy retort and keeping any sarcasm from her tone, Katie said, 'I'll try not to.' If they were going to have to spend what might turn out to be many hours a day together in cramped quarters, it was no use being anything other than friendly.

Katie knocked on the last door before the restaurant car and Churchill's gruff tones called, 'Enter.'

She opened the door to find the great man already in his pyjamas and sitting up in bed, the omnipresent cigar dangling from his mouth. Thankfully, she was getting used to him in his night attire and didn't allow herself the smallest hint of a blush. The compartment was far more cramped than she'd expected and the light was dim, but she could see the bedspread on the narrow cot was already covered with papers and files, though she noted the famous red box was nowhere in sight. On his bedside table, precariously placed, was what looked like a brandy bottle.

'Ah, Miss Valentine. Take a seat.' The Prime Minister vaguely looked round, waving a tumbler. 'Actually, there isn't one. You'll have to sit on the end of my bed.' He leaned forward and patted the space where she should go. 'Just don't bang into my feet.'

Gingerly, Katie let herself down at the end of Mr Churchill's bed, perching on the edge. This was becoming more surreal by the minute. She flipped the cover on her notepad and held her pencil ready. Suddenly, the train gave a mighty jerk as it grumbled its way out of Euston Station, causing the brandy bottle to fall and Katie to almost lose her balance. She grasped the side of the Prime Minister's bed, then bent to retrieve the bottle along with several papers that had fluttered to the floor.

'We need to send this telegram to the President,' he began, not seeming to have taken any notice of the mishap as he gulped down the last of his drink, 'in answer to his kind invitation to visit him and Mrs Roosevelt at the White House.' He gave a little smirk. 'Well, if I'd waited for his reply we still wouldn't be on our way—' He broke off. 'No, Miss Valentine, don't take that last bit down or it will cause havoc.'

'I haven't taken down anything yet,' Katie said, grateful he was so focused on his wording that he hadn't reprimanded her.

'No, no, of course not.' He cleared his throat. 'Heading is MOST SECRET – all in capitals.' He removed his cigar for a few seconds then allowed it back in for a few puffs. The smoke drifted towards her in the cramped space.

Katie desperately swallowed the tickle in her throat. She mustn't disturb his thinking in any way. She took down the preliminaries, then he came to the nub.

'Weather permitting, I hope to be with you on the twenty-second of December in time for your further kind invitation to join you and your guests at the White House for dinner that evening and will keep you updated as to progress.'

Given the time lapse, they'd obviously be sailing across the Atlantic. It was good to have that confirmed, and she couldn't help a little frisson of excitement at the idea of being one of the first people to know the Prime Minister's plans. She only hoped to God the enemy wouldn't discover them.

He dictated a few more letters. By now she was making the shorthand strokes by the feel of shaping them rather than by sight. As usual, he asked her to read everything back, only changing something minor in the President's telegram. At one point she had to hold her pad close to her eyes.

'You are not wearing your spectacles,' Mr Churchill said sternly.

'I know. I forgot to bring them.'

'Do not forget them next time,' he barked. 'Strain on your eyes.'

'I won't forget.'

He grunted. 'I think that's all the dictation for tonight. I don't need it returned until we're on the *Duke of York*.'

With relief, Katie stood up. 'May I get you anything before I go, sir?'

He shook his head. 'No, I have the valet see to that.' He peered closely at her. 'You'd better get some sleep. We'll have plenty to do on the voyage over.'

'Thank you, Mr Churchill. Goodnight.'

She quietly shut the door behind her, then walked swiftly along the corridor until she came to her and Louise's compartment. Even before she'd opened their door, she heard the sound of Louise snoring her head off – fit to wake the entire train!

Wishing she had earplugs to numb the roar of the engine and Louise's snoring, Katie turned over in the narrow bunk for the umpteenth time. At first she thought the movement would rock her to sleep but it seemed to have the opposite effect of making her feel more awake, not to mention the thrill of this being the first lap of travelling to the United States of America. She must have eventually drifted off, Katie thought, as she was jerked awake by the sound of male voices outside the door. She peered at her watch but couldn't make out the time. It didn't feel much more than five, but perhaps this was the best time to use the cloakroom facilities before the whole train woke up.

Gripping the short ladder to steady herself against the rocking of the train, she descended the few steps until she felt the floor beneath her foot. Careful not to disturb Louise, whose snoring had turned into heavy breathing, she pulled on her dressing gown and picked up her sponge bag, then tottered along the swaying corridor, anxious to keep her balance. As she approached the next carriage, she glanced down, marvelling at

307

the rails below looking as though they were rushing backwards. Heart in mouth she prayed the juddering carriages wouldn't open a gap just as she stepped across the vibrating platform that joined the two.

Without mishap she arrived at the right door and slid it open.

Good. As she'd hoped, there was no one around. She quickly washed and cleaned her teeth, then made her way back to her carriage. Louise, a sleep mask on top of her head, was endeavouring to sit up. She blinked as Katie entered.

'*You* were early.'

'Thought I'd beat the crowd,' Katie returned.

'And did you?'

'Yes, there was no one about.'

'I don't suppose there was. It's not even half-past five.'

Katie ran her tongue over her lips. 'Oh, how I could do with a cup of tea, but I don't suppose they'll be open yet.' She glanced at Louise. 'I think I'll get dressed and see if any of the staff are around.'

'You do that so I can have another forty winks.' Louise pulled her mask down and flopped back against the pillow.

'Do you want me to bring anything?'

'No. I don't bother with breakfast so long as I can have a ciggie.'

Katie quickly dressed, picked up her handbag and found her way to the restaurant car. There was no sign of life inside although a few of the passengers walked by as she was peering at the notice on the window.

Breakfast 7 a.m. to 9 a.m.
Lunch 12 noon to 2 p.m.
Dinner 6 p.m. to 8 p.m.

A young naval officer said, 'Good morning', and read the notice, then tutted. 'I could do with a coffee right now but I reckon we'll arrive in Scotland by the time they start serving breakfast.'

Katie's heart leapt. Strange how Baxter had also travelled north yesterday. She wondered if his conference was in Scotland. She'd never been but it was doubtful she'd see anything of it.

She brought her thoughts back to her current situation – where could she while away a whole hour? She didn't even have a book with her. But she *did* have her shorthand notepad in her handbag. And this was a train for the special purpose of carrying the Prime Minister, so there was sure to be a compartment somewhere with a typewriter and some stationery. She'd be able to show some initiative in not wasting any time and deliver Mr Churchill's dictation as soon as they boarded the ship.

But when she went in search of a spare typewriter and asked one of Mr Churchill's aides, he said, 'I only know of one, and that's in His Nibs' bedroom.' He saw her crestfallen expression. 'But we'll be in Scotland in about twenty minutes,' he added, 'so it's probably best to get your belongings together.'

She decided to take his advice. When she'd finished packing and found Louise's powder compact – under the woman's pillow – she opened the compartment door into the corridor and peered through the grimy window. A rush of excitement swept through her when she glimpsed the sea from one of the windows in the train's corridor. Minutes later Mr Churchill's special train shuddered and juddered, its brakes squealing as it came to a reluctant halt.

One of the train crew stuck his head in the carriage.

'All change,' he said.

'Where exactly are we?' Katie asked.

'Prince's Pier Station, Gourock.'

She'd look on the map later to pinpoint it. For now, she gathered her belongings. She and the rest of the junior staff held back as the Prime Minister alighted, closely followed by his Chiefs of Staff together with his personal and private secretaries. Katie recognised Sir Charles Wilson, Mr Churchill's personal physician, and wasn't sure whether to be alarmed or relieved as there'd been rumours in the War Rooms that the Old Man was becoming tired. She noticed several photographers with cameras poised waiting amongst the crowd to welcome their Prime Minister. So much for keeping Mr Churchill's trip a secret, she thought.

A feeling of pride swept over her to be so privileged as to work in such proximity to this great man. She only hoped he would return to London having nurtured the friendship and gaining continuing support of the President that were vital for the next phase of the war.

Chapter Thirty-Seven

Katie hoped she would never relive such an experience in her life again.

Those first days, between bouts of the most terrible seasickness, she was certain the HMS *Duke of York* would break into pieces as it tossed and rolled on the waves, valiantly fighting gale-force winds. Then, desperate for air, Katie would grope her way onto one of the decks, choking back the nausea as waves, each more violent than the last, mounted the deck in an angry, foaming river. On one occasion, she spotted Mr Churchill wandering along with his cigar in his mouth, deep in thought, seemingly oblivious to the vicious weather. She so longed to speak to him – to tell him she was sorry she hadn't been able to do any work for him – but she didn't trust her stomach. Besides, he had other more important things on his mind than being bothered about who was going to turn up to take dictation.

The only saving grace – if you could call it that, Katie thought, pulling a face – had been Louise, who'd shown no sign of sickness at all, no matter how fierce the storms, and announced to all the Chiefs of Staff that she was fit and available to take any dictation whenever they needed her, though stressing that obviously the Prime Minister had first call. He'd rung for her several times and on each occasion Louise returned to the cramped cabin they shared, assuring Katie she was not to worry or feel any guilt whatsoever.

'I've taken care of all the PM's work this morning so no need to worry.' Louise's beam of triumph grated on her every afternoon when she returned to the cabin where Katie was lying prostrate, listening miserably to the same words.

Please God, stop this ship from rolling.

'And it might be some comfort for you to know you're not the only one,' Louise droned on. 'Even some of the crew have been sick over the side of the ship.'

'Well, at least I haven't done that.'

'No, thank goodness, but you've spent most of the week being best friends with the lavatory.' Louise grimaced. 'Well, I'm only grateful that I have an iron stomach and can carry on normally – as does our Prime Minister. The rolling ship hasn't affected him in the least – probably all the brandy he lines his stomach with,' she added with a smirk.

It didn't matter how much she tried to bat away the mean notion, Katie couldn't help thinking Louise was enjoying all this, hoping she would go on feeling ill so she could step in permanently as one of Mr Churchill's personal secretaries.

On the fourth day, when Katie opened her eyes from yet another restless night, the churning in her stomach seemed to have diminished. She blinked herself properly awake. Had the storm abated? She tried to swallow but her mouth was dry. Yet for once she didn't have the dreaded nausea. But what she did desperately need was a cup of tea.

'I'll see you later after I've finished the PM's work this morning,' Louise said as she finished getting dressed. 'What about you? Do you want me to bring you anything?'

'No, thanks, Louise,' Katie said, sitting up. 'I'm much better so I'm getting up and going in search of tea.'

'No, no, you just lie there. You need to rest. *I'll* bring you a cup of tea.'

'I've had enough rest,' Katie said firmly. 'I want to do the job I was asked to do from now on.' She hesitated. She'd have to say something more to remind Louise that she'd only been standing in for her. 'I know you've had to work twice as hard to cover for me and I really appreciate it but you have your own commitments to the Chiefs of Staff.'

'Huh. They have personal secretaries who can keep up with their output. But *you* –' Louise reached up and laid a sympathetic hand on her arm '– mustn't even *think* about work.' She paused. 'The PM did ask how you were yesterday and I told him you were still very poorly and had to remain in bed. He said there's no need for you to rush back.'

Did he really say that? Or was it something Louise had made up?

'Louise, I'm getting up,' Katie repeated, 'and I'm going to resume working for Mr Churchill because that's why I'm here.'

'All right,' Louise said huffily. 'But I'd better be on my way. He'll be expecting *someone* to turn up – and as I'm the one who's ready, it might as well be me.'

She gave the door a little slam – or was that her imagination? Katie wondered, as she flung back the cover and climbed down from the bunk. She was becoming more than a little tired of Louise.

In the restaurant she was pleased to recognise the waiter.

'Two rounds of toast with scrambled egg, please,' she said. 'And a large pot of tea.'

'Right you are, miss. If I'm not mistaken, I haven't seen you here since the first day.'

'I've had terrible seasickness.'

He tutted. 'The injection didn't work then?'

'Injection?' Katie echoed. 'What injection?'

The waiter raised his eyebrows. 'You don't know?' Katie shook her head. 'It's known as Devil's Breath and is especially for sea sickness. If you haven't had the injection, it's difficult to fight a queasy stomach. Three-quarters of the passengers have been affected and even some of the crew but most of them managed to get back the following day because it normally works.' He looked at her. 'You know, even if you're feeling better it might not hurt to go down to the sickroom and ask for it. It'll stop you keeling over if the storm starts up again.'

'Devil's Breath.' Katie gave a weak smile. 'That just about describes how I feel. I *am* better but, as you say, it might be sensible.'

But when she made her way to the sickroom and asked for the injection, the nurse shook his head.

'Sorry, but we've had such a run on Scopolamine we're almost out . . . we're saving the last for anyone who suddenly becomes really ill, but I'll give you a little packet of barley sugars. They'll help to quell the nausea.'

Katie doubted she could rely on Louise to inform Mr Churchill she was better again, she thought, sucking one of the barley sugars on her way to the deck to get some air that afternoon. Louise plainly wanted to carry on working for the Prime Minister as long as possible. She bit her lip. Her only recourse was to tell him herself. He might even be roaming on the deck right now. As she struggled to heave open the door to the deck in a sudden gust of wind, she spied the very man. What a stroke of luck! He was striding up and down and from the short distance she could see his lips moving. She hesitated. He might be annoyed to be interrupted. Baxter had once remarked that the PM's pacing up and down and talking to himself usually meant he was trying out different ways to resolve a difficult decision. She wavered.

Go on, her inner voice ordered her. *He can't shoot you. If you don't say anything, you might as well hand over any secretarial duties to Louise from now on.*

No! She couldn't stand the gloating if this happened. Screwing up her nerve to approach him, she made her way slowly across the deck.

The sea might be much calmer but the waves were still lively enough to take her by surprise.

'Oh, Mr Churchill, can you please spare a moment?'

He stopped abruptly and swung round, giving her a sharp look. Her stomach burbled.

'Yes, what is it?'

She swallowed. 'I've come to tell you how sorry I am that I was ill but I'm better now and can resume work whenever you need me.'

To her relief, his face broke into a grin. 'Well, Miss Valentine, Miss Chalmers told me only this morning you were still incapacitated and couldn't take your head off the pillow, but you look to me in fine form.'

'I am now,' Katie said through gritted teeth, a vision of Louise's somewhat smug expression distinct in her mind.

'Good!' The Prime Minister beamed, his face close up reminding Katie of a mischievous Renaissance cherub. 'That means you can join me and the others this evening in the cinema. They're showing two of my favourite actors – Clark Gable and Spencer Tracy in *Boom Town*. One of the best things about watching a film – takes your mind off world problems. We meet at 21.00 hours. Don't be late or you'll miss the beginning.'

She'd vaguely heard Louise mention that the PM liked to watch American films in particular, one after the other into the early hours.

'Thank you, sir, I'd like that.' She hesitated, hoping she wasn't being presumptuous. 'And when would you like me to start work?'

'Tomorrow at eleven a.m.' He hurled the butt of his cigar accurately into a bucket some yards away. 'Perhaps you would be so kind as to tell Miss Chalmers she's free to work for anyone else who needs her,' he added as he teetered off.

Katie held on to one of the rails of the deck, pure pleasure that she'd overcome her nervousness rolling through her. She couldn't help a jubilant grin spreading as she peered over at the rushing waves. At least they weren't anywhere near so high as they had been, often crashing right over the rails and onto the deck. At the moment the water was streaming behind her in a thick, foaming, relentless path. A thrill caught her off-guard. It was only now, when she felt so much better, that she could appreciate how magnificent it looked. And how privileged she was to be here chatting to the most important man in the British Isles – who had just invited her to join him in the cinema this evening! She'd definitely be there. But more importantly, she couldn't wait for tomorrow morning to work for him. It was just a nuisance that she'd forgotten to ask where he'd be. She also had to tell Louise that her services wouldn't be necessary from now on – a conversation she was not looking forward to.

She went back to her cabin and to pass the time, decided to write a letter to Baxter, which she'd post when she arrived in Washington; that is, if she was allowed to send mail from there. The Basildon Bond pad in front of her, she unscrewed her fountain pen and began.

My darling,

Just seeing those words in blue ink made her insides quiver. She'd never written them before to any man and yet with Baxter it seemed so right. How she longed for him to be with her right this minute. How she wanted to tell him everything she was doing and seeing. Hardly aware she was doing so, she pushed the tip of her tongue between her teeth in concentration, and continued:

I hope the conference is going well.
I know I wasn't able to tell you at the time, but I was

asked to accompany a group from work and we left the day after you.

It was a comfortable train and although I worked, we did manage a break for a superb cold supper. I'm now on the high seas, having just come through some rotten weather which affected me badly, but I'm much better now and working again. There are some interesting people on the ship but how I wish you were here, too.

I long to feel your arms around me, holding me close. Your lips on mine.

Was she being too forward? Katie frowned. No, he would be happy she still felt the same way. But where was their relationship leading to? They'd never spoken of marriage and babies but she was certain it would all come in good time. Right now, there was a war on. Mr Churchill rarely let his mind wander into anything else but victory at all costs – with the exception of American films, that is, she decided with a grin.

'Are you going to watch the film this evening?' Katie asked Louise at supper in the ship's dining room that same day, steeling herself to tell the woman that she herself would be working for Mr Churchill the next morning.

'No. I've been once to please him but it didn't finish until past three in the morning. They weren't that good either. All cowboy films.' A frown wrinkled Louise's normally smooth brow. 'Why? Are you going?'

'Yes, I thought I would.'

'Well, I hope you don't let the side down by being sick again.'

'I told you I'm better. I'm beginning work again for Mr Churchill tomorrow morning.'

This time there was no mistaking the woman's displeasure as she stared at her.

'Oh. Who notified you of this arrangement?'

Katie feigned a look of surprise.

'Why Mr Churchill, of course.'

'When did you see him?'

'This afternoon after lunch – on the deck.'

'I see,' Louise said, making it sound as though she didn't see at all.

'He told me to pass on the message that you're free to work for whoever needs you.'

Louise clamped her lips together.

'Thanks for letting me know.' And with that she stalked out of the room.

Katie looked after the disappearing figure. No, she hadn't imagined anything. Louise was not at all happy that her temporary work for Mr Churchill had come to an end. Worse, she seemed downright jealous of her.

At five to nine, Katie entered the room that had been fixed up for the voyage especially to show the Prime Minister his beloved films every evening. Apparently, he liked to have company when he watched them. To her surprise there were at least fifteen men chatting – but no sign of Mr Churchill. The minutes ticked by and there was some tutting and looking at watches. At nine-thirty, with still no sign of him, Katie was wondering if he would ever turn up when the door flew open with a crash.At the entrance stood the great man dressed incongruously in what everyone called his romper suit. With cigar hanging precariously from the corner of his mouth, and to Katie's amusement, he chortled, 'Winnie's here! You can roll the film now.'

It was a Western as Louise had predicted, but Katie couldn't help becoming immersed in the complicated plot. When the credits came up at the end, and thinking it had all been great fun not just watching the film but glancing at the Prime Minister watching it, obviously enjoying himself hugely with all the smoking and the downing of three or four large brandies, Katie stood to go. She quickly sat down again when two men looked her way. No one stirred. Another film followed immediately. Oh, no. It was already gone eleven. It would be one in the morning before she got to bed. Stupidly she'd taken a seat in the middle of a row instead of at the back where she would have been able to slip out quietly. She groaned. Oh, if only just one chap stood up, she could follow him. The credits of the new film were now showing, though she hadn't caught the title. There was nothing for it but to sit it out.

After about twenty minutes she noticed the man beside her had his head bent and seconds later she heard him snore. She stifled a giggle. It seemed an eternity before the film came to an end.

'Just one more,' Mr Churchill cheerily announced, 'and then you can all go home to bed.'

At this point Katie decided she was going to be brave. Thankfully, the Prime Minister sat in the front so he had his back to everyone.

'I need some air,' she whispered to the man on her other side. 'Will you please excuse me?'

Making a vow that she would never again be caught up in one of Mr Churchill's film nights, she tiptoed out of the room.

Chapter Thirty-Eight

Making sure she had everything she needed including her glasses, Katie decided the following day to begin searching for the Prime Minister well before eleven o'clock. One of the aides said he hadn't seen him, another said he was in a private dining room in what would likely turn into a long meeting, and yet another said he was in his quarters having a bath and had made it clear he didn't wish to be disturbed. Katie couldn't help a grin. She definitely didn't want to disturb him in the middle of his ablutions.

'He's in the radio room listening to the BBC,' an officer told her when she stopped him. 'I've just come from there.'

She followed his directions and tapped on the door. There was no answer so she opened it. There was only room enough for the two men sitting with their backs to her, facing a wall chock-full of radios piled one on top of the other with workspaces underneath. Relieved, she recognised the back of the Prime Minister's bald head.

'Mr Churchill?'

Both men twisted round.

'Oh, eleven o'clock already?' the Prime Minister said.

'Coming up, sir,' Katie replied.

He turned to the other man and muttered, 'Well, that wasn't the news I wished to hear,' then glanced at Katie. 'You'd better follow me, Miss Valentine.'

He led her to a small room marked PRIVATE and put a key in the lock, then when they were both inside, proceeded to lock it again. Gesturing to where the typewriter stood, he invited her to be seated.

'We have much to get through,' he told her. 'I have four important memoranda to dictate for a start.'

'Mr Churchill, I've been thinking. Couldn't I put it straight onto the typewriter? I'm sure I could keep up with you and it would save a huge amount of time.'

He peered at her through spectacles perched on the end of his nose.

'Hmm. Not sure,' he grunted, then seemed to change his mind. 'All right. We'll give it a go.'

He sounded so doubtful that for a few moments Katie wondered if she'd been too rash. Suppose he spoke unusually fast with no hesitations? She'd feel a fool having to admit that she wasn't keeping up with him. Then she told herself not to be so ridiculous. Of course she could keep up with him. She was used to his style of dictation now. Sitting at the machine, she reached for the paper and carbon for a copy.

'Memorandum number one,' he said, 'and all to go to the three Chiefs of Staff.'

Katie inwardly groaned. Each memo would need four carbon copies. One mistake, five corrections. With slightly trembling hands she rolled in the wodge. By now she was used to a memorandum not being a few paragraphs but these four were all at least 2,000 words each. The content was obviously extremely important – mostly about strategies that the Western Allies were to adhere to during the next phase of the war and involving some names she recognised such as General Montgomery's. It sounded complicated and intricate, causing her to be even more in awe of this great man striding up and down the modest room. His words and sentences were so effortlessly chosen, it seemed to Katie, as he rumbled on, giving precise details to the three top officials of the Army, the Navy and the Royal Air Force, who must carry them out meticulously. Anything deviating from the plan could have disastrous consequences, he warned at the end of each one.

She was relieved when she'd added the final words to the fourth memorandum.

Heaving her shoulders to her ears and pulling them back, she blew out her cheeks. Oh, for a cup of tea.

'I believe we've finished them, Miss Valentine,' he said, 'and we'll see if this new method has actually saved us time.' He gave one of his sly grins. 'The proof will be in the pudding if you can read it all back accurately and I don't spot any mistakes when I initial them.'

This was it. Katie took up the first sheet she'd typed what seemed hours ago and began reading. Thankfully, the Prime Minister had spelt out all the proper names for her.

There was a knock at the door. He raised his head.

'Shall I get it?' Katie asked.

He grunted and nodded and she jumped up and unlocked the door.

A young man stood there, hesitating.

'Well, what is it, lad?'

'Telegram, sir.' The boy put a small brown envelope on the desk and swiftly exited.

Katie watched as Mr Churchill ripped it open with a stubby finger and drew out the small sheet of paper. She noticed his eyes bulge.

'Oh, dear.' He shook his head. 'That's inconvenient – most inconvenient.'

It sounded as though the message was much more than simply an inconvenience.

'Is it bad news, sir?'

He turned to her and blinked. 'You might say that. There's been a serious train crash on the way back from Newcastle. Hundreds injured and apparently few survivors.'

'Oh, how awful.'

'Yes, it is . . . one of our chaps is involved . . . not easy to replace,' he muttered.

A band of fear gripped Katie's heart.

Oh, please say his name.

She kept her eyes fixed on him, willing him to tell her.

'Mr Churchill, who—?'

'The Chief Cartographer's missing,' he said shortly, tossing the telegram onto the floor. He glanced at her. 'Now where were we? Oh, yes, you'd just begun reading out memorandum number one.'

Katie froze. She couldn't catch her breath. The Chief Cartographer? Dear God, please not Baxter! Her mouth went dry. She tried to swallow. Baxter was dreadfully injured . . . Baxter was dying right this moment . . . Baxter was already dead. She gripped the edge of her chair. The room spun. It felt as though she were falling. She mustn't faint. And she mustn't divulge to Mr Churchill or anyone that she was in love with Baxter Edwards and he with her or they'd think she wasn't fit to do her job if she botched it up now. The Prime Minister would have no compunction in telling her she was no longer needed. She could even lose her job. Her mouth tasted sour at the thought. No. At all costs she must act normally and professionally so no one would ever guess.

'Miss Valentine?'

'Oh, I'm s-sorry, sir. It was a shock hearing that news as I know the cartographers.'

He threw her a stern look.

'I expect you do. But there's a war on and with it comes bad news. The important thing is *victory* . . . *victory* at all costs.'

He smacked his knee. '*That's* what we must focus on . . . every minute of every day. So pray continue.'

How could he be so heartless, so dismissive of a member of his staff? Didn't he have any compassion? But so far as he was concerned, Baxter now missing was an 'inconvenience' and that was all. She swallowed hard, peering at the words dancing in front of her eyes. She felt the sting of tears and didn't know how she managed to keep her voice from shaking. Once or twice she stumbled and the Prime Minister tutted, but finally, dear God, thankfully, she reached the end of the fourth and last memorandum. She drew in a jerky breath as she waited for his criticism.

But all he said was, 'Good. This new method appears to work.' Then he looked at her. 'I'm going to have my nap. You look as though you could do with one as well.'

She couldn't escape fast enough. All she could think of was to return to her cabin. To be quiet. To think. To try to calm herself. But her stomach was in turmoil, just as it had been in the storm. She bowed her head low and pulled the collar of her raincoat up to her ears.

Please let Baxter be safe. Don't let him be badly hurt . . . or worse.

She didn't know to whom she was appealing, but if there was a God, she begged to be heard.

She had almost reached the safety of her cabin when a figure in the opposite direction came hurrying towards her.

'I've been looking for you.' Louise gave a light chuckle. 'Now you're better I wanted to know if you fancy a game of ping-pong.'

Katie stared numbly at her. Oh, no. That was the last thing she wanted to do. To keep all that was churning inside her, all that was ready to spurt out from her throat at any moment, firmly in check without anyone suspecting she was worried to death. She gave Louise a sickly smile.

'I've got an awful headache, Louise. I think I'll just go inside and take a couple of aspirins.'

Louise took her arm. 'Having a game of ping-pong will make you feel much better,' she said. 'You've probably been in one of those stuffy rooms with the PM smoking his filthy cigars.'

'I don't mind them,' Katie said, 'but I do mind my headache so I need to be quiet for an hour or two and give the tablets a chance to work.'

'I'll rake up another partner then.'

Katie gave her a nod and unlocked their door. She stepped in and closed it behind her. She would do what Mr Churchill had suggested. She'd have a nap. Taking off her shoes, she undid the buttons on her blouse and removed her skirt. Then she climbed the short ladder to her bunk and crept under the sheet. She closed her eyes but the tears welled and spilt down her cheeks. Giving in, she hugged her pillow to her chest and wept.

Katie felt none of the excitement she'd expected when HMS *Duke of York* finally sailed into Chesapeake Bay, the naval station in Norfolk on the Virginian coast, and docked on the 22nd December. There was a military band to greet them playing 'God Save The King' and press cameramen were snapping photographs as the passengers disembarked to a cold and drizzly day. A cheer broke out when Winston Churchill appeared, an unlit cigar in his mouth, his fingers pointing upwards in the victory sign. But what occupied every corner of her brain, as it had for the last week, was Baxter. All she could think of was that she was being taken further and further from him and had no idea when she'd be returning. If only she could find out what happened. But maybe everyone hadn't yet been accounted for. But if he was missing, he could be dead.

Stop it! You mustn't think like that, her inner voice insisted. *You don't know what you're saying. He's probably perfectly safe and back in the War Rooms by now.*

But she couldn't help the shudder that ran across her shoulders.

She was relieved that Mr Churchill had opted to fly on to Washington with a few of his close aides, as her main fear where he was concerned was that she would break down in front of him. He had that unnerving habit of looking at people closely if he wanted to know more about them. She was told that she and the rest of the party would be taken to Phoebus railway station that afternoon and go by special train to Washington.

Although the interior of the train was plush and comfortable with its deep claret-red velvet seating, and seemed much wider than English trains, with plenty of space for her to stretch her legs, Katie couldn't appreciate her surroundings as she normally would have done. All that consumed her mind was Baxter, and whether he was still alive. But surely she would know by some instinct if he was no longer in her world? She bit her lip so hard she sensed the metallic taste of blood. If he *was* alive and well – after all, Mr Churchill said there'd been some survivors – Baxter would be upset that she was in such a state before she knew the facts. And anyway, she must act in a professional manner. She had a job to do, as the Prime Minister had reminded her.

Her stomach growled from eating so poorly on the last days of the voyage, so when one of the crew came round with cold chicken sandwiches, hard-boiled eggs and fruit, she tucked in as heartily as Louise sitting beside her.

'Mmm. Delicious.' Louise licked her lips in satisfaction as she reached out for an apple. She glanced at Katie. 'Glad to see your appetite's come back after your seasickness.'

How could she tell Louise she still felt unsettled, but not from seasickness – it was not knowing Baxter's fate. If she broke down and confided in her, it would be all round the British party in no time. And that would reach the ears of the Prime Minister before you could say 'Jack'.

'Coffee, anyone?' asked a young woman in a smart uniform, carrying a tray with a silver coffee pot and steaming jug of milk. She set it on the table and poured out the cups and Katie gratefully took one.

The hot foamy liquid gave her spirits just the lift they needed. Swallowing the last of it, she felt infinitely better. There was nothing she could do about Baxter until she had more information and even then, she had to carry on regardless.

It was midnight by the time the train arrived in Washington, where several large black automobiles were waiting to whisk them to the Mayflower Hotel. Katie peered through the window but it was too dark to see anything except fuzzy outlines of tall buildings. Crossing her fingers that she just might have a bedroom to herself, Katie alighted from the elevator on the ninth floor of ten. Her heart sank when she recognised Louise's luggage already in the generous twin-bedded room, her more modest case neatly alongside. She shrugged. Louise was the only other female. It was quite natural that the organisers paired them together. She began to unpack her case and minutes later Louise burst in. She glanced round the room.

'Looks all right, doesn't it?' she said.

'It looks positively inviting,' Katie admitted. 'I'm worn out.'

'Me, too, but if there was a party going on, I dare say I could revive,' Louise chuckled.

'Party or not, I'm getting into bed just as soon as I've cleaned my teeth,' Katie said firmly.

And try to picture Baxter as safe and being looked after, wherever he was.

327

Chapter Thirty-Nine

They keep it the most dazzling white, Katie thought, as she and Louise stood transfixed in front of the White House. What a difference from peering at an old photograph in a book. She felt honoured to be here, admiring the most important building in America. Ionic columns supported the pedimented front entrance, flanked on either side by the two-storey wings, and when she tilted back her neck, there was the American flag fluttering proudly in the light breeze.

'What on earth are those two men doing on the roof?' Louise said, screwing up her eyes and pointing to the left of one of the chimneys. 'And one of them's looking at us through a pair of binoculars.'

Katie swivelled her head and shaded her eyes with her hand.

'Trying to see whether we're bona fide, I expect.' She turned to Louise. 'They must be security men, keeping a lookout for any intruders.'

'I don't like being spied on,' Louise said sullenly.

'If I'm right, they're only doing their job.' Katie took Louise's arm. 'Come on, let's go in. I can't wait to see if it's as grand as I'm expecting. And to see where we'll be working,' she added.

At the thought, she couldn't help a small triumphant thrill as she and Louise were shown into the entrance hall. They both gasped.

Pairs of marble columns on either side, forming classical

colonnades, marched the full length of what looked like fifty feet of sheer elegance, the rich red carpet cutting a luxurious swathe in between. The ceiling was moulded, but not ostentatiously – a perfect backdrop to the exquisite, sparkling crystal chandeliers.

'Aren't we lucky to be here?' Katie's voice was low. It seemed irreverent to speak in natural tones.

Louise nodded. For once she was speechless.

When Katie explored the layout of the White House the following day, she was surprised to notice that certain areas looked remarkably like the Cabinet War Rooms. There was even a replica of the Map Room: enormous maps showing the daily updated situation of the war hung on the walls of the Monroe Room, named after James Monroe, a former President. Her lips curved in amusement. This redefining of one of his host and hostess's rooms could only be down to one person – her boss. Seconds later, however, her happy mood collapsed. The Map Room. Where Baxter often worked when he wasn't in the Annexe. He would have been the one in charge of setting it up if he'd been chosen to accompany them to Washington. It must have been considered that it was more important for him to stay in Britain and head the conference. She swallowed hard. How she longed to be able to ask Mr Churchill if there was any news of his Chief Cartographer. But it was impossible.

She didn't see much of Louise as they were both kept extremely busy, and up until the small hours of the morning, taking dictation along with two of the other personal secretaries to Mr Churchill and his Chiefs of Staff. Katie was glad. Her concentration helped distract her teeming, relentless mind from spilling over.

She still didn't know quite what to make of Louise. The girl

329

was friendly enough, yet . . . oh, she didn't know what followed the 'yet'.

A busy week passed. One morning, just before Katie was about to go down to breakfast, Louise handed her an airmail letter.

'I spotted this in our pigeon-hole.'

Please let it be from Baxter.

Trying to sound nonchalant, and not examining it, she said, 'Thanks, Louise. Did *you* have any post?'

'No,' Louise said abruptly. She glanced at the envelope in Katie's hand. 'Is it from home?'

Katie turned it over. Her shoulders slumped in disappointment. It was from Ursula. The Whitehall address had been crossed through and the Mayflower Hotel in Washington written in its place.

'Yes, it is.' She stopped, not wanting to explain about her German stepmother.

'I'll leave you to it then,' Louise said. 'See you in the dining room.'

When she'd gone, Katie took the letter-opener on the desk and slit open the envelope. She drew out the thin sheet of paper and read:

Meine liebe Katharina,

Katie's eyes widened. Goodness! Ursula had written the entire letter in German. She quickly scanned it.

> *I hope you do not mind my writing to you in German but I can express myself better in my own language. We did not part very well and now your father and I do not even know where you are – only that you have gone abroad. I do not want to think of you in any danger. Will you be home for Christmas? I hope so. How I long to put my arms round you and tell you how proud I am of you and the war work*

330

you are doing – but most of all how much I love you. I know I have never told you this before. Always, I hung back, not because I did not feel the affection but because I did not want to inflict myself on you. That was mostly because I felt guilty that I was pretending to be your mother and how angry and upset you would be when we told you that I was not. That is why I kept putting off the dreadful day. At least you now know the truth, even if it is very painful for you to accept. If I had been your natural mother our relationship would have been so very different. But you have always felt like my true daughter in my heart and I have loved every minute caring for you. Now you have become a beautiful, independent young lady so I must have done something right. One day, after this terrible war ends, I am sure you will find a good man to marry and have children of your own.

I try to think that there was one thing – I taught you my language as I would have done my own flesh and blood child. That always made me feel closer to you when we conversed.

Wherever you are and whatever you are doing, I pray to God you will come back to us safely. Never forget that I love you and I always have – since I first set eyes on you when you were not even a week old. I thank Judith every day for giving you to us to love and to cherish for ever.

Deine Mutti,

Ursula

P.S. Do not worry for Tanny. He misses you but I have grown fond of him and he has become a wonderful companion.

Katie blinked. She had to read the letter again – there was so much to take in. Aspects of her stepmother she hadn't realised.

This time she read it more slowly. And when she came to the part of a husband and children of her own, she could only sit on the edge of the bed, her fists clenched as she pushed them against her eyelids to stop the flow of tears as she wondered whether she would ever see Baxter again.

This couldn't go on. She was in Washington for a purpose. She found a handkerchief to blow her nose, then went to the mirror over the wash basin. Her eyes were red and puffy. She splashed her face with cold water and reapplied her lipstick, then stuffed the letter in her handbag. She needed time to think about it and how to answer it.

In the dining room, Louise waved at her.

'I've saved you a place,' she called.

Katie groaned inwardly. She didn't feel like making small talk with Louise but felt she couldn't ignore her, so she nodded and walked over to the serving table and gasped in surprise. There was a variety of cereals, cheese, slices of ham, sausage, bacon and boiled eggs. There was no sign of rationing. The enticing smells made her mouth water and she helped herself to the cooked dishes, then poured a mug of coffee from one of the large metal pots, and carried the tray over to where Louise was sitting. She took the seat opposite.

'Your eyes are all red.' Louise said, gazing at her. 'Was it your letter? Is something wrong at home?'

'No. I'm probably a bit homesick.'

How lame that sounded. How untrue. Except for Tanny – but her stepmother had allayed her fears on his behalf – and the usual worry about her father's deteriorating health, she didn't miss her home at all.

'You're sure it's not Mr Baxter Edwards you're pining for?'

Katie's head jerked up. This woman was not going to let it go. And she obviously didn't know he was in that train crash. She must keep her voice neutral.

'Whatever gave you that idea?'

'I just wondered,' Louise said, her blue eyes innocently wide.

'Well, wonder on.'

'Oh, so-reee,' Louise drawled. 'Didn't mean to offend.'

Katie was relieved when a man of medium height, who from the solid look of him wouldn't stand any nonsense, appeared at the table and broke the silence.

'Good morning, ladies. May I join you?'

'Oh, do,' Louise trilled.

She patted the chair on the other side of her. He introduced himself as Peter Whitney, one of the Prime Minister's detectives, and proceeded to entertain them with the latest witticism from Mr Churchill that the President couldn't follow.

'He puts "KBO" at the end of all his letters.' Peter grinned. 'And apparently Roosevelt asked one of his aides what it meant. Of course the bloke being American as well had no idea, so he had a quiet word with his English counterpart who roared with laughter and said: "Keep Buggering On". The aide was shocked at the use of such an expression to a president.'

Louise couldn't stop giggling but Katie simply smiled, put her knife and fork together, then stood up.

'There's a pile of work waiting for me at the White House so I'd better be going.'

'Oh, that reminds me,' Peter Whitney interrupted. 'Which one of you works for the PM?'

'I do,' Katie said, noticing Louise roll her eyes.

'He's having one meeting after another today with the President, and there won't be any Minutes of any of them. Roosevelt doesn't care for recording any notes – he's the opposite to the PM in that way – thinks the written word can be incriminating. Anyway, he said if I ran into you this morning, to tell you you won't be needed today until late this evening. Eight o'clock sharp, he said.'

'Oh, thank you for letting me know,' Katie said. She suddenly had a thought. It was too bad Louise was there but it couldn't be helped. She'd go mad if she didn't find out something sooner or later. She couldn't ask Mr Churchill but Peter Whitney, being a detective, might be just the person. 'I don't suppose there's any more news of that recent train crash in the north of England, is there?'

'You mean the one coming from Newcastle?'

'Yes.'

Louise's curious eyes were upon her but it was too late.

Peter Whitney sucked in his breath. 'Dreadful business.' He hesitated, then said, 'I don't know how you knew about it, though I'm sure I can rely on you ladies for your discretion, but we've decided not to leak it to the press for morale purposes.'

'Oh, we wouldn't dream of it,' Louise interjected. 'What happened? How bad was it?'

Ignoring her, Katie persisted, 'But is there any fresh news?'

He puffed out his cheeks. 'Yes, they've found more people but they're either dead or seriously injured. And still a dozen or so missing with no sign of any of them – including one of our chaps.'

It was as though her heart had actually stopped beating. Katie stared at Peter Whitney with horror. A dozen people missing. And Baxter was one of them. Tears stung her eyes and she tried to blink them away. She mustn't break down in front of a stranger . . . or Louise, who would never stop questioning her. But it took all her willpower to mutter an 'Oh, dear, how worrying for their relatives', before she said she really must go.

'So that's what all the mystery was,' Louise announced when she came upon Katie just before lunch in the hotel's small library, bent over one of the desks with Ursula's letter open ready to answer it. She'd hoped the woman wouldn't track her down but

Louise had an uncanny ability to turn up like a bad penny. Katie twisted her neck round.

'What do you mean?'

'You know perfectly well – that train crash. And Baxter Edwards was on it, so Peter told me.'

'Yes.'

'No wonder you've been acting strangely.'

'Look, Louise, I'm trying to write a letter so just drop it, will you?' She turned back to the blank sheet of paper.

Louise peered over Katie's shoulder. '*Deine Mutti, Ursula,*' she quoted with a gasp of surprise. 'Your mother's a *German*?'

She made the word sound dirty and Katie winced. Then a twist of anger tightened her chest.

'Louise, it's none of your damned business what nationality my mother is.'

Louise snorted. 'That's as maybe, but it's certainly a turn-up for the records.'

'And what's that supposed to mean?'

'I mean, does everyone here know about your parentage? The PM, for instance. And I don't suppose the Americans working with him in the White House would be too impressed either if they knew.'

Don't rise to Louise's taunts.

Katie looked up at her. In a measured tone she said, 'My dear Louise, those who count – *they* know.'

She waited until the door slammed behind her before she took up her pen. It was only then that she realised for the first time since the 'betrayal', as she couldn't help calling it, that not only had she stuck up for her stepmother, but she'd acknowledged to Louise that Ursula was indeed her *mother*.

Chapter Forty

It didn't matter what time of the day or night Katie worked, there were the sounds of teleprinters, copiers and typewriters, and telephones ringing non-stop. Officials were constantly hurrying to and fro with dispatch cases, rushing into one meeting immediately followed by another, where she produced what seemed like acres of typewritten reports, memoranda, Minutes and telegrams – all under the name the Prime Minister had given to the Washington Conference: ARCADIA.

As soon as the media reported that the British Prime Minister, Mr Winston Churchill, was in Washington, there was a stream of deliveries from well-wishers: presents in the form of clocks, pocket watches, bow ties, an assortment of champagne and whisky and hundreds of boxes of cigars, few of which were Havanas – the PM's favourite, reported Louise. But most ostentatious of all was an enormous 'V' sign, taller than Mr Churchill himself – constructed of lilies, carnations and irises. Katie bit back a smile. No matter how many times his aides told him that the backward 'V' sign he used – with his palm towards himself – meant something completely different and very rude, he refused to change it. She wondered if the Americans understood the difference.

Before she knew it, it was Christmas Eve.

The Americans certainly went all out with their decorations,

Katie thought, as she breathed in the warm sweet smell of pine and admired the two Christmas trees standing like sentries, one on each side of the front door of the White House. Inside, a wreath hung on each window on the ground floor, and the main hall was filled with the most beautiful claret-red poinsettias, far bigger than ones she'd seen at home. More sparkling Christmas trees adorned a few of the grander reception rooms and the west hall upstairs.

She would have been so thrilled with all this, felt really Christmassy, Katie thought, but hanging over her was the thought of her dearest Baxter. Oh, if only she could know what had happened to him, where he was, if he was miraculously one of the missing who had now been found. She swallowed hard. There had to be some news soon. And then she remembered what that detective, Peter Whitney, had said. It wasn't going to be leaked to the media because it was so serious and would be bad for the British public's morale. But surely Mr Churchill would be advised if there was some news. Katie sighed. It was the not knowing that was the worst. She hadn't stopped writing to him but she'd never had a reply. Could he really be—? No, she wouldn't allow herself to think that terrible word.

You must never give up hope, Katie, until you know for sure.

She'd write him another letter. It would make her feel closer to him. Just as she was poised with her pen in hand, Louise rushed into the room. She glanced over to where Katie sat and frowned.

'Put that away, Katie, or we'll miss all the fun. Hundreds of people are getting together on the lawn where there's the hugest Christmas tree I've ever seen – it's lit up like a fairground.'

'I was going to give it a miss.'

Louise tutted. 'You'll do no such thing. If you do, you'll regret it for ever. The PM's going to give one of his speeches and no one can give a speech like him. They'll be spellbound. Roosevelt is down for one, and one or two others – then carol singing.' She took Katie's coat and hat from the coat hooks. 'Come on, buck up. Just fling this on.'

She didn't bother to tell Louise that she already knew the bones of the speech as she'd typed it out and heard Mr Churchill practise it. But she also knew he wouldn't bother with the notes once he had what he wanted to say in his head and he'd ad lib to fit the occasion. Louise was staring at her expectantly, tapping her foot. There was no use arguing when she was in this mood.

By the time the two girls arrived, the front lawn of the White House looked as though thousands rather than hundreds had gathered. Louise pulled her through the crowd, some of the guests turning to grumble. but when they heard the English accents of the two attractive women, they laughed and edged away a few inches to let them through. Louise steered her to the side of the lawn where they had a closer view.

At nine o'clock President Roosevelt began by welcoming the Prime Minister, Winston Churchill, and other British guests. He spoke about the American and British and Russian alliance, finishing by saying that with such a strong team working together, there was no doubt in anyone's mind they would defeat the Germans. When it came to Mr Churchill's turn, the Prime Minister removed his cigar for once and cleared his throat. There was an immediate silence.

'I spend this anniversary and festival far from my country, far from my family, yet I cannot truthfully say that I feel far from home,' he began. He admitted it was a strange Christmas Eve with 'almost the whole world locked in deadly struggle', but that the children should not suffer because of it or 'denied their right to live in a free and decent world'. He then drew on his cigar and talked a little more about the children and how they must have fun this Christmas, and that the grown-ups also should forget the war for this brief period. He finished with: 'And so, in God's mercy, a happy Christmas to you all.'

There was a roar of approval and thunderous clapping. Katie felt as proud as though she'd rehearsed him. She blinked back the tears. What a marvellous man. How lucky Britain was to have him in charge.

But the next day, contrary to his speech the night before, the Prime Minister and the Chiefs of Staff appeared not to notice it was Christmas and that adults might like to enjoy a few pleasures. Katie and Louise were both called in to work a six-hour shift.

'Christmas bloomin' Day and we're having to work,' Louise grumbled.

'I think we've got off lighter than I expected,' Katie said.

'There's a party going on for some of the junior staff this evening and I want to go.'

'Yes, I heard about that,' Katie said. 'When's your shift?'

'Six in the evening 'til midnight – when it'll be nearly over.'

'Well, mine is twelve noon to six in the evening, so I'll swap with you.' Katie paused. 'I don't suppose it matters so long as one of us turns up.'

'You'd do that?' Louise's face was one big beam of delight. 'I would have thought you'd want to attend. We haven't had any sort of leisure time since we got here. It's been all work and no play, making this Jill a very dull girl, and besides, I fancied dressing up in our glad rags.' She threw Katie a direct look. 'Are you sure you don't want to go?'

Katie hesitated. She'd been rather looking forward to wearing the beautiful shot silk evening dress Ursula had altered for her. Now, she'd have to explain that she'd never had the chance to wear it and her stepmother might think she'd not worn it on purpose. Then she scolded herself. Why must she keep analysing their relationship? And how she felt now since she'd read Ursula's letter? None of it helped at all. She stared at Louise's eager face.

'I might have put my head in the door for half an hour or so, but I'm not that bothered.' Katie kept her voice nonchalant.

Louise's beam faded. 'Look, Katie, we had a bit of a set-to the other day and—'

'I've already forgotten it so I suggest you do the same.'

'If I can return the favour, Katie, you've only got to ask.'

Katie hesitated. Louise was very friendly with Peter Whitney but she was already suspicious about her feelings towards Baxter. She'd know instantly Katie wasn't asking merely out of curiosity. If only they were genuine friends, Katie thought sadly, and she could rely on her to keep it to herself.

You won't rest until you find out about him – whatever the risk.

It was true. She'd have to take the chance. Peter Whitney was her last hope.

'Katie?'

Katie forced herself to look directly at Louise. 'There *is* a small favour you might be able to do.'

'Oh?'

'Do you remember I asked Peter Whitney about the train crash that time we first met him?'

Louise stared at her. 'The one that Baxter was on?'

'Yes.'

'Why, have you heard anything?'

Katie gulped. 'No, nothing more since he said there were still some names that hadn't been accounted for.' Tears pricked the back of her eyes.

Louise narrowed her eyes. 'And you want me to ask Peter if he's heard any news?'

'If . . . you wouldn't . . .' She felt her heart pound. '. . . mind, Louise.'

'You're in love with him, aren't you?'

Katie tried to speak but her throat felt constricted. She could only nod miserably.

'No need to answer,' Louise said in a surprisingly sympathetic tone. 'Leave it to me.'

That evening, just as Katie thought she'd be able to snatch a sandwich after working solidly for several hours with only a cup of coffee and a bar of Hershey's chocolate to keep her going – not exactly the sort of Christmas dinner she'd pictured in America, where there was no rationing, she thought grimly – one of the junior aides handed her a telegram still in its sealed envelope.

'For the PM ,' he said. 'Can you get it to him immediately?'

Her heart leapt. Could it possibly be some news about Baxter? But Mr Churchill had given her strict instructions not to be disturbed. But it was a telegram. Whatever it referred to, the Prime Minister must be told. He never mentioned which room they would be holding their meetings in, and she knew it varied, but by chance she'd seen his short stocky figure amidst clouds of cigar smoke disappear into the room next door to the Monroe Room that was now his new Map Room.

Raised voices filtered through into the hallway, one of which was Mr Churchill's. He sounded in a belligerent mood. Oh, dear. She braced herself and knocked on the door. There was a sudden silence. Then a voice called out, 'Enter.' Gingerly, she opened it and stepped in. There were only four men in the room, and she was taken aback to see one of them was President Roosevelt himself, smartly dressed in a charcoal suit. It was the first time she'd seen him this close to. Mr Churchill's head snapped up.

'Well, Miss Valentine, what is it?'

'It's a telegram, sir. I didn't know whether it was important.'

'Wait here while I see if there's any reply.'

He skimmed the telegram and she saw the blood drain from his face.

Dear God. Have they found Baxter? Was he . . . ?

The Prime Minister slapped the paper on the desk in front of him, then swung round to the President.

'Hong Kong has just surrendered to the Japanese,' he growled.

Oh, no. Not another piece of bad news. And on Christmas Day.

He turned to Katie and barked, 'No reply.'

At nine o'clock the following morning, Katie drowsily awoke after a fitful night, having been disturbed by Louise at two in the morning. The woman had gabbled on about the party and who she'd been introduced to and had danced nearly every dance, until, in the end, Katie had told her to for goodness' sake be quiet and go to sleep.

She sat up and, yawning, stretched her arms above her head, then reluctantly tucked her feet into her slippers. At that moment she saw someone slipping a note under the bedroom door. There was no envelope, just her name scrawled on a folded piece of paper telling her that Mr Churchill requested her presence immediately in his private office, though it wasn't his writing.

Katie grimaced. It was Boxing Day. But the Prime Minister had already mentioned, to his glee, that it wasn't celebrated in America.

Just my luck.

But there was no use grumbling. If the war hadn't happened, she doubted she'd ever have had an opportunity to even visit the United States of America, let alone work in the White House. Making no sound in the dim light, she washed and dressed, but as she brushed her hair, she knocked Louise's jar of Pond's Cold

Cream off the dressing table. Biting back a swear word at the clatter, she stooped to put it back in its rightful place.

Louise jerked upright. 'Wha's going on?'

'Sorry, Louise. I knocked a jar off the dressing table.'

'Where are you off to this early?'

'Mr Churchill wants me right away.'

Louise groaned and lay down again. Then she jerked upright.

'I asked Peter about Baxter. Sorry to say he'd heard nothing more, but at least that's better than hearing any bad news.'

Katie drew a shaky breath. 'Thanks for asking anyway,' she said as she quietly shut the door behind her.

'We'll begin,' Mr Churchill announced without any preamble when she entered his office, though he did give her a nod. 'Telegram to Clement Attlee and Alan Brooke – same one.' He cleared his throat. 'Things have moved very quickly. The President has obtained the agreement of the American War and Navy Departments and the Chiefs of Staff Committee have endorsed it. Be ready to inform the Prime Ministers of Australia, New Zealand and South Africa. I will tell Mackenzie King in Canada in person before returning to England.'

So he's going from here to Canada, Katie mused. Would she be going, too? You never knew with the Prime Minister – he was so unpredictable. Even when he was dictating, it wasn't unusual for him to change his mind halfway through. If she and others in the party were left behind, would he return to Washington or go back to England from Canada? She tried not to imagine there would be yet another delay in going home.

The Prime Minister dictated a telegram to Mackenzie King announcing he would be leaving for Ottawa tomorrow afternoon, the 28th of December.

'I'll be arriving by puff-puff.'

She looked up with raised eyebrows.

'Do you actually want me to type "puff-puff" rather than "train"?'

He gave her a knowing smile. 'No need to publicise my movements in writing.' He drew on his cigar not realising it wasn't lit. 'Never know when the Nahzees are tuning in.'

She hid a smile at what she was sure was his mocking pronunciation.

'You will be staying here with the majority of the party, Miss Valentine.' He grunted at the cigar before finally managing to light it.

'How long might you be gone, sir?'

'It depends.' Mr Churchill gave one of his piercing looks. 'Is there any reason why you would want to know?'

Katie felt her face warm.

'Um, no, not really.'

'Hmm,' he grunted as though he didn't believe her. 'We must get on – there's a lot to go through.' Then he added, 'It will only be a brief visit.'

This didn't seem the right time to ask him if he'd heard any news of Baxter before he left, especially when she'd plainly irritated him by asking an innocent question just now. Mr Churchill was responsible for vast regions of the world. Besides that, there was a rumour he was exhausted and in danger of having a heart attack and that his personal doctor, Dr Wilson, was having to keep a very strict eye on him to keep him on an even keel. Katie gulped. The very idea of anything that serious was too dreadful to contemplate. The country needed him and she must not say or do anything to add to the pressure. But Baxter might be in desperate need of *her*. Dear God, what should she do?

'Miss Valentine! Do you think we might make a start, if it's not *too* much to ask.'

She startled at his sarcastic tone.

344

'Oh, um, sorry, Prime Minister, I was—'

' – far away and not paying attention,' he snapped.

It'll never be the right time. Ask him now!

Pushing aside her fears, she blurted, 'Mr Churchill, have you heard any news of the cartographer who was missing from the train crash?'

He stared at her for long moments.

'Baxter Edwards?'

She nodded, her heart skipping a beat.

'No news,' he growled, putting his hands behind his back and gazing at the floor as he began to pace. 'Memo to Sir Alan Brooke.'

Sick at heart, Katie made the appropriate marks in her shorthand pad. Her only consolation was that she'd tried but on both occasions it had amounted to nothing. The saving grace was that the Prime Minister had more on his mind than questioning her motive.

The atmosphere in the White House changed the moment the Prime Minister left in his usual whirlwind style. It was as though the mansion breathed a sigh that it might recover from that power of energy he oozed day and night. But Katie and Louise were kept just as busy as usual with the piles of telegrams to answer and the reports from the Chiefs of Staff's meetings to take down in shorthand and transcribe – every one of them seemingly more urgent than the previous one.

'There's just no let-up,' Louise grumbled the following afternoon when Katie was getting ready to take over her shift. 'I thought we'd have a chance to see the lights and do a bit of shopping when His Nibs had gone to Canada – but no . . . we're working longer than ever.'

'Well, I suppose we're here to work and anything else is a bonus,' Katie said.

'I think we've worked hard enough to *deserve* a half day's bonus,' Louise snapped.

Katie thought she would scream if she heard any more of Louise's moaning.

'I'd better go,' she said, picking up her bag, 'I need a cup of tea and something to keep me going before I start tackling the workload.'

To Katie's delight and Louise's shout of joy, the Naval Chief of Staff told them they were both free for New Year's Eve afternoon.

'It's not even half an hour's walk into the city,' Louise said excitedly, 'so shall we miss lunch and have something there?'

Privately, Katie would far rather have gone on her own but as things had calmed down between them, she thought now was not the time to be prickly.

'Yes, a walk will do us good after all the sitting we've done lately, but I want to do a bit of sightseeing – the Lincoln Centre for a start.'

'What about the shops – if they're open?'

'That, too. So why don't we walk together to the centre – then you go off shopping and I'll do a bit of sightseeing and meet you afterwards in one of the stores for a cup of tea.'

Louise's face fell. 'Oh, no. I'll come with you. As long as I'm out of this place for a few hours and seeing people other than White House staff, I'm happy.'

Was Louise worried about being on her own in a city? Katie wondered with a sigh. It didn't look as though she'd have any time to wander around on her own.

The day was crisp and sunny. Katie gratefully drew in lungfuls of air. Oh, that felt so good after the heat of the White House rooms. Much of the walk was through the tranquil Constitution Gardens by the side of an enormous lake where ducks swam silently by. Katie glanced up to see an obelisk dominating the skyline.

'Oh, look, Louise – that's the Washington Monument. Isn't it incredible?'

'Well, it would be if we could see the man himself.'

'I don't think we have time because I really want to see Mr Lincoln's statue.'

The Lincoln Memorial site was now visible. Katie felt a real thrill to see this famous landmark in person, rather than simply studying photographs in a book.

'Phew! That was quite a climb,' she said, watching Louise struggle up the last dozen or so steps where it was steepest. 'They say it's eighty-seven steps and I believe it.'

'I'm exhausted before I even start,' Louise gasped. 'Give me shopping on flat terrain any day.'

The statue of Abraham Lincoln was housed in what looked like a Grecian temple with Doric columns and constructed of Georgia marble, so a passing American with a southern accent proudly announced. Inside, where the chambers were divided by Ionic columns, Katie picked up a leaflet describing in more detail how the statue was sculpted from Colorado Yule marble. It was with a feeling of awe that she and Louise walked into the chamber where the great President was, larger than life, not only in the marble figure itself but in what he represented. There he sat in a thoughtful pose, perfectly echoing the calmness of the lake they'd recently walked past. Katie stood mesmerised until she was aware of Louise constantly looking at her watch and blowing out her cheeks.

'Yes, very impressive but I'm ready to go,' Louise said rather loudly. A small group of onlookers turned their heads and frowned. 'You'd think this was a religious place,' she hissed.

'They do revere Mr Lincoln and he deserves it,' Katie whispered, 'so we have to be respectful.'

Louise rolled her eyes.

To appease her, and to avoid any further embarrassment, Katie swept her outside.

'All right, then, Louise. Lead on to the shops.'

Louise's face broke into a relieved smile. It was as though she could smell where the shops were, Katie thought, as half an hour later they entered the ten-storey building of Garfinckel's. As soon as they walked through the entrance, they were in a retail world of elegance, quality and luxury. Not being used to such plenty after the rationing at home, her eye fell on a glass case filled with beautiful silk scarves. On impulse, she bought Ursula a large square, shot through with greens and blues. While Louise was trying on hats, Katie admired the shining glass shelves behind the counter displaying a range of cosmetics and treated herself to a new scarlet lipstick and matching nail varnish – or polish, as the sales assistant called it. There was a variety of mouth-watering shoes and boots and handbags on a floor to themselves, afternoon tea-dresses and evening wear on another, wedding dresses on yet another – Louise, all the while, stopping to give her opinion of the latest fashion displayed on the mannequins. It was breath-taking but overwhelming.

'What do you think of this dress, Katie?' Louise held against herself an evening gown with a lime-green beaded bodice and a flounce of emerald-green feathers on the satin skirt.

'Just like the film stars wear,' Katie said, secretly thinking it was ostentatious. 'Have you seen the price tag?'

Louise turned over the small card and gasped.

'Would Madam care to try on the dress?' A saleslady in black suit and cream silk blouse floated towards them.

'We're on our way to the restaurant to take tea,' Louise said in a posh accent, 'and when I've satisfied my thirst, I'll have a think about which gowns would be appropriate for upcoming events I will be attending this coming year.'

'Of course, Madam,' the woman said, in a tone that showed she disbelieved her. 'The restaurant is on the fifth floor.' She added, 'And if Madam doesn't return, then I wish her and her friend a Happy New Year.'

'Thank you,' Katie said, finding it hard to contain her giggles at Louise being addressed in the third person. She slipped her arm through Louise's. 'Come on, let's find the restaurant.'

'What a crone,' Louise said when she and Katie had been ushered to a table in the restaurant with a skyscraper view over the city and the waitress had brought their tea.

'She knew perfectly well you weren't going back,' Katie giggled.

'I know.' Louise gave a playful smile as she took a sip of tea, holding out her little finger. 'This shop is much more expensive than I realised. It's when you put the dollars into pounds that you get quite a shock. But at least you don't have to produce ration coupons if you want to buy something over here.'

They chatted about the difference in fashion between America and England and decided England was streets ahead. When they'd both finished their tea and Katie had paid the bill, she stood up. 'I think we should call it a day.'

'Good, because I can't walk another step.' Louise screwed up her face. 'Why don't we get a cab for a treat?'

'Good idea.' But when it came to paying the taxi fare and Louise didn't offer half, Katie wondered if it had been such a good idea after all.

Chapter Forty-One

January 1942

'The PM's back,' Louise announced on New Year's Day. 'He'll be lunching with the President in an hour's time.'

How Louise always heard any news pertaining to Mr Churchill before anyone else, Katie would never know. There'd been rumours that she and one of Mr Churchill's detectives had been caught kissing but Katie hadn't taken much notice, although she'd idly wondered if it was Peter Whitney. Well, someone must be giving Louise hints as to Mr Churchill's movements. Katie shrugged. Really it was none of her business.

As soon as New Year's Day was over, the Prime Minister sprang into action and Katie worked three days in a row from morning until the early hours of the following morning. Her eyes had started to smart and she was worried her work would suffer, but so far he hadn't pulled her up on anything serious.

Louise thought they'd be able to skip off while he was away, but still the workload never stopped, and it increased as soon as Mr Churchill was back in Washington, a city now thickly covered in snow. He'd been in sunnier climes, someone had said, for a rest. Katie doubted that. From the little she knew of the man, the verb 'to rest' was not in his vocabulary and he always had a reason for whatever preposterous scheme he thought up.

But now he sported a light tan, his eyes gleamed with his old enthusiasm, and to Katie's delight, he looked quite restored.

One afternoon in the middle of January when the snow had almost disappeared, Louise stormed into their bedroom where Katie was writing another letter to Baxter. It made her feel closer to him – telling herself she hadn't given up hope, even though every day without news made that hope recede just a fraction more.

Louise threw her hands in the air. 'I don't believe it. We've had no notice at all.'

'What about?'

'Apparently we're packing up and going home *tonight*! Before we've had any time for ourselves.'

'Oh, thank goodness!' Katie blurted before she could stop herself.

Louise narrowed her eyes. 'Why are you so keen?'

'That's the point,' Katie said, not quite truthfully, realising this conversation could remind Louise of Baxter. She must steer it away. 'It's because we haven't had much chance to do any real sightseeing that we might as well go back to London.'

'Hmm.' Louise's lip curled unattractively. 'It seems to me we've missed a perfect opportunity to do some shopping that we can actually afford.'

'You mean not shop in Garfinckel's?' Katie kept a straight face.

Louise threw her a sharp look. 'I hope you're joking, Katie.'

'Of course I am – I couldn't afford anything there except to splash out for a scarf for my –' she hesitated a split second '– mother and that lipstick and nail varnish for myself.'

'Well, the decision's out of our hands, that's for sure,' Louise said sulkily.

* * *

Katie wasn't disappointed to be finally leaving America. She looked out of the window of the overnight train heading to Norfolk, Virginia. It would have been nice if they'd had a guide and been taken round Washington even just once during the weeks they'd been there, but it was too late now.

Too late, too late, too late . . . the words formed a rhythm in her head, matching the wheels of the train, that she couldn't shake off. Was it too late for Baxter? At least she'd feel nearer to him in London, even if there was still no definite news. But oh, another transatlantic crossing. She trembled at the thought of going through such a nightmare again.

It was still dark outside just after five in the morning when the train finally rumbled into Norfolk. To Katie's astonishment they were told they'd be travelling in a flying boat. And there they were, three giant clippers gently bobbing in the harbour like Venetian gondolas waiting to take excited tourists around the canals. Katie smiled at the attractive image. One of the flying boats, the *Berwick*, had a large Union Jack painted on the side, and she guessed it would be taking Mr Churchill. Once again, Louise filled in her unspoken question – they were heading for Bermuda.

While the Prime Minister was taken to the *Berwick* and they were waiting to board one of the other two clippers, Katie said in an undertone, 'Louise, how is it you always know ahead of time what we're doing and where we're going, when most of the party is kept in the dark?'

'Ah.' Louise tapped the side of her nose. 'It's not what you know, it's *who*.' She gave Katie a wink. 'That's a lesson for life itself.'

'So it's obviously someone close to Mr Churchill.'

'Obviously,' Louise repeated, a sly smile touching her lips.

'Well, go on, who is it who's such a mine of information?'

'That'd be telling.'

'I think it's that detective we met in the Mayflower Hotel.'

'You might be right – but then again, you might not.'

'Good morning, ladies.' A young RAF officer standing at the entrance to the flying boat interrupted them. 'Please go through.'

Katie's heart gave a lurch of excitement.

'Come on, Louise, we're about to have another adventure.'

Once they were inside, Louise squealed with delight. She turned to Katie. 'Oh, I could stay in here for ever, it's so glamorous.'

She was right, Katie thought, looking round in wonder at the luxurious armchair seating, the dining room beautifully dressed with white linen tablecloths and what looked like solid silver cutlery and crystal glasses. They were shown the spacious cloakroom with toilet, wash basin and large mirror above . . . everywhere spotlessly clean and shining.

'There's even a bridal suite,' Louise exclaimed, her eyes sparkling with excitement. 'Wouldn't that be marvellous, to go on this plane – or boat, whatever you're supposed to call it – on your honeymoon? I'd love that!'

Katie smiled as though in agreement.

I don't care where I'd be. All I want to know now is that Baxter is alive and well – or whether . . . .

She felt the tears threaten. She mustn't break down. She'd been able to suppress them up until now. But a whole month had passed since she'd heard the news of the crash, and there had been nothing from Baxter, and she couldn't help thinking he must be too injured to write even a postcard. And although this might be a comfortable short journey, the long and miserable one was yet to come . . . on the Atlantic.

When everyone had been seated and the pilot had revved the engines, he announced that they were about to take off and the flying time would be just over two hours.

'Enjoy the comfort because this is the last flight as a tourist clipper,' he added. 'It's due to be stripped of all its luxury for military purposes upon return to the States, so sit back and relax and one of the crew will be with you shortly.'

Louise clutched Katie's hand.

'Have you ever flown?' she said.

Katie shook her head. 'No, but I'm looking forward to it.'

'You're not scared?'

'I don't think so – but anything is better than the *Duke of York* in a storm.'

She had butterflies in her stomach but whether of excited anticipation or fear, she had no idea. She looked around at the other passengers. They all seemed unperturbed. Most of them were reading but she was too wound up to do the same. She wanted to experience every moment. The aircraft's engine began a steady hum and then they were speeding along for several hundred yards until she felt the boat lift off the water.

At that point a smiling young woman in navy-blue uniform announced that a light breakfast would be served in the dining room in half an hour.

By the time everyone had eaten the breakfast of fruit, hard-boiled eggs, toast and tea or coffee, most of the passengers, including Louise, were nodding off, but Katie was too tense even to close her eyes. Every mile was taking her nearer to home, she kept reminding herself. She had to admit she could hardly feel anything was moving. After twenty minutes or so she decided to go to the newspaper rack and removed the latest copy of *Life* magazine. On the front was a photograph of a woman in a two-piece bathing costume stretched out on a towel on the beach. Katie was quite absorbed when the pilot's voice came over the loudspeaker, making her jump.

'We will shortly be landing in Bermuda,' he announced.

Katie turned to find a startled Louise staring back at her, having just awoken from her nap. 'So you were right.'

Louise threw her a smug glance. 'Of *course* I was right. I don't give you duff information.'

Nevertheless, Katie thought Louise sounded thoroughly fed-up. Was it because she might soon have to say goodbye to the detective, or whoever it was she'd got close to?

It was a strange feeling to land on the water. The *Duke of York* was already in the harbour waiting for them. Just looking at the waves softly lapping the sides of the great ship turned Katie's stomach. She was sure she'd spend at least half the time in her bunk feeling ill. But when they'd disembarked, it seemed that Mr Churchill had other ideas so far as he was concerned, because one of his aides told them the PM had asked to stay on the *Berwick* for the entire journey back to Portsmouth, and he'd be taking a few in the party with him.

'These are the names of those who will be travelling back to Britain on the *Berwick*,' he said, his eyes lowered to the piece of paper in his hand. 'There will be ten passengers.' He cleared his throat. 'Dr Wilson, George Wright, John Robson . . . '

Katie held her breath while she counted everyone, though why, she had no idea, as there'd be no reason for the Prime Minister to include her in such a select group. Yet when the ninth name was announced, making ten with Mr Churchill, she couldn't help a sharp twinge of disappointment. She'd have to face that nightmare voyage again.

'And lastly, Miss Valentine,' Mr Churchill's aide said as he put the sheet of paper back in his briefcase. 'All ten will accompany the Prime Minister on the flight back to England in the *Berwick*.'

Katie jumped. Relief flooded through her that she'd be home in a day or two instead of at least a week on the ocean and that was so long as there were no emergencies such as another violent storm or, worse, the captain having to fend off any U-boats and zig-zag his way across the Atlantic.

'It looks like we've both got what we want,' Louise said, coming up behind her. 'I want this all to last as long as possible with Peter.' She looked at Katie with tearful eyes and gave a wan smile. 'And yes, it *is* Peter Whitney, the detective I've rather fallen for.'

Katie opened her mouth to speak but Louise held up her palm.

'He's married so it's not going to last, but at least you'll be able to find out sooner what's happened to Baxter. He's a decent chap and I'm crossing my fingers for him.'

In a strange way, Katie was glad that the *Berwick* had already been prepared for military use and there was none of the glamour of the boat she and Louise had just travelled on. It matched her mood. And oh, the bliss of not having Louise's voice in her ear all the time. Then she scolded herself. All right, the woman liked to stir a bit of trouble when she felt bored, and she wasn't entirely happy if she wasn't in the limelight, Katie thought with a grimace, but it didn't make her a bad person.

A shadow fell over her seat.

'Miss Valentine, the PM wants you for dictation.'

Katie took her shorthand notepad and a freshly sharpened pencil from her handbag and stepped across to where Mr Churchill was sitting in the front row. He looked up and gave her a cherubic smile, then thrust out his arm and patted the seat opposite.

'I hope you're enjoying the flight, Miss Valentine.'

'Oh, yes, Mr Churchill, very much.'

'Not quite so lavish as the one you came on just now, I understand.'

'I'm more than happy on the *Berwick* – with you, sir,' she added.

He beamed. 'Let us make a start then. We have plenty of catching up to do.' He took a gulp from his large glass of brandy.

He sounded tired, Katie thought. The words weren't flowing as they so often did. But by the second report it was as though he'd been injected with adrenaline. After three hours solid, her eyes began to droop.

'Miss Valentine, I don't believe even *your* skills can be expected to work efficiently when you're fast asleep.'

Her eyelids flew open. 'I'm awfully sorry, sir. I'm not usually like this.'

'Maybe if you get typing, the clatter of the machine will wake you up,' he said with a cynical grin, then added, 'as well as everyone else.' He took another gulp of his drink. 'Ridiculous that they don't have noiseless typewriters on this boat when the Americans were the ones who invented them.'

Katie didn't know how she managed to transcribe her shorthand onto the typewriter. Had she made any mistakes? There was no one she'd feel comfortable asking if they would check it with her, so she carefully peered at every single word. She let out a breath of relief. There didn't appear to be any mistakes but then some of the letters were quite hazy. Maybe the ribbon needed changing. She wondered if there were any on board, but then a wave of sleep enveloped her brain. If she could only put her head on a pillow. Fortunately, Captain Kelly Rogers, the pilot, made several announcements over the public address system, keeping the small group up to date with bulletins about their position, how high they were travelling, their speed and the time and distance still to go. Each time he spoke, he jolted Katie back to the job in hand.

Collecting the sheets she'd typed into a neat stack, she clipped each report together, then placed them on a small table by the side of Mr Churchill. She was amused to see that he had succumbed to sleep. She was just about to creep away when he juddered awake.

'Thank you, Miss Valentine.' His eyes pierced hers. 'Am I to understand they have all been checked by someone for any mistakes?'

She swallowed. 'Um, no, sir. I didn't feel I could ask anyone here to help but I've gone over everything very carefully.'

'I'm sure any of them would be only too happy to oblige.' He grunted. 'I'd better go through them with a fine-tooth comb, then.' He glanced at her. 'And you, Miss Valentine, had better ask the steward to pull out one of the bunks and get some shut-eye.'

But tired as she was, Katie couldn't drift off. Her mind was teeming with thoughts, mostly about Baxter. This happened whenever she'd finished her work and was on her own. Surely if he was dead she'd know it. But perhaps that was wishful thinking. After half an hour of lying there she sat up. It was no good. She'd do better to ask one of the crew for a cup of tea to pull her round, and then see if Mr Churchill had any more work for her.

She was amused to find Mr Churchill signing a few of the pilot's bulletins and handing them round to his fellow passengers.

'And one for you, Miss Valentine,' he said, handing her the small sheet of paper.

She couldn't help a smile of delight to see he'd scrawled 'Miss Valentine' on the top and 'W. S. Churchill' at the bottom, with the date, 16th January 1942.

If I ever have children, I'll certainly have some stories to tell them.

She felt her heartstrings tighten. She'd never really thought about children until she'd fallen in love with Baxter. His were the only children she would ever want, and she didn't even know if he still existed.

You have to stop this! She forced herself to imagine Baxter being looked after, whatever injury he might have suffered, and refused to think anything different. Feeling a little better she rose to her feet. She'd stretch her legs and find that cup of tea.

The hours slowly ticked by.

'Do you realise we are fifteen hundred miles from anywhere?' Katie heard the gravelly tones of Mr Churchill, this time addressing his doctor.

'Heaven is as near by sea as by land,' replied Dr Wilson.

The Prime Minister chortled.

It was an odd feeling to be floating in the air so far from land, but the weather had been kind up to now, and the flying boat seemed to be on a smooth path. They'd been served excellent food with plenty of snacks during the twenty-four hours they'd been in the air, and now, according to a clock on the wall, they should be nearing home. The pilot had continued to keep them abreast of the weather and told them they would be landing in Plymouth harbour. Shortly after, he announced they would be making their descent.

Oh, the relief to think she'd be touching water in a few minutes' time. She wished they hadn't had to pull down the dark blinds when they left America's air space so as not to be spotted by enemy planes. It would have been interesting to see how the clipper came in to land. The pilot broke into her thoughts.

'We've got quite a bit of fog,' he announced, 'so I'm afraid we've drifted slightly off course in the night. We'll have to make a bit of a U-turn northward.'

Dear God, he must mean we've been heading for France! Katie grasped the arms of her chair. The part of France which was occupied by the Germans! Her heart thumping madly in her chest, she looked round the cabin. There were a few mutterings but most of the men continued reading. But she noticed several didn't turn over a page.

The minutes felt like hours. The cabin had settled into an eerie calm. No one spoke. Everyone stubbed out their cigarettes. Even Mr Churchill's cigar was no longer glowing.

Katie squeezed her eyes shut, her heart beating furiously in her ears. Oh, they couldn't crash. She was too young to die. And they had the Prime Minister on board. The man in whom everyone had such faith. If they lost Mr Churchill, then they might lose the war!

But after a quarter of an hour or so, the sweetest words rang out.

'We're now approaching the English coast!'

Her eyelids shot open. But knowing they were now back on track and, according to the pilot, visibility had somewhat improved did nothing to stop Katie's stomach somersaulting at every turn of the flying boat as it circled around Plymouth harbour. Five minutes later, to her intense relief, Captain Rogers landed the clipper on the water as gently as if the sea were a soft cushion.

The Prime Minister and Dr Wilson were immediately escorted off the flying boat by military guards and disappeared. Katie rubbed her eyes, which were sore from a whole day and night of no sleep. Now she faced having to adjust to the British winter clock.

Katie and the rest of the group showed their passports, went through Customs with no one having to open any cases, and out to the two sleek black motorcars that one of Mr Churchill's personal secretaries had announced would be waiting to take them into London.

'However, you will have to find your own way home from there,' he'd added, 'but the good news is that you won't be needed for forty-eight hours, which will give you all a chance to rest.'

Chapter Forty-Two

It was mid-morning by the time Katie climbed into a taxi, dazed from the long journey and no sleep, the time difference, and the drained feeling of not knowing if she would ever set eyes on Baxter again. Hardly aware of how much time had passed since she'd alighted from the flying boat, she arrived at her front door. The driver sprang out, removed her suitcase and set it down in the porch. She smiled gratefully as she paid him with an extra two shillings. It had been expensive but worth every penny. Her house key was somewhere in her handbag but she was too tired to search for it. And anyway, it would be too much of a shock to suddenly walk in without their having any idea she was home.

She rang the bell, her stomach churning as she braced herself to face her stepmother after all the misery, anger and hurt that had transpired between them. But it would be good to get things on a more even keel. Being away for over a month had given her time to reflect on the whole situation from everyone's perspective and realise no one could take all the blame, least of all Ursula. The trouble was, she hadn't come to terms yet with the woman she'd always thought of as her beloved Aunt Judy, and how she had casually given her own daughter away without even attempting to see whether she and Dad could make a go of it. Wanting to be a free spirit simply wasn't a good enough reason.

She shook herself. She could never put herself in Judy's

shoes to understand the reason so there was no point in torturing herself by raking it over and over in her mind. But Ursula was different. She was alive and had poured her heart out in that letter. Katie gave a deep sigh. Where her stepmother was concerned, she'd have to play it by ear.

But it wasn't her stepmother who answered the door, it was Dad, his jaw dropping in surprise. Tanny pushed past, barking wildly with joy.

'Have you missed me, old boy?' she said, patting his silky head.

The dog's tongue lolled out of his wide, grinning mouth. 'Woof.'

'That means "yes",' Katie laughed.

Oscar's face broke into a beam as he pulled her and her case inside, then hugged her.

'We hoped you'd be home soon,' he said, 'but I don't suppose you had any way of letting us know.'

'I didn't.' Katie removed her coat and hung it on the stand in the hall. 'We were literally told one afternoon that we would be going home that evening.'

'Did you come by ship or fly?'

Katie hesitated. Surely it would be all right if she told him.

'It was train and then flying boat.'

He whistled through his teeth.

'Good gracious. You must have been in the lap of luxury on one of those. They say they're kitted out fit for a king.'

'Apparently they were in ordinary times, but the military took over when the war started and stripped out the luxury items – at least they had in Mr—' She broke off.

Her father regarded her. 'I think I can gather who you came back with, love. And it makes sense to give more space for the military, and reduce the weight.' His eyebrows pulled together.

'Come on through, Katie. I should think you're gasping for a cup of tea. I'll put the kettle on.'

'Where's Mu . . . Mother?'

Her father's mouth thinned from her stumbling question but he didn't comment, except to say, 'She told me she wrote to you when you were away.'

'Yes, she did.'

'I think she was trying to mend the rift.'

'Dad, if you don't mind, that's between the two of us.' She glanced at him. 'Is she in the sitting room?'

Did he hesitate?

'No, she's in bed.'

'But it's much too early for her to be in bed.' She threw him a sharp look. 'Is anything wrong, Dad?'

'Let me go and make the tea.'

Why hadn't he answered her question? Maybe he was disappointed that she was still bitter, from the way she'd called her stepmother 'Mother'. She bit her lower lip. If so, she had to admit there was a grain of truth in it. She'd probably got one of her sick headaches, Katie thought. When this happened, she'd be laid up for two or three days with the curtains pulled. Yes, that would probably be it.

Five minutes later he came in with a tray of tea and a piece of Ursula's *Käsekuchen*. She remembered, somewhat guiltily, that yesterday was their wedding anniversary.

'So has she got one of her headaches?' Katie said, while cutting a piece of the German cheesecake with her fork.

Her father cleared his throat.

'I wish that was all she had.'

A sense of foreboding surged through her body.

'What is it then?'

Her father looked at the floor. 'She's been having pains in her stomach. They got so bad that I took her to the hospital a

363

month ago – it was just before you went to America. They've done some tests –' he glanced up and she saw his Adam's apple rise and fall '– and I'm afraid it's . . . cancer.' His voice trembled on the last word.

Katie's stomach contracted. That terrible word that people could hardly bring themselves to utter. She'd never expected anything like this. She looked down at the forkful of cake she'd been about to put in her mouth and instead laid it back on the plate. 'Why didn't you let me know?'

'The results weren't back until you'd gone.'

'But she wrote me a letter and never mentioned it.'

He looked at her. 'She didn't want you to worry or be distracted, Katie. She knew how important your work was. Besides, she wanted you to enjoy your time abroad.' He sniffed, then blew his nose loudly.

Dear God. He was really upset. She remembered something Ursula had written in the letter to her about him forgiving her for not disclosing the fact that she could never conceive. Maybe he loved his German wife far more than she'd ever realised. She tried to swallow but a lump had suddenly formed in her throat.

'Oh, Dad, I'm so sorry.'

'*Are* you, Katharina?'

She saw his eyes glisten with tears.

'Yes, I am . . . truly.'

'But you haven't forgiven her, have you?' He paused. 'And I mean without reservation.'

Katie heaved a sigh. 'I'm trying to.'

'She's been waiting patiently for you to come home, Katie. She doesn't want to die without your forgiveness.'

Fear made her shiver. 'She's not going to die, Dad. We'll get her the best surgeon to remove the tumour. And we'll . . . ' She trailed off when her father shook his head.

'It's too late, I'm afraid. The doctor at the hospital told me in private that she has very little time left. And we've hired the best nurse for her day-to-day care to make her last few weeks – possibly only d-days –' he cleared his throat '– to make her as comfortable as possible.' His eyes flicked to hers and then cast down again. 'In fact, the nurse has just gone to the chemist to collect a prescription.'

Days? Dear God. It could happen that soon?

'When did she make the cheesecake?'

'She has a good day sometimes and you know how she loves baking. She says it calms her down. She made it two days ago, ready . . . '

'. . . for your wedding anniversary yesterday,' Katie finished.

Her father looked surprised. 'That's right. You have a good memory. We managed to have a nice evening in spite of everything, but she overdid it and she's been very tired yesterday and today.' He hesitated and glanced at her. 'But her main worry is not seeing you before she dies.' He put his hand to his face.

Katie swallowed hard. 'Dad, I—'

'Just go up and see her,' he said. 'She might be asleep but these days she's a light sleeper. The pain won't allow her to have a good night's sleep, but she'll wake up right away when she knows it's you.' He blinked. 'Katie?'

'Yes, Dad.'

'Be kind to her.'

Katie wasn't sure her knees would support her as she climbed the stairs, Tanny following. This was dreadful. She tried to think of what to say but her mind was numb. Tanny nudged her leg for attention.

'Tanny, go back downstairs,' Katie admonished. 'I can't have you barking around her.'

His tail between his legs with disappointment, Tanny snuffled his way instead into her bedroom.

Gently, she tapped on her stepmother's door.

'Katharina?'

Katie had entered quietly, the scarf still wrapped in Garfinckel's tissue in her hand, but her stepmother heard her. She tried to heave herself up but fell back on the pillows with the effort. Katie rushed over and pushed them behind Ursula's back as she propped her up, using one of her father's pillows for extra support. She kissed her cheek and pulled up a chair to the bedside.

'How did you know it was me?'

'I know your footsteps.'

Katie looked down at the parched face, the skin stretched over the lovely bone structure, and blurted, 'Dad's told me you're seriously ill. He's in shock . . . and so am I.' She gently took her stepmother's hand and Ursula closed her eyes as though savouring her daughter's touch.

'You're still young,' Katie added, though in only a month she could tell her stepmother had aged.

Ursula's lids fluttered open and she gazed at Katie. 'You must not feel sorry for me, Katharina. It is something I am ready to bear.'

Was it her imagination, or was the colour already fading from Ursula's beautiful blue eyes?

Katie gulped. 'I'm glad I know now. I'll ask to take some extra time off work and—'

Ursula raised her hand a few inches off the sheet. Even that small effort seemed to stretch her to the limit.

'*Nein*. You must not. You are there for a special purpose. To help put an end to this *schrecklichen* . . . ' She broke off, searching for the English word.

'Terrible war,' Katie finished.

Ursula gave her a wan smile.

'I forget my words sometimes and blame it on my illness. People then take pity. It helps me forget the guilt I feel – just for being German.'

'Mutti, you mustn't apologise for being born a German,' Katie said, not realising she had gone back to her old way of addressing her stepmother. She impulsively put a hand on Ursula's arm, which now lay motionless on the counterpane. 'The German people are basically good. It's only a small number of Nazis who are evil and destroying the lives of anyone who doesn't uphold their sickening beliefs, but unfortunately ignorant people think they represent normal Germans.'

Ursula gave a weak nod.

'I know that with my heart, but it fights with my head.'

'Well, then,' Katie said firmly, 'you must listen to your heart – because that's where the truth lies.'

Suddenly, Katie was aware of what she was saying. Wasn't she giving advice to her stepmother that she hadn't taken herself? Her resentment and anger were simply because she hadn't been told the truth about her maternal heritage. Logical response. But if she searched her heart and looked now at the woman lying so ill in bed, Katie realised that the person she now called her stepmother had been in every sense a mother. It wasn't true, what she'd thought about Ursula taking her as her own child out of guilt. She might not have often shown it but she'd accepted another woman's child as her own. She'd looked after Katie, cooked wholesome meals, made many of her clothes, taught her her own language, worried about her, and had been so much more of a mother than Judy could ever have been capable of. Like a bolt of lightning, Katie accepted that her stepmother had loved her from the week-old baby she'd been when Judy had handed her over, trusting Ursula to do the right thing. And Ursula had. With all her heart.

Be kind to her, her father had said.

'Mutti,' Katie said, and this time she was aware of addressing her in the old way, 'I'm sorry I wasn't kind to you when I knew the truth about Judy.'

Ursula twisted the edge of the blanket. 'It was understandable . . . no more than your father and I deserved. We should have told you years ago. He wanted to. I hope I explained why in the letter I wrote to you.'

'You did . . . and now I understand. Judy was the mother who gave birth to me, but *you* are the mother who was . . . who *is* my true mother in every sense.' Katie's voice broke on those last words and tears streamed down her cheeks.

'Please don't cry, Katharina. You have just told me the words I have longed to hear. And best of all that you call me "Mutti" the way you always did.'

Katie stood and leaned over the bed and put her arms around her mother's thin shoulders. Just then she caught sight of her parents' wedding photograph on her father's bedside table. Strange she'd never noticed it before. But it was Ursula's wedding dress that made her take a sharp breath. It was the same dress she'd altered for Katie to take with her to Washington. Tears sprang to her eyes. She gulped, then without thinking she said:

'I love you, Mutti, for taking me and caring for me all these years. I realise I always have. And thank you for loving Dad,' she added.

'*Ich liebe dich ebenfalls*,' her mother replied, then added, 'I love you, too,' as though worried Katie would think she couldn't bring herself to say the words in English. 'You will never know how much.' She hesitated. 'Let me give you a kiss.' She pecked Katie's cheek. 'I only wish I was strong enough to hug you.'

'It doesn't matter, Mutti. None of it matters any more. I just want us to concentrate on making you as comfortable as possible. Oh, and I have a present for you.'

'For me?'

'Yes. I bought it in a very posh department store in—' She broke off. 'Well, I can tell you now I was in Washington, home of President Roosevelt.'

Ursula's eyes widened and then she smiled.

'You don't have to worry, Katharina. Your dad and I guessed where you were and who was there also.'

Katie couldn't help smiling back as she put the small packet into her mother's hands.

'Will you open it for me?'

Katie unwrapped the paper and the silk scarf flowed onto the bed. Ursula fingered it, her expression alight.

'Katharina, it is beautiful. My favourite colours. You knew that by the dress I altered for you.' She tilted her chin. 'Did you wear the dress?'

'No, I never had a chance. We didn't stop working and were too tired to go out most evenings.'

Her mother gave a slight nod. 'It does not matter. The opportunity will come.' She frowned. 'Oh, Katharina, did Dad tell you there is a letter for you on the bureau? I believe it is from that nice young man, Mr Edwards.'

A letter from Baxter! Katie's heart leapt.

'Why don't you go downstairs and read it.'

'I don't want to leave you just yet,' Katie said.

'I'm tired, *meine Liebling*. I am ready for the best sleep I have had for a long time.'

'Are you sure?'

'Yes, I'm sure.'

'Have you everything you need – water or . . .'

'I have everything now I could ever wish for.' Her blue eyes suddenly brightened as she smiled at Katie. 'You must have missed him when you were away in America.'

Katie swallowed hard. 'I have missed him.'

'Then go and read your letter.'

'All right, then. I'll leave you to rest.'

'Just one thing I long to ask,' Ursula said.

'Anything.'

Her mother took in a breath as though to make sure she spoke all the words she wanted to say.

'I know you cannot tell me about the work you are doing,' she began, then coughed.

Katie handed her the glass of water on the bedside table.

'Thank you.' Her mother took a few sips. 'But your father and I always had a strong feeling you are working somewhere close to our splendid Prime Minister.'

She took hold of her mother's hand.

'Mutti, you and Dad are right. Not only am I close to Mr Churchill, but I have been doing actual work for him in his office so I have got to know him . . . just a little bit.' She smiled. 'And you are right about that, too – he's a remarkable man, and very human.'

Ursula's eyes flew wide.

'Oh, Katharina, you must tell this to your father. He will be so proud of you . . . as I am.' Her voice faded on the last words.

'I'll leave you in peace, then.' Katie bent to kiss her mother's cheek.

Her mother's eyes had already closed.

Katie ran down the stairs and into the dining room, where letters were kept in a rack on top of the bureau. And there it was. She turned over the envelope but the date was blurred. Heart pounding, she put her head in the sitting room where her father sat reading his newspaper.

'Dad, I'm just going up to my room for a few minutes to read my letter,' she said.

He looked up. 'Oh, yes, I meant to tell you. You take your time, love.' He winked. 'I believe it's from that young man we met.'

'It is,' she said.

'Did you clear the air between you and your mother?'

Katie nodded. 'Yes, we did.' She hesitated. 'I do feel ashamed of the way I behaved, Dad.'

'You were shocked and hurt,' her father said. 'Forget it. If your mother has, then that's all that matters.'

'She has. She seemed really happy – especially as I called her "Mutti" again.' She blinked away the threatening tears.

'Yes, she would have loved that.' Her father took up his newspaper again. 'Well, you go and read your letter and come down when you're ready.'

'I will.'

The letter was burning in her hand as she ran back up the stairs and into her room where Tanny rushed up to lick her hand. She gave him a pat, then sat on the edge of her bed and tore it open. She pulled out the thin sheet of paper and scanned the date: *19th December 1941*.

She began to read.

My darling Katharina,

I hope by the time you read this you will be looking forward, I hope, to spending Christmas with your parents. Just hope you're not missing me too much! I don't want you to get a swollen head but I'm missing you like crazy. But that will all change soon as I'll be on my way back tomorrow and will post this in London if you've gone home for Christmas. If not, I'll see you in person which would be marvellous.

I can't wait to kiss those luscious lips, but more than likely I won't get the chance until Christmas is over and we're back in the routine.

Bye for now, my sweetheart.

Baxter XXX

Her chest felt tight, her eyes now dry. Baxter hadn't known she'd gone to the States, let alone Washington, when he'd written this. And of course he hadn't known that his train was going to be involved in a fatal crash.

Tanny sat by her feet and put his paw on her lap, his golden eyes looking troubled.

She bent down to him.

'Oh, Tanny, I'm so miserable. I wish I knew what's happened to him.'

The dog nuzzled his head against her calves. Then his head shot up and he cocked his head on one side.

'What is it, boy?'

He looked at her and whined, then rushed to the door, still whining and looking round at her. She frowned and he gave a short bark, then went up on his haunches and pawed at the closed door.

'Did you hear something, Tanny?'

He gave a long, drawn-out whine.

Mutti. She must have called out for something but her voice was so weak now. Berating herself that she hadn't heard, Katie leapt to her feet and was out of the door and into her mother's room.

Her mother's eyes were closed. She was asleep, her hand still in the folds of the silk scarf. Tanny trotted in and sat quietly nearby. She put an arm around her mother's back, feeling the bones beneath her fingers, as she tried to lift her to a sitting position.

'Mutti, you must have been having a bad dream. It's all right, I'm here. Let me help you up and I'll get you some water.'

There was no response. She gave the shoulders a gentle shake. Tanny came closer to the bed, softly whimpering. In a daze, Katie gently took her mother's hand. It was still warm. But she knew – and Tanny had known before her – Mutti was dead.

Waves of misery and disbelief swept over her. How was it possible that it could have happened so quickly? Tears streaming down her cheeks, she carefully laid her mother's head back on the pillow. She'd never again see Mutti's sapphire-blue eyes, so often looking anxious these last few months, ever since she'd disclosed her true relationship to her daughter. A cloak of guilt engulfed her. She took in a jerky breath, her mouth parched.

'Come on, Tanny,' she said softly. 'We must tell Dad.'

By the time her father was back downstairs, Katie had made a pot of tea. Such a stupid thing to do, she thought, as she carried through the tray into the sitting room, but she needed the comforting ritual of a familiar chore. And he would need one as much as she did, she reasoned. He was sitting in his armchair gazing at the fire in silence, clutching a half-completed glove. Her mother's knitting. She swallowed hard.

'Dad?'

He looked up with tear-filled eyes that were red and swollen and held up the glove. 'She was making this for a soldier. She's made a dozen pairs already . . . and socks as well.' He broke down and sobbed.

Katie set the tray down and rushed over to him, cradling his head in her arms. He stayed quiet for a few moments, then raised his head.

'Oh, dear, I'm sorry, love, but I can't stand the thought I've lost her.' He pulled his handkerchief from his pocket and wiped his eyes.

She'd never known her father to cry and it unnerved her.

'I've made us some tea.'

'Oh . . . yes.'

He held out a hand that trembled to take the cup.

'I'll put it on the table.'

'Thank you.' He put his head in his hands for a few moments. 'I did grow to love her, you know,' he said in a broken voice, 'but I never told her. I just hoped she knew.'

Katie smiled gently at him. 'I'm sure she did. And she loved *you* – with all her heart.'

He stared at her. 'How do you know?'

'She tried to explain the circumstances of my birth once but it was too soon after I found out, and I didn't want to listen to her. But I remember all of it now. She said she fell in love with you when you were her tutor teaching English. And that she felt you'd grown to love her over the years. Not only that, Dad, it was every time she mentioned you. I could tell by her tone. It always softened.'

He shook his head. 'You don't know how happy I am to hear that. And to know you and she were friends again.'

'Not *just* friends, Dad . . . but mother and daughter.'

Chapter Forty-Three

Katie and her father spent the evening quietly talking about Ursula. Looking at her father's distraught expression, hearing the tremor in his voice when he said her name, she realised he was as shocked as she was that it had happened so very suddenly, even though he'd known the end was coming. But to think Mutti had died on the very day she'd come back from America. Katie shuddered, dreading the thought that if Mr Churchill hadn't added her name to his list to go home on his clipper, she'd still be on the ship . . . and wouldn't have had the chance to say how sorry she was to the woman who was her mother in every way but blood. She would never have forgiven herself. As it was, she wished it could have been different. She'd acted like an angry child, barely considering how Ursula must have felt, a young woman who would never have her own children, and only too thankful to take the little new-born into her heart.

There was a long silence as they both tried to make sense of everything. Then Katie said:

'I'll have to ring work and tell them what's happened, Dad, as I shan't go back until after the service.' She wouldn't use the word 'funeral'. It was too final.

'I can manage, Katie. You're needed at work.' He gave her a wan smile. 'Besides, I've got Tanny for company.'

She argued but it made no difference.

375

'If you're absolutely sure, then I'll be back to help when there's a date fixed.'

'Your mother wanted it to be very simple. You know how she kept herself to herself most of the time.'

Because she didn't want to disclose her German-ness.

'There'll only be her friend Joan and a couple of neighbours. They've all offered to help – and I shall let them.'

'What about her parents?'

Her father grunted. 'It was no use writing to them because there's no postal service between the two countries.'

'Oh, of course not.' Katie sat quietly for a few moments. Then she said, 'Was Mutti very upset not to be able to contact them?'

'No. She said she'd cried all her tears over them years ago.'

Two days later, when she was back in the War Rooms, Katie's mission was to find out if anyone knew anything about Baxter – if by some miracle he was back at work. She'd seen the Prime Minister rushing off to a meeting an hour ago but she couldn't possibly question him. No, the place to go was the Map Room Annexe. Barnaby and Tom were bound to know where their colleague was.

She knocked on the door but there was no answer. She tried it and looked in. Then the Map Room itself. No one around. Perhaps they were at a meeting. She couldn't wait for hours to know. Biting her lip, she suddenly spotted Roz coming out of the typing pool, then turning into another passage off the main corridor. Without thinking, Katie flew along after her, not caring about being reprimanded – even by the Prime Minister himself.

'Roz,' she called.

Roz turned. 'Oh, hello. I see you're back.'

Katie ignored Roz's smirk.

'Have you heard any news about Baxter?'

'Why don't you try the Map Room – they should know.'

'I've been to the Map Room and the Annexe but no one's in.'

'Who told you about the crash in the first place?'

'Mr Churchill. I was taking dictation when the telegram came.'

'Then ask him.' Roz looked pointedly at her files. 'You must excuse me.' Then to Katie's astonishment, Roz added, 'Good luck, Katie,' in a softer tone before walking briskly away.

Katie looked after the stiffly held retreating back, wondering if Roz would ever enjoy life. But she'd actually wished her luck at the last moment. Perhaps there was a human side to the woman after all. And she'd take Roz's advice. She was down to take dictation from the Prime Minister in his room after his nap later this afternoon With any luck he wouldn't snap at her like he did the last time she'd made the same enquiry.

It was strange how she no longer felt uncomfortable or embarrassed in the Prime Minister's bedroom, Katie thought, as she sat at the desk typing while the great man himself finished putting on his socks and shoes, at the same time dictating a letter to the President. After she'd typed for more than two solid hours, with just a sip of water now and again while Mr Churchill had downed at least two large tumblers of whisky, and she thought he'd stopped to consider how to word the next bit, he told her that would be all.

She massaged her back and neck. The chair was just an ordinary one and not comfortable for long spells of typing. She might have a word with Miss Nicholson about the chance of having a proper typist's chair brought in. But for now, she only had one burning question in her mind.

Before she could open her mouth, Mr Churchill said, 'Was everything well at home? No bombing nearby?'

'No bombing,' she said. 'But my mother . . . she d-died just a short time after I came back from America.'

'Oh, dear. I'm very sorry to hear that. I presume you still have your father.'

'Yes. He's in the Home Guard but he's taking care of everything at the moment and insisted I should go back to work.'

He lit a fresh cigar. 'It's just like putting on a play. The show must go on. And the war doesn't stop for anything – family included. Your father would know that.'

'Yes, he does.' She drew in a deep breath. Now was the time. 'Mr Churchill, I'm sorry, I've already asked you this, but now we're back in England, have you heard anything further about the Chief Cartographer who was caught up in that railway crash?'

He took his glasses off and blinked, then placed his glasses halfway down his nose again.

'Young Edwards, you're talking about?' He stared at her with those all-seeing, all-knowing eyes. When she nodded, he said, 'Bad business, that.'

Dear God, no.

She pulled her stomach in tightly to stop herself from fainting.

'So h-he's d-dead.' It wasn't a question.

'No, no, child, he's not dead. He took a wallop but he's out of hospital and in a convalescent home. I plan to see him this week.' He gave a sly grin. 'Shall I say you asked after him?'

Relief and joy flooded through her. He wasn't dead. He was alive. He was all right and recuperating. Her cheeks warm at the Prime Minister's mischief, she answered, 'Oh, no. I just wanted to find out if he was all right as he was one of the people missing and of course I knew him . . . as I do all the cartographers,' she added quickly.

'Hmm. Well, he certainly took a blow to his head and had a

severe case of concussion. Didn't know where the devil he was when he awoke in hospital. I believe at one point he didn't even know his own name. But it'll come back in time, I don't doubt.'

He unnerved her the way he was looking at her.

'Miss Valentine, I've heard rumours that you are in love with Wing Commander Baxter Edwards.'

Katie jerked upright. She hadn't expected this. How could she lie when he was staring at her like that?

'Yes, Mr Churchill, I am.'

'Does he know?'

'Yes.'

'And how does he feel about it?'

'He said he feels the same.'

'Then you must waste no time in seeing him.' He frowned as though thinking. 'Mrs Goodman will have his address.'

She blinked away the tears.

'Thank you, sir. Thank you very much.'

She gathered her bag and closed the door quietly behind her. What an incredible man. And sensitive in unexpected ways. She was almost at her office when she heard her name.

'Ah, Katie. Good to see you back.'

It was Barnaby, looking more serious than she'd ever seen him.

'Oh, Barnaby, do you know where Baxter's been sent?'

'Come into the Annexe.'

She followed him in. He went over to his desk and flipped the pages of his diary.

'Ah, here it is.' He scribbled the address on a scrap of paper and handed it to her.

'How is he?' Katie breathed. 'Have you seen him?'

Barnaby's handsome features hardened. 'Yes. Actually, I've just come back from the convalescent home. Physically, he's doing well. Mentally, he's not in too good a shape.'

'Well, I suppose it will all take time,' she said. 'I understand it was a nasty blow to his head.'

'That's all healing nicely. But I do wonder if it's jolted his brain somehow as he's really quite distressed.'

Her heart plummeted.

'Has his memory come back?'

'So you know about that.' She nodded, hardly daring to breathe. He looked at her. 'It's partly back but if you could see him, it would be the best possible medicine.'

She swallowed. 'Why do you say that? Did he mention me?'

Barnaby was silent.

She looked directly at him.

'That means he didn't,' was all she said.

Chapter Forty-Four

It was just as well that she'd been on the graveyard shift, Katie thought, as she was able to have most of the next day free without asking for any time off. She'd need that later. She could get to the convalescent home and back to work in a day, now she was on such an early morning train to Haywards Heath. She'd looked it up on the map and seen how close it was to Lewes, near where he'd been brought up.

As usual the compartment was packed with soldiers but at least the train hadn't stopped because of an air-raid alarm. With the address safely in her coat pocket, she stepped down from the train onto the platform that the conductor had announced was Haywards Heath.

She'd been in such a hurry to leave the train that she hadn't had time to button her coat. Now she pulled it together and fastened it, adjusted her hat and scarf and hurried out of the station. The town was unknown to her so she wouldn't even try to work out bus timetables and stops. The taxi rank was where she needed to head.

Outside it was raining and there was only one taxi in the rank. She ran forward but was beaten by a man in a raincoat holding an umbrella, who was rushing to the window to speak to the driver.

'Oh, please . . . I'm in a dreadful hurry,' Katie gasped.

He swung round.

'Sorry, miss, I'm sure my journey is just as urgent.'

'I'm seeing my boyfriend. He was in a train crash. He's lost his memory. He's in—'

He stood back. 'You'd better jump in.'

'I can't thank you enough.'

He smiled, the rain dripping from his umbrella as he folded it. She bent low to sit in the back seat and he joined her.

The driver twisted his neck round. 'Where to, miss?'

She unfolded the piece of paper.

'Stanton Manor. It's—'

'I know it,' he interrupted. 'Going a bit out of the way for our other passenger.'

'It's all right.' Her rescuer removed his hat and looked at her. He grinned. 'Take the young lady where she needs to go and then carry on with me.'

'Right-o, sir.'

'You're very kind.' Katie took her purse from her bag, but he put his hand on hers and pushed it gently aside.

'No, I don't want the fare. It's the least I can do in this bloody war.'

After only ten minutes by Katie's watch, the taxi crunched up the winding gravel drive through an avenue of elm trees to the convalescent home. After saying goodbye and thanks again to her rescuer, Katie walked up to the main entrance. Stanton Manor was an imposing Jacobean building in its own beautiful grounds, but she barely appreciated it, so intent was she on seeing Baxter. Taking hold of the heavy knocker, she let it fall with a crash. As she heard footsteps coming towards the door, her head was still crammed with images of him. How would she find him? Would he be pleased to see her? Or had his personality changed since the crash, so that he no longer loved her? She thrust away the terrifying thought. The door opened and a smiling young nurse, clipboard in hand, stepped forward.

'Do come in. This weather is appalling, isn't it? You need to take that wet coat off.'

Katie's heart lifted. 'Thank you,' she said as she removed her coat and put it over her arm.

'May I have your name and the patient's name?'

'Katharina Valentine. I'm visiting Mr Edwards – Mr Baxter Edwards.'

'Ah, yes.'

The nurse glanced at the clipboard then frowned. She looked up.

'Your name's not here. Do you have an appointment?'

'Um, no. I didn't know I'd be able to come until the last moment.'

The nurse's mouth tightened. 'I'm afraid you must have an appointment.'

'But—'

'What is your relationship with Mr Edwards?'

'I'm – he's my – well, we're engaged to be married.'

It was a lie, but she didn't care.

'So you're his fiancée?'

'Yes,' she said firmly.

The nurse smiled again. 'Well, in that case, I believe we can make an exception to the rule.' She paused. 'Follow me. I think I know where he is.'

As they walked along the hallway, the smell of Dettol, though faint, reminded Katie that Stanton Manor, once an elegant country house, was now used for a completely different purpose. Instead of the walls being adorned by famous artists, as she might have expected, there were posters of events taking place, signs pointing to various rooms, and photographs of some of the patients, most of them sporting a cheerful smile. She loitered behind the nurse for a few seconds to see if Baxter was in any of them but couldn't see any sign.

She glanced through open doors at the elegant rooms beyond with their chandeliers and moulded ceilings. Then they went down another hall, until the nurse finally stopped outside a closed door saying: LIBRARY – QUIET, PLEASE.

'Could you wait here for a few moments, Miss Valentine?'

A minute later the nurse came out, her previous friendly demeanour noticeably absent.

'He's here,' she said, 'but he didn't seem to know who I was talking about.' She kept her eyes fixed on Katie. 'He said he didn't have any fiancée.' She paused and must have seen the stupefied misery in Katie's expression. 'I'm sorry, but we can't let anyone in unless the patient already knows them – unless they're medical staff, of course.'

Of course, Katie thought numbly. She'd come all this way on a wild-goose chase. It was too frustrating for words.

'We have a small café on the premises for patients where they can take visitors,' the nurse said in a more sympathetic tone, 'if you'd like a cup of tea or something to eat before you go.'

'Thank you, I would.' Anything to be allowed to stay a bit longer. To think what to do. To see if there was a way . . .

The nurse accompanied her to a bustling café where people, mostly young men who Katie presumed were in the services, chatted with one another as they drank tea and coffee. Several were on crutches, and one man had a bandage around his head and over his eyes. One of the other patients had hold of his arm and was talking quietly to him. For a horrible moment she thought it was Baxter. Then she realised the man wasn't as tall and had a much slighter build.

'I'll leave you to it,' the nurse said. 'But make sure you sign your name when you leave.'

'I will.'

Thank goodness her every move was not now being watched.

Katie went to the counter and asked for a cup of tea and a shortbread biscuit. She took it and, aware of curious glances, sat as far away from everyone as she could. Oh, how good that tea tasted. She finished it and was debating whether to order another when a voice said, 'Are you waiting to see anyone?'

A man of around thirty with a moustache and dark hair swept back from his forehead smiled down at her.

'I was,' she answered, trying to keep any bitterness from her tone, 'but I didn't know until the last minute I was coming and because I didn't make an appointment, they said I couldn't go in.'

'Who are you visiting?'

'Baxter Edwards.'

He nodded. 'One of the newer patients.' He looked at her. 'Friend of his or relation?'

'He's my boyfriend. We fell in love just before the accident.' She looked him squarely in the eye. 'I just need to know if he still feels the same, but no one will allow me to see him, even when I lied and said I was his fiancée.'

'I know Baxter,' he said unexpectedly.

'You do?'

'Yes. He's a decent bloke. Had a rough time in a train crash, I understand. Got a bit of a memory problem.' He glanced at her. 'And one of the nurses would have told him your name, which by the way is—?'

'Katie Valentine.'

'Mmm. Nice name. Sorry, I haven't introduced myself. Norman Jackson at your service.' He gave a small mock bow. 'The thing is, did they say where he is now?'

'Yes, he's in the library. But it's no good. He denied all knowledge of a fiancée . . . which in a way was right, I suppose. We're not actually engaged yet, but I'd have thought he'd have put two and two together.'

Norman Jackson threw back his head and laughed.

What was so funny?

'I'm sorry, Katie, if I may call you that. I bet a bob to a tenner I know what's happened. He's trying to remember people and events as accurately as he can so he can be truthful with his consultant, who's monitoring everything. But he can't recall being engaged to be married. His brain isn't linking things fast enough to grasp that it's you, and that you used the term to boost your chance of seeing him.' He briefly touched her arm. 'Stay there and leave this to me.' He disappeared.

Patients didn't have the authority to break any rules, Katie thought, as she sipped a second cup of tea, so what could this Norman Jackson do to help? But at least he was kind enough to try. She briefly closed her eyes, dreading leaving the convalescent home and not seeing Baxter for herself. She'd tried – really she had.

The café door opened and closed at intervals. She stopped looking towards it. What was the point of raising her hopes? More people came in. This time she looked up, to see a woman with her arm in a sling – and behind her Norman Jackson. The woman went to the counter. Norman caught her eye and sent her a beaming smile then stepped aside. She saw who was following him and gasped. Baxter!

Her heart beating madly in her ears, she half rose, but Norman waved her down. He took Baxter's arm and led him over to where she was sitting.

'Let me introduce a friend of mine, Katie,' Norman beamed. 'This is Baxter Edwards.'

Katie cast an anxious look at Baxter. There was a deep angry scar on his forehead running into his scalp. He wasn't smiling. In fact, after giving her the briefest of glances and a nod, he wasn't doing anything. She looked up at Norman, who shook his head in warning.

'Sit yourself down, Edwards,' he said. 'I'll go and get you some tea.' His eyes fell on Katie. 'Can I get you something else?'

'No, thanks.'

At the sound of her voice, Baxter looked at her more directly and his forehead wrinkled in puzzlement.

'I know you, don't I?' he said.

Feeling her heart would break into pieces if she didn't keep hold of herself, she said, 'Yes. You know me well, Baxter.'

'I do?'

'We work at the same place.' She lowered her voice. She mustn't let anyone hear her tell him but she had to help him remember. 'You and I work close to the Prime Minister.'

Relief crossed his face. 'Oh, yes, that's right.'

Good. At least he remembered that.

'That damn fool Chamberlain.'

Oh, no. She took his hand and he looked down at the two hands touching, almost in wonderment.

'The Prime Minister's no longer Neville Chamberlain,' she said slowly. 'It's Winston Churchill – you must remember him, with his perpetual cigar.'

'Oh, yes, now I remember.'

But she didn't think he remembered at all; he was just saying it to appease her.

She kept hold of his hand and was grateful that he'd made no movement to pull away.

'We became friends at work,' she said.

'Yes, I thought so.'

Katie looked at him hard. He didn't look that much altered. A little thinner – his face in particular. But his eyes had lost their twinkle. Their teasing look. Their laughter. She could have wept.

'Loving friends,' she dared say.

He gave her what looked like a sad smile. 'Oh, that's nice.

I wish I could remember more. You look such a pretty girl to be loving friends with.' He breathed out a deep sigh. 'Will you help me?'

Dear God.

'I'll try, Baxter.'

But even saying the words, she knew it would be impossible. As soon as she left the building she wouldn't be able to remind him of how they loved one another. How they'd been so happy together. Oh, it was too cruel. But she had to have faith. She'd heard of people with amnesia and in nine cases out of ten, things gradually came back to them. But what if he was the tenth?

Stop it. He needs help. And you won't be giving him any with that frame of mind.

'Tea up,' Norman said, placing a cup in front of Baxter.

He took it and swallowed half in one go.

'Do you have good food here?' she asked him, more for something to say.

'Oh, yes. It's very good.' He paused as though trying to find the words. 'I've lost some weight, you know.'

'Yes, I can tell,' she said.

'Really?' He glanced at her. 'How long have you known me?' he said.

Katie blinked. 'We've known one another for several months.'

'Oh?' He shook his head. 'I wish I could remember.'

The three of them were silent until Norman said, 'Well, I'll leave you to it for a while.' He stood and glanced down at her. 'What time do you think you'll be leaving, Katie?'

She peered at her watch. Drat! It was getting more difficult to see the small numbers. She opened her bag and took out her glasses case, then put them on.

'I probably won't stay much longer,' she said. 'I have to work this evening.'

'I often worked in the evenings,' Baxter put in unexpectedly.

'Sometimes right through the night.' He seemed to do a double-take as he stared at Katie. 'You know, you remind me a lot of a girl I once knew who couldn't read my writing. I told her she should get her eyes tested. She did, and next time I saw her she was wearing glasses!'

Katie gasped, then pretended it was a cough so as not to let him see her surprise at his recollection. She didn't know how she stopped herself from blurting out, *That was* me, *Baxter. Can't you see –* I'm *that girl.*

No! He had to work it out for himself without any hint from her. She swallowed hard. It was the only way to know for sure he really did remember who she was – and that he'd once loved her.

Chapter Forty-Five

On the train going back to London, Katie tried to read her book, but it was impossible. All she could think of was that Baxter didn't recognise her – only that she reminded him of another girl. But at least the other girl was herself, Katie thought, though it didn't give her much reassurance. She hadn't stayed long after that. The only small comfort she'd taken was when she'd said goodbye to him, still in the café, and he'd looked at her with almost a probing look, and replied, 'I do hope you'll come and see me again . . . soon.' His eyes scanned the room. A few patients darted curious glances towards their table. 'Some of the blokes here seem surprised I have such a pretty girl visiting me.'

Was that only so he could show her off as some kind of trophy? Or was it that he genuinely wanted to see her again?

She arranged her features in a pleasant but neutral expression as she rose to her feet and extended her hand to him to shake. He stood and took her hand in his and a buzz of electricity shot up her arm. She saw him flush as he let her hand fall. So he felt something, too. She was sure of it.

'Will you do that?'

'Yes.'

'Promise?'

He was appealing to her. She could see it in his expression.

'Yes, I promise.'

She had to turn away so he couldn't see her eyes brimming

over with tears. She rushed out of the door and walked swiftly along the corridors until she came to the entrance. Not even saying goodbye to the receptionist, she heaved open the main door just as a voice called, 'Oh, miss, you haven't signed the book!'

She didn't bother to look round. All she wanted to do was escape from this place where Baxter was trapped for goodness knew how long. Trapped both physically and, worse, mentally. Katie looked at her watch. If the train was on time and there weren't any delays she should be able to squeeze in an hour to see her father – make sure he was all right.

'Hungry, love?' he said after giving her a hug. Tanny was barking joyously and licking her hand to pieces as they went into the sitting room.

She ran her tongue over her lips, realising she'd had nothing except two cups of tea and two shortbreads since early this morning.

'I am, rather.'

'I'll make you a cheese on toast.' He gave her an apologetic smile. 'I'm not much of a cook. I left all that side of things to your mother.'

'She was very good,' Katie said. 'I wish she'd shown me some of her recipes.'

'She would have done if you'd asked.'

'I suppose so. I probably wasn't that interested, if truth be known.' She looked at him. He'd aged suddenly. 'How are you coping, Dad?'

'All right, I suppose. It's not easy. But Mrs Shelton often brings me a bit of lunch.' He stood abruptly. 'Speaking of that, I'd better go and do it. I haven't had anything myself yet, and it's getting late.'

She followed him into the kitchen with Tanny trotting behind, ever hopeful.

'I miss her terribly, you know,' he said, his back to her as he put the toast and cheese under the grill.

'I do, too,' Katie said fervently. 'I keep thinking she's going to walk in at any moment.'

'And tell us to for goodness' sake leave her kitchen,' her father finished, and they both chuckled.

After they'd had their modest lunch, he suddenly said, 'How's that young man of yours?'

Without warning, all the pent-up emotion she'd held inside herself while on the train bubbled to the surface, and tears streamed down her face.

'Oh, Dad, he . . . well, he's not my young man, as you call him, any more.'

'What are you talking about? Have you had a row? If so, don't worry. All young people have one – even us older ones from time to time. Clears the air.' He looked at her. 'Do you want to tell me about it?'

'I'm not sure what good it will do. And it's not what you think.'

'Tell me anyway.' He lit a pipe and watched her.

After she'd briefly told him about the train crash and going to Haywards Heath to see Baxter that morning, he looked thoughtful.

'Used to happen a lot in the last war,' he said. 'Mostly due to the men in the trenches seeing their mates get blown to pieces beside them. They sometimes spent the rest of their lives having nightmares and desperately trying to block out such visions. I've had that myself and I wasn't so exposed as they were, poor blighters.'

Katie swallowed hard. Her father had never said as much as this before about the Great War.

'Was *your* mind affected, Dad?'

'We were all affected one way or another. And a direct blow to the head can easily cause amnesia, which can go on for months.' He looked at her. 'But it usually comes back, so I shouldn't worry.' He puffed on his pipe. 'What's his mobility like?'

'He seemed to be walking naturally but his speech is slower, though clear. But mainly it's his memory. He thought he was working for Chamberlain so I had to put him right. And he knows he once knew me but has no idea how close we were.'

'Then try to see him as often as possible. Something you'll say will suddenly prompt him to remember more.'

'I'm planning to go every other day this coming fortnight when I don't start work until eight in the evening – and I'll come and see you and Tanny in between.' Then she stopped. 'Is there a date yet for Mutti's service?'

'Not yet, love. I'll let you know as soon as I hear.'

Katie smothered a yawn. Then another.

'Why don't you go upstairs and have a nap?' her father said. 'Apparently even Winston Churchill is a big fan of them.'

She wouldn't tell him she knew. That she sometimes had to work around his naps. It was different from telling her mother. Mutti had gone to her grave with her daughter's secret.

Katie was as good as her word and two days later was back at Stanton Manor. This time it wasn't the same nurse but a woman clad in a grey serge dress with white apron and cap, two scarlet bands above white cuffs denoting her status as Sister. Her mouth was tight as she opened the door wider to allow Katie in out of the cold and into the reception hall.

'I've come to see Baxter Edwards,' Katie said, trying not to feel intimidated and giving her a smile.

The woman didn't smile back. Instead, she snapped, 'You can't see him at the moment . . . he has the doctor with him.' She looked at Katie with small sharp eyes. 'Yes, I thought it was you.' Her tone was challenging. 'Miss Valentine, isn't it?'

'Yes, I'm—'

'There's no need to explain yourself,' the woman interrupted. 'I understand you came here under false pretences two days ago, saying you were his fiancée when clearly you are not, and Mr Edwards confirmed it.'

Katie opened her mouth to protest, but the woman put the palm of her hand in the air.

'Furthermore, Miss Valentine, you saw Mr Edwards illicitly, thanks to the irresponsibility of one of our other patients, whom I have reprimanded. Not only that, but you left the premises without signing the register. We cannot tolerate that sort of behaviour here. Security is paramount. This is a well-run establishment and I intend to keep it as such.'

'I'm really sorry,' Katie said. 'It was all rather too much to take in. He half recognises me and I know I could help him make some headway in getting back to normal if you would only allow me to visit him.'

'I'm sorry, I cannot.'

Katie spotted her name badge.

'Sister Dawson, it's really urgent that—'

A short, stockily built doctor was passing by at that moment. He sent Katie an appreciative glance.

Did she dare? In front of Sister who stood there ready to bar her way? Yes, she damned well would. If she could question the Prime Minister about Baxter, she could tackle *anyone* about him, however superior they believed they were. She put a hand on the doctor's arm and he stopped.

'Oh, doctor, I'm a close friend of Baxter Edwards and wondered whether you might have any further update on his condition? I'm most anxious about him.'

'I've just this minute examined him.' He smiled at Katie. 'Would you like to come to my office and I can answer your questions in private.'

Before Katie could answer, Sister Dawson broke in.

'I've told her, Doctor Cameron, that she can't visit him. Nurse Bell told her that her name didn't appear on the day's appointments two days ago, so she lied and pretended she was his fiancée so she could make a false entry. Mr Edwards denied all knowledge of having a fiancée. Then unbeknown to us, she sneaked into the cafeteria and managed to persuade Norman Jackson to drag him from the library, where he was perfectly happy, and into the noisy cafeteria, which always confuses him.' She paused for breath. '*And* she didn't sign the register when she left, so our security was severely breached.' There was a note of triumph in her voice.

Doctor Cameron looked at Katie and frowned. 'Is this true?'

Rage against this harridan of a woman, who was surely supposed to be sympathetic to the plight of the patients, burned in Katie's throat. But she *had* to keep calm or her chance of visiting Baxter would disappear for good. 'Yes, but I can explain why—'

'I'm afraid Sister Dawson is right about security, especially as we're at war,' he interrupted. 'We can't bend the rules or we'd have mayhem.' Softening his tone, he continued. 'If a bomb hit us, we wouldn't have any record of your being here. Your grieving parents would have no knowledge of where you were and you wouldn't want that to happen, would you?'

'Of course not. But I was desperate. You see, I think I'm the only one who can truly help him. We fell in love just before the accident,' she carried on, ignoring the tut of disapproval from the Sister, 'and I'm the only one who can bring back memories of how happy we were.' She looked up at him imploringly. 'Please, doctor, let me help him.'

She waited. She could see by Doctor Cameron's hesitation that he was wavering.

He swung round to the rigid Sister Dawson, her face thunderous, daring him to challenge the rules. 'Things can sometimes go awry when we're in a stressful situation, Sister, and I'm sure this young lady meant no harm.' He turned back to Katie. 'Come with me, Miss . . . ?'

'Katie Valentine. And thank you so much, doctor.'

Sister Dawson snorted and turned on her heel. Katie couldn't help feeling her own moment of triumph when she caught the confounded expression on the Sister's face. She followed the doctor to his office. Once they were inside, he gestured to a chair on the other side of his desk.

'I'm really sorry I seem to have upset Sister Dawson,' Katie began when she'd sat down.

He shook his head. 'As I said, the war makes everything difficult. People are on edge much of the time and you can't blame them. But let me update you on Baxter Edwards, as he's one of my patients, and also one of Mr Winterbotham's – one of the consultants.' He paused. 'Unfortunately, he's not here at the moment but I can give you a good idea of how Edwards is doing.' He went to the filing cabinet and removed a file, then flipped through the first few pages. 'Ah, yes, this is what I was looking for – his state of mind when he first went into hospital. Apparently, one of the first things he said was: "Has the war ended?" He gave her an ironic smile. 'But he's certainly improved since he's been with us.'

She swallowed hard. 'When I managed to see him for that short time in the cafeteria, he thought it was Mr Chamberlain, not Mr Churchill, who was the Prime Minister, and that really worried me.'

He nodded. 'The trouble is, amnesia patients lose all sense of time. And don't forget, he's only been with us a month. Since then he's come on by leaps and bounds.' He paused. 'How did you find him when you came for the first time the other day?'

'He didn't recognise me – that's the most upsetting bit. He just said I reminded him of a girl he used to know, when I'd put my glasses on to read the time on my watch.' She gave him a wan smile. 'And that girl was *me*.'

Dr Cameron smiled. 'It's surprising how sometimes a small detail will open a whole window of memories. I shouldn't worry too much,' he said, echoing her father's words. Then he leaned forward, his elbows on the desk, linking his fingers. Looking straight at her, he said, 'Now tell me precisely your relationship with him.'

'We met at work and fell in love,' she said simply. 'Then my boss sent me abroad and while I was away I heard the news about the terrible train crash . . . there were many deaths and quite a few missing. Also some survivors. But his name wasn't down on the survivors' list.' Her lower lip trembled and she bit it to hold it steady.

Dr Cameron nodded. 'Yes, we were told that by the medical staff at the hospital he attended, but when we've tried to jog his memory about it, he's just looked bewildered.' He gave a sigh. 'I believe his mind has blotted out what his brain processed that day, in order to protect him mentally, but that doesn't mean it will be a permanent condition.' His eyes met hers. 'By the sound of it, you're by far the best person to help him by visiting him as often as possible and talking to him about daily matters at work.'

'Oh, I can't do that, doctor.' Katie's voice rose in disappointment. 'We've both signed the Official Secrets Act.'

He raised his eyebrows. 'Mmm. Sounds as though you both have interesting wartime jobs.'

'We do. But we're not allowed to talk about it to anyone else, even those we work near to – and certainly not to each other.'

'More and more mysterious.' He ran his finger down his bumpy nose as if in deep thought. 'You seem to have had some difficulty getting in to see him that time – and I should think today with our stern Sister Dawson.'

'I hoped I'd be able to persuade her but I must admit it didn't look likely . . . that is, until you happened to walk by.'

He gave a wry smile. 'It's called "good timing".' He opened a notepad, scribbled something and handed it to her. She read:

Stanton Manor 21st January 1942

Please allow Miss Valentine special attendance to visit Baxter Edwards whenever I, or Mr Winterbotham, see fit. In my opinion, this should be as often as possible as she is in a unique position, having known him both at work and socially, to help restore his memory.

Dr A. C. Cameron

What a relief. No one would dare argue with this, she was sure. She looked up to see Dr Cameron waiting for her reaction.

'I can't thank you enough,' she said quietly.

'I don't think you'll have any more trouble now,' he said, smiling. 'Even Sister Dawson can't object.' He removed a packet of Player's cigarettes from his pocket and offered her one. She shook her head. 'Very wise. And I should know . . . I'm a doctor.' His smile broadened and she smiled back.

'I really appreciate your help, Dr Cameron.' She glanced at him as she rose. 'Would it be all right if I go and visit him for a while?'

'I'm sure he'd be delighted. I'll take you there myself as he should still be in his room.'

Katie hurried to match Dr Cameron's brisk strides as he led the way, first up a flight of stairs, then along a landing until he reached a door numbered 32 with a sign: 'Baxter Edwards'. Her heart beat rapidly at the sight of his name. She crossed her fingers. *Please let him recognise me this time.*

Dr Cameron knocked and walked straight in. She followed. Baxter was in his pyjamas lying on top of the bed reading. When he saw her he put his book down, his face lighting up. For a mad moment she thought he'd truly recognised her as the girl he'd fallen in love with – until he said, 'Well, hello! This is a nice surprise. I don't remember your name but you came a few days ago, didn't you? You were with Nurse Bell.'

'Yes,' she said. 'And my name is Katie.'

You sometimes called me Katharina. But I won't mention that just yet.

'You've got a good hour before lunch,' Dr Cameron said, 'and you're welcome to have lunch with Baxter in the canteen, if you'd like.' He looked from one to the other. 'I'd better be off. I've got some even more difficult patients to deal with than you, Edwards.'

'They can't be worse than me.' Baxter pointed to himself with a grin. 'It's not possible.'

'You'd be surprised.'

Katie was comforted by their banter. Baxter sounded quite normal. Except she knew he wasn't.

On the train home she had to admit she'd made little progress. She'd tried to jog his memory about Myra Hess playing the piano at the National Gallery. She deliberately didn't mention that he'd asked her to go with him and how much they'd enjoyed it. To her disappointment, all he said was that she was a marvellous pianist and how wonderful she was to give up her time to play classical music for audiences even though a bomb might drop on them.

As she'd stood to go, making an excuse that she couldn't stay for lunch as she had to be back at work, he said, 'You mentioned when you came before that we were loving friends.' He watched her closely. 'Does that mean we had an intimate relationship?'

'Oh, no,' she said quickly, feeling the warmth spread up the back of her neck. 'We're friends in the true sense of the word.'

She hesitated. 'But we were concerned for one another . . . and, um, well, we wanted the best for the other.'

She knew she was stuttering but she didn't know how to put it any other way. It wasn't up to her to describe their friendship in detail and have him nod, and her not know if he genuinely remembered; it was so much better if he could make these observations himself.

'Oh.' He looked disappointed.

'I'll say goodbye for now.' She endeavoured to keep her tone neutral but she felt awkward. More than anything she wanted to kiss him. As though he read her thoughts he said, 'Would loving friends kiss, do you think?'

'Yes, they would.' She bent down and kissed his cheek. 'Like this.'

'I see.'

But she knew from the questioning way he looked at her that he didn't see at all. Her eyes filled with tears.

'Why are you looking so sad?' he said, making her start. He reached in his top pyjama pocket. 'Here, take this.' He handed her a handkerchief. 'You mustn't worry about me – I'm fine. I'll be out of here in no time.'

She turned and wiped her eyes on the spotless piece of cloth.

'Do you need this back?'

'No. Keep it.'

'I'll wash it and bring it back next time.'

'Ah, so you're coming to see me again.' This time he gave her the smile that she loved so much. Just for her.

'Yes, Baxter, I am.'

Chapter Forty-Six

Time didn't seem to run normally any longer. It had altered with all the shift work and her stomach having to get used to eating at odd hours, but now, even though only two days had passed, Katie felt she was being split three ways – each of them needing her time: Baxter, Dad and work. It had been drummed into her that the war and therefore her work must come first but her heart felt torn in two over Baxter and her father. Dad was always saying he was coping fine, but since Mutti died it was as though he'd had the stuffing knocked out of him. As for her, she'd hardly had any time to think about her mother, and when she did, guilt would set in, followed by numbness.

By sheer effort, she managed to push aside her worries and concentrate on work. Sir Alan was giving her more dictation than usual as Miss Nicholson was having a few days' leave, not having had any time off this past year. She was grateful that her boss was such an amenable man to work for and lacked the volatile personality of Mr Churchill, though she admired the PM tremendously and had even begun to grow fond of him. But her emotions were already running high and she didn't think she'd be able to cope with his extreme mood changes at the moment. Also, Miss Nicholson's absence left her with little time off to visit Baxter and her father and squeeze in a few hours' sleep.

'Is Baxter making progress yet, love?' Oscar said when she'd been to see Baxter for a snatched visit that morning and had decided to call in and check on her father before flying off to work for the two o'clock shift.

'He seemed pleased to see me but he didn't make any big recollection.'

'Patience, my dear – that's the key here.' He looked thoughtful. 'You know, Katie, I'd like to come with you next time you go. After all, your mother and I both liked him – he even stayed the night that time in the fog – so I might be able to jog his memory.'

'I'd love you to, Dad,' Katie said. 'I'm going again the day after tomorrow so I'll come by for you.'

'Better still, why don't I meet you there. Then you won't waste time.'

To Katie's delight it was Nurse Bell who let her in, smiling at her in recognition.

'Your father has already arrived,' she said. 'He's having a cup of tea in the canteen while Baxter is getting dressed.'

Dad didn't seem to have had any problem being allowed in, Katie thought with a wry smile.

'I'll go and join him, if that's all right.'

'Yes, of course, Miss Valentine. You know the way.'

Her father was sitting at a table talking to a younger man. He must miss male company, she thought. Being in the Home Guard at least got him out of the house for a good old chinwag, as he called it.

'Hello, Dad,' she said as he stood up and gave her a hug.

'Hello, my dear. I've been having a most interesting talk with Philip. He was shot down in his plane but, would you believe it, taken by the Germans to a French hospital where with their help, he managed to escape back to England and ended up here.'

'Remarkable,' Katie said, smiling at Philip, who hardly looked more than a boy.

The three chatted for a few minutes over tea until Katie said, 'I think he'll be ready by now, Dad.'

'Oh, yes,' Philip said. 'Your father said you're visiting Baxter. He told me you were coming today and how much he was looking forward to it.' He lowered his voice. 'I get the feeling you're his girlfriend but he hasn't quite made that connection.'

'You're right.' Katie sighed as she got up. 'He almost did, and then the idea seemed to slip away.'

'I shouldn't worry too much. He remembers more than he did when he first came here about some of the things he did before the accident.' He looked at her. 'You must be patient. These things take time.'

If another person told her that once more, she'd scream. Giving him a tight smile, she took her father's arm.

'Philip's such a nice young man,' her father remarked as they walked to Baxter's room. 'Thank goodness, he's doing well and will be ejected, as he jokingly calls it, tomorrow.'

Baxter was sitting on top of the bed fully clothed this time and looked towards the door as Katie stepped inside, her father behind her. A plump woman in a tweed costume, a little tight over her full bosom, was sitting by Baxter's bedside. She remained seated but smiled.

'Oh, I'm sorry to disturb you . . . ' Katie began, not before she noticed Baxter's smile of welcome fade. 'We'll come back.'

'I'm Mrs Norris, the almoner, but I've only just arrived so I may be twenty minutes or so, I'm afraid.'

Mrs Norris glanced at Baxter, who was listening intently. For several moments he stared at Katie. The air between them whispered . . . *it's me, Katie, the woman you love* – or was it her overwrought imagination? Then he nodded to Oscar and the spell was broken.

'Please stay.' He turned back to the almoner. 'They're

my friends.' He put his hand out to Oscar. 'Nice to see you again, Mr— Sorry, you'll have to excuse me. I'm not good at remembering names these days.'

Katie gave a start. *He genuinely seems to remember Dad.*

'Valentine. But call me Oscar. And good to see you, too, dear boy.'

Baxter frowned as though trying to piece together why Mr Valentine had arrived with Katie.

'I was just saying how pleased I am that Mr Edwards is due to be discharged next week,' Mrs Norris said brightly. 'But I do need to find out how he's going to manage.' She looked at Baxter. 'I believe the doctor's signed you off work for four to six weeks.'

Baxter nodded. 'Yes, but I don't see the need for that length of time. I'm perfectly all right now.'

Mrs Norris glanced down at her notes.

'I expect they want to be sure you're well and truly restored before you return to work.' When he didn't answer, she said, 'I believe you live on your own in a flat in London.'

'That's right,' he said, but didn't glance in the almoner's direction. Instead, his eyes were fixed on Katie.

Mrs Norris pursed her lips. 'That's not ideal. You'd be far better placed if you had someone there.'

'I don't need anyone to look after me,' Baxter protested. 'I'm perfectly all right to do things for myself now my head's healed.'

'It's more than my job's worth to send you back to an empty flat,' Mrs Norris said.

'Mrs Norris, what about if he comes and stays with me for that time,' Oscar suddenly interjected. 'I'm on my own since my wife died recently and Baxter's on his own. We can look out for one another – with Tanny's help, of course.' He winked at Katie.

Oh, no! That would be too embarrassing for words. It was bad enough when he stayed that night and we had to sleep under the same roof. This would be worse, him not knowing.

404

She tried hard not to show her dismay as Baxter's face lit up with a beam.

'How very kind of you, Oscar. I'd be delighted.' He turned to the almoner. 'Well, that's your problem solved, Mrs Norris,' he said, then glanced at Oscar. 'If you're really sure you can put up with me for that long.'

'Absolutely sure,' her father said. 'It'd be a pleasure.'

'Dad, I really wish you hadn't made that offer, even though I know you meant to be kind,' Katie said in the crowded carriage going home. Two soldiers had politely given up their seats for them. 'And it *was* kind. But it's going to be awkward for me when I'm there overnight.' She kept her voice low but everyone was engrossed in their newspapers or books.

Her father looked perplexed. 'Why on earth would it be awkward? He's stayed overnight once before and he was a perfect gentleman.' He gave her a sharp look. 'At least I assume so.'

'Yes, of course he was. But that's when he knew who I was.'

He put his hand on her arm. 'I think you're worrying for nothing, love. And being in closer contact, you could easily jog his memory by some small thing you're not even aware of that makes him remember who you are. Just act naturally and give the boy a chance.'

Katie was at work on the day Baxter was sent by private car to her house – probably just as well, as it would give him time to settle in without causing her any awkwardness. But she decided to ring her father that evening.

'How does he seem to you, Dad?' she asked when the preliminaries were over.

'In some ways you wouldn't know he had any problem – but I can tell by his eyes when he's desperately trying to recall something, though time and rest will do wonders . . . you mustn't worry, love.'

Katie briefly shut her eyes. 'I can't help it.' She didn't want to ask the next question for fear that her father might not tell the truth, but in the end she blurted:

'I don't suppose he's remembered who I am.'

The line suddenly went dead. Her heart pounded. Oh, no. What had happened? She was about to call back the operator and ask to be reconnected, when her father's soothing tones came over the wires.

'I'm not pushing him on anything . . . let him remember naturally. He'll only pretend so as to please me. But after we'd had a bit of lunch, he came into my study and saw that wall map I have of the British Isles. He stood staring at it for a minute or two, then said how he loved maps and that's why he'd chosen to become a cartographer.' Katie could almost see her father's triumphant grin. 'So I thought that was definite progress when you said he couldn't even remember who he worked for.'

'That's really good news,' Katie said, thinking it was also a good move of her dad's to change the subject. Maybe she'd spend the next couple of nights in the Dock so he and Baxter would have more private time together. Or was it that she was scared to face the fact that Baxter had no idea he'd once professed his love to her, and she'd told him she felt the same, and now he no longer remembered?

She was about to tell her father her plan when he broke into her thoughts.

'Oh, before you go, Katie, I had a letter from the undertaker saying your mother's funeral will be this coming Monday, the ninth of February.'

Four days' time. Katie's chin wobbled. Baxter had been her only agonising thought for the last week.

'They haven't given us much notice.'

'It's wartime. Things don't go accordingly any more.' He cleared his throat. 'Frankly, I shall be glad to get the day over but I hope you'll be able to come.'

'I'll make sure I will,' Katie said. 'But until then I think I should stay away and let you two talk on your own.'

'I don't think that's a good idea at all.' Her father's voice became crisp. 'He needs all the help he can get to remind him of different things by being around different people. Just carry on as you would – and that means coming home tomorrow to see your old dad . . . not to mention that cheeky dog of yours!'

Chapter Forty-Seven

The next hours weighed heavily on Katie. Once again she was relieved the Cabinet Room was holding extra meetings and she had plenty of work to do. The war effort was accelerating. Only the other day Luxembourg's government, although in exile, had declared war on Germany, Italy and Japan, but ominously, those three countries had declared war on places in South America she'd never heard of. How had one man been able to set such horror on such a scale in motion?

She deliberately volunteered to keep working right through the evening to the early hours, when she crawled into the bunk down in the depths of the building, feeling completely wiped out.

After a fitful night's sleep, she didn't look where she was going and didn't duck her head low enough when passing through the four-foot doorway leading up the two flights of stairs to the wash basins.

'Ouch, that hurt!' She rubbed the top of her head and inspected her hand. At least there was no blood but she bet there'd be a lump before the day was over. Just when she'd wanted to look her best. Well, it couldn't be helped. But it was a timely reminder that she needed to concentrate.

Miss Nicholson waylaid her as Katie was about to collect her case and handbag, ready to go home.

'Oh, Katharina, can you come into the office?'

I do hope she hasn't got more work for me. I really want to see how Baxter is now.

When they were both in her office, Miss Nicholson told her to sit down, then lit a cigarette. She caught Katie's eye.

'When Mrs Goodman first recommended you to work as my assistant and for Sir Alan, my immediate thought was that you were too young and inexperienced to have that sort of responsibility. I was wrong.' She drew on her cigarette as though to cover the discomfort of having admitted she'd made a mistake.

Katie waited, wondering what was coming next.

'Sir Alan and I want to thank you for all the extra work you've been putting in lately, Katharina,' she continued. 'And always so efficiently.'

Katie felt her cheeks flush with surprise. It was the first time Miss Nicholson had given her such a compliment.

'I was glad to do it.'

'You look tired. Even Sir Alan feels you need a rest for a few days.'

'I don't have time at the moment . . . we're too busy and—'

'Louise is back tomorrow. You need a week off.'

When Katie protested that she didn't need that long, Miss Nicholson interrupted.

'You've had nothing except the odd day here and there for the best part of a year. And you've had the death of your mother to cope with.' She gave Katie a sharp look. 'Do you have a date for the funeral yet?'

'Yes, it's this Monday, so I was going to ask you for Sunday and Monday off, if that's possible. It's going to be a very quiet, simple one.'

'Your father will need some support in the coming days,' Miss Nicholson said, 'and as next week was the week I'd suggested to Sir Alan, it will work well.' She glanced at the wall calendar. 'So we'll see you back on the eighteenth.'

'But that's more than a week,' Katie protested. 'It's very thoughtful of you and Sir Alan but—'

'I've merely included the middle weekend,' Miss Nicholson said. 'A little extra time now is far better than you having a nervous breakdown and being off for months.'

Katie couldn't prevent a sigh of relief. It *was* perfect timing and would mean she might be able to help Baxter regain his memory while also being there for her father for a few days after the service, when he was bound to feel sad.

'We are aware, Katharina, of Baxter Edwards finishing his convalescence at your home.'

Katie startled. 'H-how—?'

'It's our business to find out the whereabouts of the staff.' She gave a small smile. 'But I'm sure he's being well looked after by Mr Valentine.'

It was with some trepidation that Katie put the key in her front door only an hour later. How would Baxter be after spending only one night at her home? How would he treat her? Had her father told him that she was his girlfriend? She hoped not. He needed to come to that conclusion by himself. Before she could answer the unanswerable, there was a joyous bark and Tanny came flying up to her, woofing his welcome.

She heard a movement on the landing and looked up. Baxter was hesitating. Then he bounded down the stairs.

'Hello, Katie,' he said, helping her off with her coat. 'Have they let you out?'

She couldn't tell if he realised where she might have been in order to be let out. Oh, this was all so confusing.

'Yes,' she said. 'They've told me I'm not to go back until the eighteenth – that's over a week.'

'Good. I'm sure it will be beneficial . . . to all of us.'

She glanced at him but before she could look away, he

caught her eye. He stared at her, then shook his head as though he were trying to work out exactly who she was, and who she reminded him of. Well, she wasn't going to help him. She couldn't bear it if he pretended to remember. It would also put him in an awkward position as he'd have to either play-act that he still loved her or tell her that since the accident he'd had second thoughts and wanted to break it off.

'Is Dad here?' she asked.

'No, he's gone off to the Home Guard and didn't think he'd be back before you arrived.'

'I'll just go and put my case upstairs.'

'And I'll put the kettle on – I'm sure you're ready for a cup of tea.'

'That'd be nice.' She raised a smile for him and he smiled back but there was no twinkle in his eyes – only what seemed to her a question that he needed her to answer.

They were acting like two different people, Katie thought sadly. Perhaps she was being foolish to hope for any rekindling of their love.

Tea with Baxter felt just as stilted. She didn't know what she should or shouldn't say. He was even more silent than when she'd visited him in the convalescent home. Maybe it was because there were people around, coming in and out of his room, and now it's just him and me, she thought miserably.

But something strange happened. After welcoming Baxter boisterously, Tanny had gone to sit at his feet, almost as though he knew this person needed reassuring. Just as the thought entered her head, Baxter bent down to ruffle the dog's silky ears. Tanny looked up with an expression that would make the hardest heart melt.

'Good boy,' Baxter told him. Tanny gave a short bark. 'I think he's telling us he wants to go for a walk.' He looked at

411

Katie. 'Your dad took him earlier but I'm happy to go again – that is, if you come with me.'

Was this some kind of breakthrough? He obviously now knew she was Oscar's daughter. But he still didn't appear to have quite put everything together.

'Yes, I'll come. It'll do me good to have some air after being in that stuffy room I slept in last night.' She deliberately didn't say where.

'Yes,' he agreed, 'the air conditioning needs a complete overhaul. No one should be allowed to sleep down there.'

'So you remember the place where we work?' Katie said casually, not allowing herself to show her delight.

'Oh, yes, in the War Rooms.'

'Do you know where?'

He hesitated. 'I can see myself in several rooms. The Cabinet Room is as clear as a bell with Winston striding up and down, cigar in his mouth, pontificating as he does.'

'Do you remember what your work is?'

Baxter gave her his lopsided smile.

'Your father's map on his study wall reminded me – did he tell you?'

Katie nodded.

'I'm one of the cartographers in the Map Room, or the room next door.' He looked straight at her. 'And I remember you didn't have an office. You set up a table in the main passage.'

She held her breath. 'Go on,' she stammered.

Oh, he was so close to remembering everything now. Just remember how we were to one another, my darling, and I'll be the happiest girl in the world.

Not taking his eyes off her, he said, 'And you're one of Sir Alan's personal secretaries.' Then he drew his brows together. 'Have I got that right?'

412

'Sort of, although Miss Nicholson thinks I'm hers.' She grinned.

Oh, how she wanted to put her arms around him. Tell him it was going to be all right – he'd soon recall everything that happened before the accident.

'You and I had a coffee together sometimes,' he continued.

She jerked her head to stare at him.

'Where was that – in the poky little canteen in the Dock?'

'No, it was outside. The . . . um . . . Kettle something.' He frowned. 'No, that's not it. It was something like that.'

'You're nearly right. It was The Copper Kettle.'

'That's the one.'

'It does sound as though your memory is coming back by leaps and bounds,' Katie ventured

'But there's something missing.' He kept his eyes fixed on her, then suddenly sprang to his feet. Tanny looked up, his tail wagging hopefully. 'Why don't we both clear our heads and take him for his walk?'

They walked in companionable silence with Tanny trotting ahead, pulling at the lead.

'Shall I take it?' Baxter said.

'Do.' She handed it to him.

'Come on, boy, you've got a tough chap on the end of your lead now – someone who knows what they're doing – not some feeble woman who can't be trusted to keep up.' He looked back at Katie and winked.

For the first time since the crash, she saw that mischievous expression she knew and loved – just like a naughty schoolboy. And for the first time her heart lifted. Maybe everything really would turn out all right after all.

Up until the funeral, the atmosphere at home had relaxed, Katie was pleased to notice, even though her father was out with the Home Guard much of the time. To her amazement, Baxter had turned out to be an excellent cook. He'd laughed when she'd told him. 'How do you think I've managed to live on my own all these years?'

'Toast and baked beans?' she teased.

'Hmm. I think I'd soon tire of that.' He set today's supper dish on the table. From the wonderful spicy smells emanating from the kitchen, he'd made a curry.

Katie looked up at him. 'Did you find the recipe in one of my cookery books?'

'No, Miss Valentine, I didn't,' he said, giving her a playful tap on her cheek. 'My memory might be shaky but it hasn't destroyed my cooking ability . . . at least I don't think so, but you'd better be the judge of that.'

'It smells wonderful.'

'I just hope you like curry,' he said, ladling it out.

'I've only had it once,' Katie said, biting back the words 'with you'.

'Yes, I ordered it for you when we went out to dinner one night.' He added some rice to her plate, then clicked his tongue as he set it down in front of her with a shake of his head. 'Oh, dear, and I *did* hope you'd remember.'

'Of course I remem—' She broke off at his chuckles and stared at him. Suddenly they were both laughing uproariously.

It felt almost like old times, Katie thought, as she brushed her blonde hair in front of the dressing-table mirror, coaxing it into waves from her curlers the previous night. It made her think of the first time she ever set eyes on Baxter. How furious she'd been when he'd laughed at her attire. She'd wanted to sink through the concrete floor. She couldn't help smiling. And then realisation swept over her. Why she was wearing black. Her mother was to be buried today.

Katie drew in a jerky breath.

Oh, why did you have to die just when I finally realised how much I appreciated you – how I must have loved you all along for everything you did for me. How I nearly didn't recognise that you were my true mother in every way but blood. And blood in the end didn't count.

At least Mutti knew I loved her before it was too late, Katie tried to console herself. With that thought firmly in her mind, she pinned on one of Judy's hats. It was also black. She looked severe and harsh – not what she was feeling in the least. The coat needed something that would brighten it up but was still dressy. She had it! Going to her mother's chest of drawers, she removed the scarf she'd bought for her, and tied it softly around her neck, then checked herself in the mirror. Yes. Mutti would be pleased. She'd been the last person to touch it and it made Katie feel closer to her.

Sure that neither mother would object, she ran downstairs with a lighter heart to join her father and Baxter.

'The motor's waiting,' Oscar said. 'Shall we go?'

It was a simple service but more people turned up than she'd expected.

'Pity some of them didn't come while she was alive,' Oscar said under his breath with a trace of bitterness.

He gave a short speech about how he met his wife, making no secret of the fact that she was German, and Katie read a poem from *The Prophet*. But outside, standing between her father and Baxter in the cold wind watching the coffin being lowered into the ground, Katie's head swam with the image of Mutti being buried alive. She knew she was being ridiculous but it didn't stop the faint feeling. She pulled her stomach in tightly . . . tried to breathe in the cold air . . . dear God . . . another bucketful of earth.

As if he knew, Baxter turned to her.

'Hold on to me.' He crooked his arm.

She put her hand through, clutching his arm, and stole a glance. He kept his attention on the coffin and she forced herself to do the same. Finally, it was over and he looked at her.

'You didn't feel very well a few minutes ago, did you, Katharina?'

Katie blinked. He'd used her full name, which he had done occasionally, but not since the crash. Had he remembered – or had he heard her father use her full name?

'That *is* your real name, isn't it?'

'Yes,' she said.

I won't question him – now's not the time.

After thanking the vicar, they walked the short distance from the church to where the car was parked and ten minutes later they were all home, with Tanny wagging his tail off, barking his welcome.

Katie busied herself in the kitchen, leaving Baxter and her father to chat. Two neighbours had made sandwiches, and early that morning had delivered a large packet wrapped in greaseproof paper, a sponge cake and shortbread biscuits.

'You will stay, I hope,' Katie had said when she'd thanked them.

'Oh, no, dear, it's for you and your father, and that nice young man who's recuperating with you. But we'll be in church.'

Mrs Shelton, a widow, who'd tried to make up for the other neighbours by being extra kind, was away visiting her sister. She'd sent a card saying how dreadfully sorry she was not to be able to attend the service, but when she was back she'd pop in and see Mr Valentine and bring him a meal and do any shopping for him.

Mutti must have been deeply upset with some of the neighbours who'd almost ostracised her, Katie mused, as she poured boiling water over the tea leaves. Yet she never complained. It was as though her mother had resigned herself to the fact that they knew no better – they'd lumped her in the same category as the Nazis, the enemy, and she must have realised she would never alter their opinions. Thank goodness Mrs Shelton never wavered. At least Mutti had had one genuine friend to turn to.

The kitchen door opened and her heart turned over to see Baxter standing there looking uncertain.

'Your father's apologised but says he wants to be on his own for a bit so he's gone to his room. I said I'd bring him a tray.'

Poor Dad. She put some sandwiches on a plate and poured him a mug of tea, then handed Baxter the tray.

'Do you think he'll be all right?'

'Yes,' Baxter said, 'but it's quite understandable. He's trying to take it all in.' He looked at her. 'Rather like me when I first learnt I was in a train crash and thrown some way away, lying there for goodness knows how long before I was discovered. And when I *was* discovered, I couldn't tell them even my name. But more and more is coming back to me, thank God.'

This was the most he'd ever said to her about the aftermath of the crash. Before she could comment, he said, 'I'll take this up to him. I'll be down in a jiffy.'

She took the other tray into the sitting room and had only just poured herself a cup of tea when Baxter walked in.

'He's all right,' he said to her unasked question. 'He just wants to be quiet. But he's strong – he won't go under, if that's what you're thinking.'

'I was a bit,' Katie admitted.

They had their lunch with little conversation, but for once it didn't feel awkward. Afterwards, she cleared away and came back to find Baxter on the sofa, his eyes closed. She tiptoed in.

'I'm not asleep,' he said. 'Just resting my eyes.'

'I've heard that before.' Katie smiled as he opened his lids.

'Katie . . . Katharina, come and sit beside me.'

She did as he asked. He put an arm around her shoulders and drew her a little nearer. She felt her heart starting to beat out of rhythm.

'I still love you, you know.'

Katie's eyes flew wide at his words – so out of the blue.

'Wh-what are you talking about?'

He drew her even closer and put a finger under her jaw to bring her to face him.

'As soon as I saw you with Oscar, even though I'd forgotten Oscar's name, I knew who he was and then everything clicked into place . . . you and me loving one another. But I was worried you might have changed your mind with me losing my memory and being a burden to you, so I just kept quiet. I couldn't face it.'

'But I didn't change my mind. I won't ever—'

'Let me finish, my darling.' He kissed her forehead. 'I was terrified of the future, especially when I couldn't even remember where I worked or what I did. And then as soon as I saw the map in your dad's study, it all came back. But I'll never forget when I thought it was Chamberlain and not Churchill who was the PM. That was a dreadful blow to the little bit of confidence I'd started to build.' He gently shook her shoulders. 'Don't you see, darling, I felt worthless. And when I did start to remember and think the doctor would sign me off as fit to return to work, I worried that they wouldn't have me because I hadn't fully recovered and might slip up and say something I shouldn't. The War Rooms are the nerve centre of the country, holding the most heavily guarded secrets.' He looked at her. 'You know how it is in that place – and rightly so – and they can't risk being compromised.' He paused. 'But the doc has said he'll sign me off in a fortnight and is quite happy about me going back to work, thank God.'

Katie was silent. She'd had no idea this had all been churning round in his mind. She tried to understand how he must have felt, but how she wished he'd trusted her not to waver in her love for him. She bit her tongue to stop any such suggestion bursting out. No, the best thing was . . .

Without putting it into words, she brought his head towards her and lifted her face.

'Baxter, please kiss me.'

His kiss was deep and loving, then suddenly changed in intensity. She felt his tongue, the passion flaring. When they finally drew apart she felt as limp as a rag doll.

'Mmm.' He gazed down at her, the flashes of gold in his eyes sparking. 'That was nice . . . *very* nice.' He stroked her hair, then fingered the lump where she'd hit her head. 'How did you get this?'

'I banged it in the Dock.'

'Hmm. So we have something in common at least.' He grinned. Then his smile faded. 'You know, Katie, that first time you came to see me in the convalescent home?'

'How could I forget? They weren't going to let me in. I hadn't made an appointment so they had no idea who I was.'

'Except that you told them you were my fiancée.'

'I *had* to. It was the only way I had a chance to get in to see you. If I'd been a sister or a wife, I wouldn't have had any trouble. So a fiancée was as close as I dared go.'

'It was an outrageous lie,' he said. 'So I told Nurse Bell the truth – that I didn't have any fiancée.'

Why was he bringing this up? And why was he looking so grim?

Baxter shook his head. 'I think I need to clear that up . . . make an honest woman of you.' He stood, and before she knew it, he'd dropped to one knee and taken her hand firmly in his, looking up into her eyes. 'Katie, my love, will you marry me? Be

419

my wife and then you can see me any time of the day or night without the likes of Sister Dawson meddling.' He grinned, then kissed her fingertips. 'And even if you change your mind later and don't go through with the wedding, at least you can say *truthfully* at this moment to anyone interested that you are my fiancée – and I'm yours.'

She gave a mischievous smile. 'And what about if I *don't* change my mind? What about if I *want* to go through with the wedding, as you so charmingly put it?'

He chuckled. 'Then, for me, that will be the icing on the wedding cake.'

And for me, Katie thought, as an image suddenly rushed into her head: *the icing on the cake will be when I wear Mutti's wedding dress for the very first time on my* own *wedding day*.

But she wouldn't marry him until the war ended. She knew only too well the strict rule that married couples were not allowed to work in the War Rooms, or anywhere else in Whitehall, for fear of a lapse of security. Katie's jaw stiffened. No, she wouldn't risk being dismissed. Since she'd recently filled in as one of Mr Churchill's personal secretaries, her job had felt more important to her than ever. She would do everything in her power for as long as it took to meet the demands of the Prime Minister, and anyone who worked for him, to win the war. And when that victorious day came and the church bells all over the country triumphantly pealed out, her reward for waiting would be to marry the man who had captured her heart. Only then would she tell him her dream of setting up a home to rescue animals. She still had the bulk of the money Judy had left her and now she knew of the charity her birth mother had set up during the Great War, Katie was sure she'd have approved. But that was all in the future. For now, they had to concentrate on Mr Churchill's maxim: '*Victory at all costs, victory in spite of all terror, victory however long and hard the road may be.*'

'Katie . . . Katharina . . . what do you say?' Baxter's tone was anxious as he gazed up at her.

She smiled at him. 'Dearest Baxter, I say "yes".'

He jumped up, pulled her towards him and kissed her soundly on the lips.

'And we'll get married as soon as possible, won't we, darling? I don't want to wait a moment longer than we have to.'

She crossed her fingers behind her back.

'Yes, Baxter, I'll marry you as soon as possible.'

THE END

Acknowledgements

This first acknowledgement might sound rather unusual because it's for my two amazingly talented artisan builders, Whitney Lumas and John James, for creating my dream office to write my historical novels. Some of you already know that I love steam trains and they've built me a carriage in my garden! Well, of course it's a facsimile but it's surprising how many visitors think on first sight that it's from a real train. You enter by an authentic 1930s train door and step into a First Class compartment, which looks as though it's come from the Orient Express! That's where I can do my thinking, and research reading and editing, along with my tray of coffee on the pull-out table. Those of you who are regular readers of my books know my heroines are always travelling on trains during the war, but not in the comfort of a First Class compartment, I hasten to add! Then I walk through a glazed partition to my office where the 'real' work is done. Every morning I go into my carriage I can't help smiling – the atmosphere is so inspirational to get my head down.

But I don't write in isolation all the time. Many people are interested and kind enough to offer their advice. The first person to read my manuscript before it goes to my editor is my critique writing partner, Alison Morton, crime and thriller writer. Her beady eyes spot so much I've missed, brightly marking it with her horrid red pen. Luckily, I get even with her when it's the other way round! We call it 'brutal love' and it works a treat.

Then my two fantastic writing groups – the Diamonds and the Vestas, all published authors. The Diamonds are Terri Fleming, Sue Mackender and Tessa Spencer and the Vestas are Gail Aldwin, Suzanne Goldring and Carol McGrath. All different, all vital to morale boosting, throwing out ideas for plot holes and critiquing each other's work in progress. This is topped by our having tremendous fun, friendship and laughter washed down with the odd glass or so of wine. Being a writer is simply the best job in the world.

Dear Heather Holden Brown, unsurpassed agent for my previous nine novels at HHB Agency, has decided after decades in the successful business she created to hand it over to her colleague, Elly James, who is now my new agent. Elly has already made a brilliant suggestion for my next novel – all will be revealed in the summer of 2025!

I'm so lucky to have had Avon HarperCollins as my publishers from the very beginning and they've given me a talented and inspiring editor – namely Rachel Hart. She comes up with consistently good suggestions that I get cross I haven't thought of myself! I mustn't forget the whole award-winning Avon team of graphic designers, media experts, marketing, PR and sales. All of you have conjoined to bring my story into a beautiful book.

And finally, to you, dear reader, who has been kind enough to read my novel. If I've been able to transport you to a different era with a world at war, shining a light on young girls and women and the crucial part they played during those turbulent times, then I feel I've done my job.

A small request – would you consider leaving a review on Amazon? I get the greatest kick from knowing you've enjoyed my stories. It makes all the effort and time it takes to write a novel worthwhile. And if you would like to get in touch with me direct, please go to my website: **mollygreenauthor.com**

I look forward very much to hearing from you.

Reading List

Winston Churchill by his Personal Secretary – Elizabeth Nel

Joy's Journey: A Memoir – Joy Hunter

The Inner Circle: A View of War at the Top – Joan Bright Astley OBE

From Churchill's War Rooms: Letters of a Secretary 1943–45 – Joanna Moody

One Christmas in Washington: Churchill and Roosevelt forge the Grand Alliance – David J. Bercuson and Holder H. Herwig

Churchill's War in Words: His finest quotes, 1939–1945 – Jonathan Asbury

Churchill's Bunker: The Secret Headquarters at the Heart of Britain's Victory – Richard Holmes

Secrets of Churchill's War Rooms – Jonathan Asbury

The Turn of the Tide 1939–1943: Based on the War Diaries of Field Marshall Viscount Alanbrooke – Arthur Bryant *

Triumph in the West: Completing the War Diaries of Field Marshall Viscount Alanbrooke – Arthur Bryant *

*For anyone with more than a passing interest in the Second World War and the way decisions were made at the very top and the details of the events as they unfolded, I cannot recommend more highly these two tomes incorporating heavy use of Lord

Alanbrooke's diaries. One gets a tremendous understanding of how very easily we could on so many occasions have lost this most evil world war if it hadn't been for Winston Churchill's magnificent and tenacious will and inspiration, together with much risk-taking, coupled with the steady hand, military experience and superb judgement of Sir Alan Brooke. Not only are the two books very readable, but they are more thrilling than any novel when one realises it was all too true.

Author's Historical Notes

I've enjoyed immensely writing this novel, partly because my all-time hero, Winston Churchill, plays a major role. I've read so many books about him that I'm pretty sure I've given a fairly accurate flavour of his volatile personality: generous, sarcastic, stubborn, warm, witty, tenacious, lovable, mischievous, inspirational . . . I could go on. But overall, if we hadn't had him with his mix of clever and weak, good and bad (a human being, like the rest of us), it's extremely doubtful we would have won the war. His closest aide, General Sir Alan Brooke, Chairman of the Chiefs of Staff Committee and Winston Churchill's principal military adviser (who also appears in the novel), said in his diary that although Winston could be the most impossible man to work with and his judgement not always sensible, he wouldn't have missed those anxious years working with such an incredible giant of a man for all the world.

As always, I have kept as accurately as I possibly can to the dates on which the events of the war unfolded during the period I am writing. But there is one minor issue which requires a little explanation.

One of the typists refers to Winston Churchill's private lavatory in the Cabinet War Rooms' basement. But as I've mentioned in the novel, there was no plumbing in the basement or the Dock below. This particular door only *appeared* to be the door of the Prime Minister's private lavatory. It was kept locked with the 'Engaged' sign permanently on. (You might have noticed this if you've seen the excellent film in the setting of the Cabinet War Rooms: *Darkest Hour.*) Mr Churchill would unlock the door, go in, and lock it behind him. Inside, was a small, airless cubicle with a special clock on the wall with two hands, the black hand with London time, and the red hand showing the equivalent time in Washington. He would sit on the swivel leather chair alongside the desk, pick up the receiver of the solitary telephone and announce: 'Winnie here, Old Pal' on a pre-booked, direct transatlantic line to President Roosevelt himself! The conversation would be automatically scrambled by an enormous installation called SIGSALY that was stored in the basement of Selfridges in London. Secretly designed by a US company, it was cutting-edge technology at the time.

Winston Churchill really did invite his staff, however low in the pecking order, to his cinema nights where they felt forced to stay until the early hours of the morning when they'd already put in a 10-to-twelve-hour working day. He just loved company while watching his favourite films.

Katie's idea to have her desk in one of the alcoves off the main corridor was not exclusive. In truth, as the Cabinet War Rooms began to get more crowded over the years, several typists were seconded to the alcoves whether they wanted to be or not. Any space in the basement was always coveted.

Winston Churchill loved working in bed but he loathed staying overnight in his bedroom in the basement. He only did this four times throughout the entire war but one night he promised Clementine he would stay there as a particularly bad raid was predicted. His aide happened to be in the PM's bedroom as Winston dived under the covers, fully dressed, where he lay for no more than thirty seconds, then climbed out. His aide reminded him of his promise to his wife.

'I haven't broken it,' Winston said with a sly grin. 'I can tell her with complete honesty that I was in bed in the basement last night.'

He really did have an answer for everything!

Will helping the war effort help mend her broken heart?

Summer Secrets at Bletchley Park

MOLLY GREEN

September 1939. London is in blackout, war has been declared, but Dulcie Treadwell can think only of American broadcaster Glenn Reeves, who didn't say goodbye before leaving for Berlin.

Heartbroken, Dulcie is posted to Bletchley Park, where she must concentrate instead on cracking the German Enigma codes. The hours are long and the conditions tough, with little recognition from above. Until she breaks her first code . . .

But when a spiteful act of jealousy leads to Dulcie's brutal dismissal, her life is left in pieces once more. Is it too late for Dulcie to prove her innocence and keep the job she loves? And will her heart ever truly heal if she doesn't hear from Glenn again . . . ?

With war raging on, there are still
battles of the heart to be won...

A Winter
Wedding
at
Bletchley
Park

MOLLY GREEN

When Rosie Frost was jilted on her wedding day, she didn't
think life could get any worse. But six years later in the throes
of the Second World War, she is unceremoniously dismissed
from her dream job after they discover her illegitimate child.

Thankfully, top secret war office Bletchley Park recognises
Rosie's talent and recruits her to decipher their Italian naval
signals. Happy to be doing her bit for the war effort, Rosie
settles into her new life.

But when she spots a familiar face at the Park, Rosie's world
threatens to come crashing down once more. Can she put her
heartbreak behind her? And will wedding bells ring out across
Bletchley Park before the year is out?

Munich. September, 1938.
When twenty-one-year-old Madeleine Hamilton is asked to smuggle two young pupils to Berlin, she nervously agrees. But, when they run into trouble on the train, it is Maddie's turn to be saved by a chance encounter with a handsome man.

Bletchley Park. September, 1939.
A year later, Maddie is undertaking training in Morse code when a familiar face shows up unexpectedly. The attraction between them is as deep as it is instant, but Maddie knows one person holds the potential to harm her country and her heart – and it is her duty to protect both . . .

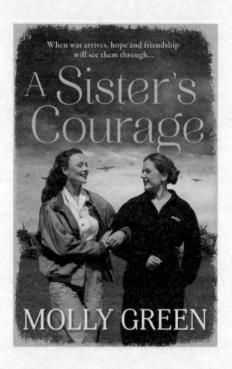

When war arrives, hope and friendship
will see them through...

A Sister's Courage

MOLLY GREEN

In the midst of war, she knew her place was not at home . . .
The most ambitious of three sisters, Lorraine 'Raine'
Linfoot always dreamed of becoming a pilot. As a spirited
seventeen-year-old, she persuades her hero Doug Williams
to teach her to fly.

When war breaks out in 1939, Raine is determined to put her
skills to good use. She enlists in the Air Transport Auxiliary,
becoming one of a handful of brave female pilots flying fighter
planes to the men on the front line.

As war rages on, she'll fight
to keep spirits high...

A
Sister's
Song

MOLLY GREEN

Her duty is to keep smiling through . . .
When World War II breaks out, Suzanne's dream of attending
the Royal Academy of Music crumbles.

Determined to do her bit, she joins a swing band that
entertains troops in some of the worst-hit cities of Europe.

Through singing, Suzanne finds a confidence she never
knew she had, and she soon wins the admiration of Britain's
brave servicemen.

But her heart already belongs to a Navy officer who is serving
out at sea. The question is . . . will they meet again?

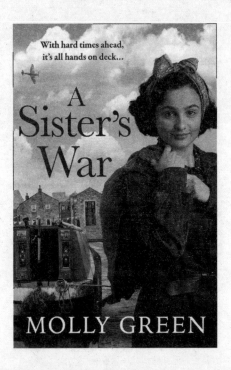

With hard times ahead, it's all hands on deck...

A Sister's War

MOLLY GREEN

Britain, 1943

Ronnie Linfoot may be the youngest of three sisters, but she's determined to do her bit . . .

Against her strict mother's wishes, Ronnie signs up to join the Grand Union Canal Company, where she'll be working on a narrowboat taking critical supplies between London and Birmingham.

But with no experience on the waterways, she must learn the ropes quickly. She's facing dreadful weather, long days, and rough living conditions. At least she isn't on her own.

In the toughest times, will Ronnie and her fellow trainees pull together? For even in the darkest days of war, hope and friendship can see you through . . .

Or why not curl up with Molly Green's heart-warming Orphans series?

LIVERPOOL, 1941

Haunted by the death of her sister, June Lavender takes a job at a Dr Barnardo's orphanage. June couldn't save Clara from their father's violence, but perhaps she can help children whose lives have been torn apart by war.

A WORLD AT WAR

When June bumps into Flight Lieutenant Murray Andrews on the bombed streets of Liverpool, the attraction is instant. But how can they think of love when war is tearing the world apart?

A FIGHT FOR HOPE

As winter closes in, and the war rages on, can June find the strength and courage to make a better life for herself and the children?

War rages on, but the women and children of Liverpool's Dr Barnardo's Home cannot give up hope . . .

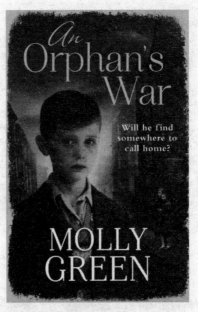

LIVERPOOL, 1940

When her childhood sweetheart Johnny is killed in action, Maxine Grey loses more than her husband – she loses her best friend. Desperate to make a difference in this awful war, Maxine takes a nursing job at London's St Thomas's Hospital.

A BROKEN HEART

Maxine takes comfort in the attentions of a handsome surgeon, but Edwin Blake might not be all he seems. And as the Blitz descends on the capital, Maxine returns to Liverpool heartbroken and surrounded by the threat of scandal.

A BRAVE SPIRIT

When offered a job at a Dr Barnardo's orphanage, Maxine hopes this is the second chance she has been looking for. And one little boy in particular helps her to realise that she needs the orphans just as much as they need her…

Even when all seems lost at Dr Barnardo's orphanage, there is always a glimmer of hope to be found . . .

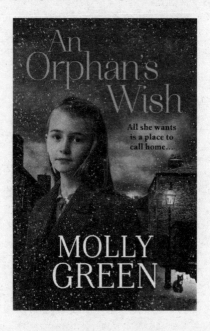

LIVERPOOL, 1943

When Lana accepts the challenging position of headmistress at a school in Liverpool, she hopes a new beginning will help to mend her own broken heart.

There are children that desperately need her help, and Lana must fight for everyone's happiness, as well as her own. But one young girl in particular shows her that there is a way through the darkness – because even when all seems lost, there is always a glimmer of hope to be found . . .